FOLLOW ME
DOWN

GORDON MACKINNEY

Black Rose writing™

© 2017 by Gordon MacKinney
All rights reserved. No part of this book may be reproduced, stored in a retrieval system or transmitted in any form or by any means without the prior written permission of the publishers, except by a reviewer who may quote brief passages in a review to be printed in a newspaper, magazine or journal.

The final approval for this literary material is granted by the author.

First printing

This is a work of fiction. Names, characters, businesses, places, events and incidents are either the products of the author's imagination or used in a fictitious manner. Any resemblance to actual persons, living or dead, or actual events is purely coincidental.

ISBN: 978-1-61296-969-5
PUBLISHED BY BLACK ROSE WRITING
www.blackrosewriting.com

Printed in the United States of America
Suggested Retail Price (SRP) $19.95

Follow Me Down is printed in Adobe Garamond Pro

I dedicate this book to the memory of Urangua "Sisi" Mijiddorj.

ACKNOWLEDGMENTS

A special group of people encouraged me and helped improve my writing. My deepest thanks to (alphabetical by first name) Adrienne Schatz, Alison Kemper, Anson MacKinney, April Moore, Arthur MacKinney, Brian Kaufman, Brigid Kemmerer, Colleen Greshock, John Duesenberg, Katherine Valdez, Ken Harmon, Ken Slight, Laura Powers, Lisa Malmquist, Lois MacKinney, Nada MacKinney, Pat Stoltey, Paula Horton, Taryn MacKinney, and Teresa Funke. Lillian, Reece, and Merrick—you're somethin' special! The biggest and best of my gratitude to my wife, Kristy Dowers.

The excellent book *Access All Areas* by Ninjalicious inspired the urban exploration philosophies of N. Jefferson Chapel in *Follow Me Down*. Jacob R. Mecklenborg's *Cincinnati's Incomplete Subway* proved an invaluable resource. John P. Maggard kindly provided informative research material about the Cincinnati Union Terminal.

PRAISE FOR
FOLLOW ME DOWN

"In this well-researched thriller, urban explorers descend into deep trouble when they uncover the buried crimes of a corrupt company. MacKinney keeps us turning the pages."
— Patricia Stoltey, author of *The Prairie Grass Murders*,
The Desert Hedge Murders and *Dead Wrong*

"This smart psychological thriller pulls readers into the fascinating world of urban exploration. MacKinney is a new author to watch."
— *Secrets of Best-Selling Authors*, www.KatherineValdez.com

"Part treasure hunt, part mystery, *Follow Me Down* is a full-throttle, urbex thriller that deftly manages plot, setting, and complex characterization. (Five stars out of five)"
— Rabbit Hole Reviews

"A thriller indeed, but also a love story, between father and son, and between Lucas and a young woman willing to risk everything. *Follow Me Down* will keep you up at night and stay with you long after the final page."
— Kenneth W. Harmon, author of *Upon the Stage of Time*
and *The Paranormalist*

FOLLOW ME DOWN

Leave me a place underground, a labyrinth,
where I can go, when I wish to turn,
without eyes, without touch,
in the void, to dumb stone,
or the finger of shadow.
~ Pablo Neruda

Follow Me Down

CHAPTER 1

Twenty feet below the shoes of Cincinnati's pedestrians lay a wilderness as remote as the moon, a wilderness that had beckoned me since I was a kid. The city had gated off the unused subway when money ran out during the Depression. But in 1945, a nine-year-old girl named Emily Langford squeezed between the iron bars, got lost in the abandoned tunnels and, in the words of a careless politician, "screamed herself to death." Afraid of another tragedy, the city council entombed the subway behind steel plates as thick as the hulls of oil tankers.

My friend Reuben and I breached the barriers before anyone else, back when I had more flexible joints. I wasn't trying to burn a corporate empire to the ground—not at first. I was only playing with matches, searching for sensations that sounded paradoxical to most people. How could I trap myself in concrete and earth, yet feel so liberated? How could I fear the cops arresting us, yet crave the thrill of talking my way free? How could I inhale decades-old vapors, some toxic, yet feel so damn alive?

Reuben said I went belowground to escape. Perhaps. The above-ground world offered nothing after my father was killed. I couldn't sleep, not when memories, sharp and bright as a wolf's teeth in the dark, jolted me awake. Forbidden places distracted me. When squeezing through a concrete fissure too tight for a deep breath, I couldn't dwell on the past.

Our route to the off-limits subway was indirect, through an abandoned train station called the Cincinnati Union Terminal.

The year was 1973.

· · · · ·

My knees and palms burned after crawling through a hundred feet of ventilation duct, but I didn't mind. We were almost in. Just beyond a vent cover was the concourse of the old train station. A familiar flutter in my gut, I checked my watch—4:10 a.m.

Reuben crawled up beside me. In the gloom, his eyes glimmered behind thick lenses. A penlight tipped with a blue swatch supplied our only illumination. Reuben was an unlikely urban explorer—a mop-topped nerd in high school and a buttoned-up insurance actuary after we graduated from Xavier. Was he quenching some primitive male thirst for adventure? "No," he would answer, "I keep your sorry ass out of trouble." True, and I owed him for that.

Something crawled across my wrist. I shook it free. "You ready?" I whispered, even though the chance of being overheard was nil. The security guard desk was too far away.

"Ask me when we're done," Reuben replied.

I grabbed from my backpack a cigar-thick gun sight I'd bought at the army surplus store for a buck, all the money in my pocket at the time, and pretty much ever since, thanks to grad school tuition and my cheapskate boss. I raised the scope to my eye and aimed through the vent cover toward the guard station at the far end of the main concourse, more than a football field away. "He's not there. I think he's making his rounds."

"You *think*?" Reuben sat so close I could smell the cinnamon from his Dentyne, which reminded me. I unzipped my pack's front pocket, retrieved a fresh pack of gum and held it out.

Reuben accepted the peace offering. "Thanks. You're still a moron."

I smiled. "Of course." I handed him the scope. "See for yourself."

Reuben repositioned his glasses on top of his wavy hair and pointed the device. "Come on, Lucas. This isn't the same as the tunnels under the student union. That *looked* like a fraternity hazing stunt, so they believed us—"

"Because we followed Chapel's rules." The late N. Jefferson Chapel wrote the ultimate how-to manual for urban spelunkers.

"But this *looks* like trespassing in a guarded building because that's what it is. We're talking serious fines, maybe jail time, regardless of what bullshit you tell them."

"I don't need to bullshit. We're not thieves. We're taking a picture, that's it." I didn't blame Reuben for being testy. My photo required electronic flash, and not just one flash but a dozen. "Why not launch fireworks from the roof?" he'd said after I'd described my plan, that vein in his neck bulging. "Every Cincinnati resident has a view of those big windows." But eventually he had come around. He always did.

I twisted the metal clips holding the vent cover and swung it open, bracing for a hinge squeak that would slice the silence. But it didn't come. I bear-walked into the concourse and stood. Blood flowed through my cramped legs. Overhead, even in the faint glow of exit signs, I could make out the scalloped ceiling with hundreds of curved indentations, shoulder to shoulder like marching centurions.

The Cincinnati Union Terminal was an Art Deco masterpiece that could be considered a museum. Or perhaps a mausoleum. Trains ruled in the '30s and '40s but gave up their passengers to the superhighways. The city shuttered the building a year ago, a sad occasion. Today, only the ghosts of long-departed travelers remained.

We padded past the station's platforms, now slabs gathering pigeon guano. A layer of dust dampened our footfalls. I caught whiffs of moist concrete and machine oil.

I sensed a sudden darkening, then a return to dim light. My palms tingled. I glanced ahead. The guard had returned and passed temporarily in front of his reading lamp.

"Shit," I whispered. I hooked my hand in the loop above Reuben's backpack and yanked us both to the stone floor. I let out my breath.

Reuben glowered inches from my face, grime powdering his lower lip and chin stubble. "What would Chapel say now?"

"He'd say *don't get caught*," I whispered. I jabbed my thumb in the direction of the nearest vestibule and belly-crawled like a soldier. Reuben followed close. We sat up and leaned our backs against an abutment. My heart thudded inside my sweatshirt.

Reuben wiped his mouth with his sleeve and held up the dusty result. "Do you know what's in this crap?" He knew I did, but he continued anyway. "Rat crap. Along with mite carcasses, mold and asbestos—all so you can take a goddamn picture."

True, but *this* goddamn picture might change a few things, and Reuben knew it.

I turned my body to aim the scope. The uniformed man floated on an island of light from the desk lamp, surrounded by an ocean of shadow that filled the cavernous interior. But thirty seconds later, he vanished into the darkness.

"Okay, now he's gone for real," I said. "We've got thirty minutes to get into the rotunda, set up, take the shot, and get back here." I clambered to my feet and took a swig of water from an old World War II canteen, a gift from my dad. Years ago, I'd hand-stitched a Foghorn Leghorn patch on the canteen's canvas case.

Reuben remained sitting, his jaw muscles bulging. "What if he wanders in while we're still shooting?"

"What if he doesn't?" I replied.

"We should've recruited a spotter."

"There wasn't time." No response from Reuben. "It's not just about the picture." An image of Dad flashed through my mind. He stood across the station's grand rotunda, his hands clasped in front, grinning, so proud to show me his favorite city landmark. "And I can't do it without your help."

Reuben stared at his filthy knees for a moment before sighing. "Okay." He stood.

En route to the grand rotunda, we passed by the security desk where I paused, curious. Our guard had been passing the nighttime hours with the Bible—The Gospel of Luke, to be specific.

"We don't have time for whatever you're up to," Reuben said.

"Just a sec." I flipped the pages to Revelations and smiled to myself. The man would return to read about scorpions, locusts and plagues.

When I looked up, Reuben frowned back. "Why do you do stuff like that?"

I shrugged. "Let's go."

Lately I'd been drawn to '50s doo-wop, the musical equivalent of comfort food. As *Earth Angel* by the Penguins played in my mind, we slipped into the train station's grand rotunda and eased the double doors shut behind us. Even in the fractured light from the tall windows facing the city, I could make out one stunning architectural feature after another. The vast horizontal space wider than NYC's Grand Central Station. The liquid curves and clean grids of glass, aluminum and limestone. The crisp, geometric Jazz Age letters, the purest symbol of the Art Deco style, labeling the ticket windows, boot black's shop,

Follow Me Down

and Newsreel Theater.

Dad used to say the building reminded him of a giant Philco radio with rounded top and vertical grill. When he first brought me, I pretended we were walking into Pinocchio's whale. The arched ceiling seemed a mile above, swirling with parallel lines of muscle. Would the creature remain peaceful as we stomped on its insides, or would the dome collapse like a bellows and blow us tumbling out to the parking lot?

That was long ago. This past year, Cincinnati's politicos decided the derelict station would make a fine shopping mall. Soon, the concourse would be razed, and the massive circular rotunda violated by Day-Glo signs, the *chink-ching* of pinball machines, and the stench of deep fryers. Teenagers in cut-off jeans and sandals would drip ice cream on the tile floors.

A number of firms had applied for the renovation job, but the winner was predestined: Drax Enterprises, the biggest and most powerful developer in the city. That figured. Drax had held Cincinnati's weak politicians by the balls since the '20s. Before long, Drax people would slither all over the place. The thought made me sick. In the courtroom six years earlier, Drax lawyers had called my father's death an accident—a lie.

I located the ideal vantage point overseeing the rotunda and slid out the tripod legs. Reuben jittered just off my elbow. I lifted the camera from the bag.

Reuben's eyes went wide. "Blumenfeld let you borrow the Leica?"

I winced. "Not exactly."

"You swiped it from *your own boss?*"

"I'll put it back in his desk before he knows it's gone." There'd been no choice. Alfred Blumenfeld would never loan it, and I couldn't trust my old Yashica. Leica was one of the best cameras on planet Earth, with razor-sharp optics. By all reasoning, the old man shouldn't have owned it because he despised everything German. The only better photo would come from Alfred's Hasselblad, manufactured by the Swedes, which he reserved for weddings. The problem was that he never let it out of his sight, probably slept with it under his pillow.

"I hope you know what you're getting into," Reuben said.

"Calculated risk." I thumb-screwed the camera to the tripod and crossed the terrazzo floor for the first flash of the sequence. Reuben waited behind. I positioned myself a few feet from the wall and angled the flash. "Shutter open."

Because of the dome's amplifying acoustics, Reuben could hear my hushed voice from two hundred feet away—a marvel that sent the same giddy chill down my spine as years earlier.

Reuben depressed the shutter release and held it down. The film would remain exposed throughout the series of flashes, which I called "painting with light."

Alfred Blumenfeld had taught me the technique. A few months back, after closing time, I was developing black-and-whites from the latest off-limits excursion. Alfred allowed employees to borrow the darkroom for personal projects. He slipped through the light barriers and hovered over my shoulder, the quarters too cramped for his aura of English Leather and BenGay. He tweezed my print from the tray and held it up, the chemicals dripping. "You screwed up the lighting." In the darkroom's red glow, his herringbone suit and floral tie looked as lifeless as his skin by daylight. He sniffed. "Never hit your subject head-on. You'll whitewash it." He was right.

I learned a lot about photography from the old man, but the lessons weren't exactly pleasant experiences.

Later, I had stuck my head into his office. "We're going to shoot the grand rotunda of the Union Terminal at night."

He sat behind his wooden desk with perfect posture, looking skeptical. "Mighty big interior. At night, you say?"

"Maybe the first time ever."

"And maybe the last." He knew all about the shopping mall project. "So don't botch it." He set aside the piece of mail he'd been reading. "Ever see those National Geographic photos of the big caves in South America, the ones you could hold a concert in?"

"Sure."

"No single flash can illuminate a space that large. You have to open the shutter and leave it open, with the film exposed the whole time. Then, in the dark, you move around and fire the flash near sections of wall, multiple times. The flash becomes your paintbrush."

Painting with light.

He described the finer points of the technique, and I hung on his instruction. When he finished, I thanked him and turned to go.

"Hey Lucas," he said, more softly this time. "Make it really good. Get published in *The Cincinnatian*, maybe *Preservation Quarterly*. You might change a few minds about that old station." I figured Alfred was sentimental for the forgotten building, but then his voice hardened. "And you might change a few minds about that damn company."

Something tightened in my gut. "You got a problem with Drax?"

He stared at me through an awkward silence, and then waved me towards the exit. "Just focus on the photo." He reached for the next envelope in his inbox.

Alfred knew about the power of photography. Years before shooting weddings, he'd been a big-time photojournalist. I'd seen his work on a high shelf in the front office in tattered copies of *Look*, *Harper's* and *The Saturday Evening Post*.

I'd always photographed our infiltrations, creating frameable trophies, the temporary made permanent. But everything is fleeting.

Alfred was right. My photo could be more than proof of our exploit. It could trigger a chain of events: I'd publish the shot, tip the scale of popular opinion, compel the city's leaders to rethink the shopping mall project, and drive a thorn in the side of Drax Enterprises.

"Last flash," I said to Reuben across the expanse. He was probably crawling out of his skin with anxiety. I hit the button once more near the ticket windows, framed by barrel-thick columns of Verona marble the color of campfire embers. I heard a *shak* sound as Reuben closed the camera's shutter. "The guard'll be back any minute," he said.

"To read about the end of days, or get scared a ghost came along and turned his pages."

"It's not funny. I bet someone's already spotted the flashes and called the cops."

I shouldered the camera bag and tried to speak with the calm of an airline pilot. "We're doing okay."

Reuben and I had begun infiltrating off-limits places way back in junior high. Throughout our college days at Xavier, we explored buildings and construction sites, expanding over time to utility tunnels, bridges, and even boats moored on the Ohio River.

Post-graduation, Reuben took a job with an insurance company, God knows why. He had a scientist's brain. I began studying toward my Master of

Gordon MacKinney

Architecture. Now, past the quarter-century mark and halfway to my M.Arch degree, I accumulated course credits as fast as Mom and I could scrape up tuition money.

Reuben and I met up mid-rotunda to stow the gear. Since we'd arrived, the vast space had predetermined our rendezvous point as if all the energies of the place converged below the dome's apex, a kind of mecca to rightfully occupy.

Maybe that's why, when the security guard squeezed between the double doors with his pistol drawn and splashed Reuben and me with a wedge of light, *he* seemed to be the trespasser, not us.

CHAPTER 2

I remember a summer evening. I figured I was twenty-five feet down, a few feet of water below me. Granddad had bragged about the thirty-foot well on his farm, how the depth meant more water, better water and colder water. I'd decided to find out for myself.

Surrounded by black stone wall, I descended further, the circle of orange sky shrinking above me with each handhold. I smelled wet, living rock.

My jeans were stiff-new from Montgomery Ward, the rubber soles of my Keds still white—new for school. Cash was tight, so Mom would've blown her top if I'd soaked my clothes.

I wedged my sneakers tight between rocks on opposite sides. The fingers of my left hand found grip on the slick stones. With my free hand, I reached down and dunked. Icy cold.

Something skittered across the back of my left hand and stopped on my knuckles. The light was too dim to see it, so I found a new grip for my right hand and gave my left a shake. The creature dropped and made a splash. Big old bug, I figured.

Everything got darker fast. I looked up. A head and a couple of shoulders leaned over the stone perimeter.

"Lucas?" It was my mom, her voice on edge.

"Yeah?"

"Lucas! Oh my God! He fell in!" She said other things but I couldn't understand, with her half talking and half screaming.

"Mom," I said, hoping to sound like it was no big deal, that I was perfectly fine, but she was disappearing and reappearing, her shrieks doing the same. Things became quiet after her last exit, so I waited and took in that heavy smell, all dirt and wetness and decay, old but also new, like the brick-lined cellar with the earth floor where my grandmother stored jars of peaches and bread-and-butter pickles. A minute passed.

"Lucas?" This time it was my father, and he wasn't screaming. "You okay?"

"Yeah."

He stayed up there for a few more seconds, not saying anything, which made me a little nervous. Then he said, almost whispering, "You didn't fall, did you?"

I considered his question and how my answer might get interpreted by the grown-ups. *Would it be better if I fell?* The way I figured, my mother was already hysterical, and she would go catatonic if she learned the truth.

"Please answer me," my father said. He sounded a bit amused.

"I climbed down."

Dad shook his head and laughed and quickly covered his mouth. "Can you come up on your own?"

"Sure." But before climbing, I filled my nostrils one last time.

That was only the beginning. I remember digging a hole in the backyard after a heavy rain and sticking my head in to find that dark, wet silence. I knew, even then, that it was only a hole, but I was going somewhere no one had gone before. Edmund Hillary, Captain Nemo—and me.

But as I stared down the barrel of the security guard's gun in the Grand Rotunda of the Cincinnati Union Terminal, I wasn't thinking about Hillary or Nemo, or the safe stillness of the underground. I was thinking about my idol, the greatest urban explorer of all time, an expert on avoiding capture.

His name was N. Jefferson Chapel, a Canadian who rose to fame when he discovered the most famous ossuary in the Paris catacombs, *Le soleil*, the sunflower, with its seed-filled center of human skulls and its petals of tibia bones. Chapel famously donned German lederhosen and knee socks during his exploits, and upon reaching the innermost point of each journey, drained a small leather pouch of Castarède Armagnac to "fortify the return."

Chapel recorded his conquests in a journal, and preferred impenetrable language. In 1953, he wrote, "Periodic encounters with property stewards wishing to detain you should be part and parcel of *la vive émotion*. If not, you play too safe and risk entering life's winter with the sweetest fruit left hanging on the vine."

I'm in debt to Mr. Chapel. Of my nine apprehensions over the years, I was freed seven times without fine or imprisonment, all thanks to his *Six Rules of Apprehension*.

We were *apprehended*, but not *captured*. Big difference. Reuben never grasped that apprehension is a process, not a moment, with the ideal outcome determined by carefully orchestrated steps.

I blinked at the guard's pistol and scribbled Chapel's rules on a blackboard in my mind, each beginning with a single word: *obey, disclose, relate, agree, inquire* and *revere*.

The guard squinted as if bringing us into focus. "You better not move." In his upper twenties like us, he wore a neutering gray uniform with *Drax Security* embroidered above a breast pocket that bulged with a pack of smokes. His long hair, likely freewheeling during off-duty hours, was greased, parted and hooked behind his ears, a good-grooming regulation from Drax. This was no career security man.

Chapel's Rule Number One: Obey. Demonstrate certainty of purpose by elevating yourself above the petty defiance of the diffident.

"No problem, sir," Reuben said, his voice flat, his fear probably tempered by his anger at me.

I took the lead. "Sir, we can explain everything."

The guard used the barrel of his pistol as a pointer, twitching nervously. "What's in the bag?"

Again, Reuben jumped ahead of me. "Only equipment, nothing more." Hmm. I wouldn't have said *nothing more*. Sounded too defensive. Reuben reached for the leather satchel hanging from my shoulder.

The guard's eyes widened. He brought both hands together on the pistol butt. "I *can* shoot you," he declared.

Well, of course you can, I thought, almost smiling, which would've been disastrous. Of the three of us, the one with the hand cannon was the highest strung.

"It's camera equipment," I said while floating my hands away from my body. "If it's okay with you, I'm going to set the bag on the ground, only touching the strap, and kick it away from us. Nice and easy."

The guard jerked a nod. "Okay." He had the roundest Charlie Brown face I'd ever seen. The bullies cruising the halls of Cincinnati's public schools had probably gorged themselves on his self-esteem. I felt an unlikely kinship.

I lowered the bag to the floor and gave it a slow slide with my foot. It closed the twenty-foot gap between us by about a third.

The guard didn't move. Wheels turned behind his moon face. What could he do? Approach the bag to inspect? Order us to back away? Radio for reinforcements? Then I noticed: no communications device hanging from his belt. Big boo-boo for a rookie guard.

I decided to help. "We'll move away a little so you can check out the bag. We're unarmed." I took four liquid steps backwards. Reuben followed my lead.

Charlie Brown faltered forward, lifted the camera bag and tipped it toward the light so he could peek inside. Apparently satisfied, he set it down. "How'd you get in here?" The question surprised me.

Chapel's Rule Number Two: Disclose. Your road to freedom may be paved with truth. Stand proud; while we do commit the victimless and recherché crime of trespass, we neither vandalize nor pilfer.

I opened my mouth to speak the truth, but then rethought. A plausible lie could work in our favor. I recalled the building's schematics at the city records office. "We got in through the executive office entrance on the east side. It was unlocked." The guard's face betrayed a flash of concern—perfect. Maybe he was responsible for locking those doors, but he could avoid taking heat from his Drax bosses, if he played things right.

The guard remained wordless, perhaps unwilling to turn us over to the authorities and expose a security faux pas.

"Sir, my name is Lucas Tremaine and this is my colleague, Reuben Klein. We're members of the Cincinnati Historical Society." Technically speaking, I was the only member—a forgivable fib. "We're here to take pictures of the rotunda by night."

Again, the guard said nothing, apparently flummoxed. After all, his partner was out of earshot beyond Pantheon-thick walls. He couldn't radio for help because he'd left the gadget behind. And he couldn't lead us through the long concourse by gunpoint because we'd bolt for one of sixteen exits, leaving him with the vexing choice of shooting unarmed men in the back or permitting their escape.

Think! How could all three of us walk away with no damage done?

Chapel's Rule Number Three: Relate. Do not presume property stewards will comport adversarially. Find the flow of their river and float with them toward a common portage.

I made my move. "Sir, it's about Drax Enterprises."

The guard's eyes narrowed. "What about 'em?"

"We would've asked permission to take the pictures but your bosses would never go along with that." This was true. Drax people knew my name and not in a good way, not after Mom and I sued the company over Dad's death. Maybe the guard would share my disdain for his employer.

"It don't matter," he said. "You're trespassing on private property."

Chapel's Rule Number Four: Agree. Your captor has the upper hand. Don't proclaim he's ignorant of the laws he prides himself in enforcing.

But I couldn't agree. The guard was wrong. We stood on public property, *your property*, I wanted to say, *your city's greatest treasure, and Drax will destroy it.*

But the guard wouldn't care.

Chapel's Rule Number Five: Inquire. Among the tedium of the watchman's devoir, your sudden presence may be the apogee of his day. He may hesitate to relinquish you to higher authority, a chance to postpone his return to work. Make a connection while buying time to devise your exodus.

"You're right," I said, "we're trespassing, but only to take pictures. We mean no harm. Did you grow up in Cincinnati?"

The guard stiffened. "None of your business."

I held up my palms. "No problem. But if you grew up here like I did, you know all about this place. I saw this building every day. When my grandparents came to visit, we waited right here to greet them. I used to stand over in that corner of the rotunda and whisper, and my dad on the opposite side could hear me like I was inches away." The guard's shoulders relaxed a little. "My dad once told me that if a couple kissed right under the highest point, they were destined to spend their lives together."

Chapel's Rule Number Six: Revere. We enter forbidden places with veneration. Your captor, spending hours each day within the same walls, may share your respect, which forms the basis for communion.

I continued. "Drax has a contract to turn this into a shopping mall. You know that concourse where you've got your desk? They'll bulldoze it." I looked to the ground and shook my head, feeling like a stage actor, and feeling the heat of Reuben's glare on my cheek. He'd always hated my verbal gymnastics, even when they saved his ass.

The guard responded. "So it'll be a mall for a time, then it'll be somethin' else. No big deal." I bristled. I'd made him feel partly responsible, so he rationalized it—diminished it. *Just a building.* But too many Cincinnatians slept peacefully with their complacency. A dazzling photo—*my* photo—of the rotunda might slap some sense into them. After all, a picture of a naked Vietnamese girl running from a napalm attack had slapped America into questioning this war.

"I'm sorry," I said, my voice now soft and deliberate. I looked toward the concentric ceiling. "I know it sounds weird, but this place always felt more like a cathedral than a train station." I glanced back at the guard. I held his attention. "You can't trespass in a church, can you? Just like the Good Book, this place is for everyone."

The guard's face registered a swift realization. "You looked through my Bible."

Chapel also said something about capitalizing on good fortune, but I couldn't remember the quote. Regardless, this was too good to be true. "I'm afraid I lost your place in the pages."

The guard blinked.

"Look, we wanted to take one last picture before it's all gone." I paused, outwardly thoughtful. "You've got a job to do. We…" I glanced at Reuben, a gesture mandated by my script. His eyes were the size of Kennedy half dollars. "We'll do whatever you ask."

"So you think I'm gonna let you go?" Score! Openly expressing a choice increased its odds of being chosen.

Now, to walk him across the finish line. "Like I said, we'll respect your judgment." My implied point: *you have choices.* Workers bridled by rules didn't feel free to choose. Furthermore, all decisions sat at a fulcrum, therefore easy to tip in our favor. "If you must turn us over to your superiors, so be it. But if you'll let us leave in peace, we will feel truly blessed."

Done. *Amen!* The defense rested its case.

But just then, another security guard—older, heavier and pissed off, with a buzz-cut and the same dust-colored Drax uniform as his colleague—muscled through the doors and halted with a slap of shoe leather, legs spread. He aimed his gun at my belt buckle. This *was* a career security man, and a real hard ass.

My elaborate construction of justification, affiliation and suggestion collapsed to the floor.

He locked his eyes with mine and barked at Charlie Brown from the side of his mouth. "Next time, Jamie, carry your goddamn walkie-talkie." Then to us, "You clowns, guts to the ground, hands behind your heads."

We'd come so far. "Sir, we can explain everything," I said.

But Hard Ass would have nothing of it. "Now!" His bellow bounced off the infinite surfaces of the dome, hammering our eardrums.

By the time I dropped to the floor, Reuben was already there, seething.

. . . . .

Charlie Brown guarded us from a safe distance, like we were pit bulls on weak chains, while Hard Ass radioed for instructions from inside the vestibule. My name stood out twice among an army of unintelligible words marching through airwave static. "Tremaine," followed a moment later by, "Yeah, *Lucas Tremaine.*"

He spat my full name, like griping about a boss over a beer. When I got in trouble as a kid, my mother would enunciate my first and last name, but gently, her anger peaking on *Lucas* and ebbing on *Tremaine,* as if remembering that boys will be boys.

These days, she would sprawl across the couch in the small house we shared, staring past me at something I could never see. In her weakened state, she didn't need me making things worse.

And neither did Reuben. I called to Charlie Brown from a cement bench along the rotunda wall. "Tell your boss to let my friend go. This was my plan. He only sets up the equipment."

Reuben sat beside me, hands folded in his lap. He didn't protest the suggestion, but frowned and whispered, "They'll unload you on the cops."

"I doubt it." I hoped my turbulent history with Drax might work to my advantage.

Reuben considered this a moment. "If they take you to Drax, try to keep it cool."

On the drive, we passed the Music Hall and the old Shillito department store, both architectural wonders. "They call it the Paris of America," Dad would remind Mom and me about his hometown. "Two hundred fifty listings on the National Register of Historic Places."

My suggestion to Charlie Brown paid off. Hard Ass pulled up to a bus stop on Spring Grove and gave Reuben a parental glower. "You dodged a bullet, Pixie. Get lost." Reuben climbed out and teetered at the curb, looking in his grimy jeans like a homeless man with no destination in mind, the pewter sky of a new day floating over his head.

Hard Ass, my camera bag close by, stomped the accelerator and screeched right at Hopple Avenue, heading toward Drax corporate headquarters.

CHAPTER 3

We lost Dad six years ago.

At the time, Mom earned what she could wrangling switchboards at Cincinnati Bell. Dad earned less painting canvases, so he started working for anyone with a checkbook, painting houses, strip malls, new construction, residential, and commercial. He called his business True Man Painting, a twist on our family name. He would pick me up from school in his work overalls—sometimes shit-colored from blends of paint—and I was embarrassed, hopping into the car with my cap pulled low. I wish I could tell him now how stupid I'd been, and how proud I am.

Over time, his client list picked up household names like Cincinnati Public Schools, First Financial Bank, and Drax Enterprises. Drax hired Dad for a project thirty miles north near Hamilton, Ohio, where the company was building a Minuteman missile silo for the federal government. Operating as a subcontractor, Dad was to paint steel doors and trim.

On a dazzling summer day at the work site, twenty-four lengths of galvanized framing studs toppled from a stack and thirteen tumbled over the edge into the multi-story concrete cylinder. Sixty feet below, Dad painted a yellow railing on a cantilevered walkway. The studs struck him on the head and shoulder. He died quickly, we were told, as though we should be thankful. But the nightmares still came, all yellow paint and blood and metal.

Even in my dreams, I knew the truth: it was no accident. Drax had committed three acts of negligence: the unsecured bundle, forklifting too close to the edge, and no protective barrier. At the time, we didn't know that Drax grew profits by cutting corners.

We needed a lawyer. Cincinnati had plenty of contingency lawyers, but they didn't want our case. The odds were long, the adversary powerful. Drax's deep pockets could keep a case in litigation for years, bleeding a law firm dry.

So we drained every penny from family savings and hired an attorney, two years out of law school with an office above a hardware store. Our lawsuit contended Drax had "not exercised reasonable care." We made headway, tracking down a Drax pipefitter who agreed to testify to lax safety practices on the job site. Another worker swore Dad's injuries occurred in spite of the helmet secured to his head.

Mom and I later learned that moments after Dad's death, a powerful force within Drax switched on, like a machine with one purpose: to shield the company from responsibility and protect its reputation. Drax's legal team and covert operators constructed a bulwark of deception and confusion. Both witnesses suddenly backed out, citing cloudy memory. New witnesses materialized from the ether, swearing to OSHA-approved safety measures and the absence of Dad's headgear.

Dad would never avoid protective measures, and our lawyer said so in court. The lead Drax attorney pressed the judge for an out-of-sequence presentation. Civil trials have softer rules, so the judge accommodated. The attorney reached into an accordion briefcase and withdrew a see-through evidence bag containing a bullet-shaped bottle of Bacardi 151 rum with an inch of liquid in the bottom. He placed the bottle conspicuously on the table and read a deposition from a worker who supposedly witnessed my father stashing the bottle in a locker. The attorney looked up from his paper and, in an Oscar-winning performance, glanced toward us sadly. "We're pained to air harsh truths when this family has suffered enough," he said to the jury, "but drink impairs judgment, and alcoholics take risks."

Dad didn't drink.

Never in my life had I come closer to throwing it all away, to launching myself across the courtroom and choking the last breath from another human being. I still imagine the protruding eyes and panic-stretched cheeks, the wet crush of the windpipe under my thumbs. But at that moment, my mother knitted her fingers in mine and squeezed.

By the time we'd primed our counterattack, Drax lawyers in their Italian suits and fifty-dollar haircuts were flanking us, pelting the jury with complex definitions of prime contractors and first- and second-tier subcontractors, wedging my father into the last group because he'd trusted a handshake over a signed contract.

As the proceedings wound down, Rudolph Drax appeared in the back row of the courtroom in a crisp suit and tie, hair parted precisely. A job-site fatality wouldn't disrupt the CEO's schedule, but a threat to reputation would. His dark eyes tracked from attorney to attorney and juror to juror, his lips pursed in indecipherable stoicism.

In the end, the eight jurors were too confused to produce the six votes necessary. The final gavel fell and Rudolph glanced in my direction. Not *at* me, but through me. Me, the son of a dead worker. Me, a liability on the company books, now offset. He rose, nodded to the lead attorney, and strode out.

Mom and I walked to the bus stop with Dad's stained reputation in a three-ring binder. At home in bed, I listened to a fly die slowly on the windowsill. I slept and dreamed that Dad and I were eating at the dinner table by candlelight. His fork fell silent for a moment, and when I looked up, he stared back, smiling wistfully, yellow paint dripping from somewhere above his hairline.

In the days after, I climbed into my hidey-holes. Mom climbed into a bottle of Valium.

Perhaps Drax couldn't be compared to a machine. A machine suggests an assemblage of parts in sync, devoid of emotion and prejudice, pre-programmed to serve stockholders.

But Drax was no machine. Drax was an organism with a central nervous system in complete control of arms and legs and feet and hands, all capable of crossing legal and moral lines as easily as boarding an elevator. The organism came to life with Walther Drax decades ago and grew stronger through Rudolph Drax. One day, it would grow stronger still through Tony Drax, the organism's fetid blood flowing from one generation to the next like sewage through pipes.

CHAPTER 4

A few blocks from the Ohio River, the Drax building loomed before us, surpassed in height by only the Carew Tower. Hard Ass double-parked before the rotating stainless steel Drax Enterprises sign, yanked me out by the collar, and pushed us into a single revolving door compartment, his protruding belly against my back. Once in the main lobby, he gripped my arm above the elbow and steered me across the polished marble floor.

I gave my arm a jerk. "I'm not trying to run off."

Hard Ass puffed his chest out, as proud as Eliot Ness parading Al Capone to a prison cell. My camera bag hung from his shoulder. He spoke to be overheard by the female receptionist. "You won't B & E our buildings anymore, not after this."

Like hell. "I sure won't." In the early morning light, his lumpy face looked like a bag of rope.

"We keep an eagle eye on things. You better remember that."

Then why did we have the run of the Union Terminal? "I sure will."

Hard Ass seated me on a lobby bench, lowered himself alongside and exhaled. He smelled of cigarettes and chocolate. He checked his watch. I checked mine—6:45 a.m. "The bosses aren't here yet," he said, "so sit tight."

A guard and his prisoner drew the attention of Drax employees reporting for work early with their shiny briefcases and noisy shoes. I imagined raising my voice to deflate their speculations. *I'm not a serial killer. I'm a graduate student in architecture who wanted to photograph a historic treasure before your employer shitcans it.*

The lobby was designed to impress. Even though the building had been built fifty years ago, Drax had remodeled the interiors every decade or so to showcase the styles of the day. From the floor to the high ceiling, taut steel cables held Plexiglas-framed photos the size of garage doors, most of them visible from the street. In one, a girl in pigtails let loose a beach ball, her mother proud in the background. In another, a beaming granny in amber goggles waved down from the basket of a hot air balloon.

The same images were scattered on billboards and bus signs throughout the city. The Drax public image had always been scrubbed, styled and displayed as meticulously as Jackie O's hairdo.

Below each photo was the Drax slogan, *Let Your Dreams Take Flight*, coined during the Depression by the company's founder, Walther Drax.

According to the business press, Walther remained vigorous and active on the Board of Directors in spite of being in his late seventies. Most managerial duties had fallen to Walther's son Rudolph. As for Rudolph's only child, Tony, I didn't know his role, but he couldn't hold any real responsibility, not the gristlehead I remembered from high school.

Back then, Anton "Tony" Drax was already considered the future of the company and heir to millions, if his fellow students didn't conspire to murder him first.

Tony and the other Princes of Cincinnati's Seven Hills would tour the halls as if they owned the place—and for all we knew, they did—and dispatch challenges with a knee to the crotch.

Off to the right was the entrance to the Drax Museum. How many companies built monuments to themselves? I'd heard from fellow grad students the museum displayed scale models of every Drax construction project. I'd never ventured in, terrified I'd find a replica of the job site where Dad died.

At 7:30 a.m., Hard Ass hauled me to my feet and led us to the elevator. He punched the call button and stood erect. Irritated by his smugness, I shifted my gaze to wall-mounted photos of the Drax Center for the Performing Arts, Drax Business School at Cincinnati University, and more. Strategically placed photos. Every visitor would see Drax magnanimity.

I didn't buy it. Al Capone opened soup kitchens, but he was still a crook.

Hard Ass was talking again. "Breaking and entering can get you two years in lock-up."

This guy loved cop jargon. "Entering, yes," I replied, "but we don't break things."

"Two years and ten Gs." The elevator doors opened to an empty car. I took a step forward but Hard Ass shoved me between the shoulder blades anyway. "Tack on another six months for wanton destruction of public property." He pressed the button for the forty-second floor, three floors from the top, near the nerve center of the company.

"We don't destroy things." The elevator felt like a cage.

Hard Ass gave a heard-it-all-before shake of the head. "That's the problem with your kind. You don't respect."

My kind? My face felt hot, a dangerous sign. Reuben had warned me.

Hard Ass continued. "Do you have any idea how much graffiti I've seen on the walls of beautiful old buildings from people like you?"

People like me? I faced him. "Look, we don't vandalize. We enter places to learn about them, and sometimes to protect them from developers like your boss who'd use the Grand Canyon as a landfill if it paid the mortgage on his Mt. Adams mansion. Now what does that say about *people like you* who follow his orders?"

I breathed hard through my nose, waiting for a reply. But Hard Ass didn't have the words. His expression was clogged with surprise and indignation. Apparently I wasn't expected to have a viewpoint, only a craving for wanton destruction.

He collected himself. "You bet I'm loyal, to the places I protect from scum."

"Instead of *people like you*, Drax should use dogs," I snapped. I counted out points on my fingers, one, two, three. "They don't take coffee breaks, they don't leave doors unlocked, and they don't lecture when they don't know shit."

The elevator car came to a stop. The doors hissed apart.

Hard Ass clenched his jaw, new lumps forming on his cheeks.

Find the flow of their river and float with them toward a common portage, Chapel had advised. I'd ignored him.

Hard Ass sliced the silence. "You won't always be in a nice crowded office building, so you better watch your back." He clamped my arm and push-pulled me out of the elevator.

We walked down a long hallway lined with doors and more framed photos. One showed Walther Drax posing alongside Charles Lindbergh, as if greatness might pass from one to another by osmosis. A few doors down, a black-and-white showed Walther attending the ribbon-cutting ceremony for the Cincinnati Union Terminal in 1933. I wanted to shout, *See? First he celebrates the place, then he destroys it.*

But these pretend words were stifled by echoes of my real words to Hard Ass, pissed off and personal. If Reuben had seen my outburst, he would've had plenty to say. *What's the point, Lucas? 'Focus on the mission,' you always say. Practice what you preach, for once.*

Hard Ass yanked open a door and gave my back another shove. I stumbled into a large, unoccupied room.

"Stay in here," he ordered. "I'll be right outside so don't get any ideas." He swung the door shut as he left.

I looked around the room. There was a small raised stage at one end, and enough folding chairs for an audience of a hundred or more. The walls were lined with dozens of sayings on huge banners. One said, *Follow your dreams… they know the way.* This was where Rudolph Drax addressed his employees.

Dad wouldn't have been proud of my war of words with Hard Ass. "Everybody in this world," he'd once said, "including rich and poor and doctors and garbage collectors, wants to feel they count for something." Then he smiled. Mom described it as a "smoothing smile," because it smoothed out the wrinkles of a bad day.

A door clicked open behind me. I turned. Hard Ass entered followed by a well-dressed young man. "Lucas Tremaine," the new arrival said with a world-weary sigh.

I knew him. Unlike his rebellious shag from high school, his dark hair was trimmed neat, off the ears and parted on the side. He wore herringbone suit pants with no jacket, a striped necktie and white button-down dress shirt tucked in snug around a toned torso. He had broad shoulders, the body of a contact-sport athlete. I'd once seen that body lift a kid off the ground by the throat.

Tony Drax flashed a chilly smile. "Don't we both have better things to do?"

• • • • •

Hard Ass cleared his throat to get Tony's attention. The two men exchanged a few words beyond my hearing.

The guard walked out. Tony spoke. "He wants me to turn you over to the police."

"I told him the truth. He didn't like that." Tony was silent, and I felt a flush of boldness. "But I don't think you'll call the cops."

He frowned. "Like hell I won't."

"Oh, come on. We both know why you're here. Your dad figured since we're old school *buddies*, I'll open up and tell you the real reason we were in the train station. Otherwise, why bring me up here?" Speculation, yes, but I watched Tony's face for a tell.

He forced a smirk. "Do you think the CEO of a multimillion-dollar corporation cares about your bullshit hobby?"

Tony was a puppet. He could neither return my equipment nor cut me loose without his father's okay. I was wasting my time.

I needed breathing room to plan a way out. I pointed to one of the banners hung high on the walls. *When everything seems to be going against you, remember that the airplane takes off against the wind, not with it.* — Henry Ford. "Your dad likes quoting famous people." More credibility by osmosis.

"We can learn from the greats."

"Is that you talking or Rudolph?" I wondered about a Type A overachiever father and a stupid brute of a son who was expected to take over the family business one day. It couldn't be a healthy relationship.

"I have to care about employee morale as the vice president of operations." He followed this with a contemptuous smile. "Are you employed?"

"Job titles come cheap when Dad owns the place. He could've labeled you Archbishop of Canterbury without a peep from his subordinates." Tony held firm. I pointed to another banner: *Life always offers you a second chance. It's called tomorrow.* "So that one helps with morale? It's patronizing. What's your employee turnover rate?"

"Our team is loyal."

"And there's no attribution on that one."

"My dad said it—in a speech to the team on our fiftieth anniversary in business."

"I feel my morale lifting by the second." I jumped to the next banner: *I believe fundamental honesty is the keystone of business.* — Harvey S. Firestone. "Who's Rudolph kidding? That's like Kissinger quoting Gandhi. Now, when can I speak with him?"

Tony faced me. "Why did you break into our job site?"

"Why is taking a few pictures such a big deal?" I switched into offensive mode, venom oozing into my words before I could staunch the flow. "Are you guys hiding something?"

"No, we're repurposing the building."

I laughed. "Repurposing? That's tidy." I held my hand parallel to the floor and flipped it over. "You're simply shifting from one purpose to another. No damage in that." I singled out the next banner: *You can never cross the ocean until you have the courage to lose sight of the shore.* — *Christopher Columbus.* "Finally, a quote that belongs in this place. Columbus brought smallpox to the New World and killed millions of people."

Tony folded his arms across his chest. "This is bullshit. Some people have work to do. Last chance. What do you want?"

I hadn't expected the question. "Look, maybe I'm a guy who can't bear the thought of a Spencer Gifts selling whoopee cushions and fake vomit in a historic—"

"City Council approved the decision to rezone that property for retail. If you got a problem, complain to the Mayor."

"Or maybe we were there to get back at the people who destroyed my family."

Tony rummaged in his mind and found what he was looking for. "We were all devastated by the accident that led to your father's death."

"Spare me the canned speech from your PR department. The point is, if our little adventure goes public, either the press will find me or I'll find them, and I'll talk about the outrage of bulldozing half a cultural landmark to create parking spaces." Tony opened his mouth to speak but I held up a hand. "But then I'll keep talking. About my father. And I'll use language like *wrongful death* and *grave injustice* and *wound that never heals.*"

"Your dad was a tier two subcontractor, not an employee. It's all in the official court record."

I waved him off. "That's a technicality cooked up by your lawyers, and you know it. But the public saw a company that doesn't give a shit about people. That's why your dad wants my family to go away. We won't."

"Then what do you want, Tremaine?"

I felt a fresh wave of heat in my cheeks. "My gear and a ride home."

"Sorry to break it to you, but we'll keep your camera bag. And if you need a ride, call a friend." He pointed to a wall-mounted office phone. "Press nine for an outside line."

There he was—the Tony Drax I knew. Hairstyle and dress of a respectable businessman, maybe, but a seventeen-year-old bully underneath.

He flashed me a smartass grin. "So you still like crawling around underground?" He sniffed the air. "I'm surprised you don't smell like a sewer."

I said nothing.

"What's the attraction?"

Defending urban exploration to Tony Drax would be like explaining a Picasso to a housecat.

Tony shook his head slowly as if marveling. "And you break into places with your buddy, Reuben Klein." A raised eyebrow, a realization. "We used to call him Ruby Jew, remember?"

My face burned red hot. I was done with this pointless back-and-forth. I wanted out.

But Tony wasn't done. He scooted a chair aside and stepped too close for comfort. I smelled his contempt like sour milk. "I don't get it, Lucas. You're a dirt-poor river rat. Always have been, always will be."

For a moment, I became a forgettable kid in cracked sneakers, squeaking down a high school hallway, stepping aside for the Princes of the Seven Hills. Something torqued into a hard ball just below my rib cage.

Tony cocked his head, play-acting deep contemplation. "And since you don't have any money, what do you need a Jew for?"

It's funny the way the brain works. Or maybe it's *my* brain, with halves that never stop fighting each other. In a millisecond, a comeback popped into one half, the diplomatic half, something about Reuben getting to be anything he damn well wants to be.

But while the diplomatic half of my brain cycled, trying to figure out what words should enter the inches of airspace between Tony and me, the other half—the impulsive half—grew tired of waiting. It issued a terse command, and the fist of my right hand obeyed.

A long second later, the man-boy who'd pummeled so many victims in the halls of Queen City High School lay on the ground, both hands pressed to the sides of his nose as if trying to hold the pieces of his face together.

CHAPTER 5

Later that morning, my one permitted phone call woke my mom. I explained what had happened. "I'm sorry, Mom. Something came over me."

"I understand," she said, her voice empty. "I'll try to get you out." She hung up, clearly in no shape to dissect my story. Her symptoms often were bad in the morning, now made worse with my troubles caked on top like volcanic ash. I realized something. I'd been cruel, like a pet owner who stays out late while his dog, bladder near bursting, must relieve herself shamefully on the rug.

Mom had been picking up part-time gigs for Cincinnati Bell whenever the switchboard jockeys went on strike. That and subbing for sick regulars.

Working 411 directory assistance suited Mom, at least now. The job was simple: incoming beep, request for a person or a pizzeria, quick look-up, disconnect, and repeat. No forethought. According to the doctors, she couldn't tackle anything more challenging for six to twelve months, maybe longer.

I spent the day behind bars sitting on an immovable steel bench that seemed inches from the opposite wall. The air smelled of wet concrete and bleach.

Unlike in the movies, I didn't share my cell with a shark-eyed, tattooed beast. I was alone, but would've preferred a bunkie to take my mind off the incessant *you're an idiot* droning between my ears. I'd verbally assaulted a security guard doing his job, and I'd physically assaulted a powerful businessman with the means to make my life hell.

By midafternoon, the jail guard shouted from down the hall, "Tremaine! Bail posted." The cell door opened automatically with a *clack* and metallic grind.

Bail? With whose money? Mom was broke like me.

I entered the jail's receiving area. Mom wavered next to Reuben, her eyes red and rimmed with shadow, her shoulders slumped.

"We can tell you about the bail money," Reuben said, "but in the car. We're late." We started walking.

"Good news, honey." Mom's eyes defied her cheerful words. "I picked up the four o'clock shift. We're just two blocks away. You can drop me off and I'll take the bus home."

She'd be on duty until midnight. "You good for an entire shift?" I doubted.

"If you tell them no, they don't call again." Temp workers were as expendable as coat hangers.

We piled into Reuben's '66 Ford Falcon, with me in the back and leaning forward between the bucket seats. Reuben pulled onto Lincoln Avenue and stepped on the gas.

Mom began. "Honey, you're not gonna like it, but we couldn't leave you in that jail. I don't know what I'd do if you got hurt." She patted her thigh, keeping a beat, a symptom.

I shifted position to catch Reuben in the rearview mirror. "Who coughed up the bail money?"

"Your boss," Mom replied. "Mr. Blumenfeld can be a very sweet man."

Reuben threw me a look of pity.

I felt a throb of pressure behind my forehead. "No, Mom, Alfred's *not* a very sweet man. He can be a real pain in the… how much?"

"Five thousand dollars," she said, gripping her thigh to control her hand movements.

"Oh God." I squeezed my eyes shut and reopened. "Does he know I took the Leica?"

"Even if he doesn't, I bet Tricia does," Reuben said. "She read it in her witches' brew."

Reuben and I graduated from Queen City High with Alfred's granddaughter. She called herself Trix back then. She'd stroll into class with a cigarette behind her ear, exuding the tired boredom of a cop directing traffic. Today, a decade later, she went by Tricia and worked the retail camera shop next to the photo lab where I worked, all part of Alfred's little empire.

Reuben gazed at me like a priest consoling a death-row inmate. "I'm afraid to ask what happened to the camera."

"Tony Drax kept it," I said.

Mom tried to turn in her seat to see me. "Kept what?"

I pointed through the front window at the Cincinnati Bell building looming before us. "Here we are. Let's talk later tonight. I'll wait up."

She gave my hand a squeeze, labored from the car, and shuffled away, the result of another withdrawal symptom, tar-like leg muscles.

I scrambled into the front seat. Reuben shoved the gearshift forward. I touched his forearm. "Wait until she gets inside. Sometimes they hassle her about her temps pass."

But they didn't and Reuben pulled away, his words also accelerating. "What if they had hassled her? Would you run over there and smash somebody in the face?"

And thus began Reuben's tirade. I had it coming. I'd almost dragged him down with me. He tossed in all the greatest hits from our more contentious exchanges:

"Have you completely lost your mind?"

"Do you ever *think* before you do something?"

"You were expecting Tony to blot the blood from his Brooks Brothers' shirt and say *sorry, you're right, and here's your stuff?*"

"Don't you think your mom has enough to worry about?"

"Focus on the mission! Focus on the mission! Bullshit."

"You didn't *elevate yourself above the petty defiance of the diffident*, now did you?"

Reuben must've liked the sound of that last one because he continued twisting more of Chapel's advice. "*We neither vandalize nor pilfer*—but we do randomly beat up people!"

Red-faced, Reuben stopped, now breathing hard.

"Are you finished?" I asked.

"No." He sounded exhausted suddenly, the insistence stripped from his voice. "I was rid of that asshole, but now he's back in my life. Thanks a lot."

"Tony's mad at me, not you," I said.

"Like that ever worked. I was always guilty by association."

I stifled a smile. We were in this mess together.

Reuben took his frustration out on the Ford, turning northbound onto Colerain Avenue too fast, the tires squealing.

I gripped the dashboard. "Where are we going?"

"Your work. Blumenfeld told your mom he needed to speak with you the minute you got sprung."

I checked my watch. Four in the afternoon. "Maybe he's already noticed the Leica's missing. Good. He'll murder me now and I won't have to appear in court."

In all the hubbub of regaining my freedom, I'd temporarily forgotten my biggest problem: a potential felonious assault conviction. Fear pulsed in my chest.

We parked in front of Blumenfeld Photography, an off-white, single-story building with a flat roof, powder blue trim and minimal windows to keep stray light from polluting the portrait studio and darkroom. Concrete planters held well-tended petunias in purples and pinks, chosen by Alfred.

Blumenfeld had owned the building for decades, expanding every few years by knocking down a wall and adding workspace. One expansion tripled the size of the portrait studio. Another made room for new developing equipment after the invention of color photography. A third tacked on the retail shop, now run by Blumenfeld's granddaughter, Tricia, bringing the total number of employees to eight, at last count.

I tried to brace myself for an ugly reckoning with Alfred, but my thoughts drifted back. "I should've kept Mom out of this," I said and reached for the car's door handle. Reuben touched my shoulder, his face a question mark behind pop-bottle optics. "Lucas, it's none of my business, but I've never seen her so bad."

Reuben knew she struggled, and that sometimes I'd drop everything because of some vague trouble at home. But he didn't know about tapering off the medications. "She made me promise to keep a secret," I said, "but her symptoms are so obvious." I paused to recheck my thinking. "Just between you and me, okay?"

"Of course."

I took a deep breath. "Dad's death pushed her over the edge. Depression, as you know, but anxiety too—I swear she's been drenched in sweat so many times, afraid to leave the house. The doctors put her on Valium."

A pause to consider. "Mother's little helper."

I nodded. "And why not? There's a Stones song about it. Couldn't be so bad."

Reuben pushed up his glasses with his thumb, waiting for the punch line.

"But those little yellow pills were designed for short-term use, a week or two max. She's been taking them for years."

"Damn."

"Six months ago, she hit bottom again. A different doctor said the pills were making her worse."

"That happened to my dad after his foot surgery. It was Dilaudid, and he had to get off it fast."

"But with Valium, you can't stop cold turkey. You'll go insane."

Reuben squinted, doubting. Movement caught my eye. Beyond the front window of Alfred's business, the receptionist set a coffee mug on her desk.

I explained. "If you go cold turkey, whatever you're most afraid of—snakes, crowds, small spaces, death—attacks you like you're trapped in a haunted house, but the ghosts and monsters aren't people in costumes. They're real and trying to kill you. You shiver and sweat and dread every waking moment until you take more pills. Or, you wash down the whole bottle with a tumbler of vodka and escape the monsters permanently."

Reuben's Adam's apple jumped as he swallowed. "I'm so sorry for her."

A magpie landed on the building's gutter, teetered for balance, and swooped down to chase off a couple of sparrows.

"She's tapering," I said. "Gradual decreases, *really* gradual, only a few percent every couple of weeks. And even with those tiny reductions, the monsters pound on her door." I recalled a bad night: Mom curled up on the shower floor in her work clothes, whimpering, hot water scalding her skin, the pain a kind of relief. "Some days I worry she'll give up."

"Would she?"

"A few weeks ago, she said her life felt optional. That's the word she used. I told her it's the withdrawal, but in her mind, the hopelessness can't be explained by tiny pills. Life scares her."

"What's she scared of most?" Reuben asked, scratching his chin.

The magpie landed in a trimmed bed of evergreen shrubs, checked for predators, and pecked at the topsoil.

"Losing me too, I suppose." I glanced back at my friend and endured a wave of guilt. "I chose a terrible time to clobber Tony Drax."

The magpie hopped to the rim of a planter and surveyed his domain.

"What did Tony say right before you punched him?" Reuben asked.

The question caught me off-guard. "Oh, you know, the usual crap, same as in high school. Me being a scumbag river rat, him being royalty. Got under my skin, I guess."

I wasn't ready to share what Tony said about Reuben. "Let's get this done." I yanked the door handle.

· · · · ·

We entered through the retail shop, a tidy operation about half the size of a 7-Eleven. Center displays stocked darkroom supplies and photo accessories like tripods and floodlights. Cameras and lenses remained in a glass case tended by Tricia Blumenfeld, the store's manager and sole clerk.

Given the way she perched on her high stool, straight-backed and attentive, a customer had to be nearby. Sure enough, there he was, reading the fine print on a bright yellow box of Kodak enlarging paper. Without a customer in the house, Tricia might've been slouched in a chair in the corner, the front door always in sight. She'd have a notebook on her lap where she'd scribble pictures or words we'd never see. I imagined sketches of vengeful she-warriors or poems about life after an apocalypse.

She watched us approach as if we were delivering a virus.

"I have a customer," she muttered and tipped her head toward the displays. She'd never admit it, but Alfred's decision to put his granddaughter in charge of the shop was brilliant. Unlike the Tricia I knew in high school, she now cared about something. The store was her baby, and she'd raised it right.

"Got it," I said. Reuben took up a cautious position behind me. He'd always coexisted with Tricia like a barnyard chicken around the farmer's dog—willing to peck but never with its back turned. "How's business?"

"What do you need?" Tricia said.

Let's see... a good lawyer, safe asylum, a ride to Tijuana. "We didn't see Alfred's car outside."

She creased her brow. "That's because he's not here."

Okay, it was going to be one of *those* conversations. Reuben sidestepped, pretending to be interested in the merchandise.

"Would you be willing to tell me where he is?" I asked.

"Sure, and after I tell you, you two should get back in your Cadillac and drive away."

"That bad, huh?"

"That bad."

"Come on, Trish. I'm trying to get through one shitty day, okay?" I wondered how much she knew. "What's Alfred pissed about?"

The customer appeared, trailing shyness, the yellow box in his hand.

"Just unofficial business here, sir," I said to him amiably, stepping aside and waiting while Tricia rang him up.

Her wavy brunette hair, restrained by a black hairband, fell to her shoulder blades. In high school, that same hair crashed about her face, blocking her brown eyes and shielding her from a world that disapproved of her scruffy looks and screw-you demeanor. Back then, only a couple of close friends squeezed past the barrier. The rest of us were assholes until proven otherwise.

One weekend last year, I spotted her across the dance floor of a Mount Adams nightclub called The Blind Lemon. She'd teased her hair into madness and tinted it purple and yellow. She was dancing with a guy who looked like James Dean back from the grave—probably her one-night stand, if you believed the gossip from back in high school.

At Queen City High, Tricia seemed to hate the sameness of American suburban teenhood. For a year, she called herself Tricks because she hated all the "Goldilocks" variations on Patricia. "But tricks are what prostitutes sell to make a living," her friends told her. So Tricia changed the spelling to Trix, like the cereal. By senior year, she was Tricia again and I forgot about her until years later when I began working for her grandfather to pay my tuition bills.

She placed the enlarging paper in a brown bag, folded over the top, and stapled it shut with the cash register receipt. She handed over the package and smiled as if she'd been waiting all day for the man to pay a visit. "We sure do appreciate your business, sir. Have a wonderful evening."

The moment the customer cleared the front door, the warmth escaped Tricia's expression. "Look, all I know is that Alfred stormed off to the reshoot about two hours ago hollering that you're supposed to get your ass over there."

So she didn't know about the Leica, and she didn't know about my arrest. But wait. "Reshoot?" I asked, the ominous word sinking in.

"You didn't hear?" Her face brightened at the prospect of juicy storytelling.

"Chuckles fought the dip 'n dunk and lost big time." That meant film shot at a recent wedding had been destroyed, the worst possible news for a photo lab.

A few years earlier, Alfred installed *dip 'n dunk* automated color film-developing equipment to better handle the booming wedding business. Two people received training from the manufacturer: my fellow lab technician Chuckles and me. If only we'd known what we were getting into, and why the machine would come to be nicknamed *fuck 'n junk*.

Developing wedding film was nerve-racking, beginning with inserting the filmstrips into the machine, like threading needles in total darkness. Then, for the forty-five-minute cycle, we'd perch blind on a folding chair and hunger for the sounds of nothing going wrong. But every so often, things did go wrong. Something unseen would clunk and splash, and part of a twenty-thousand-dollar wedding would disintegrate in chemicals. Alfred would then drag us along to share in the agony of apologizing to the tearful bride. Dresses would be dry cleaned and tuxedos re-rented to re-stage and re-shoot the lost moments, the smiles of the wedding party stiff the second time around.

"Which scene bit the dust?" I asked. All weddings were comprised of predictable scenes, from the bride getting dressed, to the newlyweds' car dragging tin cans off to marital bliss.

"Not scene, *scenes*—cake cutting and the first dance." Tricia was enjoying this a little too much.

The dance photos would be a total loss. You couldn't restage a reception crowd encircling a dance floor. As for the cake scene, Tricia anticipated my question. "Alfred got Turetzky's to whip up a replacement triple-decker, and swore to deduct the cost from Chuckles' paycheck." Chuckles, a.k.a. Charles "Chuck" Dahlgren, only cared about four things: football, weightlifting, pot smoking and his Corvette—and the last two cost money.

"But it's not his fault," I said. "It's the machine."

"But the old man bought the thing," Tricia said. "He'll always blame human error before himself."

"Tough break. Is Chuckles here?" The least I could do is offer a word of sympathy from one lab tech to another. There but for the grace of God go I. But then again, Chuck took chances.

Tricia reached under the cash register, pulled out her notepad, and set it on the glass case. She caught me eyeballing it. "He's either at the hospital or asleep in the lab. The bleach bath splashed his eye when he tried to salvage the film. Alfred ordered him to the ER but Chuckles blew it off. He was pretty baked when it all happened."

Maybe it *was* human error. Russian roulette with the dip 'n dunk was stressful but we coped. I would play music cassettes but Chuckles would light up a joint. Because of the chemicals, the dip 'n dunk room was the best ventilated in the complex. Chuckles could ride the Rasta rocket to distant planets and Alfred would never be the wiser. And while Tricia could slay with a fiery glance, she'd never rat out a coworker, especially to her grandfather—her boss.

Reuben reappeared at my side after his phony browsing. "We better get going."

"Where's the reshoot?" I asked Tricia.

"Hyde Park Event Center on Fifteenth."

The location sounded familiar. Then it struck me. "Chuckles screwed up the Steiner-Dawson wedding?"

The bride was the client from hell—Angelica Dawson, as tyrannical as Cecil B. DeMille and no less determined to make every detail perfect, regardless of the carnage.

I was doomed. Even if I hadn't lost Alfred's prized Leica, any encounter with the old man within spitting distance of Angelica Dawson would go very badly. Could I avoid it? I imagined strolling into the lab, switching off the ventilation fans, and stretching out on the chemical tanks for a permanent nap.

Tricia must've seen something in my expression because, surprisingly, her face softened. "Look, I don't give a shit what you guys do back there in the dark, but what happened to make Alfred spout the filthiest obscenity ever to pass his lips?"

I didn't follow.

"Ass. He said to get your ass over there." She smiled. Another surprise.

She'd find out eventually. I explained taking the Leica, the train station breach, our capture, my dustup with Tony Drax, and my release that afternoon.

As I spoke and Reuben eyed the exit, Tricia listened, her expression registering the same what-a-bunch-of-idiots disgust as usual, but with one exception. She winced when I mentioned Tony Drax. Tony's reign of terror affected everyone at Queen City High, even Tricia.

"You performed a public service by laying him out," she said.

I ended my story with Alfred's five thousand dollars of bail money. Tricia tightened her brow and placed a porcelain coffee cup full of pens and pencils on top of her notepad, declaring it off limits. "You're in luck," she said. Another surprise from the ice queen.

"I don't feel very lucky."

She plucked a pencil from the cup and twirled it in her fingers like a majorette's baton. "Let me tell you about my grandfather." That statement was rare enough; she always referred to him as Alfred or "the old man," as if denying family ties. "The minute you think you've figured him out, forget it. You haven't. He's a devious old fart who never does anything without a good reason."

"I think I knew that already."

"And when it comes to money, he never does anything without a *damn* good reason. So think about it. He just shelled out five thousand bucks for you when he should've fired you instead."

"Thanks for the vote of confidence."

"He's up to something and he needs you for it."

"Like what?"

She opened the cash register with a *ching* and began arranging bills. "I have my theories. Go to the reshoot and find out for yourself. And then *don't* tell me about it, because I don't want to know."

CHAPTER 6

When Reuben and I arrived at the Hyde Park Event Center, the only cars in the parking lot were Alfred's Oldsmobile and Chuckles' Corvette. My fellow lab tech stood by a dumpster near the service entrance smoking, his head bent forward. Chuckles was one of those guys who smoked with great intensity, studying the glowing tip for the origin of the universe. Women dug this gloss of soulfulness, until they struck up a conversation.

Reuben pulled up alongside and I rolled down my window. "Hey man, Tricia said you might've gone to the hospital." Chuckles wore a collared shirt, khakis, and no-slip shoes, standard issue for Alfred's male employees. His left eye was puffy and red.

"It's better if Tricia doesn't know where I am," he said, his voice anemic and sandpapery from smokes. He flipped his hair off his neck with the back of his hand. As usual, every lock was in place, permed into tight blonde curls and long enough to touch his shoulders.

"Don't you think you better get that eye checked out?"

Chuckles snorted. "Keeping my job is a little more important right now."

"Than keeping your eye?" I considered Chuckles a friend, but he was Reuben's opposite. I tried to offer a sympathetic ear. Reuben's trials and tribulations were Wagnerian operas. Chuckles' were three-minute pop tunes.

He thumbed his cigarette against the dumpster and let the butt bounce on the asphalt. "What're you guys doing here?"

"Trying to help out. What's up inside?"

"Blumenfeld's been waiting two hours, but Her Highness is late, just to be a bitch, if you ask me."

A dark Lincoln Mark III rocked to a stop by the main entrance. Maybe it was a wedding present from the bride's father, an orthodontist in North

Avondale. A young man in a tuxedo climbed out, scurried to open the passenger side door, and stepped back. An attractive woman in a wedding dress emerged. Angelica Dawson. She was hunched over, muttering and complaining, forced to gesture with her head because her bare, slender arms held the billowing layers of fabric off the pavement. Her words were inaudible except for the occasional obscenity and one crystal clear "Because he knows I'd take him to court!"

"Showtime." Chuckles held open the side door for us.

I looked at Reuben, beseeching. "Safety in numbers?"

Reuben sighed and climbed out.

Inside, Alfred stood erect in a dapper houndstooth sport coat, razor-creased slacks and a bow tie. He held the Hasselblad close to his chest with both hands, his eyes trained on the front door except for a sideways glance to inventory our arrival. A triple-decker wedding cake waited on a table nearby. After a moment, the bride and her gown filled the doorway.

"Miss Angelica, we have everything ready," Alfred said. He would never refer to a client by first name only, but ladies' last names were troublesome because they changed mid-project. So he resorted to calling women *Miss* followed by their given names. Most clients found the practice endearing. Angelica Dawson found nothing endearing.

"I have thirty minutes," she said curtly and tramped across the room, tipping her head in our direction. "Who are these people?" For the way she said it, *people* could've been *things*.

Alfred blinked twice. "Members of my staff, Miss Angelica. I insisted they join us to help out in any way possible." Reuben's expression was frozen in unremarkable neutrality, like a desert lizard blending into the sand. Alfred continued. "We are so very sorry that—"

"Their names?" she demanded, perhaps building a roster for later depositions.

Alfred gestured a manicured hand. "This is Charles Dahlgren, Lucas Tremaine—"

"—and Reuben Klein," I interjected. "Our lab intern."

The bride singled me out. "Did *you* destroy the film from my wedding?"

Alfred was quick on his feet. "That particular employee has been dismissed, which explains our lab intern in training, here to learn what's most important to our business, *our valuable clients*." Alfred spoke this with velvety calm, bowing slightly at the waist.

Angelica's icy expression defrosted a few degrees. "All right then, Mr. Blumenfeld. I require five minutes to touch up my makeup." She shuffled toward the ladies room with her skirts still suspended above the linoleum. The groom tagged along.

"That... *woman*," Alfred whispered to none of us in particular, "possesses not one iota of humility or generosity. That's the result of life served on bone china."

Chuckles raised both eyebrows. "I think it's the result of being a bitch."

Alfred glowered. "That, Mr. Dahlgren, is why I do the talking around our customers."

"Pretty impressive performance, Mr. Blumenfeld," I said. I'd always admired Alfred when he smooth-talked his clients. "Like defusing a bomb."

Alfred squared his shoulders. "That is known as kissing up, and kissing up to me won't improve *your* situation, Mr. Tremaine."

"Oh—not my intention, Mr.—"

Alfred held up his hand to silence me. He turned his attention to Chuckles. "A flower arrangement for Miss Angelica needs to be picked up from Friedman's. Make sure the note uses apologetic language as I requested, not *happy retirement*. Understood?"

Chuckles looked worried. "Is it already paid for?"

Alfred stared back without blinking. "No."

Chuckles seemed to turn this information over in his reptile brain, no doubt wondering if he'd get reimbursed. But he caught himself. "Okay."

Next, Alfred singled out Reuben, as if everyone within reach were instant employees. "Go with Mr. Dahlgren to keep the bouquet from bouncing around in that thing he drives." Reuben nodded and followed Chuckles out the door.

Alfred faced me. "Momentarily, Miss Angelica will require our utmost attention, so I suggest you answer the following question with dispatch. Where is my Leica?"

Could he see the guilt like sunburn on my cheeks? "Temporarily detained at the corporate headquarters of Drax Enterprises." My answer felt incomplete. "Sir."

"You better hope it's *temporarily*."

"If not, I will pay for it."

"That's not possible. It's priceless. Did you ever look at the underside of the camera?"

I remembered. "Yeah. Scratched on the aluminum."

Alfred shook his head with disapproval. "That's not a scratch. It was engraved with an electric device many years ago." He watched for my reaction. I fell short. "You don't have a clue what I'm talking about, do you?"

"I know what an engraver is," I said, which suddenly sounded moronic.

"That *scratch* is the signature of Ernst Leitz, the man in charge of the Leica Company during World War II."

"A German? You've never seemed fond of Germans." Alfred's Teutonophobia was legendary around the lab. Shooting with Agfa film instead of Kodak or Ilford could get you fired. Blumenfeld once spotted me popping a BASF cassette tape into my music player. "Use Memorex, dumbhead." He slapped the eject button and dangled the cassette from his fingers like a dead mouse. "These whoresons made the poison for the gas chambers."

Alfred glanced toward the hall. No Angelica yet. He went on. "Leitz was a saint among vermin. He smuggled hundreds of Jews out of Nazi Germany. They called it the Leica Freedom Train. That's why I paid many times market value for that camera, and why we must get it back."

"Yes, sir."

"What film did you shoot?"

"What? Kodak…"

Alfred glanced skyward and exhaled. "What kind of Kodak?"

"What does that have to do with anything?"

"This is some kind of professional secret with you? Answer the question."

"Panatomic-X, but—"

"Meet me in the lobby of the Drax building tomorrow at nine a.m."

"Okay." What was he planning, and why hadn't he mentioned my run-in with the law? "Sir, about posting my bail. I just want you to know—"

"I'm ready." Angelica Dawson rounded the corner, her new husband in tow.

"Nine a.m., and not one minute later," Alfred said to me before spinning toward the bride with a freshly minted smile on his face.

· · · · ·

In spite of the past twenty-four hours, I still had classes and assignments and exams I had to pass. If I failed, Tony Drax would be right. I'd remain a dirt poor river rat.

So, after the reshoot and a cheap supper at Skyline Chili, Reuben dropped me at the main library on the Xavier campus. But instead of studying, I stewed about how my legal troubles could drive a wedge between me and my master's degree in architecture.

I took the bus home and slipped through the front door of our house around one a.m., hoping Mom would be asleep. She wasn't.

The only light came from the bulb over the kitchen sink. She lay on the couch, legs straight out, an unopened magazine on her belly. Reading had become laborious. Her doctor once told me tapering could reduce concentration to that of a three-year-old.

"Mom? How'd it go?"

Our orange tabby cat sprang from the floor to the back of the couch and curled up. Dad had adored the cat, now into her teens, so we adored her too.

Mom turned her head slowly. "What?"

"Your shift."

She waved dismissively and let her hand flop back on the cushion. "Oh, just fine, just fine. Becky Livingston had her baby so everyone celebrated and wrote cute little things on cards. I'm so happy for her."

But her eyes held no happiness for Becky Livingston or anyone else. I sat on the edge of the couch. "It's bad right now, isn't it?"

Her eyes glossed with moisture but she said nothing.

"Tell me what you're feeling."

She hesitated.

"What are you feeling right now?"

"Scared."

"Oh yeah?"

She looked away, embarrassed. "Sometimes I imagine scary things."

"I know, Mom."

"But sometimes they seem real."

"Like what?"

"You'll think I'm a crazy person."

"Crazy? *I'm* the one who crawls around in the city's digestive system. Tell me."

She fixed her gaze on the dark ceiling. "I feel hands on my shoulders, dozens of hands. I know they're not really there, but still."

I nodded.

"I know who's attached to every hand. Mother and Daddy. Your Aunt Janie. The first boy I loved… I know that's silly but it's important to me. My best friends from high school. You're there, of course, and your father."

"We're all there because we care about you."

Her eyes suddenly widened. She lifted her head off the cushion. "But every hand is dying. I don't see it happen, but I feel them turn brown and shrivel up. And then they lose their grip and slide away, and I feel dizzy, like I'm going to fall down. See?"

"Keep going."

"The hands were holding me up. And eventually I *will* fall down. It's only a matter of time before every hand is dead and there's no one there to hold me up anymore." Her head settled back. She took a deep breath.

"You stand on your own two feet."

"No I don't."

Cold swept the skin of my arms. I imagined her in her slippers on the Roebling Bridge, nightgown billowing, staring down into the black water a hundred feet below, a sparrow teetering on the rim of hell. "Do I need to worry about… you being safe, Mom?"

She understood. "I would never do that to you."

I clutched her words like a lifeline.

The magazine slid from her belly and slapped the floor. The cat's head popped up.

Mom thought a moment, her brow creased. "What if I'm still like this after all the meds are gone from my system? What if this is the real me?"

I produced a reassuring smile, as if the answer were obvious. But drugs or no drugs, she changed after Dad died. "This is not the real you. Your brain is getting used to life without chemicals." I gripped her hand, cold and damp. "You're sweating again."

"At work my legs felt like there were a thousand pins stuck in them. I wanted to kick the chair across the room, I was so angry."

"At what?"

"Nothing you haven't heard before."

"Maybe it helps to say it anyway?" I was a lousy psychotherapist.

"I'm angry at that company… and your father." She squeezed her eyes shut. "For going to work that day."

I had no reply. Venting my own anger wouldn't have helped.

"I'm not happy with you either, Lucas. You take foolish risks. Why go near those people?"

I remembered getting into a fight on the muddy banks of the Ohio River when I was thirteen or fourteen. No clue what started it. Maybe a turf dispute, maybe a contest to find out who was toughest, me or the other guy, a zit-faced redneck who lifted homemade barbells under their carport for the neighborhood kids to marvel at.

When some other kids picked me up from the muck, my lip was split, my nose was bleeding, and my left ear felt packed with sawdust.

But I launched myself at the kid again, a puppy fighting a battle-scarred pit bull, even though it meant more of the same punishment. I had to, because going on day after day, tail tucked between my legs, would've been worse than any damage that hillbilly could've done.

CHAPTER 7

The following morning, I emerged from the revolving door precisely at nine a.m. The lobby of the Drax building buzzed with employees on their respective missions. Just beyond the bustle, Alfred stood rail straight at the receptionist's desk, a thin leather portfolio between his slender fingers. He seemed puny amidst the high walls and gigantic propaganda photos suspended overhead.

I dodged cross-traffic and halted alongside Alfred. He wore a tweed sport jacket, necktie, and breast-pocket kerchief, all in earth tones and burnt orange. His tie was perfectly dimpled, his sparse white hair oiled and secured in neat crop rows.

"You're late," he said without emotion, and then returned his attention to the receptionist, a stunning young woman with bound-up hair and a muted gray suit.

She flashed me a fleeting smile of sympathy and then said to Alfred, "And you don't have an appointment?"

"Regrettably, that is correct, Miss Danielle," Alfred said with broadcast-quality enunciation. A brass rectangle on her lapel proclaimed her name in capital letters, enough information for the old man to dial up the charm.

"Your timing is a bit awkward," she said. "There was an accident at one of our construction sites. The management team is quite occupied."

"Oh yes, we read about that in the newspaper. Very tragic," Alfred said, his expression now appropriately grave. "While we're visiting with Mr. Drax on another topic, I hope to offer my counsel regarding this unfortunate event."

I had no idea what he was talking about.

Miss Danielle punched four touchtone numbers and rotated her chair for privacy. Thirty seconds later she turned back and replaced the handset, smiling professionally. "Very well, Mr. Blumenfeld, you and your associate may go ahead. Mr. Drax will be waiting for you in room four three zero five."

Forty-third floor. I was moving up in the world compared to yesterday's face-off with Tony Drax, and now I was an *associate*.

Alfred stopped us halfway to the elevators. "I hope you were taking notes back there."

"Sir?" But I knew what was coming.

"The power of respect and decorum, with that looker at the desk. If you're going to be useful to me, you should remember that diplomacy works far better than punching someone in the nose."

Useful to him, perhaps. Diplomacy was pointless in the lab. Sweet talking the dip 'n dunk machine wouldn't spare any wedding photos or Alfred's wrath. "Which Drax are we seeing?" There were three possibilities: company founder Walther, his son and current CEO Rudolph, and finally, my former classmate. I both desired and dreaded the prospect of facing Tony.

Alfred held his words until a triad of staffers passed by. "We are seeing the Drax most likely to return my camera *if* we demonstrate respect and decorum, which I expect from you."

I was dying to make a smartass comparison between Alfred and an etiquette columnist, but I swallowed it. The old man's five thousand dollars stood between me and a jail cell.

"There is something else."

I waited.

"About what happened to your father." He turned the portfolio over in his hands. "We're here with a specific goal. Would you agree?"

"To get your camera back. *And the film.*"

"And the film. Fine. But we're not here for certain… other purposes."

"Sorry, I don't get it." But I did. He was issuing a gag order.

"Look, you have plenty of reason to pick a bone with Drax."

I sighed. "What do you want, Mr. Blumenfeld?"

"Contrition."

"What happened to respect and decorum?"

Alfred stuck out his chin. "Don't be difficult. You can accomplish a great deal by appealing to another person's sentiments."

"If you're so worried about how I'll behave, why'd you bring me along?"

"Contrition by proxy doesn't work."

"So you need me to stand there and shut up and look wracked with guilt so they'll cough up your camera."

Alfred nodded. "Exactly."

"I'll do my best," I said through my teeth.

We walked side-by-side and boarded an empty elevator car. The moment the doors closed, Alfred flipped open his leather portfolio, plucked a single sheet of paper, and handed it to me. On it was taped a newspaper clipping with a photo and about six inches of copy. "I need you to do some speed reading so you don't embarrass us in front of Mr. Drax."

"What's this?"

"I said *speed reading*. While you were sneaking around the train station yesterday morning, this appeared in the *Enquirer*."

The headline read *Excavator Crashes into Abandoned Subway; Worker Killed*.

I moved to the photo. An I-beam skeleton of a five-story building appeared in the background. New construction.

The foreground grabbed me by the throat. It showed a large piece of construction equipment, the modern-day version of a steam shovel, halfway submerged in a massive hole in the ground. The bucket and its pneumatic attachment stuck awkwardly in the air like the arm and hand of a movie ghoul escaping from the grave. The operator's cab appeared crushed, wedged against the earth as the equipment slid down.

The elevator stopped to receive more passengers.

I reread the headline. *The subway*. Regardless of the grim circumstances, the idea of breaching the long-sealed underground accelerated my heartbeat. Gravity and tons of steel had accomplished in seconds what urban adventurers had failed to accomplish in years. Would the hole provide an access route? I glanced up. Alfred was studying my reaction. I kept reading.

The accident happened in late afternoon. The excavator wasn't digging at the time but rather was crossing a small field to reach the worksite, a new hotel parking garage on Race Street. According to an onlooker, a young mother with her child, "Toby and I were watching from the playground. All of a sudden, the tread thing on one side vanished and everything tipped. Sounded like a car crash in slow motion. Just horrible."

The elevator doors opened again. Thirty-second floor. More passengers squeezed in between Alfred and me. I scanned the remaining text for one word:

Follow Me Down

Drax. I found it in this passage: "The equipment operator, Mr. Delbert Turkel, an employee of Drax Enterprises, was pronounced dead at the scene."

So this was the accident mentioned by the receptionist. This was what would preoccupy the Drax management team and potentially everyone in the company, including the employees in our now-cramped elevator.

I checked out the blank faces, none engaged in typical workday banter, because this day was not typical. But how many of them knew what I knew, that Drax Enterprises was not only responsible for the hotel parking garage project, but also for pouring the subway's concrete some forty years earlier?

The concrete that had just failed, claiming a life.

An on-the-job death reflects horribly on a company's reputation. In retrospect, any headway Mom and I made against Drax after my father's death, however small, had been because the company feared for its reputation.

But why had Alfred shown me the story? This was about more than keeping up on current events to avoid embarrassment. About more than *respect and decorum*. As Tricia had said, *he's a devious old fart who never does anything without a good reason.*

The elevator hissed open to the forty-third floor.

A small plate numbering room four three zero five was dwarfed by a large placard that said *Inspiration Archipelago*.

We entered a room as big as a basketball court, the ceiling twice normal height. I'd expected a cubicle farm, but instead workers stood around one of four islands of activity. Yes, islands, forming an archipelago. Each island was a sprawling work surface covered with the accoutrement of design: angled drawing platforms, sliding straightedges, tins of lettering stencils and X-Acto knives, and sheet after sheet of oversized drafting paper in various stages of use, from blank to blueprint.

Above each island hung more motivational posters, with quotations like *From heart and mind, to steel and stone* and *Be the architect of your enduring legacy*. The dozen or so designers in the room appeared hard at work.

I couldn't help myself. "Look at them," I whispered to Alfred. "I'll bet they're figuring out how Cincinnati's churches can be *repurposed*."

"This is an inopportune time for jokes."

"Maybe for retail. Stack up the pews to display shoes or cookware—strictly Monday through Saturday when God doesn't need the floor space."

Alfred frowned. "Focus on the mission, Mr. Tremaine."

Hey, that was my line. Or had I picked it up from Alfred?

He scanned the room and found what he was looking for, a silver-haired man in shirtsleeves. Standing and speaking to one of the designers, the man reached down and traced a line on a blueprint with his index finger.

He was Walther Drax, company founder and Cincinnati institution.

I'd never met him, but I'd seen him a thousand times. In the newspaper and on local TV he was as ubiquitous as Ronald McDonald. At every ceremony to break ground, cut a ribbon, lay a cornerstone, or seal a time capsule, Walther would be there, surrounded by local politicians and business leaders—an exclusive fraternity with a secret handshake. He'd be wearing a thousand-dollar suit and Italian wingtips, perhaps holding a polished chrome shovel, poised to scoop the first soil. But of course he wouldn't. Showpiece shovels and gleaming executives don't pierce the earth. The shovels go back to velvet-lined cases. The executives go back to idling cars and deferential drivers.

In the lobby and on the elevator, I'd considered our morning excursion as something to endure and forget. I would keep my mouth shut while Alfred groveled for the return of his Leica. We would then leave with our dignity bruised but intact. And if we groveled well, the film shot inside the grand rotunda would be safe in my hand.

But the sight of Walther, the company patriarch, brought up memories black as pitch.

During our legal battle over my father's death, I was desperate to meet the Drax man who started it all. We mostly encountered Drax surrogates—lawyers and staffers. Even after seeing Rudolph briefly in the courtroom, I'd wondered if he and Walther knew any more about my father than the speaking points written by Drax attorneys.

Jack Tremaine, 45, interior trim painter, killed by falling debris.

"A terrible tragedy. Our hearts go out to the Tremaine family."

"We're working hard to learn everything we can to prevent such subcontractor accidents in the future."

"Any additional comment would be inappropriate while the investigation is underway."

I'd fantasized about confronting Walther Drax in the courthouse lobby under the TV lights. *Did you ever learn more than your speaking points about my dad?* I'd ask. *That he was a gifted landscape artist who painted walls instead because he needed to feed his family? That he tipped even the rudest waitress because, as he used to say, "Maybe things aren't so good for her at home"? Did you learn what happened to his wife? You didn't take her life, only her reason for living. Did you learn these things, Mr. Drax?*

No, I'd never had that opportunity, and I didn't have it now as I stood beside Alfred in his quest to retrieve a camera. But then I reminded myself: the Leica still contained my photos of the grand rotunda. And however lousy the odds, those photos could deal Drax a blow.

I felt the need to prepare for a monumental encounter. Or better yet, prepare to *avoid* a monumental encounter by keeping my trap shut. "Wait," I said, but Alfred was already striding toward Walther Drax.

I followed, an electrical storm in my veins.

. . . . .

Walther looked up and recognized Alfred. He raised an index finger, requesting a minute more with his rapt designer.

I studied the business leader whose name came up constantly during my M.Arch coursework at Xavier, the man *The Cincinnatian* magazine had named "Queen City King" six times over the decades.

Walther had first made local headlines as a young businessman, undercutting old-guard firms to win the subway contract. "It's your city, your future, your money," he said to the people of Cincinnati. "Why risk tomorrow's paycheck on yesterday's construction methods?" When the city's stiff-collared elites gasped at such brazen competitive language, Walther raised his voice. "Automobiles today are sleeker, faster, and more affordable for you hard-working Americans. Should the city's projects be any different? I say no."

Walther walked toward us. Like Alfred, he was in his seventies, but this was no doddering oldster. With a full head of hair, more gray than Alfred's white, he stood erect and strode with purpose, stylish in cuffed trousers. The rolled sleeves of his starched shirt fell to mid-forearm, orchestrated to present a man of the people, never mind a net worth of fifty million dollars.

The two elders exchanged handshakes and smiles but as perfunctorily as greeting the tax accountant every spring. Even Angelica Dawson, the bride from hell, had received a warmer smile from Alfred.

Alfred introduced me as his employee and by first name only. Perhaps he feared Walther would recognize the name Tremaine from the lawsuit. Alfred had planned everything out like a stage performance, but I wasn't even a supporting actor. I was a prop.

"Our timing is far from ideal," Alfred said, "given yesterday's accident. We're very sorry—"

"Our condolences to the Turkel family," I said. "It seems strange the concrete would fail. Surely the subway was built to withstand overhead traffic."

Walther peered at me quizzically, caught off-guard, and rose to my bait. "Our equipment operator appears to have taken the wrong route to the job site, but surely that's not why you're here."

I could've gasped. He was blaming his dead employee, a predictable pattern for Drax.

Alfred intervened with a half step forward. "No, that's not why we're here," he said, more to me than Walther. "An incident occurred yesterday at another job site, the old train station."

Walther nodded. Apparently, he'd been briefed.

Alfred continued. "Two individuals were detained."

"Strange hobby," Walther said, "breaking into restricted areas to make trouble."

"That's not why we were there," I said.

Confused, Walther glanced at me and then Alfred. "What's this all about?"

"Our objective was to take photographs," I said.

"You..." Walther's eyes narrowed. "*You* sneaked past our guards—"

"Into a public building," I said, "owned by every Cincinnati citizen. So we weren't breaking in, more like visiting, before it's... repurposed."

Alfred placed his hand on my forearm, a harmless gesture from all outward appearances, but accompanied by a forceful squeeze.

Walther smiled without displaying teeth, as if engaged in entertaining but inconsequential sport. "That building is a valuable Cincinnati asset, sitting idle. The city's elected officials voted to convert it into something that benefits the citizens."

"Tony used the same words," I said.

Walther addressed Alfred. "This young man works for you?"

"A lab technician," Alfred replied. "But what he does in his spare time is beyond my control."

Walther returned his attention to me. "So you know my grandson?"

"Queen City High School. Same graduating class."

Walther's eyes lit up with realization. "I see. You're the one who met here with Tony yesterday morning." It was a statement, not a question, but it hung in the air like a bad odor.

Alfred tried again to take charge. "There was an altercation between Lucas and your grandson, which we very much regret."

Walther's eyes remained on me. "Your boss used the word *we*. But do *you* regret punching Tony in the face?"

"I'm sorry, but I don't."

Alfred drew in a sharp breath.

Walther eased up. "My grandson isn't always diplomatic. What prompted this... this altercation?"

"Look, I grew up on the floodplain where ratting a guy out can get you beat to a pulp," I said. "Tony and I will settle our differences on our own."

Alfred spotted another opening. "Lucas will also be settling his differences with the police, so enough of that. We have a small request and we'll be on our way."

But Walther's eyes stayed fixed on me. "Who are you again?"

"Lucas Tremaine." To hell with Alfred's muzzle order. Walther was going to hear my father's last name. I scrutinized the deep lines on the man's face for any hint of recognition, but saw nothing. *We* were nothing. My stomach twisted into a knot the size of a football.

"I've come for my camera," Alfred blurted.

"Wait a minute." Walther seemed amused. "This is about a camera?"

"A rare camera," Alfred said, "with great personal and historical value. Your security detail retained it when Lucas was brought here."

Walther turned to me. "You used your boss's camera to take pictures of our job site?"

"The grand rotunda."

Walther tipped his chin up. "For what purpose?"

I'd anticipated this point in our conversation, had even rehearsed a little speech, the perfect blend of explanation and contrition. "Well, Mr. Drax, I'm a graduate student in urban antiquity. I'm fascinated by Art Deco styling, and the rotunda's never been photographed by night."

Walther listened intently but said nothing.

"As an artist yourself, surely you'll understand." I forced a smile.

Seemingly satisfied, Walther begged for patience so he could "look into the camera issue." He then exited to the hall and beyond our vision.

"What happened to contrition?" Alfred muttered.

"That was the best I could do," I replied.

When Walther returned a few minutes later, three men followed. They took up positions in a tidy row. Walther had summoned reinforcements.

To the left was a man with his legs spread slightly and hands folded like an at-ease soldier. He wore the Drax uniform and had six inches and a hundred pounds on me. A human gorilla. To the right was Hard Ass, wearing the uniform and a subdued grin. Dead center between the guards was Tony Drax sporting a bruise above his left cheekbone—my handiwork. He held my camera bag, which meant he held my film.

"You may have your camera back," Walther said to Alfred, "but the film is problematic."

"Wait a minute," I blurted.

"Please," Walther replied calmly. "This conversation is with your boss."

Alfred brought his hand to his chin and remained silent.

The situation was grim and getting grimmer. I'd never get a chance to reshoot the grand rotunda. Drax had probably already doubled the number of security guards.

Yet I found myself hoping Alfred would intervene on artistic grounds. *Respect artists*, Dad once told me, *because only two things separate man and animal: love and art.*

Alfred had once been an artist, years before wasting his talent on prima donnas like Angelica Dawson. He understood. Just as the great masters painted their art on canvas, photographers painted their art on film.

Respect the art, Alfred, and save the film.

"Take it," Alfred said, "with our apologies for everything that has happened."

My heart sank. There was no turning back. I'd frightened my mother, endangered my best friend, and lost my job. Even if Alfred didn't fire me, I'd quit. I couldn't work for him anymore. And then what? Nobody hires felons. The situation was hopeless.

N. Jefferson Chapel wrote about the tragic delusion of the word *hopeless*. Wedged in a stone passage sixty feet beneath Athens, as the floodwaters of a surprise storm rose to his chin and kept rising, Chapel uttered *hopeless* and prepared to breathe his last breath. Then he remembered the hollow aluminum legs of his camera tripod, potentially enough breathing tube to reach an overhead air pocket. He worked furiously. The waters receded after ninety minutes and Chapel emerged alive, the word *hopeless* re-examined. *Does one contemplate? Ambulate? Operate?* he later wrote. *Then one's exigency is never hopeless.*

I lunged at Tony Drax so ferociously his eyes shot open. He braced for another punch to the face and dropped the camera bag. I snatched it up and hunched like a fullback for a mad dash to the door. According to my plan—materializing on the fly—I'd reach the emergency stairwells and go up, not down, losing my pursuers in the massive building's infrastructure before escaping on my own terms.

As plans go, it sucked.

Hard Ass was a dough-bellied slug but he moved surprisingly fast. He reached me as I tore open the door to the hall. His hand clamped my wrist. His arm collared my throat from behind. I tipped backwards. Gorilla dove for my legs.

"On the ground like I showed you," Tony barked. "On the back—wrists and ankles."

Tony had ordered one of his favorite maneuvers for immobilizing a victim. I remembered it well. He'd used it in high school on Reuben before humiliating him in front of twenty half-dressed boys in a locker room.

Hard Ass and Gorilla obeyed, lifting me off the ground and lowering me to the floor until the tiles flattened my shoulder blades. Hard Ass yanked my arms up over my head and pinned my wrists. At my other end, Gorilla clamped my ankles. Like a Gumby, I'd been bent into a big letter H. I writhed but to no effect. As Tony knew well, the human body's pulleys and levers are useless in such a configuration.

With a nod, Walther gave his grandson the go-ahead. Tony placed my camera bag on a nearby island and turned his body slightly to make sure I had a good view from my ankle-height vantage point. He took out the Leica, turned it over, and then hesitated.

"I beg your pardon," Alfred said, his tone strident. "Yanking out film like a parachute ripcord works in the movies, but not in real life. You'll strip the mechanism."

Tony looked irked.

Alfred went on. "They stopped making parts for that camera years ago. Please. You must depress the underside release and then rewind the film. Only then, you simultaneously press the door safety release and pull up the center spool, but *gently*."

Tony turned the tiny handle until we all heard the familiar *fwak fwak fwak* of a rewound and free-spinning film canister. He then yanked up clumsily on the return capstan, almost dropping the camera. The metal lens cover clattered to the floor.

Panicky, Alfred leaped forward. "You will *not* destroy my camera, young man." He grabbed the Leica from Tony's hands and deftly manipulated the controls until the back door clicked and swung open. He reached in, retrieved the film, and placed it in Tony's palm. "There are things in life deserving of respect," Alfred said.

But not art.

Pouty at being usurped, Tony dropped the film canister to the tile floor and glanced down to make sure I was watching. Then he brought his heel down hard. One metal end of the Kodak cylinder shot out and spun to a stop near my cheek. It was official. The film was drenched in toxic light, forever ruined.

Tony bent, fingered the carcass of the canister and flipped it toward me. It bounced off my chest and rolled to the ground. He mouthed the words *river rat* and flashed me a grin.

Back in high school, I'd seen that grin with its condescending configuration of lips and teeth. Below had been Reuben, cheeks shiny with tears, his body another big letter H.

Walther plucked the lens cap from the floor and handed it to Alfred. "I assume there will be no more of this nonsense?"

"That is correct," Alfred said, his shoulders slumped.

But I wouldn't feel sorry for him.

"Perfect response," Walther said from on high while handing Alfred the photography equipment. "Mr. Daley?"

"Yes, Mr. Drax," Hard Ass replied, still cutting off blood flow to my hands with his grip. I imagined full name combinations. Dan Daley. Don Daley. Dick Daley. *Dickerson* Daley. Nope, *Hard Ass* sounded best. Hard Ass Daley. "Please release our visitor."

Hard Ass obeyed. I rose slowly to my feet and brushed off. My face felt hot.

"Your valiant efforts to rescue your film," Walther said, "all to take some nostalgic picture? I don't buy it. For what purpose did you take pictures of our job site?"

With the loss of the film, Alfred's gag order had expired. There was nothing left to protect, nothing left to accomplish. So I chose a different speech, this one penned with acid, one phrase spewing from my mouth before the next phrase had congealed in my mind. "Not just nostalgia, Mr. Drax. You are about to destroy an architectural treasure unlike anything in the world. If you knew the Nazis were about to burn the Louvre to the ground, wouldn't you want to take a snapshot of the Mona Lisa?"

Every trace of bemusement vanished from Walther's expression as if I'd slapped him with an open hand. He squared his shoulders and I expected a counterattack. But he spoke softly, methodically. "You have more on your mind than a dusty old train station."

I promised myself to not blink or look away. "Does the name Tremaine mean *anything* to you?"

"Perhaps it would," Walther said, "if you'd get to the point."

"Jack Tremaine was my father. He worked for you, on a shoddy worksite, with negligent practices, *your* practices, that got him killed."

Walther pointed an index finger at Alfred's face. "You used our past dealings to come in here with slanderous accusations."

"Our *dealings?*" Something primitive flared in Alfred's eyes, but faded fast. He shook his head. "I came for my camera. That's all."

Walther thought a moment before showing me a synthetic smile, his eyes as cool as metal. "I remember it now. You and your mother poured your hearts into a legal action and it didn't go your way. I've felt that disappointment myself."

My heartbeat pounded in my ears. I wanted to spring from where I stood, bowl him over backwards, and smash the cold condescension from his face.

"You felt disappointment over what, a contract dispute? A quest for a lower tax rate? I lost my father. And you blamed him for what happened, just like you blamed yesterday's screw-up on your own employee."

Walther relaxed his shoulders, claiming the high ground. "I'm afraid I'm at a loss."

I laughed. "You've never lost anything in your life."

"You don't know your place, young man."

"You brainwash your employees with slogans about personal integrity and corporate responsibility, but you're a hypocrite."

Walther stared at me unblinking, his jaw muscles pulsing below his earlobes. A few seconds passed, the air between us electrified. Nearby employees gawked.

"This conversation is over," Walther said. "Mr. Daley, please escort these gentlemen from the building."

. . . . .

As Alfred and I cleared the main doors of Drax headquarters, I anticipated an earful from the old man, so I spoke first. "Take back the bail money, Mr. Blumenfeld. You bet on the wrong guy." At that moment, jail didn't seem so bad—reading, sleeping, three meals a day. Life had become too complicated.

"You think your legal troubles count for a hill of beans?" Alfred's upper lip quivered, his thin, blotched skin stretched drum tight over his forehead. "You don't know nothing from nothing, you dumbhead. It's like you give them your gun and say *go ahead, shoot me with this.*"

"What's your big idea, diplomacy? A lot of good diplomacy did back there."

Alfred's eyebrows shot up. "You called that man a Nazi!"

"Not exactly."

"Walther Drax plays golf with the chief of police every month. If he says you slandered his family name and threatened bodily harm—"

"I never threatened."

Alfred waved a hand. "Whether you did so or not, the chief will believe him because *that's the way things work in this town.* We are schmutz under the fingernail."

"And you're okay being schmutz?"

Alfred scowled and gritted his teeth. "Of course not. But for now, this is the way it has to be. *For now.* Suspend this little crusade of yours, or five thousand dollars will be pocket change compared to the trouble you'll have. Do we have an understanding?"

I was surprised at the intensity of the stick figure standing before me. *For now*, he'd said, as if privy to a hush-hush future. Well, that future would not include me.

I spun on my heel and made a bee line to the bus stop, my eyes locked on the pavement. I never looked back to check where Alfred went.

• • • • •

After my defeat at Drax, I decided to work off my frustration at the YMCA. Reuben agreed to meet me there.

The Y was okay if you didn't mind old guys strolling around naked, dangling their dicks, hands on their hips, like they were surveying a conquered land. I didn't care. Their flab reminded us to stay in shape.

In one corner of the gym, a handful of sweaty guys pumped iron and huffed themselves up for show. Out on the floor, others shot hoops in a blizzard of taunts and squeaking rubber.

I chose the pegboard climber, clutched a thick sweat-stained peg in each hand, and began my ascent, my legs dangling as counterweights. I reached the top in fourteen Mississippi seconds, not even close to my goal of ten.

"Not bad," Reuben said from below. "Now come down and do it again without touching the floor."

I did as challenged, down and up, then down again. Panting, I held out the pegs. "Your turn, smartass."

"What happened this morning?"

"Scared you can't do it?"

"Come on."

"A bunch of crap, that's what happened. Do it."

Reuben looked peeved. "You twisted my arm to come down here and now it's nothing?"

He wouldn't let up. "Okay, but let's sweat while we talk."

Reuben grabbed a twenty-pound medicine ball from a wooden rack. A basketball-sized leather orb filled with sand, the medicine ball developed the pushing and pulling strength needed for maneuvering in spaces better sized for rodents than humans.

We moved a few feet apart and began tossing the ball back and forth. With each catch, we lifted the orb over our heads, lowered to below the waist, raised to the chest, and tossed. Catch, lift, lower, raise, toss. Repeat until muscles scream.

Between gulps of air, I told the story of the morning's festivities, including the newspaper clipping of the excavator breakthrough, meeting Walther, the admission of our photo shoot, the destruction of the film, and our unceremonious exit.

"Walther knew about your dad?" Reuben asked.

"He does now."

I told it all, except how I watched the final drama from the floor, my body pinned like Reuben's body ten years earlier. I'd no more embarrass my friend than ask an old lady to model her new incontinence diaper.

The incident happened at Queen City High after gym class. I heard a shriek followed by group laughter. I ran into the boy's locker room. Reuben lay on his back in a puddle dripped by adolescent boys fresh from showering. One boy knelt at Reuben's feet and pressed his ankles together, pinning them to the wet floor. Another boy crouched near Reuben's head, immobilizing him by his upstretched arms. A dozen boys in various stages of undress had formed a circle, watching the show.

Reuben was naked, his new pubic fur strange on an otherwise hairless torso. Eyes closed but puddled with tears, he whipped his face from side to side, as if avoiding sight would transport him home and make him safe again.

"We got us a science experiment. Action reaction, stimulus response." The voice came from Tony Drax, dressed for advantage in Adidas gym shorts the rest of us could only dream of owning.

He squatted next to Reuben and gripped a janitor's broom just above the bristles. He poked at Reuben's genitals with the wood handle, flipping his penis up and down like a light switch.

"We oughta be seeing this little Heeb nozzle do something, but it stays limp." Tony scanned the faces of his audience for reactions. "Whaddaya know, Ruby Jew, you got yourself a defective dick."

Most of the boys laughed while a few glanced nervously around the crowd. Reuben now lay motionless, his face turned away, eyes pinched shut, mouth a straight line between thin white lips.

"Go play with your own, Tony," I said.

But he ignored me, pleased with himself. That was when he gave that wicked smile, all teeth, his icy eyes radiating supremacy, the same expression he flashed a decade later at Drax Headquarters after crushing my film canister.

I tossed the medicine ball to Reuben. "So Hard Ass and the big guy... kicked us out," I said, breathless. I dropped one hand to a knee and held the other hand aloft, pleading for a break. We mopped our faces with towels and sat side by side on the bleachers.

I braced myself, expecting Reuben to lay into me and tell me how *focus on the mission* had become *fuck up the mission*.

But he didn't. Instead, he got quiet, as if he pitied me, and that made everything worse. He kneaded his hands together, pondering, the muscles pulsing under the skin of his forearms like busy snakes. Strength plus endurance in a five-foot-four-inch package. I wondered how his past encounters with Tony Drax might've ended had he realized his physical potential back in high school.

He dropped the medicine ball to the floor with a dead-end thud. "What did Tony say during all this?"

"Not much. Walther keeps Puppy on a short leash."

He seemed satisfied by my telling. "So what're you going to do?"

I shrugged. "There's nothing left to do. The shoot's ruined."

Reuben frowned. "I don't get why he showed you the newspaper clipping."

"I figure Alfred was trying to look sympathetic, get on Walther's good side to rescue the camera."

"Maybe, but why bother telling you?"

"So I'd back up his little scheme, I suppose."

Reuben shook his head. "He didn't have to tell you. Why would he care if you came across looking clueless?"

"You're taking his side."

"No, you're missing something."

"It isn't complicated. He screwed me over." Elbows on my knees, I gazed at the scuffed floor, but felt Reuben staring at the side of my face. A few moments passed, the bounces and shouts of the basketball game filling the air space.

Reuben cleared his throat. "I think you need to talk to Alfred."

"Give me one good reason." I scooped up the medicine ball and held it out on my palm. The twenty pounds of downward force began a slow, blossoming burn in my arm muscles.

A renegade basketball bounced within Reuben's reach. "Does he still owe you a paycheck?" He snatched the ball and tossed it to center court.

"Yeah, a couple hundred bucks. And I owe him five thousand for bail money—"

"Which he could yank back and land you in jail, so don't piss him off."

"Too late for that."

Reuben stared at me, getting on my nerves. Then he said, "Imagine applying for a job, an assault conviction on your record for cold-cocking city royalty, and your only real employer refuses to be a reference because he thinks you're a dickhead. You ready to panhandle for your mom's recovery?"

I let my jaw go slack. "Jesus, you lay it on thick." Arm on fire, I flipped the medicine ball at him.

He caught it and pretended to nervously sweep the gymnasium with his eyes. "I shouldn't be seen in public with a felon."

"Alfred handed over the film without a peep. It was never more than a bargaining chip to get his camera—"

"Which you stole."

"Borrowed."

"Without asking."

"Whatever." I stood. "He knew how much I wanted that shot, even helped me get the lighting perfect."

"Make things right with Alfred."

I peered down at him. "Apologize? Like hell."

"Make things right before he makes things worse."

CHAPTER 8

When I entered the retail section of Alfred's business, it seemed abandoned. But no, Tricia wouldn't do that. Whenever she had to pee, she'd always grab someone from the lab to handle customers until she'd returned.

I eased past a rack of camera bags, glanced left and there she was, crouched between two shelving units. A clipboard in one hand, she perched on her comfy-dressy rubber-soled shoes, her black skirt stretched tight across her backside.

I approached. "I'm so toxic you have to hide from me?"

She didn't look up. "What's that mean?"

"You always greet your customers. But you didn't, which means you knew it was me and ducked down. You're that disappointed?"

I'd caught her but she didn't flinch. She stood and pivoted to face me, blinking her dark eyes slowly. "Disappointment requires high expectations, which I don't have of you."

I grinned, a bit relieved. The day she wouldn't yank my chain would be sad indeed. "Alfred told you what happened?"

"Yes, but I tuned out after the part where the guards wrestled you to the ground. Stopped being interesting."

"Too bad, because that was when Alfred let them destroy my film."

She tipped her head slightly. Alfred hadn't explained that condemning little tidbit. I filled in the missing pieces while Tricia listened with what barely resembled interest.

"And forget a reshoot. Guards will be all over the place." I took a breath and waited for a sympathetic reply, something like *tough break, man*.

She squinted at me. "So you think my grandfather's a pain in the ass? The line forms at the rear." She glanced down at her clipboard. Apparently our chat had ended.

"Is he here?"

"In the darkroom. You talking to him?"

"Should I?"

She shook her head like I was a dolt. "Of course. You don't have to like someone for them to be useful."

I leaned in, annoyed she'd brushed off Alfred's callousness. "Useful? You sound just like him, manipulating people to get what you want. Whatever happened to being honest?"

She propped her free hand on a hip. "You're so damn honest you can't keep your mouth shut, and now you're paying for it." This time she locked her gaze on the clipboard and didn't budge.

She was right, but I didn't like hearing it from her. I'd known her before Miss Poise and Professionalism arrived from a mail-order catalog—all paid for by Alfred. In high school, she kept all the boys at a distance, playing games with their minds and testosterone, like the time she showed up in the shortest shorts and tightest top, all hips and tits, so prized yet so untouchable. But back then, as now, I wanted her to know that not all guys were the same.

I walked away, my stomach rebelling at the prospect of facing Alfred one more time.

"Hang on, Lucas," Tricia said.

She never used my name. I looked over my shoulder. Her stance had relaxed and her eyes had cooled off a few degrees. "You know what your problem is?"

I felt the urge to say *You?*, but she didn't deserve that. "I'm dying to find out."

"You don't listen."

"Could you repeat that? I wasn't paying attention."

"Hilarious," she said. "Now here's a tip. When you meet with Alfred, spend more time listening than talking. You might learn something."

I was confused. "What aren't you telling me?"

"Nothing. I'm not involved and I don't care what you idiots do sliming around under the city."

"Under?" *Under* could only mean certain places, including the subway.

A customer bumped through the front door, looking lost. Tricia shifted her attention, ready to deliver unparalleled service.

· · · · ·

As Tricia's inventory of my flaws echoed in my ears, I made my way through the bowels of Blumenfeld Photography. According to Tricia, the building had been an ordered grid of rooms decades ago. Now it was a rat maze. With each evolution of the business, Alfred slapped up dividers, corridors, alcoves, and closets. He did things his way.

I planned to wait in Alfred's office. He wouldn't be long. Darkroom work was no all-day affair. The mind could only tolerate so much sensory deprivation.

I'd visited the old man's office on a few in-and-out occasions, never lingering long enough to notice much. But with Alfred detained, I checked things out. Daylight streamed in from a rare external window. In one corner of Alfred's big wooden desk sat the Rolodex and phone, both angled toward the desk chair. On another corner, a few 35mm film canisters aligned with soldierly discipline. Centered on the desk was a burgundy blotter, and centered on that was a blank pad of paper and a gold pen and pencil set, as parallel as highway lines. I angled the pen about twenty degrees off-center. He'd have it back in place sixty seconds after entering the room.

On the wall next to a combination safe, Alfred had hung plaques, certificates, and award photos. I eased around the desk for a closer look. *Best Visual Exposition*, 1934. *Photographer of the Year*, 1936, 1939, and 1947. *Distinguished Service in Pursuit of the Truth*, 1939, awarded by the American Press Photographers Association. *Blue Ribbon for Feature Photography*, 1947, from the Investigative Reporters and Editors Association.

I didn't get it. Why walk away from such an impressive career to babysit brides and grooms at the narcissistic pinnacles of their lives?

My eye was drawn to a photo, now faded to sepia from the light of ten thousand afternoon suns sweeping the wall. Three men in dark suits stood beaming under a sloping banner that read *Cincinnati Enquirer Shining Stars Gala*. The man at center hooked his hands on the shoulders of two other men, each holding a trophy cup. One I didn't recognize. The other was a thirtyish Alfred, eyes bright above a bushy dark mustache.

I crossed the room to a large bookcase, the wood nearly black with time.

Most volumes had something to do with photography, photojournalism, or famous photographers. The only exceptions sat on a dedicated shelf of World War II books. Some spotlighted the best photojournalists of the era, while other titles suggested closer study: the multinational politics, the arming of the Nazi regime, and America's on-again off-again involvement in the years before Pearl Harbor.

The photography books were alphabetized by artist, from Ansel Adams in the upper left to Monte Zucker in the lower right. Zucker meant nothing to me, but I admired Adams' work. I tipped a volume from the high shelf and thumbed through page after page: snowy peaks mirrored in still waters, the moon hanging over an adobe church, Yosemite rising through morning mist. Each black-and-white image seemed as varied and striking as Technicolor.

"You like the landscapes?" Alfred spoke from behind me, his tone surprisingly civil, given the circumstances. He walked with purpose, carrying a business-sized envelope in one hand and a manila folder in the other. In spite of the risk of splashed darkroom chemicals, he wore pleated slacks and a crisp white shirt, a dark blazer folded over one arm. He stopped in front of the wall safe. "Please look away."

I hesitated but then obliged and faced the bookshelf. "Some say Adams is the greatest American photographer of all time."

Alfred snorted. "Baloney."

I turned to see the old man slide the envelope into the safe, close the door, and spin the combination. "You have someone else in mind?" I asked.

"Ever heard of Paul Schutzer?"

"No."

"David Seymour?" Alfred walked behind the desk and twisted his pen back into perfect alignment. Less than sixty seconds. "How about Larry Burrows?"

That name was recently in the news. "English photographer. The Viet Cong shot down his helicopter." Soldier casualties were tragic enough, but the deaths of noncombatants—like the press, only trying to share the truth—cut the deepest.

"Killing Burrows and three other photojournalists." He dropped the folder on the blotter. "While Ansel Adams was sipping something cool and waiting for the sunlight to strike Half Dome just so, guys like Burrows had seconds between machine gun bursts to snap a Pulitzer Prize-winning photo. Calendar art sells, but—"

"Calendar art?" No greater insult for a serious artist.

"Landscapes calm the nerves in a stressed-out world. But we also need art that boils the blood. That's the work of the photojournalist." Alfred draped his blazer over the back of the leather desk chair. But he remained standing. So did I.

"If Adams is the worst kind of photographer, why keep this book around?"

"I never said worst. Paparazzi are the worst." Then Alfred broke eye contact and appeared to lose himself in a thought. "That book... an ancient keepsake, really." He spoke without the usual condescension. "A trip out west with an old pal. We visited many of the places Adams photographed."

I flipped to the inside front cover. A handwritten inscription read *Great places, great times.—R.B.*

I couldn't imagine the type of person Alfred would consider a *pal*. I knew little about the man's friends and family, except for Tricia, and she didn't seem a fair representative of the Blumenfeld gene pool.

I returned Ansel Adams to his assigned slot in the bookshelf. "So you think my pictures in the grand rotunda would've been calendar art? We weren't under enemy attack."

Alfred offered a thin smile. "You were driven by a fire in your belly, a wrong that had to be exposed. That's the stuff of great photojournalism. That's why I still have hope for you, even when you act like a schlemiel."

An ember of childish pride flared. I extinguished it. "I didn't know I'd be coming here for more lectures on my bad behavior."

Alfred slid his hand into his pants pocket. "Then let's get to why you did come here."

"I take responsibility for my actions. Besides, if you knew Tony Drax, you'd know why I decked him."

"I don't need to know him. He's a Drax, and they're all the same. They live to take from others."

"But we don't have to give them what they want—like my film."

The old man stuck out his chin and glared down his nose at me. "You called Walther a Nazi and assaulted his grandson. You think he would've handed everything over and wished us a nice day?"

Our cease-fire of civility was eroding fast. "You could've sacrificed the camera. It's only a gadget."

Alfred's cheeks reddened. "A *rare* gadget, and men like Walther Drax have enough money to purchase all the rare gadgets in the world and put them in their own museum and say *look how cultured and generous we are*."

I took a step forward, the desk between us. "You're proving my point. All they care about is their precious public image. I had the advantage until *you* threw it away. My photos could've exposed them as wasters of our culture."

Alfred studied me for an uncomfortable few seconds. Then he said, "In your estimation, what type of advantage did you have?"

I'd just explained it. "I don't understand."

"That's your problem. You don't get it."

I dismissed him with a wave. "So now you're calling me an idiot. I think I'm wasting my time."

Alfred sighed to be heard. "Mr. Tremaine, you misunderstand. I was asking an important question." He stepped out from behind his desk and came to within three feet of me, led by his sweet cologne. "What *type* of advantage did you have?"

I felt a dull pain behind my eyes. "You tell me."

"A tactical advantage, not a strategic advantage. Tactically, you might preserve the old train station. But you need a *strategic* advantage to win the war, not just one battle."

"I love that train station." Like Dad loved it.

"Of course you do." Alfred bore into me with an intensity I'd rarely seen. "But I'm talking about that fire in your belly." He jabbed a bony finger at my midsection. "The real reason you smacked that young Drax in the kisser, and called his grandfather a Nazi. The real reason you'd rather be thrown on the ground and humiliated by those flatfoots than give one inch."

I tried to respond but found no words, only memories from my childhood—the coppery taste of blood, my fists tight but small, feeling helpless.

"They cost your father his life. They blamed him. They treated your mother cruelly, and look how they treat you, saying *river rat* as if people like you have no place in *their* world."

Alfred was telling me exactly what I wanted to hear, the oil-tongued bastard, but he was right. All my life, people like Tony had been demanding an apology for my presence, as if I'd tracked dog shit across their Persian rug. I'd fantasized a hundred withering, razor-sharp retorts, my dad bearing witness. As I'd stood over Tony, his face blossoming rosy from my fist, I'd imagined my father viewing the whole spectacle from far above, proud of me for standing strong.

"You saw him call me that?" I asked.

"I've been called worse."

I recalled the stiff greeting between Alfred and Walther. Something had happened way back when.

Alfred retrieved an oversized magnifying glass from a desk drawer and handed it to me. He then reached down, flipped open the manila folder and lifted its only contents, an eight-by-ten photo sheet comprised of thirty-six separate images from a single roll of film, with each photo the size of two postage stamps. He handed it to me. "Take a look."

I positioned the magnifying glass and chose a row at random. The first photo showed a long hallway—a school or an office building, the image too small for me to make out. The next photo was closer in, showing Reuben pressing his eye to the crack between double doors. I didn't understand.

I dropped down two rows and shifted the glass right. Then I gasped, glanced up at Alfred and dropped my head again. I was seeing the Cincinnati Union Terminal's grand rotunda photographed at night, the walls painted by splashes of white light, *my* light. I felt a rush of excitement in my chest. I jerked the magnifying glass to the next image, and then the next. They were all there.

Even without the detail of an enlargement, I could discern that my gambles had paid off. Floor-level recesses balanced each other on the left and right. Arched shadows mimicked scalloped stonework. Gorgeous.

I let out a breath and looked up. "How? Tony destroyed the film."

Alfred kept his eyes on mine. "He destroyed film, that's true."

"He destroyed the film you took from the camera. I saw it."

"No, he destroyed the film he *thinks* I took from the camera."

Alfred plucked one of the film canisters from the desktop and held it at eye level. "What kind?"

I knew well the purple accent against Kodak yellow, but grabbed the cartridge anyway to read from the label. "Plus-X. One twenty-five ASA black-and-white."

"Good," Alfred said. "Hand it over but pay attention. I don't want you to think I'm reaching into my pocket or any silly thing like that." He took the film from my outstretched hand, held it in the air for a moment, and returned it to my palm.

Instead of purple on yellow, the film canister was now green on yellow. I gasped again. "Tri-X. Four hundred ASA." Flawless sleight-of-hand. "You're some kind of magician?"

The old man chuckled. "No, I'm some kind of photojournalist. It's a survival tactic. We take the pictures people don't want taken. They get mad, manhandle you, sometimes clobber you. If they don't smash your equipment, they demand your film. You oblige, acting afraid for your life as you fumble around and hand over a blank roll you've tucked in your palm. Sometimes you plead to get it back, just for show. That's how we took down Max Langdon."

The name sounded familiar.

"State senator. I snapped him pocketing a fat envelope from a corrupt businessman."

I glanced back at the contact sheet in my hand, making sure it still existed.

Alfred went on. "At the wedding reshoot for Miss Angelica, I asked what film you'd used."

I remembered. "Panatomic-X. That's what I told you. But I don't get—"

"I had to be ready with the same type. Couldn't risk someone noticing the cartridge changing color."

"You had a plan, even back then?" The scheming, brilliant old man. *Never does anything without a good reason.*

Alfred shrugged. "Only lining up options. You never know how things will go."

I replayed those last minutes in Drax Headquarters and what I'd witnessed from the floor, my limbs pinned. "But Tony tried to get the camera open. What if he'd popped the back before rewinding and exposed the film? What if he'd refused to let you touch the camera?"

"Then your work would've been lost. We got lucky."

I wanted to hug him. "*We* got lucky? I'd say *I* got lucky. Why'd you do this for me?"

Alfred turned, hooked his blazer with an index finger, threw it over his shoulder, and walked toward the door. "I didn't do it for you. I did it for me. Let's call it tactical advantage."

"What?"

He faced me from the doorway, his gaze searing. "The negatives are mine, locked in my safe. Help me turn my tactical advantage over Drax into a strategic advantage and you can have them back, maybe get them published and poke Tony in the eye." Then he pointed an index finger at me like a pistol. "I've got one more chance before I die. If you shoot off your mouth again, Mr. Tremaine, and cost me that chance, I'll burn those negatives and get you thrown back in jail, and that's just for starters."

Stunned, I stood there looking like an idiot, my mouth open. Eventually I said, "Chance to do what?"

"We get started tomorrow at nine in the morning. Don't be late." Then he left.

CHAPTER 9

The next morning, I passed through Tricia's shop on the way to Alfred's office. She stood at a wall shelf, assaulting cans of Dektol developer with a price sticker gun. She'd chosen one of her tighter white blouses.

She caught me with my eyes aimed chest high. "Don't you have enough trouble?"

"Do you know the combination to Alfred's wall safe?"

She laid down the price gun and rolled her eyes to the ceiling tiles. "You ignored my advice."

"No, I listened," I said. "I listened to him treat me like a criminal—"

"Which, technically, you are."

"—and refuse to give back my negatives."

"Which *he* salvaged." She grabbed a can from a Kodak shipping carton and slapped on a price.

"What's he up to?"

"He's sending you into the subway," she said, shelving the can with a clunk, her back to me. "Don't ask me why."

"Really?" I'd fantasized a thousand times about taking virgin steps, leaving footprints on ancient dust, like the explorers of King Tut's tomb. "Where the excavator fell through?"

"Too late for that." She gave the next can a deft one-handed flip to rotate the label. "There's a utility portal no one knows about. Just one, locked tight, but somehow he knows got the access code. He knows everybody and his brother."

Subways had long carried utilities—water, gas, phone, and power, running along ceilings and walls. But once Cincinnati ran out of money and a little girl died belowground, the city voted to seal everything off. Utilities were yanked out and rerouted. "A portal?" I said. "Why does Alfred tell you all this stuff and I'm left guessing?"

Tricia met my eyes once again. "He tells me squat."

"Then how'd you find out?"

"I listen." She glanced at her watch. "It's two minutes after nine. You're already late."

· · · · ·

As I wove toward Alfred's office, I wondered if an opportunity or a setup lay ahead. I didn't trust him, but he hadn't exactly lied, only withheld the truth.

Now he wanted me to trespass in the most forbidden zone in the greater Cincinnati area. Why?

He'd spoken about winning "this war with Drax," but maybe he was toying with me. He knew about my family's relationship with Drax. Maybe I was just another Miss Angelica to him, someone to manipulate with words, and Alfred always knew the right words.

He had a guest in his office. They stood alongside the big desk, now covered by a jumbo blueprint of the subway system. I'd recognize it from across a basketball court.

Alfred said, "This is Mr. Smith." The newcomer smiled awkwardly at Alfred and then blinked at me through thick glasses, each blink like the closing and opening of a mechanical aperture. Then the man's gaze dropped too quickly to the floor.

"Pardon my asking," I said, "but is Smith your real name?"

Smith was around Alfred's age, seventy plus, and pint-sized. Except for a few white wisps like weeds popping through a parking lot, his head was bald and pasty, with a cropped fringe horseshoeing the back of his head from one ear to the other.

Smith joined his hands under a volleyball of a belly and deferred to Alfred to address my question. "Mr. Smith agreed to help us under terms of anonymity," Alfred replied.

"Help us how?" I asked.

"He's a master-level structural engineer, the best in the business, and I've known plenty."

The man threw Alfred a silent nod of appreciation for the endorsement. His lips seemed misaligned so his mouth resembled a squashed W.

"Why are we here?" I asked.

"To bring down Drax Enterprises," Alfred replied with the seriousness of divorce court.

I snorted. "Is that all? Then why do we need all three of us?"

Alfred frowned. "Mr. Tremaine, this will go a lot smoother without your sarcasm." He took charge of the agenda. "Drax's business model is simple. Bid high, do low-quality work, and buy the protection of the lowest politicians. Same model as far back as the Depression, but we could never prove it."

"Who's *we*?" I asked.

Alfred said, "The newspaper, interested parties—some of them long dead by now. We're doing this for them too."

Smith acknowledged this with a reverent dip of the head. Did this guy speak?

"So you're sending me into the subway through a utility access portal," I said. "Sounds risky."

Alfred glanced at me with suspicion. "How do you know about the portal?"

I shrugged, stepped up to the blueprint, and scanned it. "Seems most likely. That's how Reuben and I got into the Rochester subway. But why not use the hole where the excavator broke through?"

Alfred remained wary. "No longer an option. They sealed it off immediately. Classic Drax—put the kibosh on further investigation."

Smith cleared his throat. "Two hundred cubic yards of control density fill," he said, his voice more high-pitched wind than sound. He stared at me without waver, like a cat peering down a dark alley.

"You mean dirt?" I said.

Smith nodded.

Why do some people need to complicate things? "Still, I thought all access portals were welded shut in the forties after that girl died." In a flash, I imagined her choking with hysteria, crawling like an infant, each direction a dead end in that miles-long black labyrinth.

"Not all portals," Alfred said. "One remains, and that's our golden ticket."

"To do what?"

Alfred began pacing, hands behind his back like an academic, head hung like he was drawing inspiration from the carpet. "Drax welcomed the panic after that child died. Go ahead, seal it up. Their invoices had been paid in full, and they had plenty worth hiding under tons of soil."

"But their subway work would never be used," I said. "Terrible for the image."

"Worth it," Smith said, his magnified gaze unrelenting.

Alfred stopped pacing. "We studied Drax's original bid for the subway project, all in the public record." He held up a thumb and index finger an inch apart. "From the table of contents to the closing summary, it was a work of fiction."

My skepticism was rising like the temperature in the office. "None of us are authorities on public works projects."

Alfred glared at me. "Just like you're no authority on saving old train stations. Now will you please listen?"

I gave a half nod.

Alfred continued strolling. "We talked to people who worked on the project. Distances, thicknesses, weight-bearing characteristics, piling depths, materials—all fudged, and all with inflated price tags. Drax could pull it off because of bribes and bid rigging."

"If the bid was such fantasy," I said, "expose it. Get your old friends at the newspaper to publish it."

Alfred shook his head. "No data. We need hard figures that compare what they built to what they bid. For now, we have no documented evidence of fraud, just hearsay, and no district attorney will lift a finger on gossip, especially in this town."

I held up a hand classroom style. "Why didn't the city order an independent audit? Every big city expenditure has procurement oversight."

Smith and Alfred exchanged glances like seasoned cops watching the rookie fumble a pair of handcuffs. "Independent?" Alfred chuckled. "There is no *independent* when the entire system is corrupt. Auditors were on the take just like the politicians."

"Ready for the good one?" Smith said, his eyebrows bouncing.

I was ready for something to counter my growing doubt.

Alfred explained. "The Drax proposal promised overhead reinforcement to prevent breakthroughs from above."

Smith said, "Ironic."

Yes, the irony was sickening. "Doesn't the excavator breakthrough prove crappy work?"

Alfred and Smith again exchanged all-knowing smiles. I was growing weary of being the tagalong. Alfred reached into his briefcase, produced a section of newspaper and handed it to me. It was the business section of that morning's printing, a small article circled in ballpoint pen.

I scanned and got the gist in a hurry. Rudolph Drax, company president, blamed Turkel's death on two factors: the excavator operator who "became confused about the proper route to the construction site," and "the effect of decades and moisture on the subway structure." He went on, "even our best public works projects require ongoing maintenance."

Drax had begun the process of blaming anything and anyone—blaming time, blaming Mother Nature, and of course, blaming its own employee.

"Why won't someone challenge him?" I asked, expecting no answer.

"City Hall won't," Smith said.

"Keep going," Alfred said, wagging a bent finger at the newsprint in my hands. "The best is yet to come."

I read on. Rudolph concluded the interview with a declaration. "The safety of the good people of Cincinnati cannot be assured if they continue to drive, walk, and live above the aging underground system. Our engineers have studied the situation carefully and have reached a unanimous recommendation. The tunnels must be filled in. We encourage our elected officials to take action before another family suffers as the Turkel family has suffered."

I looked up. Smith gawked at me as if I had a hundred dollar bill taped to my nose. "Their goal is to fill in the subway?" I asked.

Alfred stopped pacing with a scuff of a wingtip shoe. "Dandy way to bury their crimes."

I took a deep breath. Too much had happened too fast, including Turkel's death just days before. "What a stroke of luck for Drax," I said, "the horrors of *not* filling in the subway, played out in broad daylight for the city to witness, as if the underworld is waiting to swallow up their babies."

Smith turned up the corners of his mouth, but his eyes remained flat. "Maybe not luck."

I tilted my head and regarded the strange little man. "You mean they forced the breakthrough intentionally?"

Smith balked. "Speculating. It's just… everything about Drax seems intentional. Guess who's going to win the fill-in project."

I stepped to the window and considered his words for a moment before speaking. "So Drax bids a puffed-up project forty years ago, builds hazardous tunnels on the cheap, pockets a pile of public money, thanks their lucky stars when the Depression mothballs the tunnels, and now stands to make another pile of money covering up their own fraud?"

"Yup," Smith said. I turned to see him rocking back on his heels.

"How much fraud?"

Alfred scratched his scalp. "By our estimations, Drax overbilled by threefold—minus a few kickback payments."

"Gotta grease the moving parts," Smith said.

But my mind wasn't on city finances or public safety. It was on the Turkel family. Sympathetic relatives would be with them, keeping them fed, trying to fill the silence. But soon, visitors would return to their lives, leaving the widow and children alone. The slow shock of what they'd lost would settle around them like nighttime fog. They'd cling to what he left behind—the smell of his clothes, the memory of his voice—but those things would fade, leaving only the grief.

I blinked hard, as though it would clear the image from my mind. Would Drax intentionally bring about the death of a worker? I imagined Dad painting in that pit, and me shouting a warning.

Alfred was still talking. "The biggest public works project in Cincinnati history stuffed Drax pockets. The money they stole laid the financial foundation for the Drax that owns the city today."

"And it'll be their undoing," Smith proclaimed with bush-league bravado, despite a voice like a squeaky toy.

Suddenly, the three of us seemed so ridiculous, so impotent. We were Alfred's Avengers, including a washed-up photojournalist with delusions of a comeback, a monosyllabic propeller-head from the days of ciphering and slide rules, and a perpetual student with nothing certain in his future except a courtroom appearance. I wanted to laugh, or maybe cry.

"What about statute of limitations?" I asked. "You can't hold someone responsible today for a forty-year-old crime."

Alfred nodded his agreement. "True, and we worried about that. But a man just died because of that crime. The clock starts over, *if* we can prove fraud."

"And how, exactly, are we going to do that?"

· · · · ·

"Measurements," I said to Reuben's confused expression. "That's how Smith answered my question. One word—measurements. The guy's verbally constipated."

"Unlike you." Reuben forced a cough. "Measuring what?"

That evening, after my meeting with Alfred and Smith, and after making sure Mom had taken her proper bedtime dosage, I had rendezvoused with Reuben at one of the first places we'd infiltrated, the forty-nine-story Carew Tower, a 1930s gem that inspired the design of New York's Empire State Building.

"According to Alfred and Smith," I replied, "precise measurements taken at key points throughout the subway could be Drax's Achilles' heel."

· · · · ·

"Yes, measurements," Alfred said. He stepped behind his desk, bent at the waist, and tapped the blueprint with his finger. "Mr. Smith here can explain the technical details later, but here's the upshot. Your measurements, combined with Mr. Smith's triangulations, will reveal fraud. At the least, the DA will launch an official investigation. But if we're lucky, he'll bring charges."

"You have reassurances?" I asked.

"Yup," said Smith.

"From the DA?"

"Yup," said Smith again, looking too smug given the outlandishness of the conversation.

I needed more. "Are you *sure* the calculations will prove fraud?" I glanced at Smith. If he said *yup* again, I might smack him.

Alfred appeared to understand the importance of my question. We were heading down a dangerous path and couldn't afford to hit a dead end. He met my eyes straight on. "Drax's crimes are real, and your measurements will prove it."

· · · · ·

"Do you believe Alfred?" Reuben asked.

We were perched on a greasy service platform with our feet dangling above forty-nine stories of elevator shaft. Above us, twin twenty-horsepower GE motors hummed and paused. Gear works clicked. My scalp tingled from subsonic vibration. Below, the elevator car approached and retreated, each stopping point a mystery except to the passenger who'd punched the button.

I peered down at the latest ascent. "Yeah, I believed him. He drips information with an eyedropper, but he doesn't lie." The car continued to rise. I pointed into the shaft. "Think it's headed for the penthouse?"

Reuben squinted down, gauging. He nodded. "I smell money."

For the next few seconds, the elevator car consumed the floors below us with a rush of oily wind and a screech of cables. Forty-six, forty-seven, forty-eight… My ears popped from air pressure changes. Overhead, something pneumatic hissed and the bottoms of our sneakers settled in the car-top layer of gray dust, like boots on the moon. We exhaled involuntarily.

"Penthouse," we said as one, but it was a whisper. Elevator passengers tended to freak out when they heard voices in the ceiling.

No matter how many times I'd experienced a fast-rising elevator threatening to smash us into hamburger, my cerebral brain always lost out to my limbic brain. I'd reassure myself the car would stop in time, but animal instinct forced me to lean back to save my worthless hide.

Over the past few years, a deviant fringe of our weird hobby had begun riding elevator cars and subway trains like surfboards. I'd read of their grisly deaths in the idiot obituaries, Darwin's cruel culling at work. I never understood the appeal. How could you enjoy the ambience of a place while whipping through it at breakneck speed?

"Wait a minute," Reuben said, puzzled again, as the elevator car dropped away. "The newspaper suspected fraud years before the subway was sealed, right?"

"Right."

"If all they needed were measurements, why didn't they squeeze past the gates and get the job done? Why wait forty years?"

I grinned. "That's exactly what I asked."

• • • •

"Technology," Smith replied. Then he deferred to Alfred to fill in chasms of meaning.

"Back then, usable measurements would've required an entire survey crew with chains and ropes and tripods," Alfred said, "and it still might not have worked. The magnetics under the city are topsy-turvy. True North appears in three or four different directions. Without bearings, surveys aren't worth a tinker's damn."

Alfred prompted Smith with a dip of the head. Smith reached behind the desk and hoisted a box about the size of a lawyer's briefcase. Screwed together from unfinished plywood, it looked too much like a science fair project from junior high.

Smith placed the box on the desk, snapped open a latch and withdrew a foot-long metallic gadget, cylindrical, about three inches in diameter, and painted flat black. A rectangular plate ran its length containing a series of carpenter's levels with their characteristic liquid-filled glass tubes and sliding bubbles. Smith beamed proudly, as if he'd built it himself.

• • • •

"He built it himself?" Reuben asked.

"Nah," I replied. "Borrowed it from an old colleague at Ohio State. Helluva favor too. Those things cost big bucks."

"What *things*?"

"An experimental laser."

Reuben looked at me as if I'd grown tusks. Lasers were fantasy weapons from comic books and sci-fi movies. "Okay, I get it. You'll blast your way into the subway."

"Hang on. The laser's pinpoint of light never spreads out. You place it flat against a wall, ceiling, length of track, anywhere, and it paints a perfect dot on another surface, and that could be a foot, a hundred feet, or even a mile away."

Reuben oozed skepticism. "Until you turn off the laser. Don't you still have to measure around the dot the old-fashioned way, with a measuring tape?"

"Not if you take a picture of it. You following this?" I grinned. "Smith will do his calculations based on where the laser dot appears in photos—*my* photos."

Understanding spread on Reuben's face like sunrise across a landscape. Alfred chose me for good reason: I could infiltrate places and I could wield a camera. And lucky for Alfred, five grand of debt and the threat of a return to jail put me firmly under his thumb.

"Smith worked it all out," I went on. "The blueprint shows a couple dozen spots throughout the tunnels where measurements have to be taken. The steps are easy. One guy levels the laser against a wall and fires the beam at a distant surface, a quarter-mile away in a couple of places. Try that with a tape measure. The other guy photographs where the beam hits and records—"

"Other guy?"

"Um, yeah. I forgot to mention. You're part of this."

. . . . .

Smith and Alfred watched me, waiting for some kind of decision.

"I can't do this alone," I said.

"Of course," Alfred said. "Reuben?"

I nodded.

"Can he be trusted?"

The question raised the hairs on the back of my neck. "Can *you* be trusted?"

. . . . .

"Can we trust him?" Reuben asked, and then answered his own question with a head shake. "He threatened to get you thrown back in jail, and he's holding your property hostage."

I was glad to hear the word *we*, even though Reuben hadn't officially signed on. I peered down the shaft. The elevator car was a distant piston, pumping in slow motion.

Reuben kept talking. "What if we're caught? He could deny any knowledge and hang us out to dry."

"He won't get the subway negatives until we're free and clear, and he *really* wants them."

A few wordless moments passed, the machinery whirring and clacking around us.

Reuben spoke up. "Why does Alfred give a crap about some filed-away investigation at the *Enquirer*? He hasn't worked at the paper for ages."

Good question. Drax had been a business bully for decades, hurting others far more than Alfred Blumenfeld. But the old man was hell-bent on exposing Walther and his Machiavellian progeny.

"I don't know why. But I've got to find out."

CHAPTER 10

On the bus ride home, I made a quick detour to Xavier's main library, business publications section. I spent five minutes thumbing through trade rags, found what I'd come for, and headed home.

I ambled from the bus stop toward our house under dim light from streetlamps, stepping around dented garbage cans placed at the end of driveways. Instead of a curb, the street's edge was a ragged strip separating the cracked asphalt from the weed farms we called lawns. Flies swarmed at my approach and I found the source on the ground: a dead rat, his gray body curled into a comma, his front paws hooked like a begging dog's. His eyes were swollen and black, licked dry by the flies.

A river rat. Like all residents of the floodplain, the creature was one of too many, grinding through his days, venturing forth from necessity with no choice but to accept the risk.

I tweezered the carcass between two sticks and laid it on a pile of leaves under a shrub, a better resting place than the gutter. To see me at that moment, the neighbors would've thought me off my nut. They might've been right.

Our house came into view. I noticed a familiar vehicle parked in front, Alfred's Oldsmobile, the high beams painting my path, bugs swirling in the stretched cones of light. He waited behind the wheel.

While surprised at the sight, I was glad to see him in our neighborhood. Maybe he'd take a long look at our two-bedroom matchbox house with its sagging gutter, peeling paint, and yard the size of a Mount Adams powder room. Maybe he'd believe me the next time I argued for an extra dime of hourly pay.

As I came close, Alfred killed the engine, labored out, and steadied himself with one hand on the car. This surprised me, since he rarely exhibited his age. I tried to read his mood. He'd issued my marching orders back at the office and I'd complied without protest, so all should've been arranged. But I couldn't be sure. He could barricade his true feelings behind a smile, as he'd done with Miss Angelica.

I halted with the open door between us like a shield, not that Alfred presented a physical threat. He only threatened my art, my livelihood, and my freedom. Maybe I wasn't glad to see him in our neighborhood after all.

"Don't worry, I'll do it," I said, resting both hands on the top of the door. "And if Reuben doesn't come to his senses first, he'll help. So what's the problem?"

Alfred spoke as if an eavesdropper lurked on the deserted street. "I need a favor."

"Why not? Friends do favors for each other."

Alfred ignored my sarcasm. "I didn't want to ask in front of Smith."

"His name's not Smith. It's Angelo Russo. Are you ready to treat me like a partner instead of *the help*?"

Alfred stared at me in silence for a moment, less surprised than contemplative. "He goes by Angie. How'd you find out?"

"How many master-level structural engineers do you think work in southern Ohio?"

"Not many."

"That's right. A tight club. So when this club gets together every year for their award dinner, everyone fits in the group photo for the regional trade publication." I crossed my arms. "His name was in the caption."

Alfred's eyes softened. "He's extremely valuable to this project, and he's extremely nervous. Drax crushes its enemies. Smith has more to lose."

"Compared to whom?" I was tired of feeling like the chimpanzee NASA sent into orbit, an asset as long as I pushed the right buttons to dispense my peanuts. Safe return to earth optional.

"Please continue to call him Smith, okay?"

"Why does he stare at me like I have two heads?"

"Because he sees a kindred spirit."

"Say that again?"

In the glow from a fluorescent streetlight, Alfred's cheeks looked sunken, his skin fish-belly white. "He lost someone too. His only child. Years ago in a car accident. He knows what you've suffered, but he doesn't know how to say so."

Alfred stopped talking to allow the weight of his words to slam full-on into my chest, leaving reverberations. I uncrossed my arms, suddenly self-conscious. "I'm sorry. We can call him Frank Lloyd Wright if you want."

"Then why'd you look up his real name?"

"To make a point. If fabricating a name is your idea of protection, we're all doomed. I identified Russo—"

"Smith."

"Sorry. Smith. I found him in five minutes, and I'm a guppy compared to the Drax sharks swimming all over this town, on the payroll and on the take. If we're going to protect ourselves and our families—" I jabbed a thumb toward the house "—we've got to do better than phony names. I learned it the hard way. Drax stops at nothing to identify their enemies and destroy them."

Alfred's eyes flared with a primitive fire. "Think twice, young man, before lecturing *me* on the extreme measures Drax will take to win. Understand?"

His reaction surprised me, but I refused to look away. "What did they do to you?"

"Lucas?" It was my mother's voice, and she sounded afraid. I turned to see her upper body silhouetted behind a window screen.

I waved and raised my voice. "I'll be there in a moment. Will you make sure the cat has water? I forgot this morning." Her shadow disappeared into the house. The day settled on my shoulders like wet canvas. "What's the favor?" I said to Alfred. "I'll do it."

"There's a subway spur."

I knew about spurs—dead-end tunnels. Some were intentional, for parking unused train cars. Some were accidental, an abandoned route or an insurmountable construction challenge. "Only one? I counted four on the maps."

"Well, there might be five. But I need you to find out."

I narrowed my eyes. "But we've got the blueprints. They show four."

"Rule number one. Believe nothing you see, read, or hear, even on official documents. The subway was not only a Drax project, it was highly controversial and political. Powerful people had ample reason to disguise the truth, and they still do."

"Sure, they might pad their invoices, but why hide a cul-de-sac?"

Alfred skirted my question. "Midway between Adolphus Avenue and Ptarmigan. If it's there, it's on the west side."

"What do I do with it—*if it's there?*"

"Nothing. It'll be gated off. Take pictures through the gate. Multiple angles. Now…" He aimed his index finger at my nose. "Do I have your full attention?"

I tried to appear unimpressed. "A hundred percent."

"Don't go past the gate." He relaxed a touch. "You probably won't be able to anyway."

I angled my head and raised my eyebrows. Gates didn't stop urban adventurers, but I left it alone.

Alfred continued. "If it's there, then I'll tell you why I'm interested."

"And if it's not there?"

"Then you and I didn't have this conversation." He reached into the breast pocket of his sport jacket and produced a folded piece of paper. "You'll need this."

I took the note and kept my eyes on his, awaiting an explanation.

"It's a map to the utility access portal, and the combination to two locking mechanisms. Memorize everything and then destroy the note."

"Like on *Mission Impossible?*" But Alfred didn't get it. "It's a TV show."

"I don't have a TV."

Reuben had asked whether Alfred could be trusted if we ran into trouble. "The show always starts with a famous line," I said, "*Should you be caught or killed, the Secretary will disavow any knowledge of your actions.*"

Would Alfred disavow us? I waited for him to offer a hint of reassurance, but he didn't. Instead, his gaze drifted past me and up toward the smoggy, starless sky. Then, with one hand on the door and another on the steering wheel, he grimaced himself into the seat.

"One more thing," I said.

Alfred peered up, his hands ten-and-two on the wheel, knuckles like marbles under cracked leather.

"Does Tricia know we're going into the subway?"

Alfred looked surprised. "Tricia?" He shook his head at the absurdity of my question. "She barely knows a Polaroid from an Instamatic."

I buried a smile. Clever girl.

. . . . .

Mom usually fell asleep thirty minutes after taking her nighttime dosages, but not this evening. Her hands were burning up, another side effect of tapering off the drugs. The doctors called it akathisia. Mom called it torture, as if a colony of parasites marauded under her skin. Lying back on the pillow, she stretched and flexed and wrung, her fingers individually manic. Her breath came in short bursts, eyes wide with agony.

I sat on the edge of the bed, took her hands in mine and kneaded them, firmly at first but then gentler as the meds short-circuited her synapses. After fifteen minutes, her eyelids settled and she slept. I eased her hands to the bed covers as if placing a needle on a record.

That night, I dreamed I was in an underground void with unknown danger to my left and right. Survival lay beyond the darkness where a sky-blue orb hung barely above the horizon. My father stood between me and the distant portal, his slim body sideways, his silhouette recognizable by a noble nose and dense stack of hair. He turned toward me for a few seconds before shifting his attention to the blue ball. I had to reach him, but how long could he wait for me?

I took one step and then another, unsteady on my feet. I peered down at ebony slickness stretching from my boots to where the dim light failed. The floor undulated as if a million fist-sized organisms beneath the glossy membrane battled each other for another inch of space. I broke into a run, the unseen creatures shrieking and crunching under my feet. Ahead, my father ran too, but away from me, toward the blue beacon. I stopped and my father stopped as well. I took a single step, testing, and Dad mimicked my movement. Desperate, I bent at the waist and sprinted. Dad did the same, the distance between us never narrowing.

I awoke to find myself in the easy chair across from my mother's bed, the same chair I'd slept in after Dad died. I'd been there to comfort her—or at least that was my rationalization.

"I needed you, Mom," I whispered. "More than you needed me." But my mother was asleep, breathing softly. Her right hand paddled under the bed sheet every few seconds.

I shivered. My dream had left me coated in sweat, and it had left me with dread, wedged like a ten-pound stone into my rib cage.

Out in the living room, before I could stop myself, I picked up the phone and called Tricia.

"Do you realize what time it is?" she said, her voice hushed and jagged from sleep. Her throat constricted as she stretched. An image flashed in my mind, shallow streams of muscle flowing the lengths of her calves and thighs. Her sloping exhale ended with her workaday voice. "What do you want?"

"I—I need to know why he's going after Drax."

"No you don't. Just take the measurements."

"See, that's my point. You know things, like the measurements, which were supposed to be secret. I'm putting my neck on the block for that guy."

"No, you're running an errand." She spoke as if I were a slow child.

"If we're caught, jail would be the least of my problems," I said. "Drax could go after my family." I thought of my mother, asleep, under the gaze of an intruder. A chill climbed my spine. "I have to know why it's so important to him."

"Can this wait? I have to get up early to stock shelves before opening time."

I felt I was banging my head against a cinderblock wall. "He's your grandfather. He's always been part of your life."

"Wrong. He's like a parole officer. I don't care what he does."

The handset felt hot against my ear. "Bullshit, Tricia. You're always saying *I don't care* and *I don't want to know*, but then you snoop around behind his back. He thinks you know nothing about this—this *project*."

"That's the way I like it."

"Why keep secrets from him? What's he holding over your head?"

Tricia said nothing. I decided to try a different appeal, from beneath her, peering up. I lowered my voice to a near-whisper. "Look, I know I'm a fuck-up."

"Join the crowd."

"You're not a fuck-up. You run that shop like a real pro."

She sighed. "I mean join the crowd of people who know *you're* a fuck-up. Hang on a minute." I heard sounds of her telephone handset in motion, muffling against skin, brushing against fabric. I imagined her shrugging into a bathrobe, her breasts shifting beneath the terrycloth. A door clicked closed. Was she with someone? Had she exited the bedroom so she wouldn't wake him?

Her voice returned at regular volume. "Listen up, Lucas. If what I'm about to tell you comes around again, from Chuckles or the other guys, I'll mess you up." Her tone had the cold clarity of a steel blade.

"You don't need to threaten me." I paused a second. "You can trust me." I hoped she believed me. I meant it.

She cleared her throat. "I got in trouble a few years back. Did some bad things. Don't ask me what because I'll never say. The judge gave me a choice—prison or full-time employment in the family business, under close supervision. My dad owned a Sunoco station."

"That's a no-brainer."

"But my parents said *lock her up and teach her a lesson*. Alfred took me in."

"So you must've had a good relationship with him."

Tricia gave a dry laugh. "No one in my family had a good relationship with him. They pushed him away. Still do."

"Even his kids?"

"Kid—my dad. They talk once a year during Yom Kippur."

"I don't get it. Alfred's a control freak, but he's not a monster."

"Not always."

If only temporarily, Tricia was no longer Trix, the high school renegade with the rainbow hair and go-to-hell glance. No longer the buttoned-up professional with disregard for anyone but a paying customer.

"That's why I'm twenty-seven years old and have a legal guardian." She gave a bitter laugh. "Looks like we have something in common after all—Alfred has both of us by the balls. If you don't cooperate, you land in jail. Same as me."

She was right. We shared the same need-hate relationship with the old man, and therefore the same motivation to get the upper hand. I tried again. "What did Drax do to him?"

Another pause. I pictured her mouth a millimeter from the phone. In the dead stillness of the night, I heard her lips brush the mouthpiece. "Don't tell him I told you."

"You've got my word on it."

"For what it's worth."

That stung. "I've never done anything to hurt you."

She countered without missing a beat. "Forget about it. Drax destroyed his career as a photojournalist—made sure no publication would hire him."

"Why?"

"Does it matter? Business is a jungle, and businesspeople are predators. Here's my advice. Have fun underground doing whatever you do, take the damn measurements, and get on with your life."

My life. *For what it's worth.* "Can I trust him if we get in a jam?"

"Maybe, maybe not. Like I said, he's my parole officer."

"You're not helping much."

"That's not my job."

. . . . .

Like every Cincinnati kid, I grew up hearing subway lore, from the plausible to the absurd. The big kids told the little kids that the subway's trapped air carried cancer like pollen. That the tunnels contained warring colonies of rats as big as toasters. That one spur, a dead-end tunnel, housed "corpses stacked like cord wood." That last story was never told without those five ominous words, turning our skin to ice.

And every Cincinnati kid knew the story of Emily Langford because it was taught in schools to terrify us into obedience.

The Great Depression struck. With the subway's concrete barely dry, public transportation money shifted to other needs, like food and shelter for a desperate population. City leaders voted to mothball the underground system. Transit workers bolted iron gates over street-level entrances to dissuade the curious from venturing down.

But even as early as the 1930s, my predecessors in off-limits exploration worked their way into forbidden places. The underground sang a siren's song, and the iron gates were no match.

In 1945, the year World War II ended, a nine-year-old girl followed a group of these explorers into the depths. Emily Langford's tiny frame squeezed easily through gaps widened by the leaders. She trailed them for a time, unnoticed, before detouring solo toward Ludlow Avenue Station. She became lost among the straightaways, junctions, and dead-end spurs. Desperation eroding her judgment, she crawled into the narrower maintenance passages used to service the transit tunnels. Before long, her flashlight batteries expired and darkness entombed her.

Days later, rescue crews found her body curled into a ball on a tiny patch of dusty concrete. The cause of death might've been dehydration or exposure—I don't recall—but the rumor mill preferred a more sensational explanation, that terror had squeezed the life from her heart. Even as a young kid, I had imagined Emily, with dirt-covered knees and a rumpled dress, crying out in vain from that black pit of hell.

If little Emily had been a poor man's kid like me, the public might've brushed off the tragedy. But her uncle was a city councilman with ambition and press connections, and his cry of anguish echoed across the Seven Hills. In turn, opportunistic journalists milked the incident for peak circulation, with sensational headlines like *Subterranean Terror*, *Treading on Our Innocents*, and *The Shame beneath Our Feet*. A politician confided to an associate at a city council meeting, unaware of a live WKRC microphone nearby. "One can't help but wonder if the girl quite literally screamed herself to death," he said, and the city shuddered as one.

The mayor, with the wet-eyed councilman hovering over his shoulder, appealed to a primetime TV audience. "Never again. Our children must be protected. The relic subway must be sealed."

And sealed it was, tighter than a tomb. Wherever possible, road crews paved over street-level entrances. Elsewhere, welders affixed steel plates "as thick as the hulls of oil tanker," an excessive mandate of a city ordinance scribbled by panicky politicians. Nobody, the authorities declared, would enter the subway again.

CHAPTER 11

By the time subway access required acetylene torches, the underground had become off-limits. But Alfred had learned about a surviving utility portal, so only one thing stood between us and El Dorado: a plan. "A good job is only as good as your plan," Dad once chided me when I was a teenager. I'd assembled a bed in the living room, only to realize I couldn't fit it through the bedroom doorway.

For any first-time infiltration, Reuben and I usually divided up the planning tasks, with me in charge of getting us in and out, and Mr. Science in charge of keeping us alive in between, researching toxic fungi, explosive gases, and other natural or man-made nastiness.

We rendezvoused at the YMCA to compare progress. After running the indoor track and heaving medicine balls, we seized a corner table in the canteen and spread out our notes.

"We need a spotter," Reuben announced.

"You're nuts. How do we train somebody in three days?"

"Train?" Reuben rocked back in his chair and planted hands on hips. His forehead glistened with sweat. *"Hey, newbie, holler if anyone follows us.* There, I just gave the entire training."

"We're not roping a plebe into this. Wouldn't be fair to him." I tapped a stack of notes. "What'd you find out?"

"You go first," Reuben said, but something in his obtuse expression left me uneasy.

"We go at midnight, late enough for quiet streets, but not too late for a couple of students with their backpacks to be heading home after studying."

"Sounds reasonable."

"And we drive."

Reuben frowned. "License plates guarantee *I'm* identified, unless you're planning on buying a car for the first time in your life."

I couldn't afford a Hot Wheel and Reuben knew it. "Buses are spotty after midnight and riders get noticed. We'll park in a residential neighborhood and walk the last half-mile."

That seemed to satisfy him. I continued, feeling a bit like the eager lieutenant at the colonel's briefing. "Alfred wants the first descent to be a trial run. A few measurements to let Smith validate his triangulations. If they add up, we go back and shoot the rest."

I wasn't ready to tell Reuben about Alfred's "favor." No reason to stoke his anxiety when the mystery spur probably didn't exist.

I also didn't mention photography equipment. Reuben didn't care anyway. But I did. Earlier, I'd thrown a Hail Mary pass and petitioned Alfred for the Hasselblad. "Would you send Sir Edmund Hillary to the peak of Everest with a flea market camera?"

Alfred had flashed the smile of a superior. "Forget it, and you can forget about the Leica too."

I'd left his office determined to find a creative solution. I wasn't about to trust the greatest photo shoot of my life to the old Yashica.

"Okay, no more stalling," I asked Reuben. "What'd you find out?"

He gathered himself up. "Every man-made tunnel from Anchorage to Zanzibar is ventilated. The subway isn't, and hasn't been for decades."

"I know that."

"Gases accumulate."

"I also know that." I wiped my face with a gym towel that smelled like the inside of a suitcase. "What gases?"

Reuben held a thumb aloft. "Methane, for one. Flammable as hell."

I shrugged. "Any cave can naturally accumulate methane." I was tipping toward an idiotic argument, that natural meant benign, as if rabies from a raccoon was less fatal because the furry rascals had such adorable faces. "So we avoid open flames. No big deal."

"Oh really? So no use of unapproved electrical devices that might generate a spark," he said, his sarcasm splashing, "like a laser soldered together in some geek's basement?"

"The Ohio State physics lab is no Romper Room—"

Reuben cut me off with an open palm, the attitude gone. "A little methane is nothing compared to our biggest problem."

I tensed and waited.

"Hydrogen sulfide."

My stomach lurched. "But the subway should be dry."

Reuben shook his head. "It would be, if it were maintained."

I swallowed hard. "Sewer gas? You sure?"

"It's a sealed chamber branching close to the Ohio River, and that means ready moisture, and that means organics, and that means *decades* of anaerobic digestion."

Again I said nothing, this time waiting for a usable explanation.

"Which means poison gas," Reuben said, "maybe enough to arm a regiment." An apt comparison; the British fired canisters of the stuff into trenches in World War I, the enemy's gas masks useless against it.

Dark and dank places with static air contain plenty of gaseous hazards, including ammonia, methane, carbon dioxide, sulfur dioxide, and nitrogen oxide. But none of these strike fear in the hearts of urban explorers like hydrogen sulfide for one key reason: it methodically disarms the victim's natural defenses.

Also known as *stink damp*, hydrogen sulfide reeks like rotten eggs, but not for long, as the gas kills the victim's sense of smell. The stench seems to vanish. Fooled into complacency, the victim becomes disoriented and dizzy. Memory fails. Judgment fails. A clear mind would order the body to run to save itself. But the afflicted mind swears the danger is gone, or perhaps was never there. Effects could hit in seconds.

In September 1968, the bodies of three London adventurers were found beneath Dumfries, their faces inexplicably serene. The postmortem revealed hydrogen sulfide poisoning. With presence of mind, they would've found safe air and survival a two-minute crawl away.

Reuben scratched his chin. "I can put up with a lot. Crawlspaces, dripping acid, rats up my pants leg. But not stink damp."

I didn't need to remind Reuben of one more sinister characteristic of hydrogen sulfide. Heavier than normal air, it collects down low. The upper half of a still chamber can be as safe as a nursery. But drop down to crawl and you might never get up.

"We plan our route super carefully," I said. "Steer clear of the river."

Follow Me Down

· · · · ·

I showered off the workout while Reuben stayed behind with a blank page, a ready pencil, and a pronounced V at the center of his forehead.

I reemerged twenty minutes later, having failed to unknot my stressed shoulder muscles with near-scalding jets from the shower head. Reuben no longer sat at our table, but our paperwork remained. The room was vacant and cluttered as if evacuated in a rush. I followed the sound of whooping and jeering coming from down the hall. I pulled up behind Reuben and a circle of spectators.

On the floor of the lobby between burnt orange vinyl sofas, a small Asian man I recognized pressed the cheek of a big Teuton to the scuffed tile.

Andy Luong, a bantamweight with Fab Four-style black hair, was on the bigger guy like a backpack, a full nelson, his fingers braided in the guy's hair, his legs ratcheted around the guy's waist.

Andy first started showing up at the Y a year earlier. We showed him how to shoot hoops, not that he had a prayer, but he tried. His compact, muscular body did better with the medicine balls.

"So get this. The idiot calls Andy a Jap," Reuben said, "but Andy says he's from Vietnam and keeps walking. So the guy calls him Cong. You know, like Viet Cong? Of course, the moron wouldn't know Hanoi from Hoboken. Andy explodes and takes the guy down. Every time he tries to get up, Andy bends his neck until he screams. It's pretty impressive."

Reuben and I shouldered into the circle of bodies, dropped to a knee, disengaged Andy's fingers from his prisoner's hair digit by digit, and pointed the adversaries in opposite directions. Andy, eyes blazing, proclaimed to everyone within earshot, "I no VC, *got damn*, I no VC."

Reuben and I exchanged a knowing glance, and I drew close. "Small guy, sharp, strong as hell, afraid of nothing."

Reuben nodded. "Yeah, he'd make a damn good spotter."

CHAPTER 12

Mom had already been in bed for two hours when Reuben pulled up in front in his decaying Falcon. But I'd never complain about a car that had probably shuttled me thousands of miles since high school.

I dropped into the passenger seat. "You okay?" I asked, assessing Reuben's mood. Cloudy with a chance of rain.

He gnawed the inside of his cheek, thinking. "Remember in grade school when those big kids said we'd each get a Three Musketeers if—"

"If we dropped a bag of dog shit on Coach Vaughn's porch and rang the doorbell? Yeah, I remember."

Reuben glanced right. "That's about how I feel right now. You?"

I looked out at the blistered paint on the car's hood. "About the same." Dread and excitement battled in my gut, leaving me fidgety.

Reuben stepped on the accelerator. "You agreed to do it, not me. I can't stand Three Musketeers bars. That stuff in the middle—"

"Nougat."

"Yeah, like sugared sugar with sugar on it. Nauseating."

I was glad to hear a bit of regular Reuben, even though his lightweight words defied his pinched expression. "We never collected our candy."

"Duh," he said. "No time when you're running for your life."

"What breed was that anyway? German shepherd?"

He shrugged. "Probably part wolf."

We rode in silence until pulling up in front of Andy's apartment complex. A decent place. I wondered, suddenly, how immigrants forced to start over could already be doing better than Mom and me. Then I felt angry at myself for comparing.

Andy emerged within seconds, dutifully climbed in the back seat, and waved a greeting.

A few days earlier, over a table in the Y's canteen, Reuben and I had told Andy everything we knew. If he was going to join our band of subway pioneers, he had to do so with informed consent. We told him about our train station photos, my run-in with Tony Drax, my release from jail on Alfred's bail money, the rescue of our film followed by its imprisonment in Alfred's wall safe, and the need for underground measurements.

I didn't mention Tricia. It wouldn't make sense. *Former social spaz despises the grandfather who saved her from prison but studies his every move.* Or, *buttoned-up retail manager wants to be left alone but sticks her nose where it doesn't belong.* No, Tricia made zero sense.

At one point around that table, I'd given a weighty pause to make sure Andy was listening. Then I said, "Drax will do *anything* to protect itself. Do you understand what I mean by that?"

"No problem," Andy had said, his face surprisingly unconcerned.

We parked the Falcon on an anonymous side street, hopped the squat fence behind an elementary school, and scrambled up railroad ballast to twin tracks running east and west, an ideal route to the portal. With scarce overhead lighting, no foot traffic, and neighborhood houses tucked behind fences and high bushes, we traveled the half-mile unobserved, all the while quietly talking. Through Andy's broken English, Reuben and I learned more about our newest member.

Communist loyalists in South Vietnam had begun overtaking border villages, assuming an imminent Viet Cong victory from the north. Dissenting clans were targeted, and Andy's uncle was murdered, his corpse dumped in the village fountain for public viewing. Andy, his parents, and younger sister escaped to Cambodia and found their way into the US under asylum status.

No wonder he shrugged off Drax. Apparently, when you've seen such horrors and escaped the Cong by night, corporate corruption didn't seem so scary.

I spotted our destination up ahead, a squat moonlit building no bigger than a one-car garage. Constructed of tornado-proof brick and painted beige, the structure had no windows, only a single steel door. I gestured us into a crouch at the downhill edge of the ballast. "Let's sit tight for a minute to make sure we're alone."

Andy looked curious. Reuben looked with surprise at the building. "What the hell's that?"

"You were expecting a manhole cover with *to the subway* painted on top?" I said. "It's a Cincinnati Bell switching station for this neighborhood."

"Why do you know?" Andy asked.

I explained my mom's jobs with the phone company. "Switching stations are part of basic training, like dial tone." Then I explained dial tone. Andy received my tutelage with interest. "The portal's below that building."

Reuben asked, "Why was it never sealed up?" Moonlight refracted through his glasses and sliced his cheekbones with white shards.

I grinned. "You'll love this. Before they welded everything shut, they rerouted the utilities, but with an exception—City Hall. The election was coming and the politicians didn't want their service disrupted."

"Empty promises to be made, arms to be twisted, and palms to be greased," Reuben said, bitterness riding beneath the surface of his words. "So the subway still carries phone lines into City Hall?"

I nodded in the dark. "A handful. You still doing okay?"

"IHOP's open all night. Maybe we buy Andy some pancakes after this insanity." He bumped his shoulder against Andy's.

Silence settled around us, except for a few crickets and the odd night bird rustling in nearby shrubs. We were good to go. I led the way.

The door to the switching station was secured by an embedded circular plate with a four-digit combination lock dead center, like a thumbwheel mechanism under the handle of a briefcase, but bigger. Nine thousand nine hundred and ninety-nine combinations—secure enough. I entered the digits I'd memorized from Alfred's crib sheet and we were in. As the door clicked behind us, I released a pent-up breath.

The only ambient light was green and spare, coming from refrigerator-sized machines lined up in the room's center. Cooling fans rushed steadily, interrupted by the *clacks* of metal switches and staccato *clicks* of rotary calls going through. Reuben and Andy awaited my move.

I followed the swath from my flashlight. On the floor behind the machines, a rectangle of cream-colored linoleum was framed in aluminum and earmarked with a recessed pull ring. It was a trap door, just as Alfred had learned from some phone company insider he refused to name.

"If that flimsy flooring's the only thing blocking our access all these years," Reuben said, "I'll shoot myself."

"Don't count on it." I yanked the pull ring and the panel rose easily, one edge anchored with a piano hinge. I pointed my flashlight down into a four-foot square hole with rebar ladder rungs cast into one wall. The hole bottomed out at a circular object like a manhole cover, the steel smooth, with a single pull-handle and the same four-digit locking mechanism.

I descended the ladder, dialed in the second memorized code, and tugged. The portal swung open easily, as if we were expected. No drumroll, no Sousa flourish, no sunrise horns like in *2001: A Space Odyssey*. Only a smell that reminded me of Granddad's stone-lined well.

CHAPTER 13

Even though we'd come on a mission, I couldn't let duty overshadow the experience. To urban explorers coast to coast, the Cincinnati subway was Mount Everest upended, and I was among the chosen few.

As I hopped off the lowest rung to the tunnel floor, I wanted to scream *We made it!* at the top of my lungs. Perhaps momentous proclamations were in order, like when Neil Armstrong pressed mankind's first footprint into terra luna. Or maybe I should've celebrated the moment in solemn reference, whispering questions to the dark void and sensing answers of infinite wisdom.

Reuben shattered my reverie. "I don't smell it. Do you?"

I closed my eyes and breathed in what I expected: limestone, silica and other elements of public transit construction, but the aromas were touched by an electric arc as raw as nature, even though the last underground voltage had sparked decades ago from the utility lights of Depression-era laborers. I drew a deeper breath and detected faraway vegetable wetness—hot, alive, and unnerving. "No, but there's moisture," I said, "so we have to be careful." We'd told Andy about hydrogen sulfide, but he'd reacted as if we'd shared a weather forecast.

"That reminds me," Reuben said. He rummaged in his pocket and retrieved a fistful of fine chain. He untangled three necklaces from the clump and handed them out, each with a shiny new penny dangling. "Wear it over your clothes." He demonstrated.

"For good luck?" Andy asked.

"Far from it," Reuben replied. "Stink damp discolors copper. Think canary in the coal mine. We watch each other's penny. If it discolors, it might be too late." Reuben's choice of words included too much Hollywood drama.

"Then what good from it?" Andy asked.

"I said *might*." Reuben's voice echoed off the vertical surfaces. "Which implies the possibility of *might not*."

Andy smiled in spite of the morbid subject matter.

After positioning Andy at his watch post near the access portal, Reuben and I walked down the straightaway, flashlights in the lead, our footsteps damped by the layer of dust like a sheet of felt. Twelve feet above the floor, the concrete ceiling curved gently where it met the walls, as if sized for a gigantic loaf of bread cruising between stations.

Smith had selected three locations for taking measurements. We'd be testing laser distances of twenty feet, a hundred feet and, finally, a quarter-mile down an arrow-straight section of tunnel.

We entered one straightaway that paralleled another, and I imagined passengers catching glances across trains, their line of sight interrupted by concrete columns as if watching a flickery old movie.

I stewed as we walked. I had three items on my to-do list, but Reuben knew of only one, the measurements. He'd suffer the others but not without complaint. I decided to let one cat out of the bag.

"Alfred wants us to run a little errand." I went on to explain mystery spur number five. "If it exists, we're supposed to take pictures through a gate, nothing more."

Reuben glanced at me like a truant officer who'd heard it all. "What do you mean *supposed to*?"

"Come on. Aren't you the least bit curious?"

"That's your justification for anything boneheaded. Do as Blumenfeld asks, okay?"

I peered ahead into the dark. "If it's real, we can decide then." Didn't Reuben realize the rarity of this moment, of this place? I thought of the citizens overhead, settling for their excitement in the corridors of a shopping mall.

The route to our first stop mapped perfectly to the blueprint stored in my brain. My confidence rose.

The first measurement required lining up the laser on a major support pillar and firing the beam against a curved wall. According to Drax's bid submitted long ago, both surfaces were to be precisely engineered. Smith's triangulations, if valid, would tell the truth.

We dropped to our knees and began unloading equipment. I brought the camera into the light and braced myself for Reuben's reaction.

"Where the hell did you get that?" His words felt like a jab in the ribs. He was referring to the gorgeous Nikon F-series Photomic SLR in my hand.

I rummaged idly. "It's got a one point four Nikkor lens. Perfect for low light."

"That justifies theft?"

I wouldn't go that far and he knew it. "Borrowed it from the school."

"Without asking. You're becoming predictable."

I slid on the flash unit. "Forgiveness is easier to get than permission."

Reuben sighed and hoisted the laser from his pack. "Don't we have enough trouble?"

In truth, my old Yashica would've done Alfred's job well enough. But I needed premier optics for another purpose, and before long, Reuben would have to be told.

"Can we debate this later?" I asked.

Reuben shrugged and stood. He pressed the laser flat against the pillar, aligned an orange hash mark with a concrete edge, and leveled the device with surgical precision. I followed Smith's instructions to make sure the photo included twin reference points on the wall and floor.

"Fire," I said. A green dot, bright enough to stand out under the flash's white, appeared about five feet above the floor. I pressed the button and heard the *sh-wacka* of a state-of-the-art SLR.

Measurement number two went equally well, the laser distance greater. My only challenge was blindness after the flash, short-lived but unsettling.

We walked ten minutes southeast, rounded a turn, and peered into uninterrupted blackness. I ran my thumb in a concrete seam that separated a curving wall from another long straightaway. "That's your spot. Align on the vertical, level, and fire right into the black."

According to Smith, the quarter-mile distance would put to rest any doubts about his methodology.

I headed out. "I should be down there in five minutes, but give me ten, okay?"

Reuben rolled his eyes, but he understood. A few silent minutes alone weren't enough to connect with a place, but I had to try.

I arrived at my destination, eased the straps from my shoulders, and laid my pack in the dust. Leaning my back against the wall, I let my body slide down until my butt settled on a wedge of grit accumulated over decades. I clicked off my flashlight, closed my eyes, and listened.

I let the low-frequency thrum, now familiar and always present, seep into my head and chest. Something skittered along the ground a few feet out. I leaned my head back against the wall. Alfred's to-do list could wait a few minutes.

I thought of Dad. I wanted to talk with him, to let him know where I was, and that his awkward kid had accomplished something special indeed. I allowed my heart to drop its guard and believe for a moment that I wasn't alone, that maybe the dead could choose their haunts. If so, then Dad would join me at that moment, holding strong against my back like a rock wall. Impulsively, I pressed a finger against the artery in my neck, under my jaw, as Dad had shown me when I was young. *It feeds that big brain of yours,* he'd said smiling, his fingers in my hair.

A ripple of anger spread in my chest. With Dad's help, maybe Drax would pay for what they'd done.

The scratching sound came closer until the cuff of my jeans jostled a bit. My new friend was bold. Good for him. With a tug, my visitor attempted to steal a swatch of denim for his nest.

"Sorry," I whispered and shook my leg. "No free samples."

Skit skit sounds trailed off beyond my hearing.

"Gave up too soon, buddy." I stood. Back to work.

My flashlight revealed crisp tracks leading toward a fissure in the wall, but no intrepid tunnel mate. Judging by the prints, he was a good-sized rat. Big as a toaster? Close enough.

I took my position, advanced the film, and aimed. "Ready when you are," I said, my volume only slightly elevated in the cathedral-like acoustics.

Seconds later, the green dot appeared on the wall. *Sh-wacka.* As with each firing of the flash, I became temporarily blind, my field of vision filled by reversed ghost images of what theoretically still existed.

Time to tell Reuben.

"We've got to capture it before it's too late," I told him at our rendezvous point.

I'd made the decision the same day Alfred had mentioned the surviving utility access portal. I had to photograph the subway. Time was short. In spite of Alfred and Smith and their grand scheme, Drax would likely win—they always did—and fill in the underground system, burying it for all time.

I told Reuben how I'd use the same technique as in the train station, the shutter held open, painting with light with progressive flashes carefully aimed in total darkness like giant brushstrokes, but this time with a colorful twist.

I paused and waited. After the disastrous shoot in the Union Terminal, I expected an earful.

"Think Andy will wait that long?" he said, his eyes flat behind prismatic lenses.

"You already knew?"

Reuben nodded as if it were obvious. "Yeah, the minute you whipped out the Nikon. You wouldn't take a risk like that for Blumenfeld. Besides, you don't need Nikkor optics for what he wants." He glanced away. "So let's get this done."

"You're letting me off the hook mighty easy."

"I am?"

I lifted my hands and gestured around us. "It's this place. You're distracted."

"But we've been in way older places." For a moment, Reuben lost himself in a thought. Then he said, "It's the isolation, like being on another planet. Kind of gets to you."

We picked up Andy. He'd stood watch long enough to rule out followers.

I'd chosen the photo-shoot location in advance by studying the blueprints. The Rookwood station would give me everything I needed to compose images worth publishing in the local press, photos that might wake the citizens of Cincinnati from their stupor.

When we arrived, every eye-catching architectural feature was as I'd hoped: arched support columns lined up like paraders, an infinite straightaway to the east, a gently curving tunnel to the west, and a filigreed marble staircase rising out of sight.

Reuben sniffed the air, testing. I met his eyes. He shook his head.

"Me neither," I said, and we shared a moment of relief. No stink damp, not yet.

I swapped out the film, careful to seal our progress in a lightproof aluminum film can. I loaded up Kodachrome-X sixty-four ASA, crisp, bright, and thirsty for light. Reuben extended the tripod, screwed on the camera, and gave Andy a crash course in blind photography with the shutter locked open.

I worked on composition, starting with a photo I'd been arranging in my mind for days. It was to be a classic one-third, two-thirds ratio, naturally balanced for the mind and pleasing for the eye. The left third would feature the stone staircase rising up, and the right two-thirds a platoon of sentry columns vanishing into infinite blackness.

The photo would need excellent depth of field, crisply focused both up close and far away, and that required a tight aperture on the lens and lots of light. But this time, the light would be rainbowed, great gorgeous Technicolor splashes with each firing of the flash.

I'd thought long and hard about palette. The gray of concrete was inevitable, so I wouldn't fight it, but work with it. The perfect complement would be cool blues and purples and the endless violet variations in between. For the flash unit, I'd brought a set of glassine filters with every anticipated hue.

We doused our flashlights. Reuben opened the shutter. I groped along in the dark—no penlights that might streak the film with exposure. I fired, recharged, swapped out filters, cleared my bleached vision, and kept moving. Each composition took ten or fifteen minutes. For the last photo, I fumbled down the lightless straightaway until my fingertips stung from abrasion, as I fired through a lineup of filters. Before long, I was a half-mile from my friends and felt as if I were standing on the dark side of the moon. Throughout the shoot, I'd visualized my creation: a depiction of man's journey from birth to death—ambitious, the way art's supposed to be.

· · · · ·

Following the map in my brain, we journeyed southeast past the Avondale and Tippin Street stations to reach the straightaway Alfred had described, the one with the possible fifth spur. From a bird's eye view, we'd pass close to the Ohio River and a greater risk of airborne toxins.

Reuben took point. I hung close behind with Andy. We ambled down the most gradual of inclines, almost imperceptible, but I had no doubt where a marble placed on the floor would roll.

Without warning, Reuben's outstretched arm clotheslined me in the chest. He'd stopped dead in his tracks and backed up on the double, taking Andy and me with him.

"I smelled stink damp," he sputtered, breathless. "No doubt."

I sniffed to test. No rotten egg aroma. "I don't. False alarm?"

Reuben's mind zoomed ahead, leaving Andy and me blinking. "I knew the air down here was still, but not *this* still."

"I don't get it," I said.

He lifted the lanyard and penny over his head. "Get out your scope." I did. Reuben wadded the chain into a clump and tossed it forward with a softball underhand. Then he trained his flashlight's beam toward the foreground twenty feet out. I rotated the ring on the scope for close targeting. The penny came into view, a speck of a circle but clear enough. The copper surface transformed with undulating bands of color—violet, blue, green—like a sheen of motor oil on calm water.

I passed the telescope to Reuben. "Why did you smell it and we didn't? You were only a few feet up ahead."

"Up ahead, yeah, plus I'm shorter," he explained. "I dipped into it first."

Andy made a quizzical expression.

Reuben elaborated. "There's *zero* air movement down here, so when hydrogen sulfide settles in the low spots, it's like a pond of water. Keep your head above the surface and life goes on. Dip below, like I started to, and you drown in poison. The difference between life and death can be inches."

Andy absorbed our ghastly analysis with his usual stoicism, and I wondered if I was witnessing some cultural Teflon, a shield against war's emotional battering.

"Come to think of it," I said, "this is the closest we've been to the river."

Reuben reached a conclusion with a single nod. "The copper doesn't lie. Looks like Blumenfeld's mystery spur will remain a mystery. Let's back out of here."

"Not so fast," I countered. "I know a detour."

· · · · ·

In twelve minutes, after passing through two transit tunnels and three service passages, we arrived at the north end of Alfred's straightaway. Above us, Adolphus Avenue. Ahead of us in the darkness, a fifth spur—maybe.

To find it, we progressed the length slowly, eyeballing not only the west wall as Alfred had instructed, but every flat and crease we could see. We soon reached the Ptarmigan Street Station, the stairs rising to the steel understructure of a road. I couldn't help but think of the breach that killed Delbert Turkel—the groan of buckling metal, the ground rising up, the walls of the excavator's cab folding in on Turkel's chest until the next breath couldn't come.

Along the way, we'd encountered no spur, no openings whatsoever, not even a ground-level rat passage.

"Alfred got played," Reuben said. "Or he played us."

I shook my head. "If you were there when he mentioned it, you'd know. For whatever reason, this is no joke for Blumenfeld."

I started back in the direction we'd come, but this time hugged the west side. Reuben and Andy followed close, Andy curious, Reuben fidgety.

Around midpoint between the two stations, I pressed my flashlight against the wall and exposed the surface like sunrise across a plain. Tiny cones of shadow trailed pimples in the concrete.

"There." I pointed with my chin. "It's irregular. Andy, hold this."

He took over flashlight duty as I caressed the wall until brushing a half-inch wide indentation. It ran in a vertical line about eight inches long. I tested a hunch and felt a similar line about a foot and a half to the side. I was touching the outer dimensions of a good-sized brick embedded in the wall.

"This façade is some kind of filler over cinderblock," I said. "That's weird. The entire subway is poured concrete, but not here."

"Meaning?" Reuben asked, even though he knew what it meant—he was growing testy.

I scratched my chin. "It means this was added later, with lots of hard work to make it invisible and hide whatever's behind it."

"We take no picture?" Andy asked.

But we had to. Explorers were supposed to work past an obstacle, not retreat from it.

I mapped our progress to the memorized blueprint and thrust an index finger. "There's a service passage entrance by the stairs at Adolphus. A back door maybe?"

Except for the rare crossover from one artery to another, service passages ran parallel to the main transit tunnels. We could loop around to enter the spur from behind.

My assumptions panned out, taking us through a three-foot-wide service passage for about a minute before reaching the unexpected: a gate. With vertical bars four inches apart and mortared into the ceiling and floor, the frame wasn't going anywhere. The gate itself, however, gave me hope. It hung from three sturdy hinges on one side and a lock on the other with a key mechanism I'd seen before. It dated to the first half of the century and could be sprung with the right tools.

A lesson from the journals of N. Jefferson Chapel, explorer extraordinaire: *Take pause before stowing locksmithing accoutrement in your attaché. If apprehended, your avowal of innocence will fail, for those who carry the kit of a criminal will be availed as such.*

But on this occasion, I'd ignored Mr. Chapel. If we were caught in the forbidden subway, no *avowal of innocence* would save our criminal butts.

I retrieved my locksmith's tools from my pack, plucked a number fourteen, worked the keyhole for thirty seconds, and *click*—the gate opened like the arms of the one true love. Andy was impressed. Reuben wasn't.

"Dust clogs the steel stops," he said. "A good whack probably would've done it." Killjoy.

We advanced, with me on point. In less than a minute, my hunch proved right. Obviously, we'd paralleled the main transit tunnel because we emerged behind the makeshift wall. Except on this side there was no stucco veneer, only bare cinderblock expertly masoned into permanence. We swept our flashlights to the right and revealed the spur's unlikely contents: wooden crates constructed of roughhewn lumber, and lots of them.

"What the hell?" Reuben said. Andy's eyes widened.

I thought of an old Rory Calhoun western where the bad guys sold repeating rifles to the Indians, their contraband transported on flatbed wagons in similar crates. Still, these were bigger, six or seven feet long, and a couple of feet wide and deep. If they contained armaments, these were big guns indeed.

The crates had been arranged neatly, five side-by-side to form a row, and five rows stacked to the ceiling. Twenty-five crates to a stack.

Follow Me Down

But how many stacks? I shined my flashlight down the narrow walkway separating the pile from the rightmost wall. The beam petered out before reaching the far end of the spur. "There might be hundreds of them."

I rapped on the side of one crate, hoping for a revealing reverberation, but learned nothing. "Sure as hell isn't subway construction equipment." I swatted at possibilities in my mind. "Piping maybe, or I-beams? But never packaged like this, as if for a cross-country trip."

Reuben shot me a glare. "You can't break into them."

I pressed my lips tight before saying, "We couldn't photograph between the bars of the gate like Alfred wanted. The gate was an opaque wall."

"Your point being?" Reuben had begun circling my argument, looking for vulnerabilities.

But I plunged ahead, making things up on the fly. "We had to improvise at the locked gate, so… now we've entered a period of improvisation." I winced. Sounded weak to me too.

Reuben dismissively waved his hands in the air. "You'll do whatever you want anyway."

I wasn't going to come this far, technically break the law multiple times, and then settle for a souvenir photo of the outside of some wooden boxes. But would I tell Alfred about the contents? That depended on what we found inside.

I took off solo. Reuben stayed put. So did Andy, looking like a kid adrift between quarreling parents. I turned my body sideways to fit through the passage, the stacks at my chest and wall at my back. Humming the refrain from *There Goes My Baby*, I tapped containers as I walked, counting, and scanned the ground before me for something that might serve as a pry tool.

By the end of the spur, I'd tapped thirty-one stacks, which totaled seven hundred seventy-five crates. If they contained weapons, there were enough for a battalion.

I crossed over behind the stacks and headed toward my friends via the other side of the spur. Along the way, I grabbed a greasy wooden handle jutting from the dust and flecks of concrete. It was a screwdriver, a medium Phillips with mangled teeth. A flathead would've been better, but as Dad used to say, *generals strategize, soldiers improvise.*

"You're crossing a line," Reuben said upon my approach.

I scaled two rows of crates like massive ladder rungs and peered down at him. "We crossed a line when we dialed a stolen code and trespassed on phone company property." What was that old expression? *In for a penny, in for a pound.* Too stuffy. I tried my own variation. "Why settle for a bite when you can eat the whole cheeseburger?"

Reuben glowered. Andy blinked.

I kept climbing until I reached the top. On hands and knees, I perched about six inches below the sandpapery ceiling, studying the crate below me. Splintery slats ran the length, each maybe three or four inches wide and anchored with nails, not screws, which meant my crude pry tool might buy me a peek inside.

I wedged the Phillips and gave it a pull. A finger-sized chunk of wood burst into shards. The slat hadn't budged.

I placed my flashlight on the adjacent crate and pointed the beam toward my work space. I shifted to a sturdier slat and tried again. The nail screeched. I adjusted my angle, yanked, and opened a gap large enough to wedge in my fingers. I pulled up hard. *Crack.*

"Success," I said, but heard no reply. Reuben was probably pouting, while Andy hunkered down in the DMZ between combatants.

The slat had broken somewhere down by my knees, creating a shadowed opening a few inches wide and a couple of feet long.

"If you tell me you're not curious, you're lying through your teeth." I reached for my flashlight and caught a whiff of air freed from the depths of the crate—dusty and dead, like a tree stump so old and petrified the bacteria had given up. I shined the beam into the gap.

Two black eyes like bottomless holes in the earth stared back at me. But instead of the rodent eyes of the rat I'd laid to rest under a shrub, these eyes were human.

I sucked in air and lurched up with all the strength in my abdomen. The back of my head struck the rock-hard ceiling with a force I felt in my earlobes. I saw stars and toppled forward into a lightless pool.

• • • • •

"Lucas!" The voice was Reuben's, sounding a mile away. "You okay?"

I blinked my eyes open but saw nothing, only darkness. I breathed in a stale scent, like an old canvas tent after years in the shed. I winced at pain in my cheeks, a sharp edge on both sides, as if elevator doors had closed on my face.

Then I remembered. A dead body, a visage, those vacant eyes. I jerked both arms into push-up position and heaved. Wood splinters pierced my palms. I rose and freed my face from the opening in the slats, abrading my cheeks in the process.

After knocking myself stupid, I'd been an inch or maybe a millimeter from the corpse, eye to eye in the dark, or eye to empty socket—I didn't want to know how close, and I sure as hell wasn't going to check.

Reuben's head popped up above the edge of the crate. I wanted to reach out and clutch his arm, his head, anything. But he was busy and businesslike, directing his flashlight, exploring the gap I'd temporarily occupied.

"No wonder these crates are bigger," he said, as if remarking about a rock formation.

"Bigger than what?" I said with a cracked voice between gulps of air.

Reuben assessed me and clapped my shoulder. "You'll be okay. Bigger than a coffin, that's what. They each hold two bodies. Maybe more underneath. See?"

"No, I don't want to see."

"There's a pair of feet next to the guy's head."

I rolled away as if doing so might erase my memory. But I would never forget. The hair a spray of dusty wire. The toothy mouth twisted in a grimace of pain. The skin no longer skin, but an ashen membrane stretched over skull like leather on a saddle.

I swallowed back a wave of nausea. "They were true all along."

"What were?"

"The stories—when we were kids." I squeezed my scraped cheeks between both hands. "Corpses stacked like cord wood."

CHAPTER 14

As I lay in bed, my leg muscles spasmed and my brain swirled with unwanted images. I'd gotten home after four a.m. and resigned myself to insomnia. I stared at the ceiling and imagined what I would demand from Alfred. My eyelids drooped a few times, but shot open at a recurring scene: a ragged corpse, spring-loaded at the waist, popping up in a cloud of dust.

With the last wake-up nightmare, I swore Alfred would receive nothing from us—no film, no help, no nothing—not until he coughed up answers. Why were hundreds of bodies discarded in the old subway like so much human inventory? Was Drax somehow involved? Why did Alfred apparently know about them? What else hadn't he told me about our half-baked mission to topple Drax?

A chair scraped the kitchen floor and I glanced at my alarm clock. Almost eight a.m. I had to get moving to catch Alfred at the studio before the day's shoots swallowed him up.

I showered, shaved, and pulled on clean pants and a tennis shirt Mom had ironed, even though it came from the dryer wrinkle-free. I didn't mind. In her on-again, off-again state, pointless motion was better than no motion at all.

I entered the kitchen. Seeing Mom in the morning was hard. She'd always been the early riser in our family, first to greet with a smile and some comment about the plan for the day, her eyes sparkling. But that light had dimmed.

She wasn't alone. A woman sat at the table with her back to me, a faded paisley scarf taming disheveled, gray-streaked hair. She hunched in a frayed brown overcoat. A river rat like us, I figured, a neighbor or hopeless petitioner for road repair and stepped-up cop patrols. Maybe an old friend.

Yet Mom wasn't smiling as she would to an old friend. "Lucas," she said, gesturing with a drowsy hand. "There's someone here you'll want to meet." The woman turned.

I recognized a familiar story in every detail of her face. A half-smile that stopped at the lips and never rose to the eyes. The slightest of nods, a perfunctory acknowledgment that required little energy. Vertical lines that ran from brow to chin, discernible only to the knowing eye—the telltale signs of hidden suffering.

The woman stood slowly and extended her hand. I took it in mine. "You're Mrs. Turkel, is that right?"

Surprise registered momentarily but then drained. "Yes, that's me. You're wondering why I'm here."

I gave a small shake of the head. "I know why you're here. We have something awful in common, don't we?"

A hand to her mouth, the woman broke down crying, her shoulders rising and falling. I wrapped my arms around her and squeezed as if I might smother her pain. But I held her for myself as well; communal relief helped, if only for a short time.

"I wish there was no reason for you to be here," I murmured.

"Me too," she replied and sniffed her sobs into submission.

I let go and we both sat at the table. I knew what she was going through, the protocol of loss. The initial shock and waves of reckoning. Opening her crippled heart to the closest few while politely dispatching obligatory sympathies from friends and acquaintances.

My words would have no more impact than a sip of cool water, but no other words sufficed. "I'm so sorry for your loss."

"Thank you." She smiled that tepid smile, her eyes like empty cups.

My mother leaned in. "Louisa, tell Lucas what you told me."

The woman squared her shoulders. "They told my husband where to drive that machine."

"The excavator."

She nodded.

"Who told him?"

"A company man."

"How do you know this?"

"People saw what happened."

"Who?" I hoped for an answer a court of law would accept.

Louisa looked down and gave the slightest shake of her head. "I know their names. They told me in respect for my husband, but only with their names kept private. Delbert would never betray a friend, and I honor my husband."

So noble, and stupid. "They're protecting their jobs?" I rapped the tablecloth with my knuckles. "Some things are more important than jobs."

Louisa frowned. "Maybe they protect more than jobs."

I broke eye contact and fought off intruding memories of long wooden crates stacked floor-to-ceiling, leathery skin so taut. A few moments passed in silence. "These people… they heard your husband receive orders?"

Louisa nodded. "Heard and saw. The operations manager walked over to speak to Delbert. These men couldn't hear that part because the engine was running. But then my husband raised his voice to object because the order made no sense. The manager pointed toward the open field and shouted, *Go that way or go get another job*." Louisa pantomimed with her arm rail straight, her index finger leading the way.

"Operations manager?" I said. "His name is Tony?"

The woman nodded without a word, as if speaking the name was somehow forbidden.

"His name is Tony Drax," I said. My mother's sunken expression told me what she was thinking. It was happening all over again. First our family and now another.

It starts with a tragedy, maybe negligence or maybe intention. Then comes the cover-up and the blame game—blaming circumstance or blaming the victim. And if the truth emerges, like the head of a small animal popping from a burrow, stomp it. Strangle it. Tie it off. Then all that survives is the lie.

I reached across the table and placed my hands on top of Louisa's. Before I could stop myself, I said quietly, "Drax will pay for what they've done. I promise you."

· · · · · ·

Nine hours after making Louisa Turkel a promise I had no idea how to keep, I was in the darkroom at work printing color proofs of a wedding reception. Why brides submitted to the garter-removal ritual was beyond me. "It's like she's making an announcement," Chuckles had once said, talking like a thirty-three

RPM record on the sixteen setting. He touched his thigh and moved his finger north with each stage of the performance. "This is my leg. And this is my garter. And boys, this part up here is now officially closed for business."

When I emerged into waning daylight at 5:45 p.m., I verified that all employees had headed home. Then I returned to the darkroom, locking the door behind me.

Around six the following morning, I held in my hands the fruits of my night-long labor: a dozen immaculate eight-by-ten color enlargements of the subway, a beguiling underground realm only a handful of living Cincinnatians had ever seen. I slid these into a manila envelope and scribbled on the outside, *To Features Editor, Cincinnati Enquirer Newspaper.*

Then I sat down at the Smith Corona in the bookkeeper's office and typed.

Dear Good Sir:

For reasons you will soon understand, I wish to remain temporarily anonymous. However, if you must converse with me in order to act upon the envelope's contents, you may call 258-1772.

I represent the group SOS, as in Save Our Subway. We oppose recent efforts to destroy a precious historical treasure and potential solution to the Queen City's burgeoning traffic problem. We encourage a city-wide debate of the pros and cons of restoring our subway and, finally, using it to carry passengers.

We hereby grant the Cincinnati Enquirer exclusive rights to publish these brand-new and unprecedented photos for a period of 48 hours.

If you choose not to exercise these rights, we will extend a similar offer to The Cincinnati Post. But please act. A publication as fine as the Enquirer should be telling this important story.

Thank you kindly,
President, Save Our Subway

I proofread my note, slipped it into the envelope alongside the enlargements, and sealed the flap.

If everything went as planned, the newspaper editor—a thirty-year man at the Features desk—would dial the number but reach no one on a Saturday, only the answering machine for Blumenfeld Photography. Knowing Alfred from the old days, the editor would assume the unnamed president to be either Alfred or someone he trusts—no additional credentials required. Then, with the forty-eight-hour clock ticking, the editor would publish on Sunday, the day with the highest circulation and a color insert.

I felt a twinge of guilt for impersonating Alfred but shook it off. He'd put me through plenty and, technically speaking, I hadn't lied. I could be reached at that phone number, and if such a group existed, I'd be president.

But none of that mattered. Drax's efforts to kill the subway had to be stopped, or at least slowed down.

My call to Reuben woke him up.

"Where the hell were you last night?" he said. Damn. Slipped my mind. We were to meet with Andy to plan the final measurement excursion.

"Sorry, but something happened." I told him about Louisa Turkel and my plan for newspaper exposure.

Reuben clobbered me with silent disapproval before saying, "It's too personal for you, clouding your judgment."

"Drax has to be stopped—"

"Which we're trying to do by building a legal case."

"Public awareness could slow them down."

Reuben snorted. "The public ignored that subway for forty years, and pretty pictures in the paper won't change that." A pause. "Drax will figure out who took the photos."

"Not necessarily."

"Know what this is all about?"

I said nothing.

"Revenge. You'll do anything to hurt Drax because they hurt you, but you're not considering the collateral damage."

Dad knew nothing of revenge. He'd once stood straight-backed at the fence as our neighbor cursed a blue streak. Our dog had ripped up his petunia bed. Unflappable, Dad apologized and promised to replant every flower. He fetched a spade a moment later while smiling off the neighbor's red-faced tirade.

"Movie heroes seek revenge," I said to Reuben, "but Mom and I were too small for that, like ants on the sidewalk. *We* were collateral damage."

"And what you're doing makes you big? Yeah, big enough to become a Drax target."

"They'll find out about us eventually."

"Better be worth it."

I let Reuben have the last word. He needed it more.

Arriving downtown by bus, I delivered the manila envelope to the Enquirer building on Vine Street. The receptionist reassured me the Features Editor would receive the materials within the hour. I hit the street.

On my way out of Alfred's studio, I had glanced at the weekend shoot schedule tacked to a corkboard by the receptionist's desk. Beginning at 8:30 a.m., Alfred would be photographing the Yancey/Griffith wedding at the Netherland Plaza Hotel, an eight-hundred-room beauty first opened in 1931. I knew the old building's elevator shafts, steam tunnels, and service corridors, but this time I strolled through the front door.

I plopped in a burgundy leather chair in the lobby to await Alfred's arrival. My last visit had been by night during a remodeling closure. Now, by morning light, I admired the gorgeous French Art Deco styling, rich oak paneling, and two-story ceiling murals. I tipped my head back to take it in. One mural showed bounding gazelles, another a reclining nude with Michelin Man fat rolls.

"Your attire is ill-suited for this hotel."

I awoke to see Alfred standing over me, poindexterish in a checkered sport coat and bow tie.

"And that butterfly under your chin is?" I replied.

"You've no business advising me about fashion. You look like a ruffian. Aren't you supposed to be anywhere else?"

"I was up all night."

"What on earth for?"

I didn't feel like explaining. Maybe I was doing to Alfred what Alfred had been doing to me: not wanting to explain. "Tony Drax intentionally sent that excavator over the subway to force a collapse, without considering the danger to the operator." I explained my conversation with Louisa Turkel. "But the witnesses are too scared to testify."

Alfred responded without hesitation. "Then nothing's changed. We need the subway measurements. Have you processed the test photos?"

I squeezed the upholstered arms of the chair. The leather squeaked. "Did you hear me? They essentially murdered that man. That doesn't bother you?"

Alfred slipped a strap from his shoulder and set his camera bag on the ground. "You're emotional because of similarities to your father's death. But our strategy—*strategy*, not tactics—hasn't changed. We must prove fraud and shoddy work leading to that man's death. Then we'll have a case. Smith must validate the test measurements." Alfred held out his hand, palm up.

No film without answers. "Your mystery spur…"

Alfred's eyes widened. He withdrew his hand. "Yes?"

I scrutinized his face. "It exists, behind a wall. Someone tried to hide it, but we got in through a back door. It's filled with stacks and stacks of wooden crates."

Alfred said nothing, his expression obtuse.

I pressed. "What's inside them?" He had to know the answer, but would he lie?

Again, he said nothing. His gaze followed my face as I rose from my chair, but I realized he was mentally absent, looking through me to a place or time I knew nothing about.

Then his eyes filled with tears. I wasn't expecting that.

I paused, disarmed, before trying to press further. "What's in those crates?"

An elderly couple nearby lowered their newspapers to glower, but I kept going. "Sooner or later, Mr. Blumenfeld, you're going to tell me what this is all about. Might as well be now."

Alfred snapped out of his reverie. "Discretion would serve both of us well."

I leaned in and lowered my voice to a whisper. "Okay, then I'll answer for you. Dead people. Hundreds of them. We pried open a crate. Bodies stacked like cord wood, just like the ghost stories every kid has heard around the campfire since before I was born. But *not* since before *you* were born. So why are they down there?"

Alfred dropped his gaze to the floor. A tear broke free, rolled down his nose, and splashed on the parquet floor. "You've upset me. I'm unaccustomed to being assailed so abrasively. You should learn some manners." He leaned over and picked up his camera bag. "I have a wedding to shoot." He walked away.

What had just happened? Sure, I'd been direct, but I had a right to know. Hell, maybe we three had broken into a crime scene. Then it struck me: I'd just witnessed another of Alfred's Oscar-winning performances.

I caught up with him and blocked the path to the ballroom. "*Unaccustomed?*" I said, spraying disbelief. "So now you're all sensitive? Bitch brides like Miss Angelica slice you up every day and you practically thank them for it. And you actually *care* what those idiots think. Me? You don't give a shit what I think. So kill the act and stop ducking the question. Why the bodies?"

Whatever had upset Alfred thirty seconds earlier had apparently vanished into the lobby's paneling. The man before me radiated clear-eyed confidence. "I'll explain, but keep it to yourself or you'll ruin all the campfires yet to come." He took a breath. "It's a potter's field."

"A what?"

"Remember your Bible studies?"

I snorted. "I'm afraid not."

"The Bible speaks of a potter's field as a burial ground for indigents—homeless people. During the Depression, there were thousands of them, and many died on the streets. Everyone was broke, the city included, and proper burials cost money. When unidentified bodies showed up at the morgue, there was no money for proper disposal."

The story was too fantastic to be made up, especially on the fly. "They dumped dead hobos in the subway?"

"Technically speaking, they buried them—an important legal distinction. City code required below-ground disposal, but the law said nothing about covering a corpse with dirt. The unused subway was a dirt-cheap loophole, so to speak."

"It's heartless—barbaric."

"But not so unusual for Cincinnati. Check your history of the 1832 cholera outbreak. Corpses were dumped into a potter's field next to an orphanage at the corner of Twelfth and Elm Streets."

"But there are hundreds of them down there."

"The Depression lasted more than a decade. The coroner was saving money. Why stop a good thing? They figured they'd relocate the bodies eventually." Alfred looked away. The elderly couple had retreated to their newspapers. "That obviously never happened."

"Why keep it secret?"

He appeared to consider my question for a moment. Was he acting? "It was nothing to be proud of. And besides, corrupt governments can keep secrets when they want to." He smiled at me. "I'm sorry the truth's not so nefarious after all."

Yeah, not so nefarious *if* I were hearing the complete truth—unlikely from

Alfred. "So you drove all the way to my house at night to ask a favor, just to prove the location of some old burial site?"

"I appreciate your efforts," Alfred said, checking his watch. "But I'm late. May I please have the test measurements?"

Somehow Drax was involved with the cadaver warehouse, another reason for their rush to kill off the tunnels. But the explanation wouldn't be coming from slippery Alfred. "I'll process the film tomorrow," I said. "You'll have everything first thing Monday morning. Then can I have my negatives from the train station?"

"I'll tell Smith we need his methodology verified by Monday night." Apparently my question was too absurd to acknowledge. "Rudolph is already calling in favors at City Hall to fast-track the subway burial."

I remembered the envelope I'd delivered to the newspaper. "Something tactical might happen to slow him down."

Alfred shot me a suspicious look. "What's your meaning?"

I didn't feel like explaining.

CHAPTER 15

I awoke Sunday to the aroma of coffee, but Mom wasn't around. She'd placed a note next to the percolator: *411 regulars went on strike, so they gave me some 12-hour shifts. I packed my dosages and I'll ask Dorothy from work to double check. Proud of me? I can do this! Back tonight 9ish. I love you.*

I bounced two blocks to the Hasty Mart, grabbed the Sunday *Enquirer* and slapped it on the glass counter as the teenage attendant gawked through a frame of stringy hair.

"I gotta find the key to last week's crossword," I said, dismantling the newspaper. "It's killing me." I located what I was looking for. My heart leapt out of my chest.

The *Enquirer's* Sunday magazine, a pint-sized glossy called *Cavalcade*, was the only color insert besides the funnies. The cover before me displayed the best shot of my subway straightaways. Rings of blue and purple from my flash alternated from the near periphery to the shrinking distance and vanished into a black rectangle. Within that sat the perfect headline: *Buried Treasure?* I flipped to the article and continued my manic survey. My photo of the staircase at Rookwood Station anchored the center spread, encircled by smaller images.

Off to the side, a callout box recounted the ghastly story of nine-year-old Emily Langford and the fear-fueled decision to seal the underground.

I scanned coverage of the subway's origins, the recent deadly collapse, Drax's proposal to fill in the tunnels from above, and the emergence of opposition from "a citizens' group calling itself Save Our Subway."

I chortled and looked up. The store clerk stared back.

"I'll be damned. A female sheep is called a ewe." I slapped coins on the counter, tucked the newspaper under my arm, and pushed through the door.

By late morning, I was back in the darkroom fulfilling my promise to Alfred and glad to be the only employee in the building. No one around to puzzle over the unusual eight-by-tens hanging up to dry.

The photos of the test measurements appeared to have worked, the laser dots and markers clearly visible.

While wiping up the countertops, I heard the main entrance buzzer. Odd. I snaked through the maze of junctions and corridors and edged one eye around a wall to peer across the reception area. A slender young woman at the door shielded her eyes and peered in for signs of life. A nervous bride perhaps, hoping for an early peek at her proofs.

But when I unlocked and swung open the door, two well-dressed men stepped into view. A wave of cold raised the hairs on my arms.

First to appear was Tony Drax. When our eyes met, he twitched as if zapped by static electricity. Maybe flattening his face had left a memorable impression.

My breath caught in my throat when I saw the third visitor. Rudolph Drax. Tony's father and the company's supreme commandant. More powerful than Walther, the fading patriarch, and far more powerful than Tony, the dubious heir apparent.

Behind them in the parking lot, exhaust swirled from a black four-door limo. I spotted the driver in outline, but any other occupants hid behind tinted windows.

Tony regained his composure. "This is Lucas Tremaine, the guy who cold-cocked me."

"I understand that," Rudolph said, even-keeled, "but let's focus on the matter at hand." Like Tony, he wore a white dress shirt, no jacket, and dark tie. But unlike Tony, who rolled his sleeves, Rudolph secured his at the wrist with gold and onyx cufflinks. Either they'd dressed for church or captains of industry didn't get Sundays off.

"Tony deserved worse," I said. Speaking restored a bit of strength and focus. "He made an extremely offensive remark about a close friend."

Rudolph neither inquired further nor offered a defense. "I don't believe we've ever met face-to-face." He extended his hand. "I'm Rudolph Drax." His gray-fringed black hair was TV-ready, his self-assurance bolted in place.

I flashed open palms like twin stop signs. "Better not—darkroom chemicals." Shaking a Drax hand would violate a personal oath. "We've met in the past, through our lawyers." Rudolph registered no reaction. "What's this all about?"

While Tony fidgeted, Rudolph presented a flyweight smile. "Sorry to drop by unannounced. We tried phoning, but no answer."

"I've been here for hours," I said. "No ringing phones."

Rudolph raised his eyebrows at the woman but said nothing.

"I'll make sure we have the right number on file, Mr. Drax," the woman said, contrite.

"Please meet Miss Nolan," Rudolph said to me, "my new assistant." He emphasized the word *new* as if offering an excuse.

"Rachel Nolan," the woman said with a perfunctory smile while clutching an oversized leather notebook to her chest. She was beautiful, with hesitant dark eyes and chestnut shoulder-length hair parted on one side. Considering the statuesque receptionist at the headquarters building, perhaps CoverGirl features were a checkbox item on the company's job application. I felt the urge to offer employment advice: *anywhere but Drax.*

Rudolph took charge. "I thought we might talk for a few minutes. You disagree with us on multiple fronts, which is understandable—our projects are often controversial. But we believe in open communications. Might even narrow our differences."

I stared back, incredulous. I wanted to pluck the gold pen from his shirt pocket and plunge it into his neck, and a genial conversation wasn't going to change that. "Sure, let's talk." My tongue felt oversized in my mouth.

"May we come in briefly?" Rudolph asked.

I dismissed a small impulse of caution. With Tony uneasy in my presence, Miss Nolan unsure in her new job, and Rudolph playing the peacemaker, the threesome seemed harmless. I held open the door and gestured toward the waiting area.

"I understand you're in graduate school," Rudolph said as he selected a chair around a table stacked with *Popular Photography*, *Brides* and *Harper's Bazaar* magazines.

"Architecture."

"I see." Rudolph sat next to Tony along one wall. "When do you expect to graduate?" I sat with my back against the opposite wall. Perched upright between us like a referee, Miss Nolan folded one slender leg across the other and readied pencil and notepad. Why so official?

"Don't know yet," I replied. "Tuition is expensive and money's tight."

Rudolph chuckled. "More like your boss is tightfisted. But then, aren't they all?"

Perhaps anti-Semitism ran in the family. "You mean all bosses?"

Rudolph evaded with a little smile.

"What do you want?" I asked, tired of the song and dance.

Rudolph's eyes met mine without waver, his face relaxed. "Your father died tragically on one of our job sites. Our condolences, of course."

I said nothing. He'd spoken as if commenting on election results. *Your dad lost the vote—tough break for your side.*

"There was a legal action that didn't go your way, and that left you unsatisfied." Translation: *you tried to sue but lost.* Slick-talking son of a bitch. True to form, he peered at the tabletop as if pondering. "I might feel the same way if I were in your shoes."

Tony weaseled into the conversation. "He and Reuben Klein broke into the train station."

"Ah yes," Rudolph said. "You disagree with our plans to repurpose the Union Terminal. Well, you're not alone. Preservation versus modernization is a tough debate."

Again, I said nothing.

"You butted heads with my son here over some photographs." No, I punched him to erase a decade of condescension from his face. "And there's another item." Rudolph signaled Miss Nolan. She reached into her notebook, withdrew a copy of the Sunday *Cavalcade* and placed it on the table between us. "You disagree with us about the future of the subway."

I picked up the insert and flipped to the subway article. "Yeah, we subscribe. Amazing photos. How do you think they got in?"

Tony snorted. Rudolph smiled and said, "Yes, how *did* you get in?"

I raised my eyebrows. "Me? You're kidding."

Rudolph leaned forward, placed his elbows on his knees and peered into my face. "Open communication is pointless without honesty, so let's not play games. You're a photographer with a passion for off-limits places—"

"You flatter me, but cities as old as Cincinnati attract people with—*a passion for off-limits places.*" I vowed to not look away. "That abandoned subway is irresistible, one of only two in the country, and the only one welded closed." I tossed the insert on the table. "I'd love to take credit, but you're barking up the wrong tree."

Rudolph shook his head slowly and smiled to himself. "We also know your boss is involved."

I feigned disbelief. "Tricia Blumenfeld?" Rudolph was thinking Alfred, but I wouldn't play along.

"As you know, Alfred Blumenfeld and his colleague started chasing ghosts in the subway thirty years ago. Then, when the reporter skipped town… well, you'd think Blumenfeld would've given up. Obviously he hasn't." He theatrically considered for a moment. "What's he hoping to find down there?"

What reporter? "I don't know what you're talking about."

Rudolph crossed his legs and stared at me for a moment before saying, "I've done too much talking. Your turn."

Elbows on armrests, Tony observed behind steepled fingers.

More silence passed. I studied Rudolph's face, his mouth with the corners slightly upturned, placid eyes, brows elevated with interest. The innocence of a choirboy.

But I knew what they were serving on a platter. Alfred's generation called it bunkum. Dad called it baloney. I called it bullshit. Tony Drax had ordered an excavator operator to take a terrible risk, and he would never act without orders from above. That meant the mastermind behind manslaughter, if not murder, was shooting the breeze with me on a Sunday afternoon. But why the silky speech? Did he really believe I would rat out Alfred and reveal the access portal?

Then the answer stared at me with big brown eyes. Rudolph's performance was aimed at Miss Nolan, her attention as sharp as the pencil scratching her notepad. She was a record-keeper. If anyone ever wanted a play-by-play account of our meeting, she would testify.

Well, two could play that game. The next sixty seconds would be etched in Rachel Nolan's memory, if not her notepad.

"Okay, my turn." I leaned in. "I'll direct this question to you, Tony." He lowered his hands, as if suddenly self-conscious of his protective posture. "Why are people saying you intentionally sent Delbert Turkel to his death?"

Tony's throat produced a sound, neither word nor complete syllable. Then his gaze jumped to his father.

Rudolph bristled. "How dare you accuse my son—"

"Then I'll ask you, Mr. Drax. What under this city is so worth hiding that you're willing to kill one of your own workers?"

But the older Drax was no stranger to hard-nosed questioning. "Please wait in the car," he calmly ordered Rachel Nolan. Flustered, the woman scooped up her materials and hurried to the door.

I raised my voice after her. "People say your employer gets people killed to get what they want. Write that on your steno pad."

Rudolph rose from his chair and approached me. Tony followed. By the door, Rachel Nolan glanced back, her expression fearful. She slipped outside.

I knew I'd gone too far, but I'd face the consequences on my feet, man-to-man, eye-to-eye. I stood.

Big mistake.

Rudolph's punch landed dead center below the A-frame formed by my rib cage. My guts felt cleaved into left and right hemispheres. I buckled at the waist. My diaphragm seized into a ball and every teaspoon of air vacated my lungs. I tipped over and hit the linoleum hard, curling fetally in hopes my respiratory system would jumpstart itself. It didn't. I worked my mouth like a fish, no air moving.

I looked up sideways through watering eyes. Peering down, Rudolph wore the smile he kept handy for television appearances, groundbreakings, and closed-door meetings with corrupt politicians. "That'll shut you up long enough to listen."

"Fuck you," I said, the words forming on my lips but producing no more sound than a faint gag.

Rudolph tugged at the creases of his trousers and squatted close enough I could see the microscopic weave of his worsted wool suit fabric. "Construction is a dangerous business," he said. "Accidents happen. Your dad suffered a tragic accident." He turned his head toward Tony. "Who's the dead Gypsy?"

"Turkel."

"Yeah, Turkel." Elbows on knees, Rudolph brought his hands together. "Turkel suffered a tragic accident." A pause. "Now, are you listening?"

I stared back.

"I don't know what you're doing in that subway, but keep it up and *you* could suffer a tragic accident. And that kike of yours—I don't know his name—"

"Klein," Tony said.

"That's him." Rudolph said. "Klein could suffer a tragic accident, and so could the Chinaman from the gymnasium." He tapped a knuckle on my forehead. "Your brain should be recognizing a pattern by now."

The front door thumped and swung open with a whoosh of air. The room appeared to shrink by half as Hard Ass and Gorilla filled the reception area. Hard Ass carried a black police-style nightstick with its distinctive perpendicular handle. He eyed me like a triple-decker sandwich and snickered under his breath.

"Mr. Daley." Rudolph peered down at me. "We came here for a business meeting, but this man attempted a second assault on my son. Fortunately, I was able to incapacitate him. Please deal with him in a manner befitting his indiscretions."

Hard Ass lifted his eyebrows with a silent question. Rudolph answered with a directive nod.

Hard Ass took a step closer and drew back his club.

CHAPTER 16

Tricia gave me the usual stare, as if I violated air she planned on breathing someday. I was stretched out on the sofa in the employee lounge. My head throbbed like I wore a skull tourniquet. "What happened?" I asked.

Sitting on the edge of the couch, Tricia began a crooked smile, suspecting a joke. She wore jeans and a casual button-down blouse. "I already told you." Her smile faded. She squinted. "If you're shitting me—"

"Why are you here on your day off?"

"I already told you that too." Her forehead creased with worry.

"How long have I been here?"

Tricia sighed, reached out, and pressed a thumb to my scalp, like testing a melon for ripeness. "That chick was right. You might have a concussion."

"What chick?"

"I already told—"

I made a stop sign with my hand. "I'm sorry. I forgot what you said." I winced from pain and begged with one open eye. "But I'll remember this time, so please repeat."

She crossed her arms. "Quick, okay? I wasn't planning on babysitting today."

I nodded. Nodding hurt.

"Some woman found you on the floor by the front door. Your head was bleeding. She helped you walk back here."

"I walked?"

"And talked too. You gave her my number. She called me and I drove over. Who did this?"

"Drax people."

"That explains it. The woman said she worked for Drax but wouldn't tell me her name."

I shook my head. Shaking hurt too. Obviously, Miss Nolan suffered a pang of conscience and drove back to make sure I was still alive. "Of course she wouldn't give her name. She's worried about the Gestapo kicking in her door in the middle of the night. Was she good looking?"

Tricia blinked deliberately. "You're not her type."

"Because she's beautiful?"

"Because she's smart. She'd hate having to talk slowly all the time."

I felt a moment of relief. Maybe Tricia's normal verbal abuse meant my injuries weren't so serious. But the iffy memory concerned me. "Her name's Rachel Nolan. Why didn't she take me to the hospital?"

Tricia huffed with exasperation. "Because the cops might be waiting for you there."

I bolted upright. Pain spurted behind my eyes. "What?"

"You attacked Tony again, and Drax is pressing additional charges. That's what she said."

I squeezed my head between my hands, hoping to redirect the pressure. It didn't help. "Now wait. She *saw* me attack Tony? Or she *heard* I attacked Tony? Big difference."

Tricia thought about it. "I'm not sure."

I felt around my forehead but avoided ground zero. "How bad is it?"

Tricia scrutinized, her lips parted slightly. "You're sporting a goose egg about as big as… a goose egg. I got the bleeding to stop, iced it, and closed an inch-and-a-half wound with strapping tape. And the whole time, you were talking to me."

I shook off a wave of exhaustion. "Did I say anything embarrassing?"

"Of course you did, which is why I figured you were okay." She brought her face closer to mine, her focal point somewhere around my hairline. I breathed in her earthy sweet fragrance as it rose from the V of her blouse. "You'll need about four stitches."

"How do you know that, Doc?"

She leaned back and met my eyes with double-dare-ya defiance. "I've learned a bit about fight wounds."

I set aside that juicy tidbit for later and focused on immediate business. "Help me get around?"

Tricia rolled her eyes. "I'm not your nurse." But she eased me to standing anyway. I teetered. She hugged my upper body and I laid my arm across her shoulders. Together we staggered and bounced off the walls through the narrow corridors. We entered the room Smith used for his calculations, his *war room*.

The marked-up photos and poster paper on the desktop and walls appeared undisturbed. I sighed my relief. "They never came in here."

Next, the darkroom.

"They're gone," I said as we entered, venting my breath. "The prints were hanging up to dry, and I left the filmstrips in an envelope on that counter. All gone." I explained about the test measurement photos and my afternoon in the darkroom. "Wait." I yanked the negative tray from the enlarger. "They missed one. Six shots, and they're good ones. Maybe enough for Smith."

Tricia frowned with worry. "Can they figure out Alfred's scheme by studying the photos?"

Drax engineers would pore over images of bright dots striking concrete walls. "I don't know. No matter what, they'll know this is bigger than subway beauty shots." My skull throbbed and I teetered again.

Tricia righted me with surprising strength. "Cops or no cops, we better go to the hospital."

"Drax might match photos to negatives and realize they left some behind." I slid the surviving filmstrip into a protective envelope. "I'm taking this with me."

"To get that wound checked, I assume," Tricia admonished.

First things first. Rudolph Drax had threatened my friends. They already knew about Reuben from the train station, but now they knew about Andy. I'd hoped he'd stay off their shit list. It seemed Drax had spies everywhere, even at the YMCA.

As Tricia tried to hide her curiosity, I called Reuben's apartment from the darkroom's wall phone and explained everything, including the threats. "Where are your folks?"

"Finger Lakes, upstate New York, shopping for retirement property. I'm good for a few more days. What about your mom?"

"Good for a few more hours. She's working a marathon shift for the phone company."

"And Andy?" Reuben's hands produced muffled friction as he gripped the telephone receiver.

"I'll call you right back."

I slapped the telephone switch hook and dialed Andy's number. Six rings, no answer. I hung up and repeated. No luck. Unease became worry. Could Drax have followed through on their threat so fast?

I got Reuben back on the line. "Nobody's home." I tried to level my voice.

Reuben knew me well enough to read my mind and pretend he hadn't. "The family's probably taking a walk. Nice day out there."

"Better safe than sorry. We're close by. We'll head over." I hung up.

Tricia glowered at me. "Who's *we*?"

"Hey, you were willing to drive me to the hospital."

"That's different. I don't want to get sued if you croak of a brain hemorrhage."

"Your concern is touching." I fondled the lump above my eye. "Your field dressing will have to hold for the time being."

. . . . .

Twenty minutes later we rang the doorbell of the apartment where Andy's family lived, but there was no response, no footsteps within.

"Andy, it's me," I shouted and pounded the door. After a few moments, the peephole darkened, the deadbolt slid, and the door cracked enough for Andy's face to appear. But this was not the fearless émigré who'd helped his family escape the Viet Cong, and who'd shrugged off the dangers of pissing in Drax's punch bowl. His face was drawn, his eyes juiced with tension.

"What happened?" I asked.

Andy slipped through the door and stood with us, his feet doing a nervous dance. Arm outstretched, he spoke as if addressing someone in the street beyond. "You go. I no go. I finished. You go now!" He scanned the grounds of the apartment complex.

"You think someone's watching us?" I asked.

"Maybe yes, maybe no," he said, quieter this time.

"Okay, we'll play along, but then tell us what happened." I raised my hands, palms open, and took a step back. "Okay, okay. We're done," I shouted. "You're not part of this ever again." Then I whispered. "We're leaving, but what the hell happened?"

Andy held up an index finger. "One minute then you go." He disappeared momentarily and returned with a shoebox. "We find outside door today." He reached into the box and withdrew a stick perhaps a half inch in diameter and ten inches long. Sand-colored, with distinctive raised rings, it was tapered at one end to a sharp point. "Viet Cong call *tra tấn thanh*, bamboo torture stick. Go in body with…" His limited English failing, Andy resorted to pantomime, pounding the air with his fist.

"Hammer?" Tricia asked.

Andy nodded and then demonstrated, placing the sharp end of the stick against his palm, and then his thigh, and then finally, his temple. "For when done."

I shivered beneath my shirt. Andy reached again into the box, this time withdrawing a Polaroid photo. It showed a slim young Asian woman strolling through a park, the shadows long, perhaps in the evening. Her hands rested in the pockets of a waist-length pea coat, her head angled as if lost in contemplation. "My sister," Andy said, his eyes now glossy and pleading. "Picture yesterday."

"Is she okay?" I implored.

Andy nodded. "But I protect." He paused to survey the parking lot one more time before shouting again. "Sorry. No more help. You go now!"

He closed the door and snapped the deadbolt.

We drove away in silence as I cursed my naïveté. I'd assumed we'd be exposed, but we'd elude with anticipation and caution. Then I played back my own words to Andy: *Drax will do anything to protect themselves.* My friends were in danger because of me—because I'd ignored my own warning. That was about to change.

• • • • •

"I can't let my mom go back to our house tonight," I said. "Too risky. Get me to a phone?" Tricia stared back. "Please?"

I expected *I'm not your chauffeur*, but she cocked her head, muttered *Yeah*, and took a screeching right at Wilmot Avenue. Within a half mile, she stopped next to a call-from-car pay phone in a Marathon gas station. I rolled down my window, stuffed a dime into the slot, punched three digits, and heard my coin rattle in the change return. A moment later, a ringer sounded.

"Four-one-one directory assistance. What listing?" The woman's voice had a smoker's scraw. Definitely not Mom.

"Sorry, wrong number." I toggled the switch hook, scooped my dime from the return tray, and repeated.

"Four-one-one directory assistance. What listing?" This time she was young and nasal, like Streisand. Another miss.

The third try failed and I apologized again, but before I could ring off, the woman said, "Look, sweetie, which of the girls are you trying to reach?"

Damn. I prayed the voice didn't belong to a supervisor. Mom's temporary gigs were fragile enough without the smudge of personal calls on company time. I rolled the dice. "Mrs. Tremaine, please."

A sigh. "Lucas, it's me. Dorothy. They sent your mom home two hours ago."

I sucked in air. "What?"

Mom's friend laughed, too removed from the danger to recognize fear in my voice. "Half the town's watching the Bengals on TV. Call volume dropped like nutso after the kickoff."

"Shit."

"Honey, I know you two could use the cash, but your mom could use the rest—not doing so good today." Dorothy knew all about Mom tapering off the meds, the violent swings between panic and lethargy, and the tremors that could make flipping through a phonebook a trial of concentration and coordination.

"Thank you, Dorothy."

We rang off. My hands unsteady, I fumbled twice before successfully dialing all seven digits to reach home. Three rings felt like ten. Then Mom answered and I released my breath. "I heard they let you go early. Everything okay?"

"Thank God they did." Her speech dragged with fatigue. "My shoulders feel like I carried a backpack for twenty miles."

According to the doctors, her symptoms would last another year after reaching zero milligrams. "Sorry. Maybe some tea and a heating pad?"

"Will do, once the gas man finishes up."

Panic pulsed below my rib cage. "What do you mean, *gas man*?"

"Or electric. I should've paid better attention. They're checking meters house-to-house."

I wanted to scream at her, but she wouldn't have understood. "And you let him in?"

"Lucas, for crying out loud. He had a proper ID card, with his photo. Why are you so paranoid?"

I had a dozen reasons to be paranoid, each more authentic than *a proper ID card*. "Mom, you have to leave the house. Go next door. Now!"

"Why on earth—"

"Because we don't have a gas line, no one checks meters on Sundays, and our electric meter's on the outside of the house." I regretted firing both barrels. "That man's no good."

A pause. "Oh." All realization for my mother seemed to be on a three-second delay. "You must think I'm a ninny."

"It's not your fault." Tapering compromised judgment. "Don't hang up the phone. Set it down and walk out the front door."

"Okay." The handset clunked on the kitchen counter, and Mom's footsteps faded across the linoleum floor. Ten seconds of silence passed. A hinge squeaked. A door closed. More footsteps approached, growing louder, and then faded again to silence. A different door closed. My stomach seized. I was seconds from calling the police when footfalls sounded again, this time coming closer. Someone lifted the handset.

"There's a police car parked on the street in front of our house," Mom said, now sounding smug, "and the gas man must've finished up because he's not here anymore."

"Mom, we don't have a gas—" I glanced over my shoulder at Tricia who was staring at me, assessing my performance. I said to Mom, "There's a cop in the car?"

"Yeah, just sitting there."

He was waiting for me. Drax had upped the charges. Ironic, since I was the one sporting the tenderized forehead. Sure, I could take my story to the police, but in a my-word-against-theirs battle, Drax would have friends in high places. I would have nobody. "Are you sure the... gas man's gone?"

I checked Tricia again. She was either tired of my mother's lethargy, or tired of me.

Mom chuckled through the receiver. "Don't you think I'd know if he's here or not? I've only lived in this house for…" But her muddled mind abandoned the math. "Besides, he left his paperwork."

Over the next minute of question-and-answer, pocked with moments of confusion, I learned that the invader had taped a standard envelope at eye level just inside the front door. It contained paper only, nothing that seemed to present immediate danger.

"Please read the note to me, okay?" I asked.

She obliged, but read the note to herself first.

I drummed my fingers on the dashboard. "Mom?"

More irritating silence followed, then, "Well…"

"Well what?"

"What on earth does this mean? The note is handwritten—says *No one is safe.*" The paper crackled in Mom's hand. "Who wrote this, Lucas?"

CHAPTER 17

Early the following morning, I returned to the darkroom. The test measurements from the surviving negative had to be printed, leaving Smith to draw whatever conclusions he could. Our next trip underground could be our last, so no more trial runs. We had to capture all evidence possible before Drax buried it forever.

I clipped the last print to the clothesline and wove my way toward Alfred's office to wait for him. I needed answers.

In transit, I spotted Tricia on a stepladder, taping up a poster for Vivitar lenses, her calf muscles taut below the hem of her skirt. We'd driven in together. My house was no safe haven and Reuben's apartment not much better, so I'd persuaded Tricia to let me sleep on her couch. She'd hesitated at first but then agreed, as long as I sprang for takeout from Madam Chow's. Cheaper than a hotel, or so I'd figured.

Clever girl. She'd failed to mention that she owned no couch, only enough stray pillows to form a patchwork pallet. But the deal was done and she'd snagged a better meal than the usual Kraft dinner. In return, I'd snagged a toss-and-turn night, waking periodically to worry about our shrinking odds of success, and stare at the moonlit walls, bare except for a Frank Zappa poster and Fritz the Cat comic strip in a plastic frame.

I'd convinced Mom to room with her friend Dorothy *just for a few days, until I can work out this misunderstanding with Drax.* I felt guilty sugarcoating a sour situation, but now wasn't the time to explain the whole sordid story. Besides, I didn't *know* the whole sordid story. Not yet.

I closed the door to Alfred's unoccupied office and inspected my forehead in the same mirror where the old man damped down renegade silver hairs and leveled his bow ties. Whiffing an echo of English Leather, I imagined him pressing an eye to a peephole nearby.

My wound site was still puffy, but Tricia's strapping tape had held. The purple seam underneath resembled a string of blood sausages.

When Alfred walked in, I was standing by his bookshelf, thumbing through a World War II hardcover entitled *Building Hitler's War Machine— Deutschmarks and Dollars.* He crossed his office at a determined clip, his hard-sole shoes tapping out authority with each step. He anchored his feet behind the desk and released his briefcase a few inches above the blotter. "I should fire you."

I snorted. "From which job, the lab gig *without* people trying to kill me, or the illegal job that doesn't pay a penny?"

Alfred plunged his hand into his briefcase, yanked out a copy of the Sunday *Cavalcade,* and slapped it on the desk. "Have you lost your mind?"

I lifted my chin. "Yes, I have. I should be on a bus to Timbuktu instead of standing here."

Alfred shook his head, his neck still rosy from the morning razor. "What were you hoping to accomplish?"

The meeting was off to a bad start; I was supposed to be asking the questions. "They already know I'm involved with the subway. That article doesn't change anything, except it might slow them down. You should be thanking me."

Alfred glared. "Drax knows you took the photos and they know you work here, so now they know I'm involved."

I waved him off. "Drax knows more about your scheme than I do. Doesn't that seem a little backward?"

Alfred ignored me. "It's your fault they came here." The old man must've buttonholed Tricia on the way in and learned about Drax's little social call to the studio. "Now you're quitting our project?"

The thought hadn't crossed my mind, but apparently it had crossed Alfred's. That could work to my advantage. "*Our* project? Interesting word choice, but you've got your project and I've got mine and they don't necessarily overlap."

"After what happened to your father, you have reason enough to bring down Drax. What more do you need?"

I braced my hands on my hips. "My friend Andy helped take *your* test photos. Yesterday, Drax threatened to kill his sister." I tried to ignore a wave of guilt but couldn't.

Sadness stretched the vertical lines on Alfred's face. "That's unfortunate. I—I don't like to hear that." He straightened his back. "But it's also unsurprising. That's how Drax operates."

I felt my cheeks grow hot. "And if they hurt her, that's okay because it's *unsurprising?*"

"I didn't say that."

"You're saying every risk is justified because what we're doing is *that* important."

Alfred stared back, his jaw firm. "What we're doing is *very* important."

Something didn't add up. "Because of bid-rigging? The rich get richer and the poor get poorer, just like always. I don't see how that's bad enough to justify a bamboo spike pounded into that girl's temple."

Alfred's steely disposition eased a bit further. "That's what they threatened?"

"They left the weapon by the family's front door, along with the girl's photo. But that's not all." I told him about the phony utility man. "My mother can't protect herself." My chest throbbed at a realization. "And apparently I can't protect her either." I took a deep breath. "Look, Mr. Blumenfeld, I want to bring down Drax so bad I can taste it. But if I'm going to put my friends and family at risk, I have to know everything."

"I never lied to you."

"That's not good enough. You were working on a Drax story with a reporter from the paper. I figure you manned the camera and your partner worked the storyline. But he mysteriously disappeared and that hit you hard because you've been on a crusade ever since. Surprised I know this?"

His old, hard eyes betrayed nothing, but he stepped to the window behind his desk and looked out.

I pressed on. "I heard it from Rudolph Drax. Don't I deserve to know as much as my enemy?"

Alfred said nothing.

"What else were you and the reporter investigating?"

Again, no response.

I took a step closer and softened my voice. "You cried when you learned we found the bodies in the subway. Don't tell me you were crying for Cincinnati's taxpayers."

Alfred's head tipped forward a few degrees as if my words had struck him, his Brylcreemed hairs neat above the collar of his sport coat. Beyond the glass, morning traffic jostled for position, but the old man didn't notice. I waited.

After ten seconds, Alfred turned toward me and brought his hands together behind his back. Clear-eyed and collected, he stepped out from behind his desk and regarded me neutrally, his lips pressed into a colorless seam. "That wound on your forehead is rather unsightly. You might bandage it for the sake of others."

I scowled, testing the tape that held my head together. "Since you were about to ask if I'm okay, I'm fine, thanks to your granddaughter patching me up." Alfred looked confused, but I didn't feel like explaining. "If you think Walther's an asshole, wait 'til you meet his son."

"I also know Rudolph Drax… an unpleasant individual. He struck you?"

"It was one of his security guys."

"Name of Valentine?"

"No, his name's Daley."

Alfred leaned in for a closer look and winced.

"Please don't do that. It feels worse than it looks." I pulled back to regain my personal space. "Who's Valentine?"

"Drax chief of security. I advise avoiding him. He served his country in the European theater but apparently wasn't satisfied with the war's end. Became a mercenary in Africa for whoever controlled the gold mines. His methods are—how to put this for polite company—*field tested*. Has an affectation for knives, I believe."

"I'll commit that to memory."

"Wise." Alfred brought a hand to his chin, thinking, and then said, "Speaking of memories, you called Walther a Nazi. Do you recall that seminal moment?"

The entire episode on the upper floors of Drax headquarters was tattooed on the inside of my skull. "I never called him a Nazi. I compared the train station to the Louvre, both subjected to invasion."

Alfred pursed his lips. "You're splitting hairs. Your point was clear."

"What's *your* point?"

"That you weren't far from the truth."

I didn't follow.

"Ever heard of the company DuPont?"

"Of course."

"How about Ford?"

The lecture was strumming my nerves. "I hope to buy a car someday, once I get a real job."

"Standard Oil? General Electric? ITT?"

"Is this going somewhere?"

Alfred flashed the weary smile of a parent with an obstinate child. "All these companies have one thing in common. They actively supported the Nazi movement in the years before World War II." Alfred paused for dramatic effect. "Do you believe it?"

It seemed inconceivable. He'd named mainstream American institutions, employing hundreds of thousands of workers, while simultaneously backing a monster?

"Hindsight is twenty-twenty," Alfred went on, "but foresight is lousy. No one knew of Hitler's territorial ambitions until Austria fell in 1938, and no one knew of his grotesque plans for the Jews until years later. Throughout most of the 1930s, American businesses viewed the Führer as the leader of a large potential market, nothing more."

"Supported the Nazi movement how?"

Alfred made a clicking sound with his tongue. "Mostly they sent money, sometimes supplies. Worst of all, they sent legitimacy. What could possibly be sinister about the Third Reich if the Wehrmacht rode into Poland in Ford trucks, and if IBM—the *company*, not just their tabulating equipment—ran Germany's national census? Never mind that the data collected was used to round up the Jews."

I flipped over the book in my hands and reread the title: *Building Hitler's War Machine—Deutschmarks and Dollars*. Alfred's World War II volumes represented more than a history buff's collectibles. They were research. "You're saying Drax financed Hitler?"

The old man painted the air with hand gestures like a professor. "The name Drax is an Americanized version of Drexler, German for lathe operator. Not a bad moniker for a construction company, wouldn't you say?"

I didn't reply.

Alfred leaned back against the desk and folded his arms. "Of course, being German in America didn't make you a Nazi sympathizer. Good heavens, half the residents on Cincinnati's north side are Prussians and Bavarians." He became stern. "But sending massive quantities of stolen money, to eventually be used to bankroll the Final Solution? That's a different story."

"Stolen? You're saying Drax ripped off Cincinnati to help finance Hitler's grand plan?"

Alfred gave me a sad smile.

"That's one helluva charge. How do you know Drax did it?"

Alfred pushed off the desk and began pacing, gaze to the floor, bony fingers interwoven behind his back. "Fast-forward to right *after* Hitler fell, when newsreels showed bulldozers pushing hundreds of murdered Jews into mass graves. The world was shocked—horrified."

The inhumanity captured in those old films altered everyone who saw it. I remembered the survivors, skeletons with barely-beating hearts, eyes empty, no tears left.

"Secrets poured out," Alfred went on, "like primal scream therapy—anything to put distance between us and the evil." He stopped walking and met my gaze. "A handful of Drax people contacted the newspaper in secret, low-level people too tortured by guilt to sleep at night. One of them worked the company's books and saw the money transfers."

"A brave man."

"Yes, but he spoke in whispers, wouldn't go public, wouldn't dare try to walk out with records under his arm. He was too scared, and for good reason. People had gone missing."

"Including one person in particular, right?" I said. Alfred shrank at the mention. "One of the reporters. Your partner."

Alfred ambled to the wall that displayed his awards, certificates, and mementos. He caressed a framed photo, one I'd noticed before. It featured two young men—Alfred and another, with thick hair and a beard that met his sideburns—receiving trophy cups from a third, presumably a boss. The banner overhead read *Cincinnati Enquirer Shining Stars Gala*, and all three men were dressed to the nines in suitcoats, vests, watch chains, and neckties. "The paper put us on two-man teams, one writer and one photographer. I liked it because I didn't just focus and shoot, I pursued leads."

"Your partner didn't mind you doing reporter work?"

"Richard? That was his name, Richard Baumgartner. No, he wasn't territorial like that. He was sure of himself, and glad to have the help. See, we were busy." Alfred reset his rail-straight posture. "They gave us bigger news items, and then feature articles, investigative stuff. We got a bit of a reputation. Remember when Councilman Freitag got tangled up with bridge kickbacks?"

Not really, but it didn't matter. I nodded.

"That was us, why we won this award." Alfred waved a hand toward the photo. "So when people started showing up from Drax desperate to make a papist confession, the editor sent them down the hall to us."

"Did you believe Drax sent money to Hitler? I mean, when you first heard it?"

Alfred wrinkled his brow in thought. "Hollywood actors can sob on cue, but not accountants. Yes, I believed it." He absentmindedly lifted a paperweight from his desk, a cast-iron caboose with cozy yellow light painted in the windows.

"Where were the cops in all this?"

"In Drax's pocket, or so we assumed. But we didn't need the cops. People opened up to us." Alfred pondered that a moment, bringing the past into focus. "Well, they did to Richard."

"To a newsman? Someone who spreads information for a living?"

Alfred scowled. "A newsman with integrity. When he promised to protect his sources, he meant it." The old man's features softened with a recollection. "He had a kind face that matched the man inside, and eyes you could trust." But the reverie vaporized. Alfred set the paperweight down hard on the desk. "One morning Richard didn't show up at the office. I never saw him again."

Huh? I'd been expecting blackjacks, garrotes, and dark sedans pulling up alongside dull-witted victims. "That's all?"

"The cops investigated, for what *that's* worth. Richard was last seen carrying a suitcase from his house and getting on a bus. The police said *no foul play*, as if that made everything copacetic."

"What'd you do?"

Alfred shrugged. "I went back to the photographer pool, shooting crime scenes and ribbon cuttings and political dinners. But I knew something was wrong."

"What makes you so sure Richard didn't just take off?"

Alfred shot me a toasty glare. "The rumor mill had it all explained. First, that Richard was fed up with risky assignments on a word jockey's pay scale. Second, that he'd gotten cozy with a leggy female journalist visiting from Buenos Aires."

"She was for real?"

"Yes." Alfred gave a small shake to his head as if dismissing the absurdity of it all. "Part of some bogus exchange program by Argentinian politicians to show they cared about freedom of the press."

"He took a shine to her?"

Alfred blasted the notion like airborne skeet. "Of course not." I was tempted to observe that horny guys routinely chased gorgeous girls, but Alfred kept going. "There was a third rumor. Supposedly Richard had uncovered a dirty money trail pointing to a waterworks contractor, and that he'd put the squeeze on the guy, saying he'd bury the evidence if the contractor paid up."

"Extortion?"

"He would *never* do that."

"So what happened?" I was beginning to feel like the straight man in a failed comic routine.

"I called in a favor from a bank manager. He discreetly checked Richard's records." Alfred lowered his gaze and his voice grew quieter, the edge gone. "Three days before he disappeared, fourteen thousand dollars was deposited to his account, with no listed depositor. Banks back then received money without asking questions. On the afternoon before he disappeared, all the money was withdrawn in cash."

"By Richard?"

Alfred gritted his teeth, still staring down. "Some pimple-faced teller swore the man looked like Richard and presented an acceptable ID." Alfred took three steps around his desk and dropped into his chair. All energy seemed to leave him, and a sadness peeked out from behind the bluster, like a man defending a woman's honor while knowing, win or lose, his loyalty would never be returned.

I placed the book on the shelf and took a chair across from him.

"The rumor mill was satisfied," Alfred continued. "Everything had been explained perfectly. Richard outsmarted a crook and escaped the nine-to-five for piña coladas and his Argentinian woman. People were actually envious."

"But not you."

"No," he replied, scrunching his brow. "The Drax investigation died with him."

"*Died* with him?"

Alfred bolted upright. "Have you been asleep this whole time? Drax murdered him. They stuffed his body in one of those boxes you found in the subway." Something in my gut churned. I remembered the body—the skin covered in dust. Perhaps somewhere in the crates, a crop of thick hair and sideburns. Dark pits that once held eyes.

But something wasn't making sense, and I didn't know how to say it without whipping Alfred into a frenzy. "Strictly devil's advocate, okay? I could see why some people would reach the wrong conclusion, couldn't you?" I gave him a hesitant glance and counted out points on my fingers. "There was no foul play, big bucks mysteriously showed up and then left as cash, and there was an attractive alternative—and I'm not just talking about the woman. I mean, who hasn't dreamed of a fresh start in some tropical paradise?"

Alfred simmered. "You don't know Richard."

"Everyone has a breaking point."

"You—don't—know—Richard."

I rose from my chair. "Oh, come on. The woman wasn't a ghost. And why carry a suitcase to the bus if he wasn't going someplace? The bank teller identified him walking away with his pockets stuffed with cash, cash with a reason for being there. This doesn't sound like make-believe."

Alfred leapt to his feet, his face crimson. "Of all people, you should know what Drax is capable of. They arranged it all. Can't you see that?"

"Try me."

Alfred stabbed the air with his index finger. "Drax deposited the money. Drax arranged to have a look-alike carry a suitcase from his house to the bus stop for the neighbor to see. Drax sent the look-alike to the bank to present a fake ID to the *greenest* teller. Drax floated the rumors and everyone gobbled them up." He caught his breath and exhaled, his shoulders sagging under the weight of his hopelessness.

There was no convincing him. Or was there? "If Richard's body is in those crates, then so is proof of foul play. There must be dental records."

Alfred gave an empty laugh. "Now you're being stupid. To the law, that walled-off tunnel is a sacred resting place for hundreds of people."

I opened my mouth to speak but Alfred shoved my words back with an open palm.

"Legally, cracking open one of those boxes is the same as exhuming a grave, so you're planning to unearth an entire cemetery? Even in a normal city, one that wasn't corrupt from the mailman to the mayor, that won't happen. Believe me, I tried."

No wonder Alfred teared up when I mentioned the crates. The city had never re-interred the bodies. Therefore, to Alfred's thinking, his former partner still lay below Cincinnati's streets, sent there by Drax's founder.

"Walther started it all?" I asked. "Backing Hitler?"

"Absolutely. Good friends with Lindbergh."

Charles Lindbergh. American hero, first to fly across the Atlantic, and the most famous American Nazi sympathizer and white supremacist. I'd seen his picture in the hallway at Drax headquarters. Beaming next to the legendary pilot was Walther Drax. "What about Rudolph?"

"He was junior at the time but already active in the company, being groomed for an executive role. His hands are bloody."

"Tony?"

Alfred thought a moment. "I don't know how much he knows about Drax's history. But evil is a cancer, and some cancers are genetic."

Three entire generations. I sighed. Our small campaign suddenly felt too small, with our shop-class laser, seat-of-the-pants expeditions, and no more safety equipment than a penny on a lanyard.

Our adversary suddenly felt too big, a multimillion-dollar corporation and Cincinnati institution as permanent as the Roebling Bridge. "DuPont, Ford, IBM," I said. "They're all going strong. Why didn't the public turn on them for supporting the fascists?"

Alfred chuckled. "The answer lies in that book you were perusing when I came in. Those companies played the public relations game brilliantly. They found scapegoats in the organization and lopped off their heads—sometimes senior managers, sometimes not. They formed task forces, pretended to be shocked at the findings, and swore to new codes of conduct. They donated millions to Jewish charities and apologized until they were blue in the face." He elevated his brows. "Which brings us to a vital point. Think Drax could pull off that kind of performance?"

Of course. Drax could and would do anything to save its skin, angling the limelight perfectly to conceal every blemish. The oversized banners hanging in the headquarters building made Drax seem like the Wizard of Oz fulfilling everyone's dreams.

"Imagine this," Alfred said. "Walther and Rudolph would hold a press conference, looking haggard from their sleepless nights trying to learn what had gone wrong all those years ago. They'd release the findings from their rigorous internal investigation. Erroneous information about Hitler's intentions had bubbled up from parts of the organization. Fact-checking had been weak. Mistakes had been made. Staring unblinking into the camera, Walther would apologize—not for crimes against humanity, mind you, but for being too trusting. Then, per the script, Walther would shed a tear and Rudolph would follow suit in sympathy for Dad's suffering. Finally, surrounded by his loyal employees—all visibly shaken by the revelations and worried for their beloved patriarch—Walther would announce the upcoming groundbreaking for the Cincinnati Museum of Jewish Heritage."

I believed every word of it. Drax could turn a PR disaster into a boon. "But a fraud conviction would change everything."

Alfred's eyes lit up, and for the first time, he looked at me as a compatriot instead of a subordinate. "Exactly. We'll paint a very different public image, one that can't be erased by their PR department. Do you understand?" I nodded. "By defrauding the city with that subway, sending Hitler the proceeds, and *never coming clean*, Drax made every Cincinnatian unwittingly complicit in history's worst mass murder." Alfred slapped his fist into his palm. "The company would never survive."

I stared at the floor for a few seconds, feeling Alfred's gaze on the side of my face. "Drax swiped the test negatives but left one good strip behind. I reprinted the shots this morning."

"Good deal. I'll tell Smith to hop to it. Once he verifies the calculations, we'll need to move fast."

In other words, *I* would need to move fast to take all the measurement photos before time ran out.

I took a few steps toward the door but stopped midway. "This may come as a complete surprise to you, Mr. Blumenfeld, but I don't like Nazis either. You could've told me about this at the beginning."

"Right," Alfred replied with acid sarcasm, "because you've always shown such discretion and judgment in what you say and do." He lifted the Sunday *Cavalcade* from his desk and dropped it into the trash can. "Now, can I trust you with what I just told you?"

I broke eye contact and cursed myself for doing so. "Yes." I slipped through the doorway into the passage where Tricia leaned with her back against a wall, arms folded across her chest.

"How long have you been eavesdropping?" I whispered.

"Since the point you described me as your damn nurse."

. . . . .

Late that afternoon, I tried studying at the Xavier library but couldn't keep from rehashing Alfred's every syllable.

I took the bus to the studio, ostensibly to get supplies for our last subway excursion: film and a spare battery pack Smith had cobbled together for the laser. But I hoped to run into Tricia. She'd listened in on my conversation with Alfred and might help me make sense of it all.

But Tricia, Alfred, Chuckles, and the rest of the staff were gone for the day, everyone except Smith. He caught me by the shirt sleeve, eyes popping with excitement behind prismatic lenses, and dragged me down the hall for show-and-tell.

No bigger than a lavatory, his office-turned-war-room was outfitted with corkboard panels on which he'd tacked eight-by-ten photos, charts, and select calculations in heavy Magic Marker for broader viewing, as if any of Alfred's motley crew could appreciate advanced trigonometry. I understood enough from my graduate coursework in architecture, but was glad to leave the number-crunching to Smith.

"According to Drax's original bid," he said, singling out my vertical shot of a weight-bearing column near Rookwood Station, "that's supposed to be a pre-cast and pre-cured double-tee, *pre-tensioned*, with spread footing and rebar for a composite structure, good for fifty thousand psf. But this is on-site poured, ten thousand max."

I had little patience for the complexities. "Great way to save money, but an accident waiting to happen. That explains why the excavator smashed through." But how much did Tony know before sending Delbert Turkel across that field? While the calculations were sophisticated, Tony's brain wasn't.

Smith gave a jerky nod. "Yup, if they cut the same corners throughout the system."

But the collapsed tunnel had already been filled in, the evidence buried—another clever move by Drax. "But here's the real question. Does your methodology work?"

Smith's broad smile revealed gray and chipped teeth. "Is the Pope Catholic? Get me the rest of the measurements. We'll prove fraud that even the dumbest jury will understand."

For a moment, I delighted in the enthusiasm exuded by this brilliant little man, a potbellied throwback who felt safer behind a phony name than the real deal, Angelo Russo. I admired his loyalty to Alfred, a difficult man to love, and I admired his strength. He'd found a future for himself despite a car accident that took his only child.

I smiled my thanks. "You'll have everything in forty-eight hours, Mr. Smith."

CHAPTER 18

I arrived eight minutes ahead of our midnight rendezvous time. Overhead, the stars and moon shined bright enough to guide our way to the access point, or as we'd nicknamed it, Alpha Portal.

The crisp scent of evergreen wafted from the woods that lined the railroad tracks. I was happy to be early, given the complexities of reaching my destination. I'd left my house on foot, cut through alleys, ridden a bus west to Covedale, and made two bus transfers while circling back. Reuben was now wrapping up his own circuitous route.

We had to assume Drax watched our every move. They knew where we lived, worked, and even where we worked out. But based on Rudolph's questions at the studio, Drax didn't appear to know about Alpha Portal. If followed, we'd lose our strategic advantage.

Synchronizing with the 12:05 a.m. westbound train had been Reuben's idea, an insurance policy, one extra element of visual distraction to prevent being seen as we slinked parallel to the tracks and slipped into the phone company's switching station.

A pebble tinked against the steel rail, our agreed-upon signal. I replied with two tinks and prowled like a commando, traversing the tracks and a wide dirt path used by service vehicles. I spotted my friend in the shadow of a bush and crouched beside him.

"Hey," I whispered.

"Hey," Reuben replied. His eyes looked sunken. Since the Drax threats and Andy's pullout, urban adventure had lost its appeal. Only the risk remained.

Reuben retrieved an index card from his jeans pocket and rattled down the supply list, finally reaching the last item. "Penny on lanyard?"

I fished mine from the depths of my collar and dangled the shiny copper.

"Check, but I don't think we'll need it. None of Smith's measurement sites get within a mile of the river, so things should stay dry." The train vibrated its approach through our feet. "Right on time."

I lowered my backpack to the ground to check the laser. Reuben tested the tautness of the camera bag's strap running diagonally from his shoulder to his hip.

Without warning, the side of Reuben's face lit up. Instinctively, I spun toward the source, a flashlight, the beam bouncing as it came toward us down the dirt access road. A resident taking a stroll, neighborhood watch, a cop? Drax?

But it wasn't an individual, rather a group of four men, no faces visible behind the blare of the beam.

"Stay where you are, Mr. Tremaine," said a voice I didn't recognize. But with the mention of my name, an open question snapped shut. They were Drax. My heart dropped into my stomach and the sweat from the backpack turned cold. Our assumptions had been crap.

I glanced at Reuben, expecting something this side of panic. But he appeared calm, as if unsurprised by this latest screw-up in a long string of screw-ups. As we rose to standing, I used my foot to shove the pack into the shadow of a bush. We could sacrifice camera equipment and scrounge up more, but not the laser.

They surrounded us within seconds. I recognized Hard Ass, Gorilla, and Tony Drax, and tried to make sense of their sudden appearance. If they'd been waiting for us, then they already knew about Alpha Portal. But that seemed unlikely. If one of us had been followed, which seemed impossible, could we keep the portal secret?

The next words came from the unknown man holding the flashlight. "What are you doing here?" he asked, his voice level. He appeared the same age as Hard Ass, mid-fifties, with a similar buzz cut and broad shoulders, but without the paunch. Instead of Hard Ass's doughy face, the man's visage was chiseled, the grooves in his forehead and cheeks craggy.

"Tony, who's your new pal?" I asked. Reuben snuffed a protest a foot from my ear, ticked at my tone. Better pissed off than afraid.

"Not new," Tony replied. "Mr. Valentine's been in charge of Drax security for twenty-seven years."

Valentine. Alfred had warned me about him. Once a soldier, then a soldier-for-hire, and now boss to Gorilla and Hard Ass. The guy probably reported directly to Rudolph, and based on his years on the job, he was around when Alfred and his partner ran afoul of Drax Enterprises all those years ago. Another pair of dirty hands.

"The fact that Mr. Valentine is here," Tony said, "means you're in deep shit." Before I could respond, Tony turned to Reuben and flashed a contemptuous smile. "Well if it isn't Ruby Jew. Last time I saw you, you were belly up and buck naked on the floor of a locker room."

Reuben said nothing in reply, but the heat from his glower should've set Tony's slicked-down hair on fire. Yeah, better pissed off than afraid.

Valentine took a step closer to me and targeted my chest with his flashlight, one of those D-cell metallic tubes a foot long. "Why are you here?" The man had lowered his voice to a menacing monotone. His jawbones angled to a bulbous chin. In the military, he'd probably dug trenches—with his face.

"Answer carefully, Lucas," Tony said. "Mr. Valentine means business."

I stared into the man's blue eyes and saw the same cool condescension I'd seen all my life, as if I and my kind didn't deserve to be anywhere, let alone here. I reimagined a scene I'd never witnessed, only feared, of my father, all dust and blood, sprawled out on a cantilevered walkway, his eyes losing their light.

The hairs on the back of my neck rose. "Owl-watching," I replied.

Valentine's eyes narrowed, and in one fluid motion, he flipped the flashlight end over end and swung the battery-filled butt at the side of my head. I ducked, but too late. The impact cracked in my ear. The blue-gray of nighttime vision blurred. I fell to my knees, swearing to myself to fall no further. Nausea pulsed in my gut. Pain erupted on the side of my head, and I sucked air in quick gasps.

The vague rumble between my ears sharpened to the real sound of the approaching train, the diesels revved for acceleration. My vision cleared to reveal Tony kneeling inches from my face. "You don't know Valentine, Lucas. Wise up or things will get worse." He shifted to glare at Valentine before reconnecting with me. "We know how you got into the subway."

"How?" Reuben said, defiant.

"They don't know shit," I said, my voice raw. I glanced down the track, the engine's single light now stark and brilliant. The train would be upon us in a minute. My mind swirled with the terrible possibilities of being outnumbered two to one, combined with a fast-approaching locomotive.

Tony gave a sardonic laugh and perfectly recited the portal access codes, digit by depressing digit.

I exhaled slowly and the pain vented a bit, along with my resolve. Had we ever possessed any strategic advantage? Every plan we'd made and every hope we'd shared had been futile.

But I was baffled too. Rudolph had asked how we got belowground. "How did you find out about the portal?" I asked Tony.

Valentine interrupted. "Mr. Drax, sharing information with these individuals serves no mission."

Tony ignored him and spoke to me, animated. "You'll kick yourself when I tell you."

I stared back without blinking.

Tony grinned. "We followed your footprints in the dust, through the tunnels. Led right to the portal." He slapped his hands on his knees and rose to stand over me.

Tony's revelation could mean only one thing. "You have another way down," I said.

Tony aimed an index finger at me. "Bingo! First smart thing you've said all day. We built the subway. Think we'd let the city seal it up without preserving access for ourselves?"

Valentine cleared his throat. "Mr. Drax, our mission."

"And forget about coming back later," Tony said, followed by a hollow chuckle. "The codes are all changed, and the phone company employee who manages them has been fired."

Something wasn't adding up, and Reuben sensed it too. "Since we couldn't have gotten in anyway," he said, "then why are you here?"

Valentine slapped his flashlight club into his palm, reclaiming authority from Tony. "Our mission is to make sure *your* mission is officially terminated." In the train's harsh light, Valentine's eye sockets were bottomless black holes.

So they'd come to threaten, or follow through on their threats. Whatever our fate, I would face it on my feet. I stood but encountered a wall of dizziness and pain. I teetered on cardboard legs, pinched my eyes shut, and willed them open again. Valentine no longer stood in front of me. He was behind, grabbing me around the waist with one arm while snaking his free hand under my armpit and then upwards behind my head in a half nelson, the entire motion complete in less than a second. I buckled forward and slammed my free elbow into his ribs, but the big man held firm and applied punishing pressure to the back of my neck. Immobilized and reeling from pain, I could only watch.

Hard Ass met eyes with Valentine, appeared to receive some kind of message, and nodded an acknowledgment. Then he, Gorilla, and Tony were on Reuben like a pack of dogs in a great blur of limbs. Reuben appeared to levitate like a volunteer in a magic show, the camera bag swinging below his torso. Tony held Reuben by the wrists, one firm hand clamped on each. Hard Ass and Gorilla each held an ankle. Reuben was helpless, his body extended into the same letter H used in the high school locker room a decade ago. He writhed in vain at the midsection, the only part left unrestrained.

"Put him down!" I screamed, but Valentine rammed my head forward and wrenched my arm up. A shriek of pain from my shoulder ripped through my nervous system.

"Ever hear of the game chicken?" Tony said. "Two cars race toward each other until one driver chickens out and yanks the wheel." Then he looked down at me, his mouth like a hungry jackal's, wide but unsmiling, teeth aglow. "We'll see how it works with a train." He forced a throaty laugh. I wanted to scream until the world stopped turning.

More wordless signals passed among Reuben's captors. They carried him over the tracks and lowered him. When his arms touched the cold steel, Reuben's jagged screech sliced through the rumble of the oncoming train.

"Let him go!" I shouted. "We're done with the subway."

"You ignored our warnings," Tony shouted back, and the three men stretched Reuben's body until his upper arms and calves lay across the rails.

Reuben stopped screaming as if relinquishing his will to forces beyond his control. Or had panic stolen his voice?

Every square inch of my skin felt on fire. I threw my weight backward to tip Valentine off balance, but he planted a heel to brace himself and punished me with another onslaught of pain.

"Game's over, Tony!" I hollered. The rumble had become a roar of diesel engines and steel on steel. Neck muscles on fire, I turned my head to peer down the tracks. We had twenty seconds at most. But then I remembered a lesson from physics class about the optical illusion of large objects in motion, how they appeared slower than reality. In an old film clip, a train crumpled a station wagon like a soda can.

Behind the glass of the lead locomotive, a human silhouette passed, disappeared, and then darted back into view.

The next few seconds felt like slow motion. I bellowed but couldn't hear myself. The blast from the train's horn overwhelmed all other sound. Reuben's captors released their grips in unison and stepped back. Tony flashed his palms at me, absurdly, as if to signal *It's all okay now.*

But it wasn't. Reuben was still on the tracks.

Distracted by Tony's pantomime, Valentine loosened his grip. I whipped my head back, caught the man square on the nose, broke free, and charged the tracks.

"Reuben, get up!" I pushed between Hard Ass and Gorilla and reached the rail bed. Reuben's eyes darted from left to right, his lips taut over his teeth in a lunatic contortion. He planted an elbow on the ballast stones to lift himself, but the attempt failed.

The train seemed impossibly close.

My heart in my throat, I leaped across the tracks and peered into the gap between Reuben and the rail. The camera bag's shoulder strap had wedged under the lip of a rail spike.

I reached across Reuben's torso, grabbed a handful of his jeans in each fist, and yanked with every muscle at my command. Reuben's body flipped and slid on stones and oiled ties until he lay barely outside the parallel lines of steel.

A hot blast slapped my face as if I'd opened a furnace door. Diesel fumes blurred my vision. The wheels of the train clacked and squealed inches from Reuben's head, snipping the leather strap like scissors through a ribbon.

"Stay low," I shouted into his ear. Tons of iron zoomed past inches away. Reuben scrambled on all fours to safety and sat up, his legs splayed in a V formation. His expression was as flat as a mannequin's. He seemed in shock. *You okay?* I mouthed.

I expected him to faint or explode with rage, anything, but not sit motionless. Then I saw why: Valentine, Hard Ass, and Gorilla were on the opposite side of the train, with the caboose still distant. Tony was on our side of the tracks—defenseless.

Reuben surged to his feet, his cheeks flushed, all traces of the terrified victim on the puddled floor of the locker room gone. His teeth were bared, as though he could rip out a throat, tear and shake until all the humiliation of the past lay in sinewy shreds.

He surveyed the ground, picked up two good-sized ballast stones and charged. Tony's expression switched from defiance to surprise. He spread his legs evasively but his footing failed in the scree.

Reuben plowed into Tony's midsection, bowled him over backwards, and landed on top of him. Before Tony could get his bearings, Reuben sat on his stomach, his arms whipping madly, each hand wielding a club of granite.

Tony defended his head and face, but he couldn't block every blow. A crooked line appeared above Tony's eye like a crack in a watermelon.

I stepped forward to intervene but hesitated. Reuben had been *Ruby Jew*, the *midget*, a locker-room plaything. So many wrongs had to be set right, but not if it meant killing Tony.

Tony grabbed one of Reuben's wrists and held it midair, a serious mistake. Reuben evaded Tony's diminished defenses and slammed a stone into his mouth. Tony screamed and jerked his face to the side. The next blow landed just above his ear.

"He's done, Reuben," I shouted. "That's enough."

Tony bucked his torso enough to upset Reuben's balance and shove him aside. Tony jumped to his feet but stood off-center. His upper lip quivered, a cragged interruption in the line of teeth, now bright red. From the gash above his eye, blood trailed to his ear and down his jawbone, as if he'd been attacked by a lunatic with a tube of lipstick. Wet patches matted his hair.

Reuben released his stone weapons to the field of ballast.

Tony staggered to a weedy spot under a tree and sat down hard, his hand pressed to his forehead. "We were only trying to scare you," he hollered.

I imagined the thoughts swirling in Tony's mind at that moment, that his world had gone crazy. That the planet's rotation had reversed directions. That river rats didn't just step aside for the Princes of the Seven Hills, they bit back.

His shoulders slumped, Tony withdrew a stained hand from his head and wiped it on his pants. Humiliation was always painful to watch, no matter the circumstances.

"I tried to warn you about Valentine," Tony yelled, his speech slurred. "You got ten seconds before the train passes and they tear you apart." Blood and spittle slapped his chin.

"Let them," Reuben shouted in return, his legs spread. Noble words, but I surveyed the moonlit landscape for an escape route.

No time. The caboose passed. A yawning worker in orange overalls watched from an open window, unaware of what the train's engineer had witnessed two minutes earlier. Then the roar faded as if falling off a cliff.

I looked sideways, expecting to see the three security men charging across the tracks. But they stood uncertain, watching a vehicle with flashing red lights barrel toward us on the dirt access road. A radioed report from the engineer must've reached the cops.

With a glance, I exchanged a complete understanding with Reuben. Under the present circumstances, any encounter with the police would go badly, especially for me. We grabbed our gear and ran.

CHAPTER 19

Late afternoon the following day, Reuben and I sat in silence around the break room table at Blumenfeld Photography. I'd stopped worrying about the police, at least temporarily. A cop had left summons paperwork with the receptionist for delivery to me, with a court date two weeks out. Reuben had verified that no police cruiser staked out our house. I'd shifted my attention to Drax's next move, my greatest worry.

Reuben stared at the wooden surface and drew invisible nonsense with his fingertip. I stared at the walls. Alfred had tried to dress up the windowless space with his favorite poster-sized wedding photos, but I was in no mood for brides and grooms in ridiculous canned poses.

"Say something," I insisted, tired of Reuben's sullenness and bored with waiting.

He glanced up, his face drawn. "I really lost it, you know? I could've killed him."

"*You* could've been killed on those tracks. Tony deserved it."

Reuben returned to his phantom doodling for a few seconds before saying, "I don't want to be a vengeful person."

I thought of the indignities he'd suffered in high school, along with every short, skinny, fat, redheaded, or poor kid. "Sometimes vengeance is all you've got left."

The door thumped and Tricia strode in on noisy heels, making her way to the staff refrigerator without glancing in our direction. "What are you two doing here?" She retrieved something in aluminum foil from the fridge and began unfolding the layers. At least she was eating. After seeing her bare apartment, I wondered.

"We're waiting for a phone call," I replied, inadvertently opening the door for a dozen questions without good answers.

She turned toward me. "Holy crap! What the hell happened?" She flipped her leftovers on the counter and approached like a spectator at a freak show. I couldn't blame her. Valentine's flashlight had left an eggplant-colored bruise running from my cheekbone to my temple. I'd spent the night on an ice pack.

"It's kind of complicated." I told Tricia about the near-disaster at the railroad tracks. When I got to Reuben's brush with amputation or worse, he looked embarrassed. I felt like an idiot for putting my friend in danger.

Midway through my story, Tricia joined us at the table, hands in her lap, back straight against the chair.

I finished and she shook her head. "You sure Alfred's obsession is worth getting yourselves killed?"

"I'm not doing this for Alfred," I replied a shade too forcefully. I was doing it for my dad, my mom, Louisa Turkel, and all the others Drax had hurt. But a voice like a shadow sometimes spoke in my head: *you're doing it for yourself, Lucas*. Sometimes vengeance is all you've got left.

Tricia jutted her chin toward the telephone. "Who's calling?"

"It's kind of complicated," I repeated.

She squinted. "Try me."

I straightened in my chair, matching her. "The only reason we got into the subway was because some phone company mole slipped Alfred the codes to Alpha Portal."

Reuben chimed in. "But Drax got the guy fired and the codes changed."

"But the new codes are stored somewhere," I continued. "We just needed to track down the mole and ask him where, but Alfred wouldn't trust me with the guy's name—"

"Can't blame him," Tricia said.

I ignored the dig. "So Alfred called the guy himself. Turns out he was so pissed at getting fired he spilled the beans. All lock combos are stored in this one filing cabinet in the facilities department in the Cincinnati Bell building on Lincoln Avenue—"

"Behind an army of security. Are you crazy?"

"We don't need to go in. We still have a mole on the inside." I felt Reuben's disapproval like heat from a tanning lamp. "My mom." Mom had offered to help, and she'd insisted. After all, Drax negligence had taken her husband and left her struggling through each day. Still, I worried about involving her, with her faculties dulled by withdrawal. Could she remember the location of the file cabinet, the color coding of the folder, and the two codes without taking the risk of scribbling them down?

Tricia pursed her lips. "Way to go, Lucas. Hasn't she put up with enough of you already?"

Yes, she had, banished from her own house ever since the bogus meter man paid a visit.

My watch read 5:20 p.m. "She ended her shift at five, right when the administrative offices closed. When she gets to the street, she'll find a pay phone and call here."

Ten seconds later, the phone rang.

Reuben and Tricia stared suspended, but for what? Maybe Reuben wanted bad news that would end our dangerous adventure. Maybe Tricia wanted further proof of my ineptitude.

I grabbed the handset. Mom's opening words stretched my mouth into an easy smile. Tricia stared while I wrote the new codes, on paper only long enough to memorize.

I hung up the phone.

Tricia wasn't impressed. "Proud of yourself?"

Not in the least. "Proud of my mom. Things aren't easy for her." I scanned the two rows of numbers.

Reuben remained silent.

"You put her at risk for nothing," Tricia said. "They know where your portal is, and they know it's the only way down. Go ahead and zigzag all over town to lose them, but the minute you drop off their radar screen, they'll surround the portal and wait for you to show up."

I said nothing. Reuben continued doodling.

Tricia pressed on. "Even if you slipped past them, you'll need hours to take all the measurements. Drax will be waiting when you come back up, and you won't get away this time."

"Maybe we don't need hours," I said. "Not for this trip."

Tricia's eyebrows shot up with skepticism. "*This* trip?"

"There's another entrance somewhere," I said. "Tony admitted it. They found Alpha Portal by following our footprints in the dust. But from where? If we can get down below, we can play the same trick—following footprints to *their* entrance."

Tricia looked doubtful. But my plan had sounded feasible earlier that day when Reuben and I hashed it out. At best, Alpha Portal was good for one more access. But another entrance could swing the odds, particularly if it was located where we assumed.

She'd find out eventually. "Guess where the other entrance is."

Tricia folded her arms across her chest. Reuben glanced at me tightlipped as if to say *You're on your own, buddy.*

"Underneath Drax headquarters," I declared, and then plowed forward to head off criticism. "Think about it. They built the subway. The Gilmore line runs right under their building. Would they trust the phone company for their access? Hell no. They'd put a hatch in their own basement." Her expression shifted from skepticism to disbelief, but I stayed the course. "Look, Reuben and I have gotten into half the buildings from the river to the expressway. We're good at it. We can get into Drax headquarters by night, find that access point, go below, and shoot every measurement Smith needs to prove fraud."

Tricia played along. "If you're so positive about a second portal inside Drax, why bother following dusty footprints to find it from below?"

Reuben spread his hands, drawing an imaginary expanse on the tabletop. "Including the adjacent buildings that Drax owns, their complex covers two city blocks, and the subway runs the longest length. The portal could be anywhere."

"We can get into Drax through utility tunnels without being observed," I said, my voice sounding more confident than I felt. "But staying hidden through a quarter-mile of Drax's basement? No way. We need a specific location."

We were back to our original dilemma. Drax watched our only way down, Alpha Portal, and they watched every move we made. They had enough sentinels for half the city, while we had only Reuben and myself.

As Tricia gnawed her lip in thought, a few long moments passed silently. Then she drew in a breath and her expression took on a playful intensity. "Your mom did well," she said and leaned in with her elbows on the table. "Who gives a shit if Drax is watching you?" She paused to make sure both of us paid close attention, her eyes lit. "They're not watching me."

· · · · ·

What did Tricia know about off-limits exploration? What if she got hurt? What if she became disoriented, or panicked? Even experienced urban adventurers could come unhinged.

But we listened to her plan: while Reuben and I would divert Drax's attention, she'd slip solo into the subway and backtrack Tony's footprints—no tangents, no delays. Where the impressions in the dust ended, she'd look up and note the location of the other portal, Drax's secret portal. Then she'd retrace her steps and get out.

Reuben didn't buy it. "They could be watching that switching station around the clock."

Tricia held firm. "Why would they? They don't know we have the new access codes."

"An assumption," he said, forever the voice of doubt.

Tricia shrugged. "I'll take cover in the bushes and wait twenty minutes to make sure I'm alone. If they show up, well… game's over. If they don't show up, I'm good to go."

Reuben shook his head. "You might not get away." Good point. If the cops hadn't interrupted at the railroad tracks, we might not have escaped.

"I might make a break for it—I'm pretty fast." She gave a lazy blink. "Or I might stick around and beat the shit out of them." She smiled but something told me she wasn't entirely joking. Then she became more animated. "Your diversion will improve my odds. They'll be watching you in broad daylight, so they won't be watching me."

As she spoke, my fears for Tricia eased and I came to like the simplicity of the plan. I also came to believe that maybe Tricia had begun to care about our crazy mission.

CHAPTER 20

We waited a couple of days before making our next move. If we were lucky, Drax might ease up on their surveillance, or believe we'd thrown in the towel.

The third day began with routine. Reuben reported to work at the insurance company, and I hit the books at the Xavier library.

I went through my motions in plain sight. After a leisurely sack lunch outdoors on the granite steps, I rode the bus downtown to Drax and swung through the massive glass and steel doors like I owned the place. The lunch hour was over, the lobby quiet except for the odd courier scurrying across the marble floor with a delivery pouch.

I paused within sight of the front desk, slid a note from my hip pocket, and noisily unfolded it. In my peripheral vision, the watchful receptionist pressed a speed-dial button and murmured something. Apparently, the lobby staff had been instructed to keep an eye out for me. Good. I replaced my note, crossed diagonally to the Drax Museum, and asked the attendant about an admission fee.

"Oh, heavens no, dear," replied the older woman with a genuine smile. "Senior management holds private meetings in the mornings, but the public is always welcome every afternoon."

I returned her smile and stepped into the museum.

I'd come to do a job, to divert the attention of our pursuers and ease them into complacency, however temporary. A simple task, I'd thought, but I hadn't counted on the impact of seeing symbol after symbol of Drax success.

An old contradiction slapped me in the face. Drax built buildings, and everyday citizens benefited from Drax projects, including schools, hospitals, and workplaces. Yet lots of developers built buildings without cheating on bids, siphoning taxpayer money, and bankrolling European dictators.

Follow Me Down

To Drax, the minute Dad became a potential lawsuit, he stopped being a human being, the red-blooded father who, night after night during my young years, checked my closet for monsters. But the old contradiction nagged.

The museum was spacious and high-ceilinged like a school gymnasium. Lofty walls continued the lobby's motif of slice-of-life photos overlaid with sayings like *If you can dream it, we can build it.*

Unlike in the lobby, the museum floor was thickly carpeted so this afternoon's half-dozen visitors wandered among the exhibits in a church-like hush. I figured Rudolph, the museum's designer, intended to elicit respect, even reverence.

Five or six dozen 3-D replicas lined the perimeter, each several feet long and intricate with landscaping and hand-painted pedestrians. Some structures were lit for nighttime with functioning miniature streetlamps and indoor fixtures glowing amber. Over other buildings, wall-mounted track lights angled like the mid-afternoon sun. Placards explained each model alongside photos of groundbreakings, girder skeletons, and grand openings attended by Cincinnati's big shots. Every image included Walther or Rudolph at various ages.

A couple and their grade-school son wandered by. For a moment, I imagined I was the boy, throwing a five-year-old's tantrum, stomping each replica into pieces as if smashing models would smash the real things.

In the room's center, the black marble surface of a huge conference table gleamed with mirror-like perfection. I imagined Walther or Rudolph sitting erect in one of the burgundy leather chairs or standing majestically at the head of the table, pitching ambitious projects to well-funded clients, embraced on all sides by 3-D proof of Drax success. Our odds seemed to shrink amidst such living legacy.

I progressed along a wall of displays, feeling like an atheist in a revival tent. I recognized the Westridge Mall edged with tiny trees like plasticized broccoli, and an acrylic Mill Creek so blue it belonged in Alaska, not suburban Cincinnati.

When I spotted the next display, something old and powerful twisted in my chest.

A faux concrete lip topped with a delicate yellow railing edged a two-foot hole, all set in a cornfield landscape. The headline on the placard read *Minuteman Missile Silo, Butler County, Ohio.* I scanned the smaller text and knew damn well what I wouldn't find. But I scanned anyway, hopeful and hopeless, my face cool with new moisture. Nothing.

"Of course not!" I spoke out loud. Heads turned in my direction. There could never be mention of my father's death, even if accompanied by bullshit words like *accidental, unfortunate* or *tragic*, because the truth would leave an unsightly smudge on Drax's hospital-white image and *we fucking well can't have that, now can we?*

Again, I imagined myself as the five-year-old, hoisting one of the steel stools used by museum guards and smashing the display into fragments of balsa wood and modeling foam. I turned my head to see if such furniture lay within my reach.

But when I did, I met the familiar eyes of a beautiful woman watching me warily from four feet away. I should have been happier to see Rachel Nolan, one of Rudolph's harem of knockout assistants. After all, she'd come back to the studio to check on me after Hard Ass clubbed me unconscious. But my rage at the silo model lingered like a dissonant gong.

"Not enjoying your visit to our museum?" she said and smiled to strip any seriousness from her question.

"*Our* museum? You ignored what I told you about your bosses. You've joined the family."

Her smile vaporized. "What are you doing here, Mr. Tremaine?"

"Is that an official question?"

"I'm afraid so."

"Let's see." I stroked my chin and pondered theatrically. "That means you're obligated to tell Rudolph whatever I say?"

"Yes."

"Do you think Rudy—can I call him Rudy?"

"I don't care."

"Do you think Rudy knows *that I know* you'll repeat whatever I say?"

"He's a smart man."

"Then surely he knows I'll say nothing but complete bullshit."

She replied instantly, unwilling to be ruffled. "He can decide on his own what to believe."

"Let's surprise him with the truth." I winked, which she didn't like, but I didn't care. "I'm a graduate student at Xavier University studying architecture. I find Drax absolutely fascinating. I want to know *everything* about *every* Drax project. You should too."

I wanted to warn her to beware her employer, that Drax money funded humanity's greatest crime, but such words would tell Rudolph too much. I also wanted her to understand, for only a second, the dust and yellow paint and stillness that clouded my dreams.

She stared back at me.

I let my gaze drift to the model of the missile silo, like an unmarked grave. My heart sank further. What was I trying to prove and to whom? Rachel Nolan wasn't a Drax loyalist; she simply had no reason for disloyalty. Barely out of school, she needed a paycheck, and Drax probably had an opening for a pretty woman. Not her fault for being pretty.

"You helped me once," I said. "You have a conscience. Don't let Drax steal that from you."

She peered as if trying to see behind my eyes. "They won't back down." Something in her face softened, and she spoke quietly. "You know that."

"Neither will I." I checked my watch. "I've been here long enough." And I had, long enough for Tricia to get safely belowground.

· · · · ·

From a bench across the street, I killed another hour in plain sight of Drax, a safety cushion of distraction to give Tricia ample time to exit Alpha Portal and fade into the woods.

We would meet at a café near the studio to share news of her progress, but not for a few hours. I welcomed the delay, a chance to depressurize. The memory of the silo model fresh, my rage bubbled and nagged and owned my thoughts.

I ambled halfway through downtown before swinging south and crossing the Roebling Bridge over the Ohio River. I paused under the north tower and stared up, remembering when Reuben and I barely made it to the top. The last few feet required us to turn our heads sideways and drain our lungs to squeeze through a slit in the brick superstructure. But our efforts paid off. By the time it was dark, downtown had spread before us like a black carpet studded with jewels, and Riverfront Stadium glowed electric white after a doubleheader.

On the Kentucky side, I dropped down into Covington and burned up time dodging litter on a riverbank footpath. I rehearsed a verbal assault on Rudolph for publicly displaying the missile silo without acknowledging, let alone honoring, my father. *You callous son of a bitch*, I said in my fantasy, and Rudolph replied, *You floating piece of river trash*. I tried to shove the thoughts from my mind but they crept back. Even my imagination could be cruel.

Around eight p.m., I stepped off a northbound bus and into the agreed-upon café, but Tricia wasn't there. I returned to the street as an ambulance raced by, its siren Dopplering and red emergency lights bouncing off shop windows and apartment buildings. I quickened my pace. In a block, I smelled the smoke. In another block, I saw it rising beyond a strip mall.

I rounded the final corner and spotted Tricia standing with her back to me, shoulders slumped, staring straight ahead at an unbelievable sight. The fears I'd tried to trivialize roared into reality. Two pumpers and one hook and ladder surrounded Blumenfeld Photography, the squat white building alive with flames at one end and dead with char at the other. One fire truck blasted water into the front lobby, and I imagined blackened desk photos of the receptionist's kids blown to bits by the high-pressure jets, the old magazines with Alfred's best work as a photojournalist shredded and soaked. The other fire truck attacked the brightest blaze with a drenching shower from above, the roof likely collapsed. Above the flames, the apartment building on the rear block swayed and shimmered in the radiating heat. I felt nauseous.

I watched for signs of life but saw only firemen keeping a safe distance and chasing flare-ups with arcs of water. No one entered the building and no one came out.

CHAPTER 21

It must've been around three a.m. Tricia's living room had no clock and if I were to glance at my watch, she might think me impatient, which I wasn't. I would stay as long as she wanted me there.

Over the past six or seven hours, we'd spoken with doctors and firemen and EMTs—each encounter draining us. My limbs felt jellied and my sinuses stuffed with cotton wadding.

Tricia's one-bedroom apartment smelled of sweat and smoke, the sweat from the two of us, the smoke from the pile of debris on the floor between us—all that remained of Blumenfeld Photography.

No one witnessed anyone rescuing the items from the burning building, and by the time the firemen arrived, the gathering was done. But Alfred must've been involved because I recognized the envelope of negatives from my train station photo shoot, and only Alfred knew the combination to his wall safe.

I broke a minute of silence. "A couple of years back, a fire whipped through the hills south of LA, burning a neighborhood one house after another. The authorities allowed residents only time enough to salvage what they could carry by hand in one trip."

Tricia stared at me with red-rimmed and sunken eyes, too exhausted to show either interest or irritation at my monologue.

"Some researcher interviewed each resident to find out what they grabbed." Tricia's eyebrows raised a smidge. "Some people took crazy worthless things, like old stuffed animals—"

"Worthless to you, maybe."

I knew what she meant. I'd gladly rescue my dad's landscape paintings from an inferno, though they'd be dispensable to someone else. "But some people became machinelike with what they grabbed—birth certificates, passports, family photo album, Grandma's handwritten recipe book." I examined my hands, sooty from unloading the debris pile from Tricia's car. "The researcher asked if they'd thought it through ahead of time, or made a list."

This time her interest seemed real, and I was glad to provide a distraction from our troubles.

"But they hadn't," I said.

"Spontaneous?"

"Yeah."

She looked down and shook her head. "I don't think I'm that... put together."

"Yes, you are. That's your grandfather through and through. It's in the genes."

She met my eyes again, the sadness back. "Smith too?"

I glanced at the heap. "Sure looks like it." The sooty pile included the corkboard panels and notebooks from Smith's *war room*.

"Who's next of kin?"

Smith had a son, now long gone. "We'll find out. His real name was Angelo Russo."

When rescuers had first arrived, they found Alfred outside on the gravel, unconscious but breathing, his retrieved keepsakes strewn nearby. He showed signs of smoke inhalation—singed hair, facial burns, swollen eyes, soot around lips and nostrils. Rescuers found Smith in a hallway. Attempts to revive failed. "Had he been carrying anything?" I'd asked the fireman, but he didn't think so.

"Maybe Mr. Smith got out all the important stuff," I said to Tricia and braced for *What's the fucking point?*

But she said nothing. After all, what *was* the fucking point? Our boondoggle to bring down Drax had never seemed so hopeless.

I eased from my chair and sat cross-legged on the floor. Alfred had used a waste bin as a last-ditch collection container. I flipped through the contents, favoring each item like a museum piece. There were a half-dozen file folders—insurance, contracts, client listings—and a thin envelope of cash. I found no awards, but he'd included the framed photo of himself and the reporter receiving their trophy cups. "That man's disappearance really haunts him, doesn't it?"

"Day and night."

I pulled out the coffee table book of Ansel Adams photographs and scrunched up my face. "I don't get it. He called it calendar art."

Tricia sighed. "Sentimental value."

I remembered what Alfred once said about the book, that it was a remembrance of a trip he took out west with an old friend. And the inscription. I flipped open the cover and reread the elegant handwriting in blue fountain pen. *Great places, great times.—R.B.*

Alfred's personal life had always been enigmatic to me, but the first full name that came to mind fit the initials. "Richard?" I said, confused. "Richard Baumgartner? The reporter who disappeared?"

Tricia showed me a weary, knowing smile, her lips pressed together.

"They took a trip west together?"

She pinched the bridge of her nose and peered at me over the steeple of her fingers. "Lucas, you can be a little dense sometimes."

Apparently so. In an instant, a dozen puzzle pieces settled from random orbit into a revealing picture. "They were more than business partners. They were…"

"In *love*," she said, leaning in, teasing, eyebrows high. "It's okay to say the word."

"Hey, I'm not a homophobe." My mind scrambled to reinterpret past conversations. No wonder Alfred never believed the rumors that Richard ran off to South America with an Argentinian bombshell. He knew Richard's heart like his own. A fresh sadness settled low in my chest. "He could've told me. You could've too! How long have you known this?"

"Forever. Like I said, my family wouldn't have anything to do with him."

"But your dad—your dad's mother—I mean, your grandmother. Alfred had a wife."

"Of course he did. That's what gay men did back then. They buried their feelings, married a woman, and pretended they were *normal*," she said, infusing her last word with derision. "But Alfred couldn't pretend anymore, and when he stopped pretending, my family treated him like a leper. Especially my dad, Mr. Macho."

We fell silent. Every time I'd asked Alfred about the subway project, he dispensed just enough information to keep me strung along. I never would've learned about the missing reporter if I hadn't threatened to quit. "He thought I would judge him?"

"He was afraid," she said with resignation. "Whenever anyone found out he was gay, they turned their backs on him." But Tricia hadn't. She'd stuck by him. Maybe she had no choice, or maybe she had some other reason.

I dropped my gaze to the sooty stack. "I might abandon him for being a condescending jerk, but not for being gay."

"But he couldn't know that, couldn't risk it. He needed you for the subway. Still does."

"Still?" I asked, hopeful. Or maybe I was trying to find a fucking point when none existed.

Her chair squeaked and I glanced up. She was already standing, her back to me. "I'll pass out if I don't get some sleep." She shuffled toward her bedroom.

"You said he still needs me to do this." I was teetering between hope and defeat, fishing for resolution. "He was hurt really bad, you know." I paused, not sure what could be said out loud. "He might not make it."

She turned toward me only partially, but enough to reveal tears pooling in her eyes. "Do it for him, or for me. Whatever works."

The relationship between Alfred and Tricia Blumenfeld baffled me, and probably always would. She resented her dependence on him and called him a pain in the ass, and *my parole officer*, yet she seemed to study his every move. Why? But before I could formulate a way to ask, she'd gone to her bedroom and closed the door.

I arranged stray blankets and throw pillows into my makeshift mattress on the floor and tried to sleep but couldn't. I flopped between wakefulness and harsh half-dreams of Tricia's living room on fire, and Mr. Smith faltering and collapsing a few feet shy of the front door. I imagined more long wooden crates, one with Tricia inside, her eye sockets vacant. During a wakeful period, the sound of her muffled crying penetrated the paper walls.

I lay on my side until I drifted off. I half-woke when I felt a warm body against mine. Tricia had slipped soundlessly into the room and spooned herself to my back. We were a perfect fit, her arm around my middle. I wanted to roll over and kiss away her tears, but I knew she wouldn't want that. So I lay still and lost myself in her warmth, and pushed away thoughts of murdered lovers and secret tunnels and ash that would bury you if you closed your eyes too long.

Follow Me Down

· · · · ·

I felt her pull away. The light of the new day breached my eyelids but I kept them closed. She moved quietly through her morning rituals and out the door without a word. I figured she wanted it that way.

I got up, splashed my face at the kitchen sink, dried with a threadbare dishtowel, and noticed what she'd left behind for me: one of our subway maps. But this map included a tiny hand-drawn X in red ink. I knew she'd found Drax's secret portal, but in the tumult of the fire, I'd never asked.

One glance told me I'd been right. The access point was located under Drax headquarters.

I unfolded a floorplan of the downtown complex I'd copied at the county's building permits department. Urban adventurers loved to brag about their physical skills as subterranean gymnasts, but their success had more to do with public records than muscles and balance.

I compared the documents and marveled at what I saw.

CHAPTER 22

Since our earliest days of urban adventuring, Reuben and I had challenged each other to bullshit our way past gatekeepers at hotels, office buildings, performance venues, and government bureaus. The trick was to play a convincing enough part to dispel suspicion.

In the lobby of the building where Reuben worked, I approached the receptionist's desk looking sheepish and a little peeved. I held up a brown paper bag containing a cream cheese bagel purchased minutes earlier from next door. "My wife left her lunch in the car."

The receptionist smiled her sympathy and pushed the lobby phone toward me.

"She's eight months preggers. Can I run it up? Won't take five minutes." I said this with a tiny grimace, as if I was responsible, which I was in my fictitious scenario. The receptionist waved me through to the elevators.

It was an empty victory. Unlike Drax, Midwest Surety had no big secrets to protect.

I arrived at Reuben's cubicle on the eleventh floor. He was hunched over printed sheets of tedium in rows and columns. "We've got to talk," I said.

Unsurprised by the sound of my voice, Reuben laid down his pencil and gazed up. "My boss, who's probably watching you right now, expects me to actually work. The gall." He became serious. "I tried to reach you last night. Where were you? Did she find the portal?"

At Tricia's apartment, in the wee hours, I'd decided not to call Reuben about the fire. He couldn't have done anything, and I wasn't ready to recount—my thoughts too fractured. "Checked out the morning paper yet?" I asked.

Reuben shook his head. "I've been racing ever since the alarm went off. Why?"

"Mr. Smith was killed last night."

Reuben's face contorted with shock and pain. He scrambled to his feet. "Let's talk in the cafeteria."

On the first floor, we found a small table near a noisy kitchen and hunched on opposite sides. I told him everything.

"How'd they do it?"

"There'll be an arson investigation, but it'll be obvious. I bet someone wearing a mask splashed gasoline and struck a match. They'll never pin it on anyone."

A kitchen worker carried a foil-wrapped tray past us and beyond earshot. "And Alfred won't recover a dime."

I nodded. Reuben had long complained about Alfred's cheesecloth insurance protection. Years of makeshift walls and corridors, never code compliant, would give any insurance company ample reason to refuse coverage. "After seeing the look on Tricia's face," I said, "I didn't have the heart to mention it. That shop was everything to her, and it's gone forever." Maybe worse, the terms of her release required working for Alfred in the family business. Was her fate back in the hands of a judge?

I gave my head a little shake, overwhelmed. Too much had changed. I sought refuge in the immediate. "She found the other portal." Reuben didn't react. "Don't you want to know where?"

"Sure."

"Right under the museum. I cross-checked Tricia's mark against the floorplan."

"Ironic that you were just there." But his voice was flat. He was holding back.

"Smith salvaged all of his materials. If I can't replicate the calculations, I'll find someone who can."

Reuben said nothing, worrying me.

"We've got to go back down, through the Drax building."

"They killed Smith. I never signed up for that kind of stuff."

"Smith and Alfred chose to go back into a burning building."

Reuben narrowed his eyes. "What are you saying?"

"If Drax had wanted to kill, they would've done something else. They wanted to destroy evidence, and that means we're on the right track."

"Completed measurements don't guarantee a guilty verdict."

I kept my eyes on him. "If the measurements point to fraud, the prosecutor will open Drax's books, and the people will realize they were duped. Drax lawyers can befuddle a jury, but they can't scrub Drax's reputation." Reuben avoided my gaze. "Smith gave his life to save his methodology." I dropped my words on the little table like a ten-pound stone, but it wasn't easy to do. Our ragtag army was suffering battlefield casualties—injury and now a death. "He can't have died in vain."

Reuben met my gaze with weary rebuke. "Laying it on a little thick this morning, aren't we?" He peered down again and sat silently for ten seconds. Then he straightened, pulled back his shoulders, and surprised me. "Okay, I'm in—with a condition."

"Really?"

"No more unilateral decisions, like... cracking open coffins because *you're* dying to see what's inside. From now on, we're a democracy, got it?"

"It's a deal. Ready to get started?"

"Might as well."

I could've kissed him. We'd hit bottom less than twenty-four hours ago, but the smallest hope, even one tinged with darkness, felt like a new beginning. "Good," I said. "You work on equipment and timing." I ticked off points on my fingers. "Oh, and escape routes. What about Alpha Portal? There has to be an egress override so people coming up from below can get out."

"I'll look into it. You?"

"Access. We can't go in blind. Gotta make an advance scouting trip."

"Into Drax headquarters?" Reuben leaned back and folded his arms. The first test of our nascent democracy. "Risky."

"No choice. If I hadn't scouted the train station, we wouldn't have known vent openings, guard schedule, blind spots."

"We got caught."

"We got photos."

"Thanks to Alfred." True. If not for the old man's sleight-of-hand with film canisters, the whole mission would've tanked. I imagined him in a hospital bed, tubes snaking from his mouth and nose.

Reuben brought me back. "But they recognized you outside the museum."

"Yeah, the lobby crew, but I won't go through the lobby."

"Service entrance?"

I considered. "Loading dock would be better. But timing is key. I've got to make sure whoever's on duty failed his GED."

"Playing what part?"

In the kitchen, a stack of aluminum trays hitting the tile floor sounded like a car crash. Reuben jumped in his seat. "Haven't decided," I said. "I've got to get to the basement, near the utility tunnels. I could do a phone company tech. Mom has a union jacket and I could doctor up an ID from her temp pass. Wish I could borrow one of those Ma Bell vans."

Reuben blinked slowly. "They call that car theft. Try again."

"Electric company?" But I didn't like that either. "We need more authority." Then it struck me. I grinned. Reuben looked irritated. "I'm reminded of a quote by N. Jefferson Chapel."

Reuben pursed his lips. "He wrote those rules twenty years ago."

"Jesus did his thing two thousand years ago and everyone still takes his word as gospel."

"I don't."

I waved him off. "I quote, *When a calm analysis of prerogatives proves boldness the prudent choice, be doubly bold. Audacity itself persuades, for whom but the true would be so audacious?*"

"He might've sold a few more books if he spoke English. What the hell does that mean?"

"Ever see a little dog charge a big dog and the big dog tucks his tail and runs like hell? That's the persuasive power of *doubly bold*."

• • • • •

I followed a routine for the next few mornings. First, I made sure Mom would be safe for the day, either at work or Dorothy's house; our own house was off-limits. Second, I visited the hospital where Alfred remained unconscious and on oxygen support. Third, I dropped by a greasy spoon called Mabe's located on Torrance Avenue just across from the Drax loading dock. Between sips of coffee and time-stretching nibbles of lemon cream pie, I observed.

The core eight-to-five crew was an older guy backed by his younger and greener associate. Older Wiser presented done-it-all posture and know-it-all eyes. Greenie stood erect and habitually adjusted his pants and flexed his fingers. He was my target.

At 11:30 a.m. on the fourth day, following a now-familiar pattern, Older Wiser took his lunch break and left Greenie in charge of the loading bays. I made my move.

· · · · ·

I stepped off the sidewalk and down the loading dock ramp armed with the urban explorer's most powerful weapon against gatekeepers, a credibility prop. From N. Jefferson Chapel: *When equipped with the accoutrement of a plausible profession, you hasten property stewards toward their own erroneous explanation of your presence.*

My weapon was a clipboard topped by one of Reuben's official-looking actuarial tables that only an authority could interpret, the authority being me, a mid-level inspector from the administrative offices of the Cincinnati Fire Department.

Fortunately, CFD bureaucrats didn't wear uniform blues, so I'd dressed the part in soft-soled leathers, khakis, a rumpled dress shirt, and a windbreaker—a gear satchel hanging from my shoulder. I even had an ID card, my second credibility prop—only a last resort because the peel-and-stick laminate barely hid the cuts from my X-Acto knife. To complete the effect, I tucked a Bic pen behind my ear and mentally transformed myself into an overworked civil servant with one to-do item before lunch.

I scurried in a straight line with my head down because seasoned workers never rubbernecked. Once Greenie's field of vision included my approach, I held the clipboard aloft and gave it a Miss Florida wave from the Citrus Day Parade.

N. Jefferson Chapel: *Obfuscate with information to render unnecessary any questions about bona fides.* "You guys swapped out a standpipe valve?" I asked.

"Huh?" Greenie looked confused.

I glanced at my watch. "Your man said you guys knew about this. There must be another loading dock somewhere." I looked around.

"Not really. Who said?"

I scrabbled around in the pockets of my windbreaker. "Italian name—I've got it written down. Just a sec."

Greenie stepped out from behind his checkpoint stand, hiked up his pants, and released them to his hips. "My boss went to lunch. If you could come back in a half hour—"

"What's his name?"

Greenie gave a name.

I shook my head. "Nope, not the guy." I gave up on the windbreaker and thumbed through clipboard pages. "I've got the work order right here." I interrupted my search to look Greenie in the eye. "Standpipe inspection—won't take five minutes—routine stuff."

N. Jefferson Chapel: *For property stewards, success is simply an absence of failure, and knowing is simply an absence of unknowing.* Greenie would avoid admitting ignorance about anything routine.

As if recollecting, I looked off and chuckled. "A guy the other day asked me if the inspection was necessary. Can you believe it?"

Greenie flexed the fingers of both hands.

I continued to flip from one page to the next. "So I told him, if there's a fire, our guys have to hook the hoses to *something*, and that something is the standpipe." I glanced up. "I told him, if that standpipe valve doesn't work... buddy, you got no building. You with me?" Greenie nodded. "So if Drax swaps out a leaky standpipe valve, we've got to inspect it." I thumbed further. "Bingo!" From under the clip, I yanked out my third credibility prop, a standard pink telephone message slip, and pretended to give it a quick read. "Valentine! That's the guy." I handed over the phone message from a Mr. Valentine, supposedly scribbled by a CFD switchboard operator. The message said *The loading dock crew can escort you. If they can't handle it, have them call me.* "You know Valentine?"

"Yeah," Greenie said, looking uncomfortable.

"Buzz him down if you want, but I can show you right where the valve is. Won't take five minutes."

"We don't need to call him," Greenie said quickly. "Show me where."

As Greenie and I walked, we commiserated about flaky bosses and the shackles of the eight-to-five. We celebrated the Red's strong bullpen and the promise of a frothy Hudepohl come quitting time.

We followed a route I'd memorized from Hamilton County records. We reached the standpipe, which I'd chosen for its closeness to the utility tunnels. Greenie watched on as I retrieved my Yashica, snapped an official picture, and began a little lecture. "Everybody assumes egress is all about fire escape. But fire crews gotta have egress *into* a burning building, with no obstacles to trip over. I've got to document that." Greenie didn't bat an eye.

From the depths until we returned to daylight, I flashed thirty-four photos of fire doors, stairwells, conduit-lined concrete tunnels, security cameras, locking mechanisms, ductwork, and ventilation grating. With every couple of flashes, I muttered, "Lookin' good."

Back at the loading dock, I shook Greenie's hand. "Appreciate it, uh… what's your name again?"

"Duncan."

I smiled. "Duncan. I'll tell Valentine you've been super helpful." I eased up the ramp to the sidewalk and rounded the corner.

CHAPTER 23

By the time I made it to the hospital room, Alfred had fallen back asleep. According to the nurses, he'd regained consciousness around daybreak and observed their comings and goings most of the morning, nodding answers to simple questions. As for his lucidity, the nurse told me, "Comes and goes."

I lowered into a chair and gripped the armrests as if pinning them down. Why was I on edge? Since Alfred couldn't talk, I'd be delivering information, not debating it. Surely I could handle a monologue.

Alfred's head rested back on the pillow, the bed semi-reclined. Not much of him was visible, not enough to represent an entire human being, only eyelids, eyebrows, and a patch of lined forehead above an oxygen mask. Everything else was obscured beneath layers of fabric as drab as the room. Other than our bouquet and a few green and yellow thumbtacks on a corkboard, the place was terminally neutral.

I glanced back at the bed. Alfred stared at me, eyes wide open and fixed. I lurched in my seat. His expression, however obscured, wasn't welcoming.

"I—I hope they're treating you well," I said, which sounded stupid. To hell with hospital amenities, they'd kept him alive. "I've got news," I continued, but stopped short, suddenly feeling like a cheat. Words had always been Alfred's armor, but not now. Along with damage to his respiratory system and hands, the smoke and heat had scorched his vocal cords.

Nevertheless, I had things to say—some simple, some hard, but none easy.

I started with simple. "We're going back into the subway to complete the measurements." I wanted to tell more, that Tricia had contacted Smith's former colleague at Ohio State, the one who provided the laser. That the man understood Smith's complex calculations. That he would try to pick up where Smith left off.

But I couldn't tell Alfred these things because he'd wonder *Why not Mr. Smith?* I wasn't ready to tell him the hardest thing, that Smith was dead.

Alfred lifted his eyebrows as if they carried a question.

"How?" I asked, shifting my weight off a spring poking up from the worn furniture. "There's another portal, under the Drax headquarters building."

The eyebrows deflated with disinterest or skepticism, or maybe Alfred was mentally AWOL.

I pressed on, just in case something was getting through. "It's not as crazy as it sounds. Drax HQ shares a single utility tunnel with a half-dozen downtown buildings, including the Emerson Hotel, which I know like my own closet. Guards don't mess with tunnels. Too dirty."

I felt a little silly, conversing with a man's eyebrows and imagining what they might be saying: *Utility tunnels got you into the train station, and you got caught.*

"We didn't have a spotter at the train station."

A what?

"A lookout. This time we'll have someone looking out for us."

That appeared to reassure him, but only a little. Or maybe he was tired.

My gut tightened. Our bizarre chat had reached one of the hard things that needed to be said. Alfred couldn't give informed consent in his current state, but he had to be informed.

I cleared my throat. "The lookout is Tricia."

Alfred's eyes shot open. He frowned, grunted, and raised a bandaged hand like a club, ending all speculation about his lucidity.

I stood to dodge the heat from his stare. "You don't get it, Mr. Blumenfeld. She threatened to sabotage the whole thing if we left her behind. Said she'd rat us out." We'd argued in front of my house with Tricia red-faced and balling her fist, and me terrified she'd get hurt or killed in a dangerous place where none of us belonged anymore, not even urban adventurers who once considered the subway the ultimate infiltration.

I sat down and clasped my hands to still them. "In case you hadn't noticed, she can be stubborn as hell." I risked a cautious smile. "She takes after her grandfather."

Alfred settled back on his pillow and released his eyelids as if succumbing to exhaustion. He exhaled and almost sunk out of sight among the sheets.

"She's doing it for you, you know."

Alfred didn't react.

"She loves you, even if she won't say so."

Again, no reaction.

If not Alfred, then who would she love? A sweetheart since graduation? I couldn't imagine it. But how would anyone know? Her love wouldn't be seen—she wouldn't allow it—just gleaned from a fleeting expression when she assumed no one was watching.

His eyes open again, Alfred waved his arm in a drunken figure eight. After ten seconds of this nonsense, I flagged down a nurse from the hall. She peeked at Alfred from the doorway and returned a moment later with something like a Ouija board of letters and numbers. "He wants to say something," she said, as if any moron could figure that out. She laid the board across Alfred's lap and left the room.

Alfred began maneuvering his gauzed club among the letters.

With each pause of his hand, I sounded out the result. "H—A—S—S—E—L—B—" The Hasselblad. I glanced up. "You'd trust me with your favorite camera?"

He blinked wearily and angled his head, as if to say, *I never said trust, but you may use the camera*. He went on until he'd spelled out *DON'T BOTCH IT*, the same directive he gave before our infiltration of the old train station, which we botched.

"Okay." I stood to go. "You take care of yourself, Mr. Blumenfeld."

I stopped in the doorway, recalling my exchange with Alfred's doctor the day before. *We're worried about infection*, he'd replied to my hard question. *At his age, with that lung damage, pneumonia would kill him.*

I turned toward Alfred but lowered my gaze to the floor. "I know Richard was more than a colleague. I know you loved each other and that he'd never run off to South America like everyone said and leave you behind." A nurse wheeled a clattering metal cart behind me and continued down the hall. "I'd never judge you for that. Never."

By the time I gathered the courage to meet his eyes, they'd closed again.

. . . . .

I stepped softly from the fireproof stairwell, eased down the corridor to room fourteen twelve, and tapped twice with the knuckle of my pinky finger. The door opened a sliver and then wider once Tricia recognized me.

"Hi," I whispered.

"Hey." She turned and led the way into the hotel room, her brunette hair snaking into the draped hood of a navy blue sweatshirt. She was dressed for unfettered movement in loose jeans, fitted enough to reveal the easy slope of her hips. Through the window over her shoulder, lights of downtown buildings shimmered against a black sky.

She stopped next to the writing table and tugged open the drawstring on her rucksack. "Any chance you were followed?"

"No." I'd detoured and looped back through Cincinnati streets for almost an hour. I shrugged off my pack and lowered it to the bed, queen size with a purple spread. "If you have doubts about doing this—"

"I don't."

I sat on the edge of the bed. My boots made my feet look Frankensteinian. "The Drax portal might have a combination lock, and we won't get in without codes."

"Fine," she replied curtly. "Then we wouldn't have to worry about stink damp."

Days earlier, Tricia had proclaimed, "I'm going with you," and cauterized her declaration with a don't-fuck-with-me glare. Reuben and I then taught her as much as we could about survival in forbidden places, including how to avoid hydrogen sulfide poisoning. "It triggers cortical necrosis," Reuben had said, hoping she'd look confused so he could scare her off by describing how stink damp explodes brain cells like microscopic popcorn. But she stared back half-bored, unimpressed by Reuben's mental encyclopedia.

A mass-produced hotel painting above the dresser showed moonlight bouncing off ocean waves in a crooked line of yellow smudges. "Or, assuming there's no combination lock, we might climb down the ladder into a lake of toxin," I said, a stretch—the Drax portal was far from river moisture. "So since we're going to die together, can we sit together until Reuben shows up?" I patted the bedspread.

She turned toward me, flashed a humorless smile, and joined me on the edge of the bed. She dropped her gaze to the old-time carpet, a swirl of paisley like warring ghosts.

I stole glances at the side of her face, trying to detect nervousness. She was either the greatest actress or stone-cold fearless. "You're determined to keep me in the dark," I said, my attention drawn by the upsweep of her lashes.

"About what?"

"What you're thinking. The only thing I know for sure is that you're pissed off."

"Alfred might die. Of course I'm pissed off."

"Why?" I was goading, but I needed to understand the caustic coexistence between Tricia and her grandfather.

She shot me an icy glance.

"He asks you about the register receipts and you hand over your order list, and that's about the extent of your relationship. Ever ask him about his day?"

"Do you?"

I scowled. "He's not my grandfather."

She seemed to thaw a bit. "Relationships are more than what people say to each other. There's family history too."

"You told me about Richard, remember?"

"That doesn't make you family." She rose from the bed, her back to me again. "What does it matter to you anyway?"

I huffed an audible sigh. "Okay, I get it. You don't trust anybody, and maybe that's for good reason. But we're *both* taking a big risk for that old man, so maybe you can trust me."

"Some things are hard to talk about."

"Fair enough, then I'll go first." She stood motionless, waiting. I reached into a black pit of memories and retrieved a terrible truth. "I once blamed my mom for my dad's death. Somehow I convinced myself if she'd finished her degree and landed a better job than switchboard jockey, he wouldn't have had to paint missile silos for Drax." I stopped to let the guilt wash over me and drain away. "Thank God I never said anything to her." I swallowed. "Now it's your turn."

She rotated to face me, stuffed her hands in her jeans pockets, and pressed her arms against her body as if deflecting a chill. "Nobody ever believed in me, and I'm not asking for a pity party, okay? It's just the truth." She caught herself. "Oh, a friend or two maybe, but they were clueless. No family member—not my parents, not really. But Alfred believed in me, the only one who did. Want to know why?"

I held my attention on her face.

"Because he saw himself in me, another person who didn't quite fit in. He's been an outcast in my family ever since he told the truth about Richard. And I've been an oddball ever since… forever." I leaned forward, ready to counter her self-flagellation, but she cut me off. "When he walked me into that shop and handed me the key to that cash register, everything changed. I finally fit somewhere." Memories softened her eyes. "He's a pain in the ass, but that doesn't change what he did for me."

I let a moment go by, and then said, "We can rebuild the studio and your shop."

"Not without insurance money. Alfred broke every fire code."

So she knew. "When I saw Alfred at the hospital, he understood everything I said."

She gave a sad smile. "Thanks for the pep talk, Lucas, but I talk to the doctors every day."

Two soft knocks sounded from the vestibule. I stood and took a step but she cut me off. "So yeah, I'm pissed off. The only person who ever cared is teetering on the edge, and it's Drax's fault." Her eyes radiated heat.

There was so much more I wanted to say to her. Instead, I stepped sideways and opened the door.

· · · · ·

We emptied our three backpacks into separate piles on the bedspread. Tricia's pile included the sepia photo, minus the frame and soot-smudged, of Alfred and Richard receiving their trophy cups at the *Enquirer*'s gala. Perhaps she considered it a reminder, or a tribute—I wasn't going to ask.

Reuben pushed up his glasses and held a hotel pen against a list of supplies. He read slowly. "Three spot flashlights… lantern… camera… film… laser with spare battery pack."

As he read, I shifted a few items among the three piles based on weight distribution and who needed what.

"Electrical tape… rope… lanyards with penny and whistle."

"Hang on." I snatched up and doled out the lanyards.

Tricia looped the lamp chain necklace over her head and flipped her hair clear. "I understand the penny, but why the whistle?"

"In case we get split up," Reuben replied. "The sound carries further than a shout."

"Walkie-talkies don't work?"

"In buildings, but underground range is only a few hundred feet."

"That sucks." But she didn't seem concerned.

I settled the new copper coin and chrome referee's whistle against the outside of my shirt, remembering our encounter with Hard Ass and Charlie Brown in the train station. "It might suck for Drax. Their security guys stumble around without their radios. Could work to our advantage." *Tactical advantage*, Alfred would say.

Reuben poked the inventory list with the pen. "Probably better keep going. We need to be belowground before midnight." He looked down. "First aid kit… compass… Swiss Army knife."

Tricia picked up the red gadget with its distinctive plus-sign logo. "Not much of a weapon."

Reuben frowned. "It's a tool, not a weapon."

Tricia released the knife with a dismissive flip. "Did you guys consider something bigger?" For a moment, our planning efforts seemed as puny as the knife on the bedspread.

Reuben stuck out his chin. "They carry firearms and we're debating blade length?"

"Maybe *we* should carry *firearms*," Tricia said, mocking Reuben's choice of words. I'd been worrying about keeping her safe from Drax, but not about keeping Reuben safe from her.

Your turn, Reuben told me with his eyes.

"Our best weapon is up here." I tapped my temple. "We know the underground. Drax doesn't." Indeed, I'd memorized it all, every main tunnel, service passage, and concrete vertical tube to a street-level portal, all welded shut except for two. That reminded me. "What about escape override?"

"Alpha Portal has it," Reuben said. "We can climb out there if we need to." He jumped back to the list, hoping to get ahead of Tricia's cross-examination. But he read off the last two items with veiled disdain. "Lock picks and bolt cutters."

Tricia raised her eyebrows. "Problem?"

I leaned against the back of the desk chair. "If you're captured with break-in tools, you can't talk yourself out of it." Then to Reuben, "But we've been over this. To hell with appearances. We need every advantage, and they already know we're bad news."

Tricia hefted the bolt cutters and turned them over in her hands. Like a two-foot-long pair of pliers made of cast-iron pipe and hardened steel, the tool could snap any padlock or chain we'd ever encountered. "Now *that's* a weapon."

Reuben squeezed his lips together before saying, "Can we load up, please?"

I finished distributing our gear among the packs. Tricia wanted to carry the bolt cutters. No one objected.

CHAPTER 24

From the hotel lobby, we followed the service corridor and slipped behind the Emerson Hotel's kitchen. My watch said 11:43 p.m., and other than the tympanic echoes of a handheld sprayer blasting a cooking pot, we encountered no signs of life.

We dropped two floors using the staff elevator to the hotel's basement—familiar territory to Reuben and me from two previous infiltrations. I'd been playing *Come Go with Me* in my head and the refrain was getting on my nerves.

"That one." I pointed at a steel door and stepped around a stack of collapsed buffet tables. "It was unlocked last time."

I twisted the knob, swung open the door, and slipped through to a stairwell lit in icy fluorescent. Reuben and Tricia joined me. The walls reeked of cigarette smoke, and a butt-filled coffee can perched nearby.

"Useful fact for urban explorers," Reuben said to Tricia. "Occupied buildings are more accessible than vacant ones because people get sloppy."

We tapped down the steps until the smokers' landing, now distant, offered little light. We reached the utility tunnel and switched on our flashlights.

Reuben continued his instruction. "This tunnel's been shared for most of the century by six downtown buildings, including Drax."

Instead of showing irritation at Reuben's lecturing, Tricia seemed distracted by our surroundings.

I lit up a straightaway with my flashlight. "Drax is down that way."

"You sure?" Tricia asked.

She could be forgiven a little skepticism. "Never hurts to verify," I said. "But in this case, yeah, I'm sure."

No wider than a car, the concrete passage was lined with all manner of pipes and conduits bolted in place to survive the apocalypse and colored red, black, and bare metallic, carrying water, gas, electric, phone, and sewage.

We walked single file with Reuben on point, Tricia second, and me at the rear. I sniffed and picked up hints of concrete dust, oil-based paint, and animal decay, probably rodent. But I detected no moisture, not that I expected it. Unlike the subway beneath our heels, utility tunnels received occasional air, visitors, and maintenance.

We arrived shortly at the locked gate separating the Emerson from the old Carmichael office building. With lightweight chain-link and a corroded dime-store padlock, the barrier would've passed a lazy inspection, but not kept out intruders. I scrambled for my picks but Reuben extended a hand and gave the lock a forceful yank. It snapped open.

"Things aren't always this easy," I said to Tricia.

We heard something like fingertips brushing a grocery bag. I shifted my beam toward a fat rat waddling with purpose along the wall. Tricia dragged her index finger along a pipe and squeaked the chalky residue against her thumb, exploring the texture. *As space is canvas and sensation acrylic*, wrote N. Jefferson Chapel, *let curiosity fill your palette.* I found myself hoping Tricia's senses were excited, that she'd feel Chapel's *la vive émotion.*

The gate separating the Carmichael from Drax property was built of wrought iron with bronze fittings and a combination lock twice the heft of the gym locker variety. Chapel boasted that he could spring combos like a safecracker, his ear against the back, listening for hiccups in the mechanism. I'd tried once or twice but heard sound as steady as snow tires on asphalt.

Reuben and I exchanged glances. We had reached a key decision point in any infiltration.

Tricia was already retrieving the bolt cutters. She held them suspended, and then noticed our hesitation. "What now?" she said irritably.

"We're a democracy, right?" I asked.

Tricia waited for further explanation.

Reuben directed his flashlight straight up to give a lantern effect. "If we cut the lock, there's no more leaving without a trace. Then if we have to abort, for whatever reason, they'll know we made it this far and block any other attempt."

Tricia looked annoyed. "Should we give a little speech or something?"

I winced.

"I'm just saying," Reuben replied, deflated. "Little decisions can have big effects."

"Fair enough," she said without generosity. "It needed to be said and you said it." She wriggled the tool's hardened steel blades over the shackle and scanned our faces. "Any objections, voters?"

There never was a choice. The padlock was a reality to be dealt with. Reuben and I submitted. Tricia squeezed the long handles together. The lock spasmed and settled limp against the hasp.

The significance of entering Drax territory registered in my stomach with acidic churn. I counted paces down a straight tunnel until we reached a metal door on our left. Just beyond, according to my reconnaissance photos, lay the standpipe valve I'd "inspected" as Junior Fire Marshall.

"Once through, stand with your backs against the near wall. There's a security camera but a stack of boxes gets in the way."

"What if someone moved them?" Tricia asked.

Good question. "Everything was caked with dust, so I figure they were stored for the long haul."

She seemed to accept the logic. I dug out my lock picks and got busy as she watched on. A minute later, the doorknob spun freely in my hand. We doused our lights and squeezed into a hallway barely lit by an exit sign. I exhaled.

To determine the portal's location, I'd had to triangulate across three sources of information: floor plans from county records, the subway map where Tricia had marked the underside of the portal, and my recon photos. All of these I'd spread out in a private meeting room at the Xavier library and attacked with pencil and ruler until the answer emerged.

Tricia and Reuben stared at me as I slid my conclusion from a pocket and reviewed the notes.

I poked my index finger toward the exit sign. "Stay upright but hug the wall. When you get to the T, drop to a crawl to avoid the camera and turn right. Go about thirty feet to a door on the left. Big storage room. We regroup in there."

The long hallway had picked up a few more storage items since my last visit, but nothing we couldn't crawl around. As we did, a door slammed somewhere out of sight. Nerve endings seemed to sizzle throughout my body. Reuben dropped to his belly like a soldier under fire. Tricia followed his lead. I pressed my finger to my lips, a pointless gesture; we were too scared to breathe, let alone speak. I heard blood rushing in my ears. Hard-soled shoes clopped down an unseen hallway. Still as statues, we waited and listened. The footsteps grew fainter. Another door slammed, more distant this time, leaving us in silence.

"Clear," I whispered. Our hands-and-knees parade continued, each of us doubly aware of the audacity of our trespass.

Chapel's best advice for avoiding capture was to infiltrate when your presence could be explained as innocent. You might claim to be a tourist to a museum or historic site who took a wrong turn in search of the restroom or parking garage. But at three in the morning in the dark recesses of a private company, while toting burglars' gear, Chapel's advice meant nothing. The greenest guard would call the cops or the director of security. I compared those two possibilities. Landing with the police would complicate my legal woes, but landing with Valentine… I shuddered as a shadowy image filled my mind: three corpses vanishing under tons of dirt as Drax relinquishes the first subway tunnel to Mother Earth.

Once inside the storeroom, I scrambled to my feet and clicked the door behind us. I'd seen the contents only in passing during my earlier visit. Now I took my time, swinging my flashlight in a slow arc to reveal the props of self-promotion, including giant banners stored in rolls. I imagined their headlines: *Coming Soon, Grand Opening* and the ubiquitous *Let Your Dreams Take Flight*. Portable staging lay nearby in tidy piles, ready to give Walther or Rudolph a platform for speeches and ribbon cuttings.

I swung my light further and my heart lurched in my chest. Bright, sky-blue eyes peered back, fixed and framed in a perfect face with lips the color of watermelon flesh. She was ready for the office with a bell-shaped hairdo and pink two-piece suit, apparently delighted to see me. And she'd brought her fun friends.

Tricia strutted to the klatch of mannequins—men and women, all adorned and attentive—as if challenging them to a brawl. "If I'd known this was a formal party."

My lungs decompressed while Reuben shrugged off our plastic companions. "Drax is building the Northridge Mall. Must use them to stage in-store displays."

Tricia lit up the face of a Jane Fonda look-alike. "You know what really creeps me out? You could drench her in gas and strike a match and she'll keep right on smiling." She held her gaze on the mannequin for a moment too long, appearing lost in thought. Then she slowly lowered her hand to her side and followed the flashlight's circle to the floor. Her shoulders slumped.

I risked a hand on her forearm. "They'll pay for what they did to Alfred."

"They better," she replied without looking up.

Was that a challenge to me? No time to think about it. My light struck a steel door at the far end of the storeroom. "We're close."

A stubby hallway ended with one more door, locked but easily picked. We crowded into a compact utility room that smelled of solder and burnt flux, with wall-mounted conduits running vertically and horizontally. Whirring machines on a raised platform displayed the Ma Bell logo.

"Code violation," I said, "putting power and telecom so close to a water line." I remembered something Alfred had said about corrupt inspectors. *Drax doesn't manipulate the system. They* are *the system.*

I took a few steps to the edge of a square in the floor, a steel plate, four feet on each side, with raised crisscrosses, secured with hasp and padlock along one edge. Tricia produced the bolt cutters and snipped like a seasoned pro. Reuben cast aside the fragments and yanked skyward. I readied my light, my heart accelerating.

All three of us peered into a concrete shaft almost identical to the passage leading to Alpha Portal. Thick rebar rungs cast into one wall descended into darkness. I redirected my light straight down. Ten feet below lay a circular hatch in the floor. At its center was a wheel-like locking mechanism resembling those I'd seen in submarine movies.

Tricia flopped to her belly with her face over the edge. "No combination lock." She twisted her head to find confirmation in my expression.

"Doesn't look like it," I said, "but let's make sure."

She led the way down, the sinews of her hands rippling as she grasped each rung. I flashed Reuben a grin. Nothing about our mission was guaranteed, so by God, we'd celebrate even the smallest victories.

At the bottom, I jockeyed for position among backpacks, limbs, and adrenaline. Reuben remained standing in a corner so I could crouch next to Tricia for a closer look. Heat and musk radiated from her body in waves of exhilaration. She clutched the chrome ring with both hands like the steering wheel of a tractor-trailer rig. She tested the resistance. The wheel began to rotate. She gave a hesitant smile and applied more pressure. More rotation.

Instinct forced my line of sight to the horizontal line separating wall from floor. I gasped. "Wait!" I slapped my hands on top of Tricia's and bore down. "Don't move it."

"What?" Reuben spoke above me, his voice breathy in anticipation of bad news.

Tricia's hands relaxed beneath my grip. I let up and exhaled through my nose. Extending an arm, I traced the ninety-degree angle at the base of the wall, beginning with a small hole that emerged from the concrete. My moving finger displaced a wedge of dust to reveal a small gray wire that disappeared again into another hole near the edge of the hatch. "It's alarmed."

"We're not turning back," Tricia declared.

I shifted my weight from one leg to the other, my boots hissing in the grit. "I never said we were." I glanced up at Reuben. "We're a democracy, right?"

Reuben gave a single grim nod.

I met Tricia's electrified gaze. "We can't get in and out undetected."

"What happens if we cut the wire?" she asked.

"It's a closed circuit," Reuben said. "We'd open the circuit and trigger the alarm, probably a flashing light at the security desk."

I caressed the glossy beige surface of the bulbous hatch. "Somewhere underneath are a switch and the rest of the wire. If this were a window, we'd break the glass, reach through, and run a patch cord to keep the circuit closed."

Tricia considered that. "How soon will the guards notice the light? I mean—how many security guards stare at their consoles all night?"

"Problem is, we can't know," Reuben said, his tone labored. "We might trigger an air raid siren."

I studied the wire further. "Old circuitry. At least we aren't dealing with fresh security measures. Maybe the guards are tuned out."

But Reuben wasn't up for my cheerier assessment. "This is Drax, secretive and paranoid." He tipped his head toward the floor. "Trust me, if we pop that hatch, they'll be all over us."

Tricia sat back cross-legged and folded her arms in front of her chest. "We're not turning around."

"Let's think scenarios," I said. "That guy we heard walking around might be the only guard, or maybe he's got a buddy, but there can't be more than two."

Tricia seemed to expect a revelation in my words. "When they see the alarm, what are they going to do? Run over here, drop into seven miles of black, and start stumbling around with their guns drawn? I doubt it."

"No, they'll get help first," Reuben continued with glum certainty. "Which means we'll have Valentine and his goons after us."

Tricia perked up. "But that buys us time. They'll need a half-hour or more to get across town."

I played out more scenarios, first in my head and then out loud. "The rebar ladder keeps going below the hatch. We can rope the lid closed from underneath. That might buy us more time, especially if the night crew is afraid to test the hatch until Valentine shows up."

Tricia's eyes glowed with anticipation. "How long would ropes hold them off?"

I flexed my fingers. "They'll try to pry it open—"

"If they can find something to pry with," she said.

Reuben said, "They'll dismantle the hatch."

"*If* they brought the right tools." She kept up the pressure.

Reuben made a clicking sound in his cheek. "Too many assumptions. Plan for worst-case—thirty minutes extra delay."

Tricia's eyes pleaded with mine. "Can we shoot all the measurements in one hour?"

Our triad was looking less like a democracy and more like two warring political parties with one independent voter—me. "I don't know." My number-crunching had been inconclusive. Depending upon the route taken and how well we could divvy up the duties, completion time varied from forty-five to ninety minutes.

"Maybe they'll wait for Tony," Tricia said hopefully. "He lives in the hills."

"You're dreaming," Reuben said. "What if they send another crew to Alpha Portal and block our exit?"

Tricia scrambled to her feet and brought her face too close to Reuben's. "What if they don't?" she said, her voice more growl than speech.

Reuben stood his ground. "So now I'm not allowed to imagine possibilities?"

I rose from my crouch. "Look, it's a safe assumption the security people won't think about Alpha Portal. It's miles away, they scrambled the codes, and probably won't know about egress override. Can we agree on that?"

"Yes," Tricia said and eyeballed Reuben.

He nodded reluctantly before straightening his back and declaring, "Regardless, they could break our ropes in minutes, choose the right trail of footprints, and we're in deep shit."

"Or they could wait an hour with their thumbs up their asses and then what?" Tricia said. "They'd be entering your territory—*our* territory—seven miles of transit tunnel and even more side tunnels to lose them in. What good are their guns if they can't find us?"

Reuben protruded his jaw. "An electronic flash in total darkness tends to attract attention."

"I'll be spotter," Tricia said. "Isn't that why you brought me along anyway? I vote we go."

"Oh really?" Reuben replied with double-barrel sarcasm. Then to me, "I vote we *not* commit suicide at this time."

Tricia huffed. "You're refusing?"

"I never said that. I'll support the group decision." Reuben leaned toward me. "That makes you the tiebreaker, Lucas."

Reuben and Tricia watched me with their individual hopes, Reuben that I'd calculate our slim odds and order a wise withdrawal, Tricia that I'd be as stupid as ever and order *once more unto the breach*.

I slipped off my pack and lowered it to the floor. "The clock doesn't start ticking until we open that hatch, right?"

Tricia said, "Quit stalling."

"You don't want me deciding." Had they forgotten my track record? "I decked Tony Drax, called his grandfather a Nazi—"

"Which you were right about," Tricia said.

"—and led us into an ambush by the railroad tracks, almost getting Reuben killed."

My imagination ran headlong into a dark future. A pulse of fear tightened in my chest. I saw Tricia on her back on subway concrete, immovable walls rising to an impenetrable ceiling. She stares up warily. Drax men circle like jackals in an underground world without rules, consequences, or exits, a world soon to become seven miles of unmarked grave.

I glanced at her face, her fury as indomitable as gravity's pull.

Was I any different? Like gravity, Drax's assault on my family pressed down on me until black, venomous rage oozed out. Who was I kidding? There'd be no thoughtful calculation about the pros and cons of attack versus retreat.

"Look, we're not deciding on going now versus later," I said, the air in our four-foot-square concrete shaft heating up. "There is no later. They'll find our trail of broken locks and weld everything shut." I took a breath. "So, we decide to do this now, or give up permanently. Got it?"

"Understood," Reuben said. Tricia stared at me, her jaw set with wordless resolve.

"Then why pretend we're deciding?" I asked rhetorically and peered hard into Tricia's eyes. "You'll go no matter what we decide because of what they did to Alfred, your only real family." She blinked her acknowledgement. "And I have to go for the same reason." Because of Dad, because he had nobody looking out for him. I returned my attention to Reuben. "But you don't have to do this."

Reuben recoiled as if I'd backhanded him, his eyes flaring open. "What kind of bullshit is that? You think after all these years I'm going to run away?"

I shook my head. "That's *not* what I'm saying. It's just…" Something became crystal clear in my mind, something I should've realized long ago. "I'm done putting people in danger, that's all."

Reuben retreated to a tightlipped silence. Wisely, Tricia said nothing.

I listened to our breathing and my own heartbeat. Tricia twitched with nervous energy like an athlete before the final competition. Reuben bit his lip and darted his eyes, the telltale signs of a methodical mind on overdrive. "Then I'll spare you the trouble," he said.

"What?" I responded.

"It won't be your decision." Then his face dropped from my line of sight.

Before I could come to my senses, Reuben had gripped the hatch's steering wheel, twisted it, and pulled hard. The portal flew open. Off in the distance, a metallic alarm shredded the night.

Reuben glanced up and flashed a wry grin. "The clock just started ticking, I'd say."

CHAPTER 25

I pulled down the hatch overhead and the alarm bell faded to a faraway buzz. I found myself in a vertical tube not unlike a submarine conning tower, but made of concrete, not steel.

Reassured by the density of the barrier above, I got busy with ropes as my comrades waited below.

"What's taking so long?" Reuben called up.

I tugged on a double knot. "I'm tying them individually so breaking one won't unravel the whole thing. Make yourself useful up here, okay?"

I pressed myself into the corner as Reuben paralleled me on the ladder. Together, we strung and secured six rope lengths from the hatch handle to multiple rebar rungs. A good investment of precious time.

I began my descent. "I bet they'll have to dismantle the assembly to get through the hatch."

"Knock on wood," Reuben replied.

We dropped into the thirteen-foot-wide transit tunnel. Our flashlights created a cocoon of gloomy gray that faded left and right to infinite black. The combined aromas of natural and man-made substances made me think of unlit matches.

Under different circumstances, I'd rejoice in such glorious *vive émotion*, but not this time. A relentless countdown in my brain drowned out all sensation but anxiety, prodding me toward one overriding goal: to squeeze progress from every minute. Yet as I scanned our stone passage, my goal seemed more elusive than ever. Tricia was nowhere to be seen.

Reuben snorted his disapproval. Responsible urban adventurers never set out solo without notice.

"Listen," I said. We cocked our ears and picked up the fast rhythm of a runner's footsteps. In unison, we swung our flashlights toward the sound. Tricia came into view rounding a steady bend, broke stride, and trotted to a halt in front of us.

I jumped ahead of Reuben to prevent a verbal skewering. "You scared us."

Tricia's chest heaved with inhales and exhales. "Sorry."

Reuben glowered. "What were you doing?"

She pointed at our feet and swept her arm outward. "Making footprints." Her ragged line of smeared impressions faded into the void. "There's a junction down that way—"

"Dorning and Fourteenth," I said.

She wiped sweat from her forehead with the back of her hand. "Yeah. I bet I put down a quarter-mile, including popping in and out of a bunch of service passages."

I swatted Reuben's shoulder. "Brilliant, huh? They'll trip all over themselves trying to follow us."

Reuben eased but stayed quiet.

"Come to think of it," I said, "we ought to shuffle the sequence of measurements."

Reuben's disapproval returned. "Now you think of this?"

"She's got the right idea," I said. "If we hit all the undisturbed territory first, we put down fresh footprints and get Drax confused."

No one protested.

I set our pace at a brisk jog. We arrived in minutes at the first of the remaining measurement sites from Smith's plan, with Tricia no more winded than Reuben and me.

"Same as our rehearsals." I cradled the Hasselblad like a Fabergé egg, sensing Alfred's oversight from the world above the streets. Reuben held the laser against a wall while Tricia verified placement with the glass levels and their sliding bubbles. Upon receiving her A-OK, I tripped the shutter. *Sh-clack.*

We improved our technique, soon spending no more than a minute or two on each measurement, keeping our dialogue efficiently on-task.

"Set. Balanced?"

"Clockwise one degree—in position."

"Got it."

Sh-clack.

Travel time became a factor. During one jog, I rehashed my calculations to balance expediency and disrupting as much new dust as possible.

After twenty minutes, I became convinced the overnight guards had waited to test the hatch until their bosses arrived, and only then encountered our ropes. I imagined Valentine berating his subordinates for their lack of battlefield initiative.

After thirty minutes underground, we'd moved a mile from Drax headquarters, executed seven turns, and detected nothing behind us.

After an hour, we completed the last measurement.

"That's it," I said, snapping the Hasselblad's lens cover into place. "Maybe they never made it past our ropes, or maybe they did but took off in the wrong direction."

Reuben checked my enthusiasm. "Maybe toward Alpha Portal to block our escape."

Indeed, success lay approximately two miles to the northwest. I flipped over the Hasselblad to access the catch. "Lights out, just in case." In total darkness, I carefully rewound the film, clicked open the camera back, withdrew the roll, and felt all around to verify a lightproof seal. "Clear."

"What are you going to do with that?" Tricia asked once illumination returned.

I sensed something lurking behind her question and squeezed the roll tighter in my hand. "Protect the hell out of it. Why?"

"If we get caught," she said, "they'll confiscate our stuff, including that."

I searched Reuben's eyes for signs of comprehension, but picked up only stifled bemusement.

Tricia continued. "You guys suck at holding on to film."

No need to remind me, the train station debacle too painfully fresh. "You have an idea?"

"If you can handle it." Tricia held out a cupped hand. "Film, please."

Generals strategize, soldiers improvise, went Dad's old saying. Besides, our democracy could overrule if her idea fell flat. I surrendered the film.

Tricia straightened her back. "You'll need the electrical tape."

Curious, I lowered my pack to the ground, dropped to one knee, and rummaged until I produced the roll of black plastic tape. When I looked up, my mouth fell open.

Tricia had spread her legs slightly so that her jeans, now freed at the button, had stopped their descent at her knees. With her left hand, she held the roll of film against the inside front of her left thigh about an inch below her underwear.

Reuben cleared his throat, a substitute for unavailable speech. Tricia saved me from similar verbal constipation. "Tape it all the way around, multiple loops, and don't be shy."

I fumbled the tape roll.

"Look," she said, "no hiding place is safe from Drax. But this better be the last place they search."

Yeah, some soldier. I collected myself and proceeded as commanded. Beginning with the outside of her thigh—somehow it seemed safer—I adhered the leading edge to her skin and looped around while reaching between her legs with my free hand to pull the tape through, rotating slightly for clear passage. I repeated for five loops, struggling to focus on my task.

· · · · ·

Mid-jog and mid-tunnel en route to Alpha Portal, we heard the first sound, a dull metallic clunk like a wooden bat against a swing set. On instinct, we stopped, frozen.

How amazing the way a desperate mind can deny the obvious. I briefly entertained a ludicrous explanation that the steel superstructure had creaked, maybe because of temperature change.

But my theory vaporized when "Fuck!" reached our ears in a high-pressure whisper, as if someone had stubbed a toe, or more likely whacked a shin on a utility bracket. More epithets followed, directed at the loudmouth who'd blown cover.

I tapped shoulders and gestured us into the closest service passage where our sounds would stay contained. Manic-eyed and huffing, we crouched, our faces inches apart. Questions and conjecture flew in rapid-fire whispers.

Tricia: "Do they know we're here?"

Me: "No clue."

Tricia: "We were quiet."

Reuben: "Sound carries. Or maybe they saw our lights."

Tricia: "How far back does this service passage go?"
Me: "Dead-end into storage. We'd be trapped."
Reuben: "Shit."

I eased half my face around the concrete wall and scanned the darkness to where the tunnel curved out of sight, discerning only precursors to light, like before-dawn shimmers on the horizon. I rejoined the blizzard of point-counterpoint.

Tricia: "How many of them?"
Me: "Sounds like four, coming from Drax Portal."
Reuben: "Five at least. Does it matter? They're armed."
Tricia: "It matters. We can take them out."
Reuben: "Are you nuts?"
Me: "Maybe they'll stick with the main tunnel and pass us by."
Reuben: "I wouldn't risk it."
Tricia: "Of course you wouldn't."
Me: "Focus! We've got to decide."
Reuben: "Our footprints will lead them right in here."
Tricia: "How far away are they?"
Reuben: "Sound carries. Couple hundred yards?"
Me: "More."
Reuben: "Assume less."

No time for this. I checked the main tunnel again. Man-made light had begun tickling the outer wall of the curve.

I flashed two palms, double stop signs. "We've got to haul ass until we get past Concord, then regroup. Flashlights only when necessary. Follow my lead." Reuben knew the layout. Tricia didn't. I grasped her hand. "Stick with me."

We slipped into the transit tunnel. I glanced over my shoulder. One pursuer's flashlight had rounded the curve, beam lowered.

We ran shy of a full sprint, the dust carpet dampening our footfalls. I kept the wall off my right and periodically pulsed my flashlight to reassure that our path ahead remained clear.

People in the world above the streets don't know real darkness. Every nighttime alley or basement or bedroom contains a hair of illumination to orient us. Even with our eyes closed, blood vessels in our lids tint the faintest rays and reassure us we're alive. But in tomb-like darkness, we hold on to sound and touch as if those senses too might be lost.

Tricia paced me on the left, her hand soft yet firm in mine. For the briefest moment, I felt we might outrun not only the Drax search party, but all the shards of our past and future that could slice like broken glass.

An easy arc of the wall to the northeast told me Concord Avenue Station lay beyond a Y junction. About a hundred yards past the branch, I tapped my flashlight once again to alert Reuben behind us.

"This service passage runs parallel to the main and reconnects further down, so we can't get trapped." I steered her by the hand and protected her head from the low entrance like a cop loading a prisoner into a squad car. Far narrower than a transit tunnel, service passages had the same high ceilings. We crouched close and waited for Reuben's arrival. I felt her thigh warm against mine and listened to her catch her breath.

But Reuben didn't show.

"Shit." I stuck my head into the transit tunnel and listened. Nothing. Realization struck—we were in deep trouble. "I think he got confused and went left at the junction," I said. Another realization: tons of earth separated me from Reuben's ready intelligence and cool judgment. I touched the whistle draped against my breastbone—a form of communications, but only as a last resort.

"He'll figure it out and backtrack, right?" Tricia asked.

"Better be fast, before Drax lights up the junction."

We waited one minute. Two. Four. My stomach churned as time ate away our hard-earned lead. I considered racing back to find Reuben ahead of Drax, but wised up. The light or sound required to flush him out would attract Drax like flies to a carcass.

I retrieved my army surplus sighting scope and trained it on the intersection behind us.

First, a shimmer, a ghost of a light, enough to jumpstart the pulse. A concrete surface blinked blue-white and then blackened, followed by the overlapping brightness of multiple flashlights in motion.

As the figures came into view, I relayed the scene in whispers. "One... two, three... four... wait... yeah, four of them."

"What are they doing?" she asked, holding her breath for my answer.

"Just walking and talking. Can you make out what they're saying?"

Tricia cupped hands behind her ears. "No, too far away. Guns?"

"Not that I can see, but I can't see much. Hang on… They stopped—sweeping the ground, checking footprints. One is gesturing… pointing… now with the flashlight. Crap." The beam stabbed my eye through the scope. I blinked, blinded, switched eyes, and peered again. Outlines, faint but unmistakable in a crosshatch of reflected rays. "They split up. Two of them are heading this way in no big hurry. But they didn't see me." I lowered my scope and turned to her. "Let's get ahead of them. Maybe Reuben will be waiting where the tunnels reconnect."

In the darkness, I stood and grasped her forearm to help her to her feet. She rose with a rustle of denim and I felt her hands on my shoulders, her cheek close to mine.

"I've got an idea," she whispered, her breath hot against my ear. "Do you trust me?"

CHAPTER 26

The two men lumbered toward me, unaware of my presence. One was big, the other bigger, but when you're on your knees, everyone looks oversized.

Once they reached the halfway point between the branch and me, I raised my voice. "Please don't shoot! I give up."

I knelt at the transit tunnel's centerline, arms like goalposts. My backpack lay in a pool of gloom a dozen feet ahead.

A blast of light struck me dead in the face. I squinted.

"Well lookee here." The cocksure voice was unmistakable. Hard Ass.

"I'm not running away." I held motionless for self-preservation. Shrouds of darkness make people jumpy, and jumpy people do dangerous things.

Hard Ass walked like a gunslinger at high noon. "I oughta just shoot you but the boss has something else in mind. Where's Klein?"

"Lost. I tried to find him but you got in the way," I said wearily, as if resigned to defeat. "But Reuben's not part of this."

Hard Ass exaggerated a chuckle. "I fell for that bullshit at the train station and let him go. Not this time. Once we track him down, you're both dead."

My mouth went dry.

The two silhouettes came to a stop at my backpack. In the brief reflections, I recognized Gorilla playing his usual role of mute malevolence, the amplifier and enforcer of threat. And I noticed a greater danger: a gun in Hard Ass's meaty mitt. Tricia's plan had gone from questionable to improbable. *Think.*

While the pocked concrete took its toll on my knees, I teetered and watched Gorilla unzip my pack, upend it, and shake out the contents. The *thwack* of the Hasselblad against concrete shot straight up my spine. In a faraway hospital bed, Alfred must've shuddered.

"I'm not armed," I said. "So put away the gun."

Hard Ass gave his head a slow, authoritative shake. "How do I know you're not armed?" He commanded Gorilla with a nod in my direction. "Check him."

The giant reached me in three long steps, bent like a front loader, and thumped every square inch of fabric on my body with five-finger paddles. Satisfied, he straightened and stepped back.

The gun had to go. I tried to make eye contact with Hard Ass, but in the choked glow I picked up only pinpoint reflections in black sockets. "I told you, I'm not armed, and never have been. Recognize a pattern? I'm not looking for trouble." I took a gamble. "What are you afraid of?"

Hard Ass stepped so close to me I whiffed the garlic leeching through his hide. He set down his handheld so the beam illuminated my thighs. With one hand, he intertwined his fingers in my hair and squeezed as if juicing a lemon. It hurt like hell, but I wouldn't give the satisfaction of a whine. With his other hand, he pressed the barrel of the gun against my forehead. My breath caught in my throat. He spoke meticulously. "I'm sure as hell not scared of *you*."

"Then why the weapon? Since your boss won't let you use it."

Hard Ass spun the gun with a deft flip so the butt pressed against my hairline. "I *am* allowed to beat you 'til you talk like a retard," he snarled. "Now, what're you doing down here?"

That surprised me. I chewed on his words for a moment. Was only Hard Ass clueless, or his bosses too? Maybe they'd never noticed the tiny green dot appearing in each photo they'd swiped from Alfred's lab. Or maybe they'd noticed, but couldn't explain it. Indeed, the complex chain of logic—from laser measurements, to advanced triangulations, to proof of fraud, to bilking the citizenry, to funding fascism's rise—would require a mental pole vault.

I took another calculated risk. "I'll fess up, but not to you. I want to talk to Tony."

Hard Ass rocked his shoulders with a derisive laugh. "You're wasting your time. Mr. Drax is in charge here."

"Rudolph," I said, sounding spent, enough for Hard Ass to read nothing into my name-dropping, or so I hoped.

"That's what I said, and Tony doesn't scratch his balls unless Mr. Drax gives permission." Suddenly, Hard Ass slammed on the brakes and glared down his nose. "I don't like all your questions, Pixie."

"I didn't ask any questions."

The face in front of me twisted with rage. Hard Ass extended a leg to brace his bulk and shoved me backwards. I lost balance and toppled, but with enough sideways motion to whip out one leg. I kicked the man's flashlight and sent it spinning like a propeller.

I glimpsed what followed in the briefest of pulses from the rotating beam. Each image appeared and vanished fast, perhaps too fast for the guards to make sense of it all. A lithe young woman appeared in baggy jeans and a black, skin-tight top, the sweatshirt cast aside. Every muscle taut, she held the bolt cutters back and high like a batter at the plate.

More images. The tool mid-swing. Her jaw muscles bulging, eyes on fire. Impact and a muffled crack like the wet snap of a sapling. The gun mid-flight followed by clattering and skidding. Hard Ass, his face stretched with shock, mouth gaping with a piercing shriek. Then, a moment later, Hard Ass following his shoulder to the stone floor, buckled at the waist, forearm pressed to his belly.

By the time Gorilla produced a flashlight, she'd spun to face him. She drew the bolt cutters back for one more blow. But Gorilla was too far away. Two hundred fifty pounds of muscle had pivoted to fend off her attack.

I charged like a defensive lineman. My shoulder struck Gorilla's midsection with the energy transfer of pushing a stalled car. I flailed my fists at the wall of gut—once, twice. My third struck diaphragm, punched out an audible exhale, but did no real damage. The big man released his flashlight, clamped my shoulders from overhead, and wrenched my upper body. I seemed to spin in space before descending to the concrete. My back slammed down hard. Gorilla was on me before I'd restored my balance, crushing the wind from me. He swung a furious fist. The first blow struck just outside my eye with a force that temporarily stole my sight. Arms crossed overhead, I grimaced in anticipation of the next punch. But it never came.

I blinked my vision clear. Above me, Tricia had mounted Gorilla's back, her legs pretzeled around his midsection. The man wore the bolt cutter's nippers like a bow tie, the long handles V'd around his throat. From behind, Tricia pulled the handles hard. Gorilla, his eyes bulging and panicked, tried to wedge his fingers willy-nilly to relieve the constriction, but the leverage was insurmountable.

"Five more seconds," Tricia said, her voice pressurized with exertion.

Sure enough, Gorilla's face transformed from pink to red to purple. His eyes rolled back in his head and his body went limp as if his bones had dissolved. I shoved up hard. Gorilla's bulk settled sideways to the concrete in a heap.

Somewhere in the dark behind me, Hard Ass panted and groaned. I leaped to my feet with Gorilla's flashlight. Hard Ass was on hands and knees but with one arm pressed to his belly from below. He fished about with his free hand, searching. *The gun.* I lit up the weapon in the dust a yard away and grabbed it.

"Enough, Mr. Daley," I said. You never forget your enemy's name. "I've got your pistol."

Hard Ass let out a long breath and sat back, his right arm easy on his lap. "She broke my fucking arm."

"Be glad it wasn't your skull," Tricia replied as she found rope among the pile emptied from my pack. "I checked the big guy. No gun, but he'll wake up any minute now."

"Valentine will hunt you down and kill you," Hard Ass said between labored breaths.

We couldn't let them follow us to Alpha Portal, but ropes would be a temporary solution at best. Steady friction against concrete would wear through the bindings in minutes.

"I've got an idea," I said. Then to Hard Ass, "Go sit next to your friend."

Hard Ass radiated pain and outrage. "Fuck you, Pixie."

I stepped closer and dropped to a squatting position, eye to eye. "If you don't, I will rope the wrist of your broken wing and drag you over there like a bag of laundry. And while you're at it, give her your radio." I waited.

Hard Ass pressed his lips into a line, lumbered to his feet, and handed Tricia the walkie-talkie. With another painful effort, he lowered his bulk alongside the prostrate Gorilla who was beginning to stir.

"Don't wait too long," Tricia cautioned.

I slipped her the gun. "The safety is off."

"I can see that," she replied, training the pistol on Hard Ass's torso. "When we shoot them, let me do it, okay?" she said, deliciously dancing between serious and sarcastic.

I dragged Gorilla's right leg parallel with Hard Ass's until their boots touched. I bound their ankles, running multiple loops before turning ninety degrees to compress the binding.

"Ow," Hard Ass said. "You'll cut off the blood flow."

I stood, satisfied with my handiwork. "It'll get better once we start walking."

"Walking?"

I grinned down at him. "You were never in a three-legged race when you were a kid?"

. . . . .

We headed out, with our three-legged prisoner unit stomping ahead in sullen synchronization. Tricia had offered her sweatshirt so Hard Ass could jerry-rig a sling for his fractured forearm. This produced a small but welcome reprieve from his venomous threats.

Tricia and I took turns holding the pistol until I noticed that our prisoners cooperated better with *her* finger on the trigger. Apparently, bone-splitting, coma-inducing underworld Harpies commanded more respect than grad students in architecture.

The Adolphus Avenue straightaway delivered us to the Ptarmigan Street Station after twenty minutes of shambling progress. Bordered by a swirling banister, a marble staircase rose to the underside of a city street.

Tricia leveled the gun at our prisoners from a healthy distance.

"I need two minutes max," I said.

"Take your time," she replied with the confidence of a card shark. "If you hear a gunshot, no need to hurry back."

I wound my way through the service passage, picked open the now-familiar steel gate, and returned.

"All set." I directed Hard Ass and Gorilla toward the low doorway from which I'd emerged.

Both men registered uneasy expressions.

I placed my hands on my hips and vented an audible sigh. "Don't worry. Cold-blooded execution suits your bosses, not us." But never leave leverage on the table. "Unless you refuse to get in there."

Our tripod tagalongs complied, twisting sideways and adjusting their lopsided gait to the narrow passageway's twists and turns. Tricia and I took up the rear. I signaled her to remain back as the twosome moved beyond the heavy gate I'd left open.

"Make yourselves comfortable." I swung the steel barrier closed with a resounding clunk, then checked to make sure the lock was secure.

"What's that mean?" Gorilla asked, to my astonishment. I'd never heard him speak.

I dropped my voice. "At the end of the passage behind you is a *mystery spur*, a dead end that doesn't appear on any subway map." Gorilla appeared stunned, as if I'd asked him to spell *bougainvillea*.

Hard Ass looked worried. "You're leaving us here? For how long?"

His words brought to mind a question I'd been stewing about. "Have you ever been here before?"

"Of course not."

Tricia appeared beside me, curious. "In all your eavesdropping around Drax headquarters," I continued, "ever heard anybody mention a subway spur?"

"Hell no."

"Ever heard the name Richard Baumgartner?"

Hard Ass narrowed his eyes with mistrust. "Why should I tell you anything, Tremaine? You'll still lock us up."

"Get off it, Daley." I was fed up with the tough-guy song and dance, the memory still fresh of a cold gun barrel against my forehead. "Level with me and I'll share a little tip that might keep you morons alive until more morons show up."

Hard Ass dialed down the heat. "No, I never heard of… what's his name?"

"Richard Baumgartner."

"Never heard of him."

I believed him, not that his ignorance proved anything. But Alfred's theory that his lover's body rested in the crates seemed a little less plausible.

"What's the tip?" Gorilla said.

I smiled reassuringly. "Keep following the passage behind you. You'll get to a room full of wooden crates stacked floor-to-ceiling, hundreds of them."

"What's inside 'em?" Gorilla was becoming a conversationalist.

I forced a blank expression. "Bomb shelter supplies, in case the Soviets drop the big one. Food, water, medicine. Maybe a pocket knife so you can cut those ropes." I pointed to their chummy ankles.

"Leave us one of the flashlights," Hard Ass said, not quite a demand but short of polite. An hour earlier, he'd complained he wasn't allowed to shoot me dead. Now he wanted a favor.

I offered the prisoners my last advice as Tricia and I strolled away. "No need for flashlights. You'll find plenty of candles and matches, maybe even gas lanterns. Just yank up the slats and feel around inside. You'll be fine."

. . . . .

A minute later, Tricia stopped me short of the transit tunnel. "You've got one wicked streak. You better hope the big guy sticks his hand into those caskets first. Hard Ass will have a heart attack."

"Wicked streak? This from Trachea Tricia, master of the timed blackout?"

"Not trachea. Carotids. The brain blinks out quick without blood, but you've got to cut off both main arteries for the technique to work."

I couldn't hold back a smile. Surely she was in on the joke, even if every word was true.

She smiled back. "The handles of hedge shears work too, but then there's the risk of snipping off your opponent's fingers."

"You're shitting me."

She twisted her lips into a squiggle. "Actually, I'm not."

"How do you know this stuff? I mean, for real."

She shrank back a bit, as if worried how far my questions might go. Still, she pondered before appearing to reach some internal decision. "Improvisational defense. I got into a bad relationship—went fast from separation to restraining order to shadows on my curtains at night."

"You took matters into your own hands—literally?"

She lifted her face to mine, her chin leading in a kind of declaration of independence. "I didn't feel safe, so I trained until I did."

"And who'd want to waste all of that good training?"

Her new candor reversed direction. "I told you I wouldn't say what happened, so don't ask."

"I won't, but whatever you did to the guy—"

She cut me off with a scowl. "Stop fishing, Lucas." She closed her eyes for the duration of a deep breath before continuing more deliberately. "Listen, because I won't repeat it, okay?"

I nodded and waited.

"I never killed anybody, never maimed anybody, and never hurt anybody who didn't deserve it. The judge disagreed, but he never heard the truth." Her eyes glossed with fresh moisture. "He only heard what the lawyers said, and that had *nothing* to do with the truth."

How much had I told her about the Drax legal team and the damage done by their lies? Six years had passed, but the bus ride home from the courtroom felt like yesterday, holding hands with Mom so tight our fingers cramped.

"But Alfred heard the truth—from me," she said. "I held nothing back, not one detail. That was when he put me in charge of the shop." She studied my eyes for a reaction. "So does that work?"

I didn't understand.

"Alfred trusted me. Doesn't that prove I'm not a horrible person?"

As I peered back, I searched for the right words. But nothing sounded right in my head, so I touched her shoulders, pulled her to my chest, and squeezed, expecting her to push me away. She didn't.

We had no time to waste, but nothing was wasted in those seconds I held her. And I would have held her longer if not for the sound of a distant whistle, Reuben's whistle, three blasts at even intervals, the universal distress signal.

CHAPTER 27

"How many of them?" Tricia spoke from close behind with the faintest whisper. Renegade locks of hair teased the back of my neck.

I tweaked the scope's focus ring. "Four."

"Others must've come down later. Can you make them out?"

"Not yet." I lay prone, my midsection and thighs settled into the carpet of grit, the scope steady on my forearms. The subjects of my reconnaissance milled about Maggard Street Station a few hundred feet ahead, a straightaway separating us. As if expecting visitors, one of the men periodically swung a flashlight in our direction, but futilely. We lay obscured behind stacks of supplies, abandoned by utility companies when the project got mothballed.

"What are they doing?" she asked.

"Waiting, I guess. They're spread out. The guy holding the flashlight is leaning against the banister. One's pacing, one's sitting halfway up the stairs, and one's on the landing." The stale odor of sweat snaked up from my collar.

"Waiting for us?"

"Maybe, maybe not. Without radio communication, they can't know about their buddies. As far as they're concerned, Hard Ass and Gorilla are bringing us in."

The pacing man switched on his flashlight and ascended the stone stairs. He halted just below the seated man and leaned in as if exchanging a few private words. Why the secrecy? "Wait a minute," I said. "That's Valentine, and he's talking to Tony Drax. He must've arrived later."

"The other two?"

"The guy by the banister's big like Gorilla. I don't recognize him."

The exchange with Tony ended and Valentine cast his light upward toward the man perched on the landing. My throat constricted, cutting off my next breath. I twisted to face her in the dark, the dust squeaking beneath me. "The fourth guy is Reuben."

• • • • •

We needed an advantage. In desperate search of one, we zigzagged through service passages and approached the station from the southeast, the river to our backs. The effort seemed hopeless but Tricia had insisted. Overwhelming Hard Ass and Gorilla must've made her feel invincible. She'd whispered of "another sneak attack," unwilling to accept a cruel new reality. Reuben was now a hostage, and instead of two, we faced three adversaries, one of them a highly skilled soldier.

"But we have a gun," she'd said, searching for agreement in my eyes.

"You ever fired one?" I replied.

She said nothing.

"Me neither." I took no pleasure in exposing her flawed judgment, keenly aware of my many screw-ups.

Another factor became clear as we crouched in the nearest service passage to Maggard Street Station. Valentine had chosen his command post wisely to eliminate the element of surprise. We'd stand out amidst the featureless floor and walls of the straightaway.

I tested the air—a precautionary habit by that point—and a pint-sized idea tottered into my consciousness. It was a ludicrous little notion, terribly dangerous and complex, and requiring both advanced planning and rehearsal, neither of which we had time for. Hard Ass and Gorilla would soon fail to report, and Valentine would turn to Reuben for answers, extracting them by whatever means had worked against his prisoners in lawless jungles.

I should've sent the idea away, but as we huddled there surveying our hopelessness through the scope, the idea tugged on my shirtsleeve like a single-minded child.

What the hell. No harm testing my brainstorm with Tricia to gauge her reaction. As I turned to meet her eyes in the thinnest vapor of light from the station, the radio on her belt crackled to life, filling the air with military authority. "Mr. Daley, this is Valentine. Authenticate your location. Over."

We pounced on the radio as if speed could reinsert the broadcast, but slapping the OFF button changed nothing. We were as exposed as bucks in a clearing.

Fresh swaths of illumination from the station swept the ashen surfaces of the transit tunnel, searching for the source of the aberrant echo. Tricia's face lit up with fear and apology. "I'd been testing to see if maybe—I—I forgot to switch it off."

Valentine had probably been trying to radio Hard Ass all along, but now, without barriers of earth and concrete, the signal reached a receiver.

"Mr. Daley, make your presence known." Again, the voice was Valentine's, but not through the radio, rather through the stagnant air that separated us, the acoustics bringing his voice frightfully close.

Five seconds passed.

"Then my assumption was incorrect," Valentine went on. "Lucas Tremaine, you should be thankful. I lost one of my best scouts near Kanangao when he failed to suppress his walkie-talkie. A foot patrol first wounded and then executed him. Reveal yourself now and you might do better."

Another five seconds passed, my mind reeling—what to do?

"Mr. Tremaine, your bargaining position is weak. I have your friend, and if you don't comply in thirty seconds, I will cut him behind his right knee. He might bleed to death, or might not. I've seen it go both ways."

My pulse raced. I might've dismissed such a threat coming from Tony Drax—he didn't have the spine. But Valentine was an unknown at best, a mercenary lunatic at worst. I had no choice. But Tricia did. "You've got the film," I whispered to her. "Go northeast and find Alpha Portal. I can talk us out of this."

A wave of uncertainty splashed her features and she started to speak but stopped herself. The anger and determination roared back. She shook her head. "I've got the gun and the element of surprise. I'll… I'll think of something."

Valentine rendered our debate moot. "Fifteen seconds left, and don't forget to bring your companion. Clever business with all your footprints—got us all turned around. But shoe sizes are a dead giveaway."

A breeze chilled the skin on my forearms, but there was no breeze, only our lives at stake. I wouldn't risk Tricia or Reuben, not for Dad, Mom, Alfred—not for all the progress we'd made, and we'd come so far.

"One more thing," Valentine said. "Since you've got Mr. Daley's radio, I assume you've got his weapon. Hold the barrel by your fingertips and extend both hands high above your head. If I don't see this, I cut Mr. Klein."

"Okay," I shouted, my heart like a stone in my chest. I rose and stepped into the transit tunnel. "We're walking your way."

. . . . .

"Where are they?" Valentine said coldly. He stood hands on hips, legs slightly spread, boots firm as if bolted to the concrete.

I'd been trying to figure out the seating arrangement. They'd placed me dead center a few marble stairs up from ground level, with Tricia below left, and Reuben above right and out of my sight. Maybe Valentine wanted to survey their faces for evidence of lying. Or maybe he wanted to mess with our heads.

"Where are they?" Valentine repeated, his impatience amplified. Gorilla Two stood alert, halfway to the landing, his back against the winding banister. Tony Drax, black stitches above his eye from Reuben's revenge, lurked in the shadows with his arms folded across his chest.

"Why do you care?" I replied. It was a serious question. Valentine seemed to treat his subordinates as tools. Hard Ass was like a crescent wrench, adjustable but not ideal for any particular task. Gorilla was a hammer, designed to pound things. But like all tools, the men we'd secured behind an iron gate were replaceable. So why bother?

"Answer the question," Valentine said, lifting the corner of his upper lip with a canine snarl.

Then I understood. Valentine, an ex-soldier with khaki blood, had lost his subordinates to an architecture nerd and a girl. "This makes you look bad to Rudolph. We disarmed and locked up *your* men, that *you* trained." Our leverage paled compared to Valentine's, with our three lives dangling by a whim in a wild underground, but it was leverage nevertheless.

The harsh light deepened the crevices in Valentine's face and reduced his eye sockets to circular shadows. He relaxed his expression enough to allow a synthetic smile to spread across his lips. "There's a quiet city street twenty feet above us, but it might as well be a thousand miles away. You're in a war zone." He squared his shoulders and widened his stance. "No police, no kindness of strangers, no phones to call for help. And no laws. Understand?"

I said nothing.

"This battlefield won't exist in a few weeks. It'll be buried, along with whoever doesn't make it out. Now maybe you don't care. I've met enemy soldiers like that, defiant to the end. But even they cared about their buddies." Valentine took three easy steps toward Tricia, a foot-long knife retrieved from nowhere now dangling from his hand. Tricia stiffened, jaw fixed. Valentine locked his gaze on mine, waiting, the threat requiring no words.

The seating arrangement suddenly made sense. Tricia was Valentine's leverage, in full view.

I swallowed. "They're locked up in a spur." Valentine showed no reaction. Perhaps *spur* meant nothing to him. But before I could clarify, he crouched, pressed down Tricia's ankle with one hand, and laid the knife's edge against the back of her knee with the other hand. She gasped.

"Don't do that!" I flashed open palms. "It's a section of tunnel with a dead end—doesn't appear on the maps." Again, no recognition. "I'm telling you the truth."

Strangely, Valentine glanced at Reuben as if seeking validation. But then again, Reuben radiated the earnestness of Captain Kangaroo.

"He's telling the truth," Reuben said with absurd calm from behind my shoulder. "It branches from a transit tunnel but goes nowhere. They hid it with cinderblock and stucco."

Valentine lowered the knife from Tricia's leg. Her shoulders eased. I released my breath.

As if sensing an opportunity, my bastard child of an idea tugged again on my shirtsleeve.

No. Too risky. I sent the child away. "One service passage winds back to it," I told Valentine, my voice quivering, half performance and half physiological reaction to imagining Tricia's face gray from blood loss. "Your men are behind a reinforced iron gate."

"Draw me a map."

Another tug. Success would require coordination among the three of us, but that would be impossible—we couldn't communicate with each other. Or could we?

The child fidgeted.

"A map isn't enough," I said. "There's no key to the lock, but I know how to pick it." Speaking the truth felt natural and believable, even though the child had a different destination in mind, miles from our impromptu jail.

"He's not lying," Reuben said, unaware of the insistent imp. "The tools are in his bag."

On Valentine's command, Gorilla Two produced the pick set from my backpack. More validation.

The child yanked my sleeve, demanding commitment. It was too risky, but too risky compared to what? *You're both dead*, Hard Ass had said to Reuben and me. After retrieving his men, Valentine would probably finish the job. No plan was too risky against such hopelessness.

"We can show you where," I said and paused, hoping to attract my friends' full attention. "A mile and a half to the southeast."

The child smiled with satisfaction.

Reuben sighed. "Toward the river," he said, signaling that he understood, however reluctantly. But what about Tricia? I gambled on a sideways glance. She seemed preoccupied, as if plotting her own attack.

· · · · ·

Valentine designed our marching order with soldierly brilliance. He placed me in the lead, far from my companions. Gorilla Two followed me with the flashlight. Reuben marched solo in third place. Valentine and Tony brought up the rear surrounding Tricia, the meat in the middle of their leverage sandwich.

"I've seen every trick, Mr. Tremaine," Valentine said, "so don't waste your time—and don't waste your friend." He slapped the knife in its sheath for punctuation. "Anything stupid and she gets the first cut."

I needed Tricia to understand our true destination. Her life might depend on it. But how to tip her off without raising suspicion? Plodding along in silence wasn't helping.

I angled my head to one side to project my voice to the rear. "Why haven't you asked what we're doing down here like Daley did?"

Mimicking his toolbox twin, Gorilla Two said nothing.

"Shut up, Tremaine," Valentine growled.

"Well, if you're waiting for us to tell you, I wouldn't hold your breath."

Reuben signaled back with a cough. Gorilla Two shoved me hard at the base of my neck. I staggered before righting and shrugged my backpack into position.

A minute passed. The static air carried streaks of vegetable decay. With new intensity, I studied the footprints Reuben, Andy, and I had left behind, but my own shadow sliced up the view. More defined was the elevation change as we began our slow descent toward the river.

I cooked up a different angle and gave it a try. "It's all her fault," I railed into the void, my voice echoing, "her and her senile grandfather. But *no*, she doesn't say a damn thing!"

Gorilla Two's next blow sent me crashing and skidding, dust billowing, particles like colliding galaxies in the bitter light. I rolled on my side to project my grand finale toward the rear of the column. "Penny for your thoughts, bitch?"

"Shut up, Lucas," Tricia replied.

Gorilla Two reached down, wrapped his meaty paws around my neck, and yanked me to my feet.

"Okay, okay," I pleaded with hands held aloft, promising to toe the line. I resumed my lead, wracking my brain to recall our training session. Tricia had learned about heavier-than-air stink damp and how it settles in low spots like an invisible pond. How the copper coins gave a last-ditch warning. How the sulfurous stench falsely vanished as the toxins destroyed sense of smell. How the next thing to fail was clear thinking, and how the dead air of the sealed subway produced more powerful buildups than Calcutta's rankest sewer. We'd told her how our first expedition had retreated with moments to spare.

But had we told her where? My heart sank. Even if we had, the dizzying maze of featureless tunnels gave few navigational clues. Unaware, she would usher the intruder into her lungs.

A cone of glow from Gorilla Two's flashlight shot ahead and landed on a small, familiar pile: the lanyard and discolored penny we'd left behind weeks earlier before our hasty retreat. We approached the shoreline of a toxic pool. No time to pause for reflection and slow the column's momentum. I filled my lungs to near bursting, held my breath, and strode forward without hesitation because there could be no turning back.

I felt a strange resignation, impossibly at peace with our impossible situation. But no, this was chemistry eroding my judgment. Amazing! Even on the pool's periphery, the air contained hints of mind-altering poison. I shook off my euphoria and focused on each forward step.

"Who farted?" Gorilla Two said, and I wanted to laugh at such inauspicious words from the mute ox, but dared not risk an inhale. I spun to survey the column of followers. Reuben was tight-lipped and alert, having read the markings all along, his lungs also filled to capacity.

Gorilla Two's head bobbled off plumb and his eyes rolled to white. He settled to his knees as if readying for Sunday prayer. "Make do, make do," he recited to an absent listener, "and we will too." His hand relaxed and the flashlight tumbled. I snatched it up and spotlighted the rear of our column. There, the fates of Valentine, Tricia, and Tony rested on the random cadence of individual breathing.

"Trix, your penny," I cried out and fought the instinct to replace my expelled breath. The stench of rotten eggs teased my nostrils. My eyes watered. Fifties doo-wop music played from a nook in my brain.

Tricia fumbled at her chest and lifted the coin before widening eyes. She understood, but soon enough? To her left, Tony's legs wobbled at the knees. His expression blossomed as if witnessing the eighth wonder of the world. He raised a childlike gaze to the ceiling, searching for answers.

I charged toward them.

Forehead creased with fury, Valentine hollered, "What the—" before his speech decomposed to a dry gargle.

Tricia angled her head to locate me behind the glare from the bouncing flashlight. Her eyes lost their focus, balance failed. She tipped against Tony. They both collapsed at Valentine's feet in a dusty pile of limbs and denim.

The ex-soldier dropped to one knee and I feared some kind of classic combat maneuver. But his rutted face swirled with the same trippy befuddlement.

Two things had to happen fast and simultaneously. I glanced sideways at Reuben, also in motion, his face red with exertion and pleading lungs. "I'll drag her clear," I said and fended off another urge to inhale. "Get the weapons." Only seconds of oxygen remained.

I looked ahead. Valentine, his face now contorted with rage, swung his arm in a wide arc until the knife blade creased the skin below Tricia's jaw line. Her eyes flared wide with shock and horror.

I gasped, a deadly mistake.

Time slowed. The melody from an old Drifters record pierced my thoughts. My leg muscles liquefied. I tasted vinegar. I toppled forward and rolled, first to my shoulder and then onto my back. I peered skyward into black.

At night the stars put on a show for free.

I thanked small blessings, that Tricia's nightmare would end mercifully fast once blood stopped flowing to her brain.

And darling you can share it all with me.

The violin section swelled and Tricia's scream reverberated in our concrete wilderness but then ended abruptly as if lifting the needle from a record.

CHAPTER 28

Hardness beneath my back. Scratchy fingertips held to my wrist, on my neck. Letting go. Smoother hands on my cheeks, pressing and testing. Letting go.

Later, muffled voices. An angry question, a resolute reply. Damped footsteps. Scraping. Lid unscrewing from a metal canteen. Wet, easy slaps to my face with soft hands.

Light beyond eyelids, then images. Tricia and lines of worry on pretty skin, dark hair pulled back, the usual deviant locks arcing down to dance before bottomless brown eyes.

Her voice. "You in there?"

"You're alive," I heard myself say, sounding raw and metallic.

She smiled with her lips closed before flashing a pretend frown. "Bitch?"

I felt a rush of relief but she couldn't possibly notice, my face as flaccid as the rest of my body.

Reuben appeared too, his left eye socket and cheekbone rosy and bruised. I peered over his shoulder to a narrow line of light tracing the wall of the tunnel to the curved ceiling. I lay on the floor, face up, my head against one backpack, my feet elevated by another—classic Reuben medic protocol for an ailing explorer. He always knew his stuff. He squatted to one side, the knees of his jeans caked with dirt. Tricia knelt to the other side, hands draped on her thighs. Memory rushed back. Stink damp and a desperate scramble. "You're okay." I exhaled.

"Yeah." Her eyes twinkled with hidden happiness.

I reexamined Reuben's shiner. "You're attractive."

"I got Valentine's knife and dragged you two clear," he said. "The big guy started puking so I pulled him out next."

"Should've left him in the stink," Tricia muttered.

Reuben shot her a rebuke. "That's not how we do things."

"I was kidding."

I had my doubts.

Reuben shifted his weight from one foot to the other. "Valentine was next because he was lying across Tony, but half of him sort of woke up—"

"Half?" I said.

"The pissed off half." Reuben caressed his cheekbone. "He jumped up, slugged me pretty good, puffed up his chest with a big breath, and *timber*." He demonstrated with a toppling forearm. "They're both tied up against the wall"—he doubled the volume of his voice—"probably scraping at their ropes, but we'll redo them before they make any progress."

"Fuck you," came Valentine's reply.

I allowed myself a moment of silent celebration at Valentine's disgrace, his entire strike force dismantled by a habitual student, a shop clerk, and an insurance actuary. "What about Tony?"

Tricia and Reuben exchanged knowing glances.

"I got to him last, and only after dealing with Valentine," Reuben explained, "so he breathed more of it than anyone else. He's not looking so good."

I heaved myself up on one elbow. My friends tugged my shoulders until I sat cross-legged. My head felt cleaved down the middle.

Reuben had perched a flashlight on its end, casting the scene in a hazy glow. The air danced with particles raised during the battle. Bound at ankles and wrists, Valentine and Gorilla Two stared silently from across the tunnel. The big man appeared to accept his circumstances as another shift on the clock. Valentine seethed like a soaked cat.

I rubbed my temples, blinked away the fog, and sought out Tricia's gaze. "Valentine had his knife at your throat. You screamed."

"That's what Reuben told me," she replied, her voice unsteady. "I don't remember it." I read in her expression a mixture of awe and terror, perhaps reserved for those who get to peer into the precipice, turn on their heels, and walk back home.

"I saw it all happen as I was running toward them," Reuben said, now somber. "Tony held the knife away until Valentine passed out."

. . . . .

We prepared for our exodus. After my exposure, I didn't feel entirely present, more like a distant observer, so Reuben wisely assigned me the easiest task of stowing gear.

I hypothesized that a return to normalcy—consciousness, movement, breathing—could overrule the effects of the toxins, but they lingered like the acrid odor of smoke long after a house fire.

Reuben checked on Tony. The heir to the Drax fortune lay flat on his back, head propped on a rolled-up sweatshirt. He remained unconscious and, according to Reuben, exhibited a weak pulse, sluggish pupil dilation, and rapid breathing. I didn't fully understand the implications, but the furrow in Reuben's brow told me plenty.

Next, Reuben double-checked our prisoners' bindings while Tricia guarded from a healthy distance. She may not have known much about guns, but her stance said otherwise, with her legs spread and arms extended, sighting down the barrel at Valentine's temple.

We approached a decision point. Gear stowed, I knelt alongside Tony as if my own investigation might reveal a course of action. His face and lips were the color of grade school paste. I thumbed up an eyelid. The pupil danced left and right before rolling out of view. To my astonishment, his legs lurched and elongated, fingers flexed and jaw clenched. For a moment, I thought my probing had triggered something, but then I realized: he was having a seizure. I rolled him to his side to prevent choking.

The episode ended a minute later. Reuben ushered our trio into a crouch out of earshot.

"Listen good," he said. "Hydrogen sulfide poisoning has a tipping point. Stay on the safe side of it and the body fights back. But go beyond and… well, things get worse."

"How much worse?" Tricia asked, but I knew the answer.

Reuben braced himself. "He'll die without treatment."

Hope vented like air from a balloon, but Tricia defied our change in fortunes. "How can you be so sure?"

"I already suspected because he's neurologic—eyes all goofy—but I hoped he'd turn the corner," Reuben said. "The seizure proved he won't."

I wrung my hands, now pewter with accumulated grime. "The minute we clear Alpha Portal, we'll drop a dime and send help."

Reuben gave a single, definitive shake of the head. "Too many time-consuming steps. Laminar necrosis has begun, meaning death of cells in the cerebral cortex. The process can be stopped with an injection of sodium nitrite, but it has to happen fast."

I let my butt rock back to the concrete and wrapped my arms around my knees. In the days before our infiltration, I'd imagined every possible complication, and how to survive. But I'd never imagined our tiny crew of amateurs responsible for any lives but our own. I had led Valentine's party into a toxic trap, a decision I'd probably re-examine forever. But far more vexing for the moment, the immediate decision would determine the life or death of another human being.

"Screw this," Tricia blurted. "This is their problem. Valentine and Lunchmeat can rescue Tony, and we can get out of here."

"What?" Reuben countered. "We leave them tied up and hope they wriggle free in time?"

Tricia eased up long enough to consider this conundrum. "We toss them the knife and make a break for Alpha Portal. If they follow us, Tony dies."

Reuben shook his head. "You're dreaming. Valentine's so angry he'd gladly sacrifice his boss to burn our asses."

"Then we shoot him in the leg," Tricia said.

Reuben pressed on. "Can we please have a constructive suggestion?"

We were debating in circles. I had to try something. "We pass close to Drax HQ on the way to Alpha Portal."

"You mean we drop off Tony?" Tricia asked.

"He dies if we leave him here," Reuben said.

"We've established that," she said with a huff. "Ever carry a hundred eighty pounds of meat for three miles?"

Had she forgotten Tony saved her life by pushing away Valentine's blade?

Reuben said, "We can rig a stretcher."

Tricia held firm. "Ever carry ninety pounds of meat for three miles?"

"Now you're being difficult," Reuben said.

The bickering wasn't helping, and we paid a price for every passing second. "Valentine's the lunatic," I said, "so we leave him tied up and force the big guy to carry."

Tricia received this with a raised eyebrow. Reuben less so, perhaps considering my lame track record. I continued. "There's a service passage a few hundred feet before the Drax portal. That's where we part ways. The big guy has to fetch help—what choice does he have? We take off. The service passage crosses over to Adolphus. Three turns and twenty minutes later we're at Alpha Portal—" I almost said *and home free* but held off.

Reuben gnawed his lip before saying, "Let's do it."

. . . . .

We jerry-rigged a stretcher from the last of our rope, a sheet of plywood, and two lengths of pipe abandoned by the gas company.

As Valentine simmered nearby, we told Gorilla Two about his role in saving Tony. We included the caveat that his cooperation, or lack thereof, would be judged at gunpoint. He accepted our tutelage nonchalantly, as if recruited to help move a sofa.

Valentine spoke to his musclebound associate. "You help them and you're a traitor."

Gorilla Two shrugged it off. "I'm helping Mr. Drax, not them."

Perfect response, midpoint in the DMZ between Valentine and us. Was he performing? Would he turn on us at first opportunity? I thought not, detecting neither the inclination nor capacity for bullshit.

We got underway. Reuben took first shift at the rear of the stretcher to monitor Tony's health. The big man lugged up front where we could monitor him. He had to be six foot five, but he lost a couple of inches to slumping shoulders, as if he were much older. His haircut looked do-it-yourself.

My curiosity kicked in. "Been working for Drax long?"

"Couple years."

"Like it?"

"It's a paycheck."

"Know much about Drax? I mean… what they do?"

The man glanced like I had a screw loose. "They build buildings."

Yeah, that's what they did, along with a lot of hurting. But why should he need to know? It's a paycheck.

Follow Me Down

A recurring fear bubbled into my consciousness. What if once Cincinnati learned of Drax's crimes, no one cared enough to upset decades of tradition? After all, with Vietnam photos dominating magazine covers with green foliage and crimson blood, World War II in black and white seemed from another era, someone else's era, someone else's problem.

"What about before Drax?" I asked the man, relieving Reuben on stretcher duty.

Another you're-crazy glance. "What's it to you?"

"Just making conversation."

Now Tricia sized me up like I was nuts.

Gorilla Two said, "Drove truck and repossessed appliances for Save-On up in Hamilton."

That fit. About my age, he must've been a local boy, went to Queen City High for all I knew, one of those guys who'd no more speak in class than dance the Merengue. Maybe he tried out for defensive linebacker and even played a few evening games under misty lights, dreaming for a break that wouldn't come. And now, his sprout of ambition stomped to a shriveled stem, he followed orders without asking why because the answer wouldn't change anything.

The hopelessness of it all. My mind must've wandered into a dark place because what happened next struck like lightning from a clear nighttime sky.

Just shy of the final intersection before passing below Drax headquarters, a voice said, "Now," and ten or more men switched on flashlights and materialized from behind columns and shadowed entryways. One man wordlessly relieved me of my stretcher poles. Another, stinking of smokes, brought his stubbled face too close to mine. "Lucas Tremaine?"

A dozen comebacks failed me. "Yes," I replied.

"Rudolph Drax would like a word with you."

CHAPTER 29

"Now what?" Tricia said, sitting beside me and sounding more irritated than scared.

Reuben, his face in shadows, fingered the brass trim on the arms of the leather chair, the massive boardroom tabletop before him. "No choice but to wait. I counted seven guards in the hall."

Rudolph Drax was en route, according to the only thug authorized to speak to us, and he'd refused to answer more questions. When Reuben had tried to describe Tony's affliction, the guard shut him down with a brandish of his pistol.

The carpet and upholstery were as plush as I remembered, but in the darkness of the wee hours, the Drax Museum looked nothing like the place I'd visited one bright afternoon. No Cincinnatians strolled among the models, marveling at Drax achievement. No miniature streetlamps or windows glowed with welcoming amber. No tall replicas cast shadows on phony avenues from phony overhead suns.

The indoor expanse was barely lit by a few track lights, their weak rays harsh and specific, leaving most displays shrouded. Unlike the subway's intriguing darkness, this murk wanted us gone. The deserted buildings and streets exuded a quiet menace, as if I might blink and find myself shrunk, plasticized, and imprisoned within balsawood walls.

I tried to shake off the gloom with chatter. "Where do you think they took Tony?"

"Better be a hospital." Reuben pressed his hands to the table's onyx surface and left behind palm-shaped imprints of moisture. If either of my friends were terrified, they refused to mention it.

"How many doctors have actually seen hydrogen sulfide poisoning?" Tricia wondered aloud. "What if they don't recognize it?"

I was more worried about our own survival than Tony's, but she was right. Misdiagnosis could be fatal.

Before leaving us alone, our captors had methodically unloaded and arranged the contents of our backpacks in the center of the stone conference table. Odd. Was it a Rudolph request, as if an inspection might reveal something? But what could he be looking for? I reminded myself that our final measurements remained taped to Tricia's upper thigh. Drax could confiscate everything else, including Alfred's Hasselblad, if only we could save one film roll—along with our lives.

A door groaned open across the room, doubling our available light until Rudolph Drax entered and shut it more forcefully than necessary. He wore a dress shirt and slacks as wrinkled as a shopping bag, no doubt yesterday's outfit thrown on in a hurry. How telling that the great and powerful Rudolph Drax had bothered with three lowly explorers in the middle of the night. He wanted something. I had to figure out what, and then use the knowledge to our advantage.

"Your numbers have swelled," he said. "There used to be only two of you."

"No, we had a spotter before," I replied, irked at his insensitive memory, "but he quit when you threatened his sister's life, remember?"

Rudolph brought a hand to his chin. "The Chinaman."

"He's Vietnamese," I corrected and tipped my head toward Tricia. "She's our replacement spotter, but that's all she is, so let her go."

Rudolph stepped under a light at the far end of the table, revealing a placid smile. He stared straight into Tricia's eyes, though his words were meant for me. "You're lying again, Mr. Tremaine, just like you lied about who shot the subway photos in the Sunday newspaper."

Tricia jutted her chin. "I'm the granddaughter of Alfred Blumenfeld—"

"I know that."

"—who *your* men put in the hospital while burning down his business. And you killed a decent human being. So no, I'm not going anywhere."

Rudolph took a deep breath and exhaled slowly, as if trying to spread calm. "That's right, Miss Blumenfeld, you're not going anywhere, not until I get some answers."

He strolled, stopping periodically to pluck an item from among our gear—a set of lens filters, an aluminum film can, a roll of electrical tape. "Miss Blumenfeld, why is your grandfather determined to destroy me? No, wait, I already know that. He thinks we funded the Holocaust." He smiled as if remembering a joke. Then a steely expression snapped into place. "Let me rephrase. What do you three spelunkers and that useless subway have to do with Alfred Blumenfeld and his… his infuriating, self-righteous quest?"

Tricia stiffened. I wanted to whisper *don't say a word*. We didn't know what Rudolph knew, and tipping our hand could be disastrous.

The man didn't look up for an answer but moved on as if he'd posed the question rhetorically. He leaned in and hefted the laser with both hands. My breath caught in my throat as he rotated the device, examining the black curved surface. Surely he wouldn't identify it, not with our added gauges and levels.

"Your little mission is well-funded," Rudolph remarked. "Industrial lasers are expensive. A few pioneers in our industry are testing them for land surveying. I like the old-fashioned methods, but we'll see." I said nothing. Rudolph picked up the photo Tricia brought along showing Alfred and Richard receiving their trophy cups.

She leaned forward in her chair. "Do you recognize those men?" I pressed my foot on top of hers.

"You obviously care for your grandfather to carry his photo," Rudolph replied without rising to her challenge.

"They're being recognized for excellence in journalism," she said. "That's Alfred and his—" I bore down harder "—colleague at the newspaper."

I had to control the narrative, but before I could figure out how, a guard materialized at the door and beckoned Rudolph. The guard whispered and Rudolph's forehead pinched with worry.

He spun to address us. "My son is still unconscious. What happened down there?" His tone fell short of demanding, the enunciation less clipped, the edge duller. He needed us.

If we chose to, we could bargain with Tony's diagnosis and treatment to secure our freedom. We could fight fire with fire. The likes of Rudolph Drax would stoop so low without a pang.

But we wouldn't. *That's not how we do things*, Reuben had lectured Tricia.

I squared my shoulders. "He inhaled a toxin called hydrogen sulfide, same as me. But thanks to your man Valentine, his exposure was far longer."

Rudolph took in Valentine's name with a curious tip of the head, and I wondered how much he knew about his subordinate's tactics. Too many generals overlooked the excesses of their foot soldiers. He scowled. "How long were you planning on keeping this toxin a secret?"

Tricia fired back. "Our kidnappers weren't up for chitchat, so back off. Your son would be dead if we hadn't lugged his carcass on a stretcher."

Carcass. Not the best word choice. Reuben intervened. "There's an effective reversal agent, sodium nitrite. Works fast if injected."

"Are you a doctor?" Rudolph asked.

"No, an insurance actuary. We know what kills people."

I could've chuckled but dared not, not with Rudolph's expression toggling between fear and anger as if triggered by an electric jolt. I couldn't predict his next move.

But perhaps predictably, he resumed command. "You'll stay here," he said before storming out ahead of the guard.

. . . . .

We waited. Reuben and Tricia grew bored. They stood and strolled among the shadowed models of office buildings and shopping malls. I kept my seat, my head angled to keep my peripheral vision clear of the missile silo replica.

The door reopened at 4:15 a.m., ninety minutes after Rudolph's exit, and we soon understood the prolonged delay. Valentine showed first, moved to the table, claimed a seat, and crossed his arms, his haggard face wearier but still surly. Hard Ass and the two Gorillas followed and, per the pecking order, took up positions alongside the model of the Covington Mall. Standing erect, Hard Ass singled out Tricia with a sizzling glare, his broken arm now cradled in a proper sling instead of her sweatshirt.

The next arrival astonished me. Pushed in a wheelchair by his father, Tony Drax entered the room, staring straight ahead as if nothing warranted notice. Apparently the ultra-rich don't visit hospitals; hospitals visit them. To my relief, Tony must've received the injection.

Rudolph positioned his son at the distant end of the glossy table and presided from behind the wheelchair. "Let's get this over with." In their own tight circle of artificial light, Drax of today and tomorrow assumed center stage,

Rudolph more present than Tony whose gaze failed to focus on anything in particular.

"Sit down," Rudolph said to Reuben and Tricia, his tone neither accommodating nor antagonistic. Perhaps all routine board meetings began with businesslike civility. I took some comfort, entertaining a shaky hope that cool-headed explanations and well-worded reassurances might secure our release.

Reuben shuffled to the table. Tricia hesitated, resentment like windburn on her cheeks, before plopping into her cushy hot seat.

Rudolph kicked off the proceedings. "You trespassed at the train station—our job site—struck my son unprovoked—"

"Not unprovoked," I corrected. "Unprovoked was how you slugged me at Alfred's shop." The memory clenched my stomach muscles.

"You took and published photos of the subway to undermine a public safety project."

I snorted. "More like public fantasy. You wanted to scare the city into funding *your* fill-in project, and somehow along the way, Delbert Turkel lost his life."

Tony shook his head with small sideways jerks.

Rudolph appeared not to notice his son, or perhaps he'd ignored him. "And now you've injured Drax employees and exposed Tony to a deadly poison."

"No." I raised my voice. "We *rescued* him from a deadly poison." I jabbed a thumb toward Valentine. "G.I. Joe over there detained us at gunpoint and planned to kill us. We took exception."

"This is stupid," Tricia said, her tone more controlled than mine.

"What's that, Miss Blumenfeld?" Rudolph elevated his eyebrows with feigned curiosity.

She upped the volume. "I said this is all stupid. You'll stick to whatever lie fits with all your other lies." She turned toward me, exasperated. "Why argue with these people? They don't care about the truth."

"Wrong," Rudolph responded, still unflappable. "I want to know the truth." He reached into our pile of gear, picked up the Hasselblad, and held it out as evidence. "I want to know only one thing… why did Alfred Blumenfeld send you into the subway?"

Up until that moment, doubt had sapped my confidence. Surely we'd be found out. Surely Rudolph knew. He was relentless and brilliant, with limitless resources at his disposal.

But with his question, my confidence blossomed. The man apparently didn't know, and was willing to throw on yesterday's clothes in the middle of the night, roust his driver from bed, and travel to HQ to find out. Otherwise, he would've hung up the call from his security people and drifted back to sleep.

The more I thought about it, the more I became convinced. Rudolph and his thugs had dropped by Alfred's business, beaten me unconscious, and stolen our test photos, the bright green laser dots clearly visible. But they'd never entered Mr. Smith's war room. They'd never seen the subway maps and mathematical formulas plastering the walls.

They'd no doubt studied the swiped prints with magnifying glasses, trying to ascertain their purpose. But they'd fallen short. And even though Rudolph had recognized the laser for what it was, his question remained: what were we trying to accomplish in the subway?

Freedom could be ours with a believable and innocuous answer. *When equipped with the accoutrement of a plausible profession,* N. Jefferson Chapel had written, *you hasten property stewards toward their own erroneous explanation of your presence.*

But plausibility required proof. I scanned our *accoutrement* on the tabletop and the answer appeared, as if by magic. So simple.

"*That's* what this is all about?" I laughed out loud, part performance and part relief. "You're all idiots," I said, collecting my breath.

Valentine jumped to his feet, hands curling into fists. Hard Ass the brownnoser pushed himself off the wall.

Rudolph halted the security men with an open hand. "Let's hear him out." Then to me, "But it better be good."

I intertwined my fingers behind my head and leaned back. The chair squeaked. "Mother Nature put that poison down there and we would've avoided it, but guns at our backs gave us no choice." I aimed my index finger at Tony. "He got hurt for nothing."

Rudolph stepped from behind the wheelchair, his irritation growing. Convincing him without snapping his patience would be a challenge.

I gave a glance over my shoulder. "Same with Mr. Daley's broken arm. All for nothing." I shook my head as if confounded by absurdity. "You're all idiots."

Rudolph slapped his palm on the table's rock surface. "The next time you say that, this meeting's over. Answer my question."

I crossed my arms and leaned forward on both elbows. "Alfred didn't send us. He'd never do that. He hates my guts, almost as much as his granddaughter hates *his* guts—even if he's in the hospital, thanks to you. He's like her parole officer, part of a court settlement because she got her ass in trouble. She can't take a piss without asking the old man's permission." Everything I said was either a lie or a twisted truth, but the pieces had to form a plausible whole.

"Shut up, Lucas," Tricia said, roasting me with a fiery glare. I couldn't tell if she was serious or playacting, but no matter. I would apologize later.

I plowed ahead. "I don't do favors for Alfred. We risked our necks shooting the train station, and what did he do? He gave Tony our film just to get his damn camera back." Film that he later rescued from a burning building, but that detail would stay unspoken.

Rudolph glanced down at his son. "Is that true?" Apparently the details of our fracas with grandpa Walther and grandson Tony had never reached the middle generation.

Tony gave a weak nod. His glassy gaze darted randomly, the result of profound exhaustion or neurological damage, I couldn't tell which.

Tricia spun her chair toward me, her eyes brimming with emotion. "You stole that camera. He had no obligation to save *your* fucking photos." Role-playing or not, her words contained enough truth to sting.

"But he *should've* saved them," I said, sliding deeper into my role. "The art is everything, and he knew it. He believed in art once, but not anymore. So I stole the Leica, just like I stole the Hasselblad." I gestured to the camera in Rudolph's hands. "He loves that more than his own family."

Tricia brought her hands together in her lap and looked down, a tear glinting off her cheek in the weak light.

"Interesting." Rudolph laid the Hasselblad on the tabletop and again hoisted the laser, his meaning clear. "Again, why were you in the subway?"

"Painting with light," I declared without delay, not only to our adversaries but to my friends. I needed their backing.

Rudolph let out a sigh of doubt.

"My grandfather taught you that technique," Tricia said to me with believable bitterness.

"But I perfected it."

Rudolph narrowed his eyes. "What are you talking about?"

"How much do you know about photography?" I asked.

"I don't *need* to know about photography," he replied with a stiff jaw. "But *you* need to wrap up in twenty seconds."

"The subway photos in the newspaper," I explained, "with big splashes of color running the length of a long tunnel. We didn't drag a dozen spotlights belowground. Instead, we opened the camera's shutter and groped along in total darkness, firing the flash a dozen times, each time with a different colored filter, painting a single frame of film with light."

Rudolph appeared to relax his shoulders a smidge. "Okay, so that got you in the newspaper. Why do it again?"

"Because of the laser."

"The electronic flash is like throwing a bucket of paint against a wall," Reuben said with the assurance of a mountaintop holy man. "Beautiful but imprecise. The laser's different, all detail, more like drawing with India ink, only it's laser green."

Damn, he was brilliant. I wanted to applaud. Instead, I grabbed the baton. "When you lock open the lens and start moving the laser with deliberation, you're drawing, etching the film with green light." I pointed my finger at the device. "We attached those levels to guide our movements. Otherwise we'd end up with scribbles."

"But the pictures we—ended up with," Rudolph said, "had green dots on them."

"Of course," Reuben said. "Strictly test photos to determine aperture—the lens opening—so the film wouldn't get overexposed. We knew we had only one chance, so everything had to be perfect."

"But lasers cost thousands of dollars," Rudolph pressed, still short of buying what I was selling. "Do you expect me to believe no one's funding this? Blumenfeld perhaps?"

"Are you kidding?" I risked another laugh. "We didn't buy the laser, we borrowed it. I'm a student at Xavier and I pick locks. It's from the physics lab."

Rudolph paused, thinking. He glanced at Valentine who remained tightlipped. Same with Hard Ass from his outpost along the wall. But Gorilla One broke the silence with a grunted declaration. "He picks locks."

Rudolph set down the laser and rummaged further, retrieving and unsnapping my set of lock picks. "Aren't you clever," he said, unamused. He tossed the kit on the pile and became stern. "Well, good luck explaining to the dean what happened to his property. You'll be leaving it behind along with everything else, including the camera and film."

"What?" Tricia said angrily.

Rudolph ignored her and singled me out. "You're officially done sabotaging our projects. Am I understood?"

Tricia leapt to her feet. "You already took everything else he owns. You can't keep his camera!"

My mind staggered like a drunk in the no man's land between performance and reality. Rudolph had just proclaimed the terms of our release—our freedom. In exchange for a pile of replaceable stuff, we could keep our lives and the only physical object that really mattered, the roll of film that would bring down Drax. Had she forgotten? Or had the heat of our charade scorched her judgment?

Rudolph brushed her off. "You'll leave this building with only your filthy clothes. Mr. Valentine, search these river rats."

My God. I felt as if some organism had wound my intestines into a ball. Panic crept into Reuben's expression.

Valentine leapt to his assignment. "Stand up, legs spread, hands behind your head," he commanded Reuben. My friend obeyed, looking ready to vomit. Valentine dropped to one knee and began at the left ankle, progressively clapping with cupped hands up to the crotch. Reuben winced.

Catastrophe loomed. The same maneuver on Tricia would reveal the film.

After finishing the right leg, Valentine stood and worked Reuben's arms, shoulders, chest, belly, and back. Mid-grope, he ripped away the lamp-chain lanyard with penny and whistle.

I was next. As Valentine patted and squeezed with leathery hands, I wracked my brain for some intervention, some distraction. A diverting question? A threat? A suicidal attack? But nothing came. Valentine finished with me.

Tricia was already standing. But her face didn't show the panic I expected to see. Valentine loomed before her, momentarily eye to eye, as he adapted to an unexpected battlefield reality: a female combatant.

"Did you light the match that burned down my grandfather's business?" she said coolly, the curves beneath her black, skin-tight top too revealing. Valentine held his gaze on her face for a second before clapping her arms and shoulders. His compressed lips hinted at a smile.

Rudolph stepped behind Tricia, supervising the proceedings. "Miss Blumenfeld, our loyal employees do many important jobs because they believe in Drax Enterprises."

I shifted my weight from one foot to the next, utterly powerless.

Valentine took his time, circling like a predator. Shoulder blades. Middle back. Lower back. Rump.

Tricia stiffened. "It's easy to give the order, Mr. Drax, from your nice air-conditioned office at the top of the world."

Valentine circled again. Sides. Stomach. The curved edges of her bra, testing boundaries, invading with eyes as well as fingers, taking too long.

"Don't do that," I said.

"Now, why would you make such a comment, Mr. Tremaine?" Rudolph remarked with a teasing smile. "Feeling a little protective?"

Valentine's face was now inches in front of Tricia's as he kneaded his fingers in her dark hair—an absurd motion, as if she'd stashed a hand grenade in her ponytail.

But her mind was elsewhere, her eyes aglow with a primitive fire. "It takes a special kind of sick to light the match."

Valentine dropped to one knee and wrapped his hands around her left ankle.

Her upper lip quivered. "The kind of sick that steals and rapes and kills, and then goes on with life as if nothing happened. Is that you, Mr. Valentine?"

Valentine halted mid-calf and peered up into her eyes. "Call me whatever you want, young lady. But I lit the match." He flashed a contemptuous grin. "And that night I went out and had a steak to celebrate, charred on the outside and red on the inside, because that's how I like my meat." He held his gaze unblinking. "Now close your mouth and show me a pout." He waited another second before returning to his task.

Upper calf. Lower thigh. Mid-thigh.

The force of Tricia's knee struck dead center in Valentine's face with a crunch of cartilage. His head jerked up, neck bowed, Adam's apple bulging. He whipped his hand to the floor behind to keep from collapsing to his back.

"You don't get to touch me there, you sonofabitch," she hissed, her hands now balled up, legs rooted, one foot ahead of the other like a Greco-Roman wrestler.

Seething, Valentine settled to his knees and clutched his face, shoulders taut with rage. Blood oozed between his fingers, rapid breaths behind his hands.

Rudolph stepped between them and dangled a handkerchief before the man's face. "That'll be enough, you two," he said, as if scolding bickering children. Then with a chuckle, "One more agenda item and we can wrap this up before our director of security regains his manhood. A word in private please, Mr. Valentine?"

CHAPTER 30

Mopping his busted nose, Valentine trailed Rudolph into a corner for a whispered conference. I thought of the way a baseball coach walks out to a struggling pitcher mid-inning to offer encouragement, maybe point out the batter's weak spot. The player returns to the mound with fresh determination, which is what I saw in Valentine's smirk as he marched over to Hard Ass and the Gorillas to share the latest game-winning strategy.

I had allowed myself to imagine our exodus to a dark but benevolent city street, morning birds announcing the dawn, promise of a fresh start in Tricia's eyes. But no longer.

As if the boardroom table was a giant clock, the security men seated Tricia and Reuben at three and nine o'clock, and me straight ahead at the bottom of the hour. Their motions seemed so prescribed and inevitable, even Tricia complied without protest.

Once again, Rudolph materialized from shadow to stand alongside Tony at high noon, but now he cradled a bright red fire extinguisher, one of those bulky two-foot models mandated for commercial buildings. He lifted it over his head with both arms and paused to make sure we watched. He glanced down at our gear and adjusted his angle a few degrees.

"Don't do it," I said.

Rudolph's swing and the resulting impact caused Tony to lurch in his wheelchair. Shattered glass from the lens skated across the tabletop in a twinkling cone. The Hasselblad's aluminum housing spasmed and rocked to a stop, now caved and peeled like a trailer after a tornado.

I should've predicted Rudolph's Jekyll-to-Hyde transformation. He'd done the same at Alfred's shop, one minute civil, and the next minute raging on the fringe of control.

"You've had your fun," he said, breathing hard as he dropped the fire extinguisher to the floor.

Valentine and Hard Ass took up posts a few feet behind Tricia, the Gorillas likewise behind Reuben. I sat unsupervised, the threat to my friends enough to bolt me to my seat.

"Why are you doing this?" I asked wearily, belying the frigid sweat I felt under my shirt. "We answered every question—"

"With lies," he snapped. Then he smiled tightly, eyes devoid of mirth. "I must admit, I almost believed Miss Blumenfeld wanted to scratch your eyes out. But then Mr. Valentine's fingers got a little too close for comfort, didn't they?"

"She deserves the same respect as anyone else," I said.

Tricia shot me a disapproving glance. "I can take care of myself."

Rudolph laughed. "Oh, you've established that, as I'm sure Mr. Valentine would attest."

The ex-soldier neither spoke nor relaxed his spring-loaded stance.

I leaned forward. The leather groaned. "I told you, she's not part of this."

"Another lie," Rudolph said. "She's her grandfather's representative, the same as you."

I shook my head. "Why go over this again? Alfred Blumenfeld has no interest in my art, or in saving the subway."

Rudolph sized me up for a moment and then lowered his gaze as if preparing for some monumental declaration. "I don't need to convince you of anything, Mr. Tremaine," he said, his tone ominous, his rhythm metered. "But I will try, strictly as a courtesy, because you three must fully understand how deep a hole you've dug for yourselves."

I swallowed a lump and stared back.

"No one steals a rare laser, illegally enters a heavily guarded building, engages in hand-to-hand combat with armed security men, and then knowingly walks into a toxic cloud," he paused, his eyes blazing, "to take *goddamn pretty pictures*."

I had no response, and even if I did, there was no point. Rudolph had seen through my story with x-ray vision, exposing a cardboard foundation.

Reuben shot me a desperate glance.

Reflexively, I sought out the teachings of my savior from every tight pinch. But this was life or death. Whatever N. Jefferson Chapel had to offer, it would have to be brazen. *Audacity itself persuades,* he wrote, *for whom but the true would be so audacious?* Yet I doubted the advice. So far, I'd been bolder than ever. My painting-by-light story had accounted for every detail, including the test photos Drax stole, but Rudolph dismantled it.

He eased into a clockwise stroll around the oval table, tenting his fingers before his chest as if bestowing timeless wisdom. "We know your style, how you zigzag all over town before your little adventures so no one can follow you. Very clever." A pause. "But there's a downside. No witnesses. No one knows you're here."

"People know," Tricia blurted, but her tentative eyes betrayed the truth.

Rudolph brought his feet together behind her chair and spoke to the back of her head. "People like your grandfather? That doped-up wheezer in the hospital bed? He'll convince the police?" He continued his circular meander like ticks of a clock's second hand. In less than a minute, he'd demand an explanation. No, he'd demand a confession, and only the damning truth remained unsaid.

He halted behind my chair and placed his hands on my shoulders as a father might condescend to a child. I cringed. "Of course, Mr. Tremaine, your mother might save you."

"My mother has nothing to do with this."

"She's *unable* to have anything to do with it. She can barely look up a phone number."

He was inches away. How much damage could I do with my bare hands before the guards shut me down? Not enough. I gritted my teeth. "She's like that because of what you did to my father—to my family."

"Finally!" Rudolph said. "Now we're getting someplace. You don't need Alfred Blumenfeld's crusade to want me dead, do you?"

He released his hands and ambled further until he appeared in my peripheral vision, his wrinkled dress shirt puffed behind his back. "Who am I missing? Oh yes, your coworker, the hippie. What's his name?"

Valentine piped up. "Charles Dahlgren."

"That's right." Rudolph pulled in behind Reuben's chair and massaged the shiny cushion with manicured fingers. "The one who consumes more drugs than your mother and Blumenfeld combined. He'll call the cops?" He snorted, and then lowered his voice to a cold hush. "He could watch us bury you alive and still forget by the next morning."

Hard Ass snickered but then checked himself. Sweat trickled from my hairline to my cheek. *Think.*

Chapel wrote of a last resort, the urban explorer's Hail Mary pass. *When pretext comes to naught, and even lesser truth fails to soften the skeptic, beseech mercy through confession, for only the coldest soul refuses the penitent.* But that's the problem, Mr. Chapel. The soul of Drax is liquid nitrogen. The truth would bring no mercy. The truth would bury us.

The ticks of Rudolph's rotation continued. "My point, Mr. Tremaine, is that you've never been more alone." He arrived at high noon and signaled Valentine with a backhand, as if shooing a fly. Reuben cried out with pain as the two Gorillas pinned his arms behind the chair. I glanced right. Tricia's eyes stretched wide with fear. Kneeling behind her chair, Valentine had reached around to press his forearm to her chest, the blade to her throat.

"You're right, Miss Blumenfeld," Rudolph sneered, standing ramrod straight at the head of the table. "Mr. Valentine is that special kind of sick. He's killed more people with that knife than you've dated, and I don't mean to disparage your appeal. You're not unattractive for a Jewess." He shifted his attention to me. "Don't blow your last chance, Mr. Tremaine, because after he slices her throat, she'll stay conscious long enough to damn you to hell. Now…"

Tick.

My throat constricted.

Tick.

Rudolph brought his hands together in front of his body. My heart pounded in my ears.

"Why were you in the subway?"

Time's up.

"Forgive me, Tricia," I said to her, her face taut with panic and pain, her eyes wet. "Alfred would want me to protect you even if we had to sacrifice everything else." I turned to Rudolph. "Alfred Blumenfeld sent us to collect evidence to destroy you."

Rudolph smiled. "Now that wasn't so bad, was it?"

Another tick, unexpected, a moment to think, to dissect a single line from Chapel. Two words jumped out.

"Keep going, Mr. Tremaine."

I cleared my throat. "Alfred believes your father funneled money to support Hitler's rise to power and eventually the Holocaust."

Rudolph's smile vaporized. "That accusation is nothing new."

"Is it true?" Tricia challenged in spite of Valentine's blade, which bought me another tick of the clock. I thought of one more roll of the dice, but I'd be betting everything.

Rudolph huffed with impatience. "Mr. Valentine, on my signal." Tricia gasped. Reuben struggled against his captors but in vain. "Mr. Tremaine, you've got five seconds. *Collecting what evidence?*"

I gulped, rolled the dice, and leapt to standing. "You held the answer in your hand—the photograph—Alfred and a journalist investigating Drax twenty years ago." Five seconds done. Rudolph waited. I desperately splashed words. "But they weren't just colleagues, they were lovers." Rudolph's eyebrows shot up. "His name was Richard Baumgartner and, according to Alfred, he got too close to the truth and was murdered. Alfred believes his body is in the subway. After all, your company built it. And sure enough, just like Alfred predicted, you kept your own secret portal. So he came to us. We knew how to break in and we knew photography. Our job was to find Baumgartner's body and photograph it, clothes and all. Even dental work, if possible. Alfred planned to take the evidence to a cop he knows from the old days. He figured a murder verdict would bring down the company." I took a breath.

"He's right, it would."

Thirty seconds past deadline. Rudolph's stare demanded more. I obliged. "Alfred sent us to a hidden chamber filled with hundreds of corpses from the Depression—homeless people—stored in crates." Rudolph nodded to himself; he knew about the unmapped chamber. He glanced at Hard Ass and Valentine, but I couldn't catch their reaction. Had one of them nodded a validation? After all, we locked Hard Ass and Gorilla One in the spur. No time to speculate. "Alfred instructed us to find a peripheral crate with signs of tampering, but we never did."

I had placed our bets and rolled the dice. No turning back. But the upturned numbers remained hidden from view. Time to reveal. I threw back my shoulders. "Is the journalist in one of those boxes?" I stopped breathing.

If Alfred was right about Richard's resting place, then our knowledge would be too dangerous to release to the world. But if Alfred was wrong…

Rudolph studied me for a heart-stopping eternity, the ticks of the invisible second hand like spikes through my brain. Then he shook his head. "Jesus Christ."

No one spoke. No one moved.

Rudolph pinched the bridge of his nose and looked down. "You're wasting your time. That journalist isn't down there."

I released my breath and glanced right. Valentine retracted the blade a half-inch from Tricia's skin. A bloodless indentation lingered.

"Then where is he?" she demanded.

Rudolph returned her challenge with a smirk. "Probably where he'll never be found—but I wouldn't know."

"Of course you wouldn't," Tricia said.

I wedged my voice between them. "We failed. Alfred failed, which means he can't hurt you—*we* can't hurt you." I sat down. The seat cushion exhaled. "You should let us go."

Rudolph lifted his eyebrows as if the notion of our release was somehow novel. "You're right. I should." He leaned into the table, retrieved the photograph once again, and scrutinized the decades-old gala in fading sepia. "How about that. Blumenfeld's boyfriend. I never pegged him for a poof." He spoke to the air. "No wonder he's pissed off," he concluded, as if genocide wasn't bad enough. He tossed the photo with a flip of his hand. The image spun as it floated and settled among our gear. "Crazy old faggot."

Tony caught his father's attention and beckoned him close. They exchanged a few whispered words, during which Rudolph glowered at Valentine for a second or two. Then Rudolph straightened and said to Tony, "Fine." He shuffled toward the exit but turned midway to address the room. "Mr. Valentine, help Tony with whatever he needs. Mr. Daley, get these idiots the hell out of my building. They leave their crap behind. I'm going to bed. Jesus Christ." He shook his head as he disappeared into the hall. "Crazy Jew."

. . . . .

Hard Ass escorted us to the front entrance of Drax Enterprises and watched as we pushed out under a gray, pre-dawn sky—all without saying a word. Then he turned and vanished into the shadows of the lobby.

Too shaken or petrified or paranoid of the jinx to speak out loud, we walked single file to the first bus stop with nighttime service, between Adolphus Avenue and Ptarmigan. Instead of freshness to start a new day, humid air trapped the diesel fumes of delivery trucks. Somewhere below our feet lay hundreds of forgotten corpses, none of them Richard Baumgartner.

We climbed aboard the first bus to pull up. We didn't care where it was going. We needed departure. We'd worry about arrival later.

I couldn't help but judge every face for threat potential. Besides the driver, we shared the coach with a boozy-eyed teen in a Bengals cap, and a fresh-faced nurse with Cincinnati General Hospital embroidered above the breast pocket of her uniform.

We moved back to hide in the roar of the engine. Tricia eased down next to me. Reuben sat one seat ahead, his face forward.

I took Tricia's hand in mine, squeezed to quell her trembling, and turned to stare out the window. The owner of a news kiosk wiped down a metal countertop. A deliveryman in white overalls shouldered a case of tomatoes into a Greek restaurant. A city worker with a push broom waved toward a second-story window. So normal, but nothing felt normal.

Ahead of me, Reuben's head bobbed every so often as if he were arguing with himself.

I made eye contact with Tricia. "I've never done this to a woman without asking permission."

She squinted with mock suspicion. "What?"

"You'll forgive me?" I gave her no time to respond before squeezing her thigh an inch from ground zero. My fingers landed on a reassuring contour, like a roll of dimes—Kodak 120 film sealed up tight. I sighed with satisfaction. "As good for you as it was for me?" It was a stupid joke, floated in the darkest morning. But Tricia returned a wan smile, and that was good enough.

Reuben threw his arm across the seatback between us and whipped his head around. "Not funny, Lucas." His burning gaze caught me unprepared. "What the hell were you thinking?"

"We got out. Isn't that enough?"

"No! You bet our lives that Richard Baumgartner isn't down there. Where did that come from?"

"I don't know, I guessed—" I took a breath. "You'll be pissed when I tell you."

"I'm already pissed." His eyes flared.

"Chapel."

He exhaled with exasperation and looked away.

Tricia cleared her throat. "Um, what are you talking about?"

I reminded her about N. Jefferson Chapel, the father of urban exploration. "He wrote the book," I said, before reciting the quotation I'd gambled on. "*When pretext comes to naught, and even lesser truth fails to soften the skeptic, beseech mercy through confession, for only the coldest soul refuses the penitent.*"

She scrunched up her nose. "What does *that* mean?"

Chapel's thick prose used to be amusing, but not now. "It means when you can't bullshit your way out, confess and pray for mercy."

"But you didn't confess," she said. "Not to the measurements, thank God."

"No, because of two words—*lesser truth*." A dim glow on the horizon winked between buildings. "Everything I said was true. It had to be for Rudolph to buy it—we learned that the hard way with the laser as paintbrush. And it had to be confessional—he had to believe he'd won." I spoke with confidence but felt like a fraud. In truth, I'd been shooting in the dark in the museum. My friends had risked it all. They deserved better. "Look, I got lucky."

Reuben wasn't finished. "How could you be sure Baumgartner's body *wasn't* in one of those boxes?"

"I wasn't sure. But Hard Ass drew a blank at Baumgartner's name."

"Yeah, but Valentine recognized it," Reuben said.

"That made sense," I said. "Valentine was on the scene when the journalist disappeared, and maybe did the deed. But the mystery spur, by any name, seemed to mean nothing to either of them." Or had I misread their expressions? The possibilities were too dreadful to imagine. "Like I said, we got lucky. That's all."

Reuben fumed while Tricia squeezed my hand. She let a few moments pass before asking, "Since Baumgartner's body isn't down there, why does Drax guard the subway like it contains dirty secrets?"

"Because it probably does," I replied. "Drax is dirty. God knows what's down there, way more than construction fraud, that's for sure. No wonder they're so determined to bury their sins. But does it matter?" I was tired of peeling back the onion of our narrow escape.

Reuben wasn't. He stroked his five o'clock shadow, twelve hours off schedule. "What if Rudolph had asked how lasers help find human remains? What *lesser truth* then?"

I observed the passing street scene to avoid his gaze. "I don't know." But I did. My house of cards would've collapsed.

We bounced along without speaking. The brick homes and office buildings of old Cincinnati switched to the gas stations and strip malls of suburbia. I found myself imagining how the sole survivor of a plane crash might feel. Not relieved, but terrified. Cruel circumstance had spared him once, but surely the reckoning lay ahead.

An all-night Skyline Chili briefly appeared in neon yellow outside the bus window. "Anybody hungry?" Tricia said and yanked the bell cord.

As my friends descended to the curb ahead of me, I caught the eye of the nurse seated three rows behind the driver. "Pardon me, ma'am?"

She looked up and smiled. Apparently I didn't resemble the nighttime creeps who accosted ladies on public transportation.

I gestured toward the writing on her uniform. "Do you happen to know which company built the hospital where you work?"

She looked confused. My question must've sounded bizarre. "No. Why do you ask?"

I returned her smile and waved a friendly dismissal. "Just curious." I moved on but turned at the top of the steps. "I hope you have a really great day."

CHAPTER 31

The mayor concluded the ceremony and encouraged the small crowd of dignitaries, donors, and everyday citizens like me to wander about the classic train station. I skipped the guided tour by the Cincinnati Railroad Club, having explored passages and cul-de-sacs their best guides didn't know existed. And over the following weekend, in the wee hours, we'd be exploring more.

Times had changed since Reuben and I last visited to photograph the grand rotunda by night. Back then, dust on the terrazzo floor recorded the guards' rounds, and grime blurred the stars beyond the tall windows. Now, four years later, the fixtures sparkled and the Art Deco lettering above the doorways proudly proclaimed *TICKETS, TRAVEL BUREAU,* and *MOTOR COACHES*. Instead of mildew, the air smelled of fresh coffee.

I stood from the folding chair and sighed with satisfaction. Finally, the city's leaders had come to their senses. Converting this architectural wonder into a shopping mall would've been like turning the great pyramids over to Disney. With the mayor's official declaration, the Cincinnati Union Terminal would become the city's epicenter of history, art, and culture.

"I got it done," Reuben said, standing at the end of the row of chairs, "against my better judgment."

I joined him. "And?"

"So far, so good. East stairwell doors to the upper levels are wired open with coat hangers, most likely for the painters. Even if they released them, the scaffolding would get in the way."

"Nice."

The crowd began drifting toward the refreshment table, but Reuben didn't notice. "I don't have the best memories of this place, you know."

"All the more reason to make new memories. Here's a fun fact—the

President's office upstairs is perfectly round, with curved paneling, curved couch, and even a curved desk."

"Yes, I know. You told me. I'll bet the tour visits it."

I shot him my best that's-not-how-we-do-things look. "Did you check the west stairwell?"

Reuben rolled his eyes. "Oh, come on."

"Pardon me? Aren't you the one who said, *Never count on a single path to your destination*?"

"I said that?"

"No, but doesn't it sound like something you'd say?"

Reuben headed off to the west without a word—a good sign. He would've stuck around for a real argument.

I strolled to the center point below the grand rotunda's dome and peered up. I remembered the local legend, one of Dad's favorites, that lovers who kissed under the highest point would spend their lives together. I took in the three-hundred-sixty degrees of massive stone sweep and thought of our visits to this place, a sacred place, when I was a kid. We'd play a game, each standing in the perfect spot on opposite sides beneath the great dome. Separated by two hundred feet, we could hear each other's words as if inches apart.

On a whim, I walked to Dad's listening point along the east wall and scanned the crowd, pretending to be a spectator. But I focused on sound, not sight. Soon, snippets of conversation materialized between my ears with no discernible point of origin. The opposite side must've held the hors d'oeuvres table because different voices came and went with people in motion.

"… if Sullivan runs for a second term, I've half a mind to…"

"… out for at least four games with a pulled hamstring…"

"… interviewed him for the position but you know bureaucracies…"

"… isn't that the CEO of Drax Enterprises? Takes some balls to…"

My muscles tensed reflexively, the way combat veterans flinch at loud noises years after returning home.

Nine months earlier, the judge ruled in City of Cincinnati v. Drax Enterprises. The case was closed, so I shouldn't have been anxious in the presence of Rudolph—no, not Rudolph. Tony was in charge. After the verdict, under pressure, Rudolph stepped down and the business section of the *Enquirer* ran the headline, *Springtime for Drax?*

By the time I spotted Tony in the crowd, he was already striding toward me. Great. What was the point? We could reminisce about our previous encounters, all unpleasant, or dance around them. Or we could make small talk, but I didn't have the patience.

Dressed in a quiet gray suit, he no longer walked with the swagger of a prince. I accepted his outstretched hand, something I wouldn't have done before I'd delivered the completed calculations to the district attorney and thereby set the legal wheels in motion.

"You got your wish," he said with a tepid smile. No beating around the bush. His hair was trimmed neat. His left eye drifted occasionally to the periphery before snapping into alignment, his wiring shorted—a lifelong souvenir of stink damp.

"I did?"

Tony swept the expanse with an outstretched arm. "Soon to be a cultural center, perfect for this old building. The shopping mall was a bad idea."

I couldn't suppress a snort. "You defended that idea."

"And you almost broke my nose. You should be thankful we dropped the charges."

No, I didn't have the patience. I said nothing.

Tony exhaled. "Look, I'm just saying, we both made mistakes, didn't we?"

I'd punched him for good reason back then: he'd disparaged Reuben with an anti-Semitic slur. But for the present, I detected an olive branch. "I suppose we did."

A well-dressed older woman passed within spitting distance, flashed Tony a scowl, and scurried away as if he might bite.

"Your fan club?" I said.

"Layoffs are unpopular."

"Sounds like trouble at the great and powerful Drax Enterprises," I said, chiding but also fishing. "Your press release called it a simple restructuring."

"We've faced tough times before," he said with a weak smile.

That was an understatement. The Drax PR department had kept the worst news from the public, but the community of architects, of which I was a new member, could dig up dirt on even private entities like Drax. Triple penalties for the subway fraud broke the company's back financially. But far worse, once the business community learned Tony's grandfather had backed the Third

Reich, Drax became toxic. Politicians wouldn't risk their re-elections steering public projects toward Nazi sympathizers. The revenue stream dried up.

"I hear you'll be selling the headquarters building," I said.

Tony raised an eyebrow. "Says who?"

"It doesn't matter," I replied. "The sale will have to go on the public record eventually."

Tony plucked a piece of lint from the sleeve of his suit jacket. "We're raising operating funds."

"What happens to the museum?"

"Mothballed, I suppose. You're wondering about the replica of the missile silo?"

I gave him credit for remembering. "Yes."

"You can have it, if you want."

"I want it destroyed."

Tony nodded once. "Done. How's your mother?"

Hairs rose on the back of my neck. He had no right to ask. I felt the urge to say *You mean my father's widow?* The day after delivering the film, I'd moved her out of town. The ensuing years rid her mind of drugs, but not sadness. "Your father taught me a powerful lesson. The less Drax knows about my family and friends, the better."

Tony studied my expression. "I don't blame you for being cautious, but there's something you need to know. My father was a very dangerous man—emphasis on *was*."

"Why should I believe you?"

Tony shrugged. "The case is closed, so I have no incentive to lie to you, and as much as I hate the comparison, Rudolph thinks the same way. It's all about incentive."

I said nothing.

"He could be ruthless to achieve a goal, but vengeance was never a goal. If it had been, he wouldn't have let you go."

An old question bubbled up. "He freed us because of something you whispered from your wheelchair. What did you tell him?"

Tony hesitated, as if unsure. "That you and your friends weren't worth the trouble, his standard decision criteria. Normally he would've ignored me, but a brush with death bought me a little authority."

So we owed our lives to Tony Drax? I wasn't ready to accept that. "You'll forgive me if I wish your father a miserable retirement."

Another lukewarm smile. "Let's just say a man like that needs to be on center stage to be happy. He's no longer on center stage. Are you satisfied?"

"No. I wanted my father back. But—" I paused. "I guess that was never part of our plan."

"Then what was the plan?"

The question caught me off guard, but not for long. "To make Drax Enterprises pay for what it did." No beating around the bush.

"You mean did to your father?"

"We all had our reasons."

Tony considered that for a moment. "Well, you all succeeded."

I didn't get it. We'd brought Drax Enterprises to its knees, yet the company's native son showed no animosity. Was it a ploy?

"In a way," he went on, "I'm in your debt."

I was too baffled to respond.

He continued, his left eye untethered. "We're a startup now. Instead of adopting Rudolph's way, I can do things my way." He scanned the crowd. "That's why I'm here, trying to convince people Drax will be different from now on."

"But like you said, it's all about incentive. You have an incentive to say the old Drax is dead."

Another shrug. "And people will be skeptical, like you are. I'm okay with that."

No, it wasn't a ploy. I believed him, but I'd never say so.

Out under the great dome, a man in a striped engineer's cap beckoned visitors for the next tour.

"I'm sorry about Mr. Blumenfeld," Tony blurted, as if the words had been waiting in queue.

"You want me to believe you care what happened to Alfred?"

"I had nothing to do with that fire. That was all Valentine."

"Ready to testify to that fact?"

Tony said nothing.

Even from his hospital bed, with only his vocal cords healing, Alfred wished aloud to shoot photos again. But he couldn't, and everyone but Alfred knew it.

His damaged hands would never be able to load film or manipulate camera controls. The bacterial infection that took him nine days later spared him the truth.

Obviously, Tony wanted to get things off his chest. I felt uneasy with my complicity, but the man exuded unmistakable pain. "Alfred left his mark," I said. "Blumenfeld Photography is doing well, thanks to what he taught his granddaughter."

Tony leaned closer. I wanted to pull away. "There's something you need to know," he said, his expression severe. "I ordered Delbert Turkel across that field, but I never knew why until it was too late. Believe me, if I'd known…" His voice trailed off.

So much suffering. I was done tossing bones of sympathy. "A complete waste," I said bitterly, "even for Rudolph. The subway's still down there, along with whatever secrets he hoped to bury."

Tony offered nothing in return, yet he didn't seem to be holding back. Perhaps Rudolph had kept secrets from his only son.

I had a job to do. "I should get going."

"Of course, and I need to make the rounds." He turned toward the crowd but stopped himself. "One more thing. At the hearing—all the photographs with the laser spots. I don't get it. We confiscated all your equipment and patted you down. How'd you get the film out?"

"We had a courier—sort of."

"Aha!" Tony's eyes lit up. "You slipped it to someone at street level through—I don't know—maybe the welders missed a gap in one of the steel plates."

Not a bad idea, but no such a gap existed. "Exactly. But this courier is dear to me, so I'd rather not say anything else."

With a tilt of his head, Tony marveled at my revelation, red herring that it was. "Sure," he said, as we exchanged a final handshake. "See you around." He walked out of my sight.

"Right before they cleared the food table, I snagged you three meatballs and some of those little hotdogs." The voice was Tricia's, its point of origin neither ahead nor behind, neither left nor right. She was standing in my old listening point two hundred feet on the opposite side of the great rotunda.

I spoke at normal volume. "Thanks. How much did you hear?"

"Most of it. Congratulations. You didn't punch him this time."

The crowd had thinned enough to reveal her across the expanse, looking professional in a white button-up blouse, paisley scarf, and black skirt. She carried a clipboard, the ultimate credibility prop. "What'd you find out?" I asked.

"Apparently a lot more than you."

"Come on. He approached me. Running away wasn't an option."

She glanced at her clipboard. "The vent covers in the main concourse still have simple clasps. No big deal. Only one overnight guard and he's supposed to make his rounds on the half-hour. But I bet he snoozes." She looked over at me. "We'll have the run of the place."

"Even Reuben will be impressed. How'd you get all that?"

Her bright eyes beamed across the distance. "Have you forgotten your N. Jefferson Chapel? *Among the tedium of the watchman's devoir, your presence may... may...*" She tapped her pencil on the clipboard. "Shit. Well, in short, a bored guard likes a break."

"I beg your pardon, I know my Chapel. What'd you do?"

"Sweet-talked him."

What red-blooded man, numbed by tedium or not, could resist her?

She was still talking, a lovely refrain no one around me could hear. "You told Tony about a secret courier, someone *dear* to you. Did you mean it?"

"You know I did."

"Fair enough," she said, as three businessmen strolled across our line of sight and moved on. She grinned. "Then *how much* did you mean it?"

I took a deep breath and eased it out through a smile. "Meet me under the highest point of the great dome and I'll answer your question."

THE END

ABOUT THE AUTHOR

Gordon MacKinney is a decade-long monthly columnist for the *Fort Collins Coloradoan*, and has served as guest columnist for the *Denver Post*. He holds an MBA degree from the Harvard Business School and an undergraduate degree from Miami University of Ohio. He co-owns a marketing communications agency, www.lightsourcecreative.com, and resides in the foothills of the Rockies in Northern Colorado.

Learn more about his writing at www.gmackinney.com.

View other Black Rose Writing titles at www.blackrosewriting.com/books and use promo code **PRINT** to receive a **20% discount** when purchasing.

BLACK ROSE writing

Made in the USA
Columbia, SC
09 November 2017